Beyond
Silver City

David M. Sellet

Mindful Acorn Press

ISBN-13: 978-0-578-42834-5

Preface

What has been set down on paper here is
a fictionalized account based on a true story,
real people and their circumstances.
Names and corresponding locations
have been changed to protect
the privacy of those concerned.
Truth is in fact often stranger than fiction,
though possibly this might depend upon
the reader's conception of what is or is not strange.
Mark Twain once said that "The difference between truth
and fiction is that fiction has to make sense."

If the topics involved in this story pique the reader's interest
or raise life-sized questions, by all means research them
or see the back of the book for a list of further reading.
I offer many thanks to the WordsWERK
writer's group of Boone, NC.
Many thanks also to those other friends
who have read for me and provided comments:
Neta Bliss, Bruce Marshall, Monica Rector,
Lis Reutlinger, and Berkeley Brown.
I am majorly indebted to Malcolm Wood,
to Bonnie Jean McConnell, and to my parents
for believing in and inspiring me.

Part I

1.

"—this is too bizarre a story for me to make up."

It was early March in 1992—still winter around Silver City but with the promise of spring in the air, and the family was out for dinner at the Dairy Queen in town. This evening, Elizabeth Lewis allowed herself a fried-chicken sandwich but had a large salad to go along with it instead of the requisite French fries. Elizabeth prided herself on sticking to the rigid diet her doctor had prescribed—continuing with the herbal and vitamin supplements, and the food restrictions. But she and Nate took the kids out once a month for "junk-food night," partly as a treat for the boys, who seemed to think of it as some sort of gastronomic and cultural safari. Due to Elizabeth's diet, the usual family dinner lately consisted of many more vegetables, salads, and unrefined grains than it ever had before. And not always to the boys' delight. Nate himself had reluctantly become diet-conscious—and "junk-food night" was somewhat of a guilty pleasure for him also.

Once they'd sat down at the table, the youngest, Joey, saw his mother eating the salad before even touching her sandwich. And he quietly asked his father if he could have a salad, too. Nate—already halfway into his "Ultimate-burger"—got up, with a patient smile, and walked up to the counter again to order an extra salad. After which the boy seemed content. Elizabeth gazed at him across the gleaming table, smiling to herself. Joey's hair was still blonde, at eight years old, and needed a little trimming. Luke was nine, now, and had always been more dark-haired. Both were growing a little too fast for her liking. Joey, at least, still had some of that clinging childhood need for his mother. When a teenage girl from the counter brought out his salad, he immediately went to work on that before returning to his French fries. Elizabeth glanced at her boys . . . *Very cool. They're gonna be healthy, strong guys . . .* She cleared her throat slightly. "So, whaddya think, guys? I know we like the *taste* of French fries, and other fried stuff . . . but why is it we don't eat fried food, too much?"

Joey raised his eyebrows. But with a vacant expression. Luke, munching on a French fry, swallowed. "Bad oil in 'em, Mom."

Joey chimed in, "Yeah, bad oil."

Nate chuckled a little. Elizabeth elbowed him lightly. "That's *right!*" Then she added a melodramatic voice, sounding like a television game-show host (which might be lost on the boys, though they sometimes watched TV at the neighbor's house). "*You* are the winner, *tonight,* of a *BRAND-NEW CAR!*"

Luke grinned. "Ha ha. Cool! What kind?"

"Well, we'll have to see about that . . ." she trailed off.

When they returned home, it was still early evening but with the lingering sun of early spring. There'd been a dry spell, so Nate thought it an opportune time to begin turning the soil in the garden. The boys stayed out with him, puttering around in the garden area.

Elizabeth stepped through the doorway into the "earthship"—the off-the-grid, solar home they'd recently finished building—and she meandered over to the kitchen counter. And aware of only the slightest feeling of martyrdom and self-righteousness, she fixed her regular evening regimen of the anti-cancer diet and supplements. This included another (and she was sure, healthier) salad for herself: of raw cabbage, cauliflower, greens and alfalfa sprouts, with some added tofu. She made herself the bright green drink of Chlorella and Spirulina algae, and with sips of this drink washed down her supplements of Vitamin C, Echinacea, and the Astragalus root. And the mushroom extracts. The pungent taste of these supplements had been almost nauseating at first—when she first started on the diet around the time of her breast-cancer surgery, a year and a half ago—but she'd long since resigned herself to the peculiar flavors of her world now. She felt healthier with this daily regimen and knew it wasn't just placebo effect.

She looked, thoughtfully, out the screened door toward the garden, barely visible now in the dusk beyond the trailer. Luke and Joey were playing there, laughing—Luke poking a stick into the ground for some reason . . . *I want to be around for these guys, darn it. Damned straight! I wanna be around to watch 'em grow up . . .* Nate moved into view, with a shovel in his hands, some of his hair loose now from his ponytail.

Elizabeth puffed out her cheeks, watching him . . . *And who knows— maybe see him grow up, too . . .*

The small contracting company that Nate Lewis and his friend, Steve, had started kept busy. At least moderately so, even through the winter. The talking-heads of business and the stock market ruminated about how the country was experiencing a down-turn in the economy—there had been another "correction" on Wall Street. But the building trades in the Silver City area were holding their own, despite the recession and Wall Street shenanigans. The town continued to grow—albeit a little slower— attracting retirees and other newcomers from different parts of the country. People drawn to the moderate climate, college-town atmosphere, and inexpensive land that the Silver City environs had to offer. And there were outdoor activities like bicycling, camping, hiking, and fishing in the mountainous Gila Wilderness area nearby. Many decided on new construction for their homes, but some chose to buy existing houses and build additions onto them, or remodel.

Nate's business was often just himself and Steve, though at times they hired help or sub-contractors—and the company remained viable during this recession. For the most part, they'd decided to focus on remodeling construction. Neither he nor Steve had much interest in growing their business into a larger company.

One thing Nate liked about their work was the more personal business relationship he had with his clients, most of whom were couples, sometimes young families. In several cases, they were really nice folks, like the older couple for whom they were working now. Jim and Barbara Wilson were retiring to the Silver City area from the frenetic hustle and bustle of Silicon Valley, California, after Jim's retirement from a software company in Santa Clara. They'd recently bought a small adobe-style home in Pinos Altos (a country crossroads town just north of Silver City), and hired Nate and Steve to build a guest-bedroom and bath addition onto it. It was just the kind of small job that Nate had hoped their company would land once they'd become established. This job tided them over the winter and would keep them busy well into the spring.

In mid-April, Nate and Steve had just stopped for a lunch break at the job they were doing at Jim and Barbara's. The addition was going well, though some of the work was labor-intensive, especially regarding the log beams—what the locals called *vigas*—supporting the ceiling of the main room. A few minutes later, as the guys were sitting down with their lunch sandwiches, Jim, the homeowner, poked his head through a hanging sheet of plastic that covered a doorway opening into the house. "You guys want a freshener for your coffee? Just brewed some, about an hour ago. . . ."

Though Nate drank very little coffee after his morning cup, Steve was some sort of caffeine fiend. And his face brightened. A minute later, Jim appeared again with an insulated type of coffeepot. Steve, grinning, held up an unwholesome-looking coffee mug—covered with a patina made of coffee stains, sawdust, and a few other nameless things. Jim filled it. A spry cheerful man in his early sixties, he sat down on an overturned five-gallon bucket to join the men for a minute. He craned his neck to peer up at the half-finished ceiling. There were smooth logs, set two feet apart in the ceiling framing and spanning the length of the room. "Looks great, guys." He made a slight whistling sound, "Whew! Must be a bitch, getting the sheetrock up in between the beams, huh?"

Nate grinned at him. He and Steve got along well with Jim, bantering with him occasionally. *"Yep.* It *is* a bitch. And you know, Jim, your powers of perception never cease to amaze me."

Jim laughed. "I know. And that's why they paid me the big bucks in Santa Clara."

"Guess so. But . . . actually, this part isn't so bad. The real bitch is gonna be the plastering part—plastering up to the edges of the vigas. I'm hiring a regular plaster guy to do that. But it's gonna look great. . . . Like the real deal. An old-fashioned viga ceiling."

"So," Jim said, "I'm guessing you're going to varnish the beams—I mean vigas? Or coat them with something?"

Nate glanced up at the ceiling—momentarily—feeling a bit sickened of it now after having worked on it most of the morning. "Yeah. We will. We'll use a satin polyurethane varnish. If you're okay with that. I wouldn't recommend glossy varnish at all—it'll look tacky. But, yeah, they *have* to get varnished. In fact, we'll probably do that before the plaster guy comes—that'll make his job easier, too. It'll give the ceiling a clean, classy look . . . and keep the vigas from getting dusty and dirty, in the future."

"Gotcha. Yeah. Barbara's doing so well, lately . . . but I don't want her having to climb up there like Superwoman, to *dust* those things."

Nate looked at him, curious as to what he was referring. Jim's wife, Barbara, was an attractive older woman. Perky (even sexy, Nate thought), and appeared to be in good health . . . *Huh. Maybe he's just talking to himself, out loud, about something* . . . Nate shot him a sidelong glance. "What's, uh . . . What's up with Barbara? I don't know if you're okay talking about it. If not, well . . . just tell me to shut the hell up."

Jim looked at him with a twisted smile. "No, it's okay. I hadn't intended to talk about it, but it's okay. Yeah, ah . . . Barbara was quite ill, three years ago. She had a type of brain tumor, and—"

"Oh shit . . . I'm sorry, I didn't mean to pry."

"No," Jim said. "It's okay. It was kind of a rare tumor in the pineal gland—that part of the brain. Called a pineocytoma. Thank God it wasn't a malignant type. But it was giving her all kinds of trouble anyway. Dizziness, headaches, blurry vision . . . the works."

"Damn. I'm sorry." Nate frowned . . . *I wish I hadn't brought this up* . . .

But Jim's demeanor was remarkably calm.

"Wow," Nate said. "Sounds like she really went through the wringer, with that. She seems quite well, though . . . I mean, she looks great."

"Yeah. That's the interesting part. We *did* go through hell, for a while. The CT scans and MRI showed the growth, there—and a biopsy showed that it was benign. But it was still a really lousy prognosis 'cause it's considered to be too dangerous to operate, there. And it was, you see . . . it was the pressure from the tumor that was causing the problems."

"Uh-huh. Well, she looks wonderful. Is she okay now?"

"Well, she *is* okay," Jim said. "That's the funny part of it. You see, we heard about this healer, in Brazil. You don't hear much about him, here in the States. They call him Joseph of God. *José de Deus.* The people there do, I mean . . . in Brazil, and other parts of South America. And in other parts of the world, actually. He's pretty well-known—but not here in the States. Someone we know in San José, a woman with a medical condition, had gone down there to see him. And this woman told us that there's some remarkable healing work going on, at this place in Brazil where this healer, Joseph, lives. They have a peculiar sort of healing center there."

"No kidding."

"Yep. So, anyway . . . we talked on the phone with a few other people who'd been down there to see this guy. And we decided to go. You know, it wasn't looking real good with Barb's condition. Even if the tumor stopped growing . . . well, a lot of the symptoms could still become permanent. And be really debilitating. So we said, 'What the hell! We'll give it a whirl.' And so we went down there to Brazil for about two months, the first time. And we've been down there, again, twice, since then . . ."

"No kidding," Nate said, again.

"And the long and short of it is, well . . . that Barb doesn't have a tumor anymore."

A confused furrow appeared in Nate's forehead. "No shit. What? So, wait . . . you mean to tell me she's better? Or cured? Of this tumor?"

"*Yes*. I kid you not—this is too bizarre a story for me to make up. We went back to the neurosurgeon about a year ago. And they did the usual CT scans and MRIs all over again. But they couldn't find any tumor."

"No shit. I mean . . . that's *great*."

"Yes. It is." Jim had a distracted, distant look on his face. "The place is *amazing*. There are all these mind-boggling healings—and cures— going on there, every day. At this healing center, in this little town in the middle of nowhere. The people there all say it's God's work. And that's what this guy, Joseph, says. . . . That he doesn't actually heal anyone— God does it. Joseph says that all he is, is some kind of medium. And God's energy works *through* him."

Nate felt a little disturbed, hearing Jim talk about this. He muttered, "No kidding." A half-eaten sandwich lay in Nate's hand, as he looked at the man. And his gaze wandered to the pine trees outside a window.

Steve was setting his lunch-box aside and taking one last gulp of coffee. After a minute or two of silence, Jim seemed aware that maybe he was sidetracking the men at their work, and exhaled audibly. "Ah, well . . . I didn't mean to hold you guys up or anything. I guess I'm just grateful, about Barbara's health . . . and don't seem to mind jabbering about it." He stood up from his makeshift chair, dusting off his rear.

"No," Nate said. "No problem. That's awesome . . . you must be really happy about it. Far out."

Steve was repositioning one of the stepladders and picked up his tool-belt. Jim had almost reached the doorway into the house but glanced over at Steve and asked if he wanted a fresh cup.

"Well, uh . . . only if you still have some."

Jim held up the coffeepot. "It's right here, buddy, and I think it's got your name on it."

Steve smiled. "Thanks, Jim. My mug's over there." He nodded toward his mug, perched precariously in the two-by-four framed wall near the door. "You're a life-saver, my man."

After a while, Nate and Steve were back into the swing of the tedious ceiling sheetrock work. Nate was a little distracted, though, and couldn't seem to work as methodically as Steve was. He glanced over at the doorway opening, trying to discern if Jim or Barbara were within earshot. "That was some pretty wild shit—that Jim was talking about, there. . . . Huh?"

"Yep." Steve dropped his voice to a hoarse murmur. "Sounds a bit too much like California woo-woo stuff, to me."

Nate said, quietly, "I don't know, man. You've lived here long enough. You know the deal. Sometimes we hear the real story, here—in New Mexico—that they don't get, on the East Coast or the West Coast. You know what I mean? The East Coast, with its Ivy-league, yuppy, Pentagon-brainwashing bullshit. Or the West Coast, with its Hollywood and trendy, woo-woo spiritual stuff. If you read in between the lines— here, in New Mexico—sometimes you hear what the *real* story is. I'm serious. Those poor suckers—on either coast—are so fucking brainwashed by media hype of one kind or other . . . that they hardly know whether they're comin' or goin'. You know?"

"Yeah. I know. Every time I go back east, now, I feel like I can't even breathe. And everybody's tellin' me about the latest crap they've heard on TV, or on cable." Steve dropped his voice again. "But, you know, you gotta admit . . . there's plenty of flakes here, too."

"Yeah," Nate said. "True enough. But just because something sounds far-fetched doesn't mean it isn't the real deal. You know what I'm saying? I mean . . . with this healer guy, in Brazil. Now, if I lived on the East Coast I'd say this healer stuff would be too weird to be possible." He chuckled a moment. "But if I lived on the West Coast, I would think it wasn't weird *enough* to be possible. . . . The truth of it is somewhere in the middle. Like what we get, in the middle of the country. Here in New Mexico."

"Got it all figured out, huh, man?" Steve said, and he added, with some sort of southern-California stoner inflection, "What*ever* . . . *Dude.*"

For the rest of the afternoon, Nate was for the most part quiet, except when some construction detail needed to be discussed. And he felt distracted, even irritable, when he thought about what Jim had described earlier regarding this healer. He found new things to complain about, with the sheetrock details in between the vigas. And the ceiling work was taking too long. Finally, Steve frowned and set down his sheetrock screw-drill, looking at Nate. "What the fuck's wrong with you? Havin' a bad afternoon, huh?"

"Oh, nothing," Nate said, exhaling loudly. "Just feeling pissy." It was a sunny day outside, but the mid-afternoon shadows were growing long. Bright streams of afternoon sun shone through the new windows on the west wall of the addition. He looked around the room at the splashes of intense yellow sunlight, and it reminded him of a recent incident at home.

Two weeks earlier, he had come home from work and couldn't find

Elizabeth when he called for her in the trailer and then in the "earthship." The evening sun cast bright streaks of sparkling white on the plastered walls of the earthship, as he walked to the main bedroom—their bedroom. He found her there, lying on her side on the bed in a fetal position, crying quietly. Her body curvaceous and feminine, though childlike in her current pose.

"*Liz?* You okay, Sweetie?" He eased down onto the bed and put his hand on her shoulder while she wiped a tear-stained cheek with her shirtsleeve. Her light brown hair, usually braided back into a short pony-tail, looked disheveled, wiry, and brittle.

"Yeah?" Elizabeth said, in a wet, nasally tone. "I mean *no.* I'm *not* so good. There's another lump, in my breast. This time, it's on the left side—my left boob."

Nate exhaled, "Shit."

"Yep. . . . You know, Andi Sheaffer tried to—"

"I know, Sweetie."

"she tried to get me to do the regular treatments. But, no . . . I didn't want to. The surgeon said he thought they got all the cancerous tissue. Well guess what? They didn't. Or it came back." Nate rubbed her hand. Elizabeth sniffed convulsively. In a stifled voice she added, "I feel like I've run out of cards now, Nathan."

Coming back to the moment, Nate continued working with Steve—on Jim's addition—but returned frequently to this morbid reflection. He hadn't talked with Steve about his new concerns over Elizabeth's condition. And today didn't seem like a good time to bring it up, either. In the past couple of weeks, he'd talked with a close friend of his from the AA meetings in town. And with an old friend of his from Santa Fe. But this afternoon he just continued to return to the subject, like an itchy mosquito bite. He had absolutely supported Elizabeth in her decision not to go any further, with the conventional treatments for cancer—chemotherapy and radiation. In fact, he felt it was very much a reasonable choice—and felt her chances of beating the illness, permanently, were good . . . *Hindsight is always goddamn 20/20. Fuck . . .*

Steve, working opposite him on another stepladder, was putting the last screws into a piece of sheetrock they'd just put up. Nate set his screw-drill down on the stepladder and stepped down to the floor. He wore a somber expression. "Hey, man . . . I think I'm gonna call it a day. And boogie. You can stay if you feel like it. Guess you'll just have to use smaller pieces of sheetrock."

"No, buddy," Steve said. "Let's just call it. I'm good with that. We'll be finished with the ceiling tomorrow morning."

After the guys had cleaned up the room a bit and put away a few tools, Steve carried a few of his own personal tools out to his truck. Nate went into the house to talk with Jim for a few minutes. He briefly mentioned Elizabeth's illness and asked if they could come over sometime to talk about Barbara's experience with the healer in Brazil. Barbara was in the den, reading. She and Jim both thought that that same evening would be fine—if he and Elizabeth wanted to come over for a cup of coffee or tea, and talk.

2.

. . . A medium? And spirits of the dead working on people?
Holy shit . . .

Elizabeth was skeptical at first but talked with Barbara a number of times in the next few weeks. She also spoke on the phone with several people in California—people whom Barbara knew who had also been down to Brazil to see this healer, Joseph of God. Elizabeth tried to research the man, at the local library. She felt curious enough, that she finally made the long trip down to Las Cruces to use the library at New Mexico State University. A library that had a large collection of periodicals on microfilm. But there were few news stories or articles written about this man and the healing center in Brazil, and no published books about him. A mystery man. A couple of the articles were first-hand accounts published in American health and alternative medicine magazines.

Talk of miraculous healers of course raised eyebrows in the medical and scientific communities. And for a while, it sounded to Elizabeth like sheer quackery. But the more she heard and read about this man, the more she felt drawn to go to Brazil and visit this center. Almost as if she would be participating in some sort of spiritual experiment. And maybe it was simply faith healing that was going on there—or placebo effect. But she gradually felt more and more that she needed to go there and find out for herself.

"Liz," Nate said, "if you really think this is what you want to do . . . then we should do it." It was late night, after Elizabeth's trip to the library in Las Cruces. The boys had been put to bed for the night, the house quiet. The east-side door in the main bedroom was still halfway open. It had been a mild late-April day, the earthship was very warm, and through the screen door the cool evening air felt fresh and good. Nate lay on his side, in bed, with his boxer shorts on, Elizabeth lying next to him with a few copies she'd made of some magazine articles. He glanced at the articles resting on her lap. "We can swing it, Babe. You know, I've been kind of curious about this from the first time I heard about Jim and Barbara's story. Who knows? Maybe this guy is the real deal . . . and you'll be cured. Shit, that sounds weird . . . I mean, I consider myself a pretty logical guy—"

"Uh-huh?" Elizabeth said. "You are?"

"Well, I, uh . . . maybe cynical or cautious is a better way of putting it."

She smirked. "Yep."

"And I didn't mean that it sounds weird—if you were to be cured, by going to this healer. You know? I meant that it sounds weird, *me* saying that. . . . But, stranger things have happened. I think there are a lot of things we don't understand, in this world. Barbara's experience with this guy—in this town, what's it called, *Ada . . . Adelândia?* A pretty damned amazing story. It blows my mind, actually."

"Yeah. Her story *is* amazing. And some of the other stories I've heard. Yeah, the town's called Adelândia. In the state of Goiás, Brazil. I guess it's an area of hill country they call the Brazilian Highlands." Elizabeth flipped through the pages of a book she'd borrowed, simply titled "Brazil." She wondered if he was really behind her, on this . . . *Or is he just humoring me? I can't go through with this—if he's not really in it, all the way. If he's just going through the motions to keep me happy, well, this ain't gonna work . . .* "Nate . . . are you sure you want to *do* this? Go down to Brazil? And spend time in this town, there?"

Nate looked at her and took her hand. "*Yes,* Liz. Really. I think we should. And besides, I'm really curious, myself, about what's going on down there."

"You are? You know . . . my folks don't like the sound of it. I talked to 'em on the phone a couple days ago."

"I know."

"They want me to come back home—to Asheville. They say their doctor has a connection with a cancer specialist that they want to hook me up with—"

"Oh?" Nate said.

"and I could start a new course of cancer treatment, there."

"Well, I guess that's always an option. Of course, there are plenty of good cancer doctors here, too. Just not right near Silver City," he muttered, "that's for sure."

Puffing her cheeks out slightly, Elizabeth exhaled a long sigh. "They're gonna think I'm out of my mind—going down to this wacky place in Brazil. They think this is all some kind of new-age craziness we're doing."

"Liz—" Nate said, and paused. "on some level, it doesn't *matter* what they think. No cancer treatment is a sure thing, *any*way."

"I guess."

"Besides. Who the hell can really judge what's crazy and what's not? I mean, maybe we *are* halfway around the bend—going thousands of miles to see this healer guy. But hell, sometimes I think the whole world's almost completely insane. Look at what's going on in Iraq, now—with this 'Desert Storm.' And in Yugoslavia. Hell . . . going down to a little town in Brazil to get healed by a guy who says he heals people with God's help doesn't sound too crazy at all."

"Maybe not," Elizabeth said. "And it just *might* be true. . . . That there really *are* these amazing healings going on there."

"*Totally.*"

They talked for a while longer that night. And more, the next night. Within a few days, their musings, curiosity, and questions about this were gelling into a fairly solid plan. It wouldn't be cheap. Flying down to Rio de Janeiro, or Brasilia. Staying in this small town for a few weeks. Nate told Elizabeth not to worry for a second about the money. He had a little saved from his construction work, their cost of living was low, and he had full access now to the trust his father had set up. They called up Nate's mother, Janie, to see if she was available to visit from California, was able to stay and babysit with the kids while they were gone. The kids were getting older, now, and would be fine staying with their grandmother for a few weeks. And her answer was yes, she would come.

An old friend from Santa Fe, Mac, visited, a week and a half later— having heard of the unusual trip the couple were planning. On the Friday evening that he arrived, Elizabeth fixed a big dinner for the family. The earthship, this evening, smelled of the homely odors of seared meat, onions, and garlic—solid American food. A pot roast with potatoes and vegetables had cooked slowly in the oven for hours; there was also a salad and green beans. The boys apparently thought it a special treat—

having pot roast—and they hovered around the kitchen more than usual, horsing around with Mac. While the oven was on, Elizabeth baked a little tofu for herself. But when it came time to sit down at the table, she set the tofu aside and served herself some of the pot roast along with everybody else. Mac watched her serving up portions of the meat, out of a Dutch oven—so tender it was falling apart. *"Beef!"* he said, in a dramatic, deep voice. *"It's what's for dinner!* Ha ha! Did you guys ever see those commercials, on TV?"

"Yeah, right," Nate said. "I remember. Robert Mitchum, or somebody. Some guy with a macho voice. He was, like, a spokesman for the U.S. Beef Council, or something. . . . Our tax dollars hard at work, I guess."

"Now, now, buddy—" Mac said, "always the cynic."

Nobody even remotely complained about the pot roast, though. And the Dutch oven was empty by the time they were clearing away dishes. After some cursory dishwashing was done and the boys had quieted down in the next room, the three adults sat around the table in the kitchen of the earthship and talked, mostly of the upcoming trip.

Mac sipped from a coffee mug of decaf, and looked past his mug at Elizabeth. She seemed exhausted, a washed-out look to her. "Well," he said, "you guys sure are the adventurers, going off into the Brazilian jungles. If anyone was gonna do this kind of thing, it'd be you two."

Nate looked up from the map of Brazil that he was poring over. "Yeah. But it's not really jungle where we're going. The real jungle— rain forest—is to the north of where we'll be. But we'll hit that area, before we head back to the States. We're gonna go on a rafting trip down the Amazon, you see, and hang out for a while with some of those aboriginal tribes. You know . . . we'll have, like, a little cultural-exchange experience. Isn't that right, Hon'?"

Elizabeth raised her eyebrows. "Ah, yeah, I guess. But I hadn't heard about this part, yet."

"Oh, it's just a little side-trip I'm planning—" Nate winked at her. "to keep things interesting."

"I guess that would make it interesting," Mac said. "But it'll probably be interesting enough—just going to this town in Brazil. To be with this healer guy. I still haven't been able to find out much about this dude . . . but then, I haven't had much spare time to do that. I'm probably not looking in the right places, though. There are so many of those new-agey, Beverly Hills kind of health clinics around Santa Fe. . . . Surely the folks at *those* places would have heard of him." He grimaced for an instant and looked down at the table in front of him . . . *I shouldn't have said that. This isn't any joke. Shit* . . . "What I *meant* was . . . I just haven't heard or read anything about this Joseph of God, you know? But that doesn't really mean anything."

"*Nope*," Nate said, getting up from the table, with his coffee mug in hand. "Need a freshener, buddy?" Mac didn't. After topping off his own mug, Nate slumped back into his chair at the table. "No. No surprise there. We don't even watch TV here, of course." He motioned his head over to a large television on the far side of the living room area. "We only use 'the tube' over there for watching videos. Classic movies, and stuff. And educational videotapes for the guys. But, I mean, the so-called *news* that we're fed here—in the States—by the media . . . *God,* don't even get me started. It's not *news.* I mean, do we ever hear about any of the *good* things happening in the world? No. Only the bad shit, you know?"

"Afraid so," Mac said.

"We would never even *hear* about some dude in another part of the world—doing miraculous healings. Because *they* think we need to hear about the latest car-bombings in Baghdad. Or the latest stories about the 'death squads' in El Salvador—that supposedly we're against, but, oops!, our government actually created 'em. I guess horrible news is supposed to keep us interested."

"Yep." Mac half smiled and half grimaced. "And you tune in to the news, the next night—to see if anything's gotten better. As if it actually *would.*"

"Really," Nate said, climbing out of his chair. "Gimme a break. I gotta go check on the kids—be back in a few. . . . Got to make sure the guys brush their teeth before it's lights-out."

Mac took a gulp of his coffee, and looked at Elizabeth, one of his favorite female friends . . . *Beautiful* . . . *She looks a bit worn out, though* . . . "So, what d'ya think about all this? A pretty exciting trip, coming up, huh?"

"Yep," she said, "it should be. I'm looking forward to it. I guess you *could* say I've got nothing to lose."

Mac gazed at her in silence, not wanting to show the scramble of concern and sadness he felt. "I bet it'll be amazing. I've never been to South America. Been down to Mexico, twice, though. Baja California, once, on a BMW road bike. *Great* trip—if only I could remember it. I was drunk both times, though, and hardly remember a thing. Brazil's gotta be pretty incredible, though."

"Yes," Elizabeth said. "I think so. I'm looking forward to it. Even if this guy can't heal me. Or if it's too late, or something."

"Well, I don't know. I may be kind of red-necky and hardheaded in some ways . . . but I do believe miracles can happen. Probably they *do* happen . . . and maybe all the time. But we don't even notice them 'cause we're busy looking at something else."

"Yep. I do believe *any*thing's possible, in this phenomenal world. Our friend, Barbara, here—she told us about some really mind-blowing things happening, with this Joseph of God. When they were down there. People being cut open without bleeding. And not feeling any pain—without anesthetics."

"Wow," Mac said.

Elizabeth poured herself another cup, from a teapot on the table. "Really. There must be some kind of spiritual mojo—or some metaphysical power—that's going on there. He claims, that—Joseph of God, I mean—he claims that it's God's power and love, working through him. That he, himself, doesn't do the healing work, at all. . . . That these spirits work through him. He's like a medium—channeling these healing spirits. And *they* do this healing work."

"This is wild."

"Yeah, it is. Supposedly these spirits are the spirits of people who've died—and for some reason haven't moved on, yet. I guess they still want to help people in this world, and ease their suffering. Some of these spirits are doctors and surgeons who've passed on. And a few of them are saints, apparently. There's supposedly some kind of spiritual healing that goes on, while they're curing the patient's body of the physical disease."

Mac gulped his coffee, and it went down the wrong way. He coughed, "Incredible."

"It *is* incredible," Elizabeth said. "But it's also *possible*, I think."

"Oh, yeah. I didn't mean it that way. I just meant it's hard to believe.". . . *Shit!* . . . "What I meant, was—it's hard to believe, with a twentieth-century mind that's filled with the scientific understanding that we have. You know . . . of the way things work, in this world. Like, matter and energy. Cause and effect. Physics. Quantum Mechanics." Mac felt like there were the beginnings of a pleading tone in his verbal rambling . . . *Damn it! I should change the subject. I'm gonna put my foot right into my mouth. Maybe hurt her feelings. And her faith . . . in what could turn out to be some kind of amazing healing process . . .*

"Well . . . there you go. I mean, quantum physics tells us basically that everything's made up of energy, right? Or at least that it's one possibility. And apparently this healer—Joseph of God—uses healing energy to do this work. Or rather, these spirits do . . . working *through* him. God's energy."

Mac wore a puzzled expression . . . *Man. A medium? And spirits of the dead working on people? Holy shit* . . . "Wow. This could be an amazing trip."

"*Yes*. I hope so."

"I guess I *will* get myself a little more coffee, here . . ." As Mac hefted himself out of his chair, Elizabeth started to say something but stopped after a couple of words. When he returned to the table, he glanced at her. "I'm sorry . . . say again?"

She said, quietly, perhaps so that Nate wouldn't overhear, "I really don't want to go . . . just yet. *Die,* I mean."

For a moment Mac felt a suffocating sensation in his gut, and his eyes clouded for a second . . . *Damn it. I love this woman* . . . It passed, and his voice was steady. "No. Of course you don't." He looked at Elizabeth again; her face wasn't as animated as it had been when she spoke about Joseph of God. A tired, empty look in her eyes, again, and a facsimile of a smile on her lips. A thought flashed through his mind . . . *She's grasping at straws* . . . It nearly made him nauseous, and he dismissed it immediately. "No. No, you've got a lot more things to do here, girl . . . before your time's up."

"I hope so . . ."

Nate came back into the room, pulling the curtain closed behind him which blocked off the rest of the house. He exhaled tiredly, with a whistling sound, and dropped into his chair at the table again, glancing at his friend, then Elizabeth. "Man, it's nice that the kids are pretty quiet tonight. The little miracles in life, huh? Did I miss anything? Any earthshaking discussion?"

Elizabeth was silent. Mac felt distracted, tugging at his moustache. "Well, yeah. You *did* miss something. Liz and I are going to Brazil . . . and you're staying home and taking care of the guys." He winked at Elizabeth.

"Oh . . . *kay*."

"So," Mac said, "what's on the agenda for tomorrow?"

Nate halfway grinned. "Well, Liz is staying here and resting up for the trip . . . and you and I are going to a 'sweat-lodge' in the afternoon, at 'the People's Lodge.'"

"Oh, no. Not *again*, buddy." Mac rolled his eyes. "I almost blew a head-gasket the last time we did sweat-lodge."

"No, you did *great!* And you'll probably get even more out of it, this time."

"More *what?* More heat prostration? More strokes? More pulmonary failure? I don't know if—"

"Oh, hell," Nate blurted, "quit being so goddamn melodramatic."

Elizabeth giggled. "Oh, c'mon, Mac. You'll have fun." The three of them continued their conversation at the kitchen table late into the night.

≈   ≈   ≈   ≈   ≈

Sunday evening, after their friend hit the road back to Santa Fe, Nate and Elizabeth revisited the maps of Brazil, a travel guide, and Portuguese translation books. They finalized their plans, making it jibe with a calendar. Elizabeth talked on the phone the next day with her doctor, Andi Sheaffer, discussing what they intended to do. The doctor sounded skeptical—though she'd heard of two people in the Santa Fe area who had gone to Brazil to see this healer. As it seemed evident she couldn't talk Elizabeth out of it, she suggested instead that she make an appointment to see her as soon as they got back.

3.

Don't Believe Everything You Think

So, sooner than either of them thought possible, in the last week of May they were at Hartsfield-Atlanta International Airport boarding a flight to Brazil. Their flight had begun in Albuquerque—with a layover connection in Atlanta, where they boarded another jet for a direct flight to Brasilia, the capital.

Brasilia was inland, in the south central area of the vast country, and fairly close to the small town of Adelândia where Joseph of God worked. Adelândia was in the Brazilian Highlands region—with hills, mountains and plateaus, generally from 2,000 to 4,000 feet in elevation. Although at a relatively high elevation compared to the Amazon Basin, the Brazilian Highlands were surrounded by warm tropical rain forests and close enough to the equator that the weather would still be warm and humid. Even though this would be early winter, there—the dry season. From what Elizabeth had read, it seemed that even during the coldest months of the year it could still be in the 70s and 80s, Fahrenheit, during the daytime. And at night, only slightly cooler than at other times of the year.

Elizabeth had conjured up an image of Adelândia as a rustic tropical village, with jungle encroaching on all sides. Barbara, though, (and several others they'd talked with, about Brazil) said that Adelândia was actually a large town—several thousand in population. There were a few large cities nearby, like Anápolis and Brasilia, which had modern urban skylines rivaling those of American metropolitan areas.

Nate and Elizabeth had left Albuquerque in the early morning, but after the layover in Atlanta this second flight wouldn't arrive in Brasilia until late in the evening. As they flew over the Amazon Basin, the land, far below, was in dusky shadow—while the plane was still up in the sunlight. Elizabeth, sitting next to a window, could see the myriad lights of a large city below, surrounded by the primeval darkness of the Amazon rain forest . . . *Wonder if that's Manaus* . . . The pilot announced, over the PA system, that they were in fact flying over that city, a city which squatted and sprawled on the banks of the Amazon.

Thunderheads billowed up into the heights around the aircraft, lit up fluorescent shades of yellow and pink in the evening sun. With occasional flashes of lightning from within, illuminating the clouds like light bulbs. Even at this height, to Elizabeth it felt completely different from the wide-open arid land of New Mexico. Brazil was beginning to feel like a very foreign country . . . *Foreign, indeed. I don't even know the first thing about this place . . . never mind all the reading I've done. We don't even hear about South America, in our evening news. Almost like the entire continent doesn't exist. In the States, we're so isolated in some ways* . . . Nate was nodding off in the seat next to her and soon she dozed off, also. The plane was descending when she awoke, and she peered out the window into a starry night sky with the lights of a large city below rising to meet them. "Brasilia," she said to Nate, who was also stirring.

"Guess so," he said, in a groggy voice, squinting out the window. "Huh. Big city."

After collecting their bags at the baggage claim, they found a hotel close to the airport—one that they'd read about in a travel guide to Brazil. A young man who worked the front desk of the place could speak some English, and they were able to negotiate a room easily. The room had all the amenities of any modern urban hotel, with a comfortable bed, which they fell into quickly. Elizabeth had trouble falling asleep, though, and sat up in bed to read for a while. A travel guide-book. "Fodor's Brazil-1990."

The next morning was sunny and humid, and they got up late, dragging in to breakfast at the restaurant at the hotel. After their meal, a middle-aged, mustachioed gentleman at the front desk was able to give them directions to the bus station—where they could theoretically catch a bus that would take them all the way to Adelândia. But with a number of stops in between. The man spoke almost perfect English, though most of the other people milling around the hotel lobby were speaking in Portuguese. Elizabeth had assumed that Portuguese would sound similar to the Spanish that she and Nate were accustomed to hearing in New Mexico. But in fact it sounded completely different—like an unrelated and almost guttural language. They checked out of the hotel and got a taxi to drop them off at the bus station. The Portuguese translation book that Jim and Barbara had lent them left much to be desired—as they found out when they endeavored to find the correct bus line and purchase tickets.

It was a Monday morning in a strange country, and Elizabeth felt tired, jet-lagged, and more than a little disoriented. And Nate appeared to be in similar shape. The staccato and guttural sounds of Portuguese, being spoken all around them, only magnified the strangeness. Nate seemed tense, tapping his feet on the shiny concrete floor. While killing time in the bus station waiting room, they noticed a group of eight or ten people speaking English—so Nate wandered over to talk with them. He introduced himself and pointed out Elizabeth, sitting with their bags. "We just overheard you, from the other side of the room—and noticed you were speaking English. Where are you all from?"

A tall blonde woman introduced herself as Dawn. "We're all West Coast folks. I live in the San Francisco Bay area. Most of my friends, here, are Californians—but a couple are from Oregon." They were all headed to Adelândia, to visit Joseph of God. Dawn said she was their tour guide or liaison. She had been to Adelândia a number of times—by herself and with groups. "We're more than likely taking the same bus that you and your wife are. So we'll probably see more of you guys."

"That's great," Nate said.

"Do you have a place to stay," she asked, "when we get there, to Adelândia?"

"No, we don't. We don't have any reservations, or anything. This has been kind of a last-minute trip, for us."

"Gotcha." Dawn smiled kindly. "There might very well be room for you guys, you know, at the place we're staying—The *Pousada das Rosas*. There are quite a few bed-and-breakfast places around town, so you shouldn't have any trouble finding a place to stay. But I'll explain how to get to the place we're staying—the *pousada*—when we get off the bus, in town. It's reasonable. And the woman who runs it is adorable."

"*Awesome*. That would be *won*derful. So good to meet you guys." He smiled at the group, looking them over quickly, and walked back over to Elizabeth to tell her the good news. "Feels a little less like we're strangers in a strange land."

"Yeah," Elizabeth said, "that's great. They're going there too, huh? Maybe we can hang out with them, a bit, and learn more about this place." She felt too tired, though, to go over and talk with the group.

Soon the bus arrived, and it filled chock-full with passengers by the time they left the station. It would be over one hundred miles, by the

highways, from Brasilia to Adelândia. At first, the bus rolled down
dozens of blocks of city streets that looked much like any American city
except for the Portuguese street signs and occasional palm trees. Brasilia
sprawled over a huge area. In the outskirts of the city, though, the houses
and apartments had a decidedly foreign and tropical look to them—many
of them built of stuccoed masonry, brightly painted, with red tile roofs.
The bus finally got less crowded when many of the passengers got off in
a neighboring city, Taguatinga. Nate pointed out to Elizabeth that the
group traveling with Dawn was sitting together near the front of the bus.
Though no longer crowded on the bus, it was stuffy and warm despite a
few of the windows being cracked open. Elizabeth felt a ticklish bead of
sweat trickling under her tank-top shirt. After Taguatinga, she noticed the
land becoming more sparsely populated, with great expanses of green
between the towns. Only a few extensively wooded areas—but a lot of
pasture and ranch land, dotted with large, tropical-looking trees, standing
singly or in groups . . . *Hmm . . . shiny leaves, like they're some kind of
tropical evergreens. Maybe mango trees? Papaya? . . .* There were also
numerous mimosa trees—with their feathery leaves—similar to the ones
Elizabeth had seen where she grew up in the South. Here and there stood
coconut palms.

A woman with dark complexion—maybe Caboclo background
(mixed Portuguese and Indian)—sat across the aisle in the bus and
noticed Elizabeth looking around like a tourist. The woman asked
Elizabeth a question—as best as Elizabeth could figure—about whether
or not she was from America. Elizabeth nodded and said, "Yes. *Da
América.*" The woman smiled. Elizabeth looked frantically through the
Portuguese translation book, wanting to ask where she the woman was
going. Finally she did ask, though she knew her pronunciation left much
to be desired.

The woman looked confused for a moment, and then a look of
recognition crossed her face. "Oh. . . . Adelândia."

Elizabeth said, in English, "Me, too," and pointed at herself. "*Casa de
Dom Francisco* . . . Joseph of God. *José de Deus.*" The woman nodded
her head, smiling. Elizabeth smiled and went back to gazing around at
the countryside . . . *Well, my first half-Portuguese conversation—and
that wasn't too painful* . . . A few minutes later, Elizabeth stole a glance
at the woman again . . . *Wonder why? . . . She doesn't look ill at all—
maybe she lives there, in Adelândia . . .*

Looking around the bus, Elizabeth noticed for the first time that at
least a few people on board looked to be suffering from one type of
illness or another. A woman a couple of seats ahead of them coughed
quietly on a regular, compulsive basis. A few people had crutches

propped next to them on the seats. Elizabeth turned around, briefly, to look at the bus passengers behind her. She got a quick sense of several people who had an unwell look on their faces . . . *How odd. Almost like rolling hospital. But I 'spect I look a little sickly and tired, too . . .*

The bus stopped in another medium-sized city, mostly modern, called Alexânia. A few more people got off the bus, there, and a few got on. As the bus left this city, the landscape along the highway once again had a rural look to it . . . *Probably be another half hour to Adelândia . . .* Rolling hills and small mountains were visible, now, stretching to the horizon, some of them brownish with dry autumn grass. The scattered tall trees—and clumps of trees—reminded Elizabeth of films she'd seen of the African savannah. Here, away from the cities, the skies had become an intense blue. It reminded her of the blue skies of New Mexico . . . *But the clouds are different . . .* In the afternoon sun, distant billowing cumulous clouds like popcorn were visible near the horizon, as if sprouting out of the earth . . . *Tropical clouds. Tropical skies. It looks a lot like this in Florida . . .*

They passed a few farms and a couple of outlying houses, and seemed to be approaching a town, which Elizabeth guessed would be Adelândia. One of the farms was a cattle ranch—maybe a dairy—and had a number of coconut palms growing around a large tile-roofed house. As the bus rolled into the outskirts of the town she realized it was larger than the tropical village she'd pictured. Still, the town looked to have no more than a couple thousand residents. The houses were plain, though bright and cheerful in the varieties of color they were painted. *Caribbean colors,* Elizabeth thought . . . *Margaritaville . . .* Most of them were one-story houses with tile roofs. A few were tiny—called *casinhas,* or what New Mexicans would call casitas. There were also some brand-new houses and a couple of new two-story houses or apartments . . . *Maybe those are the pousadas—like B & Bs—that we've heard about . . .*

The bus stop in Adelândia was at a main crossroad in the town. Most everyone got off the bus here except for a handful of folks. Probably people going on to the next city further west—Anápolis. The little town was almost devoid of traffic, with an odd feeling in the air of everyone in the vicinity taking a siesta. A dusty car rolled slowly down the street, while a man in a horse-cart guided his horse in a large arc around the bus. Nate, hefting their bag off of the bus, staggered over to where the West Coast group was gathered—Elizabeth following with the backpack she'd brought. Dawn, easily recognizable with her blonde hair, was saying something to the group. Nate came up behind her and tugged on her shirtsleeve, his face a question mark.

Dawn turned, giggled, and began to explain to Nate and Elizabeth which *pousada* they were staying at and how to get there. But midway through the directions, she looked around and took a quick tally of her group. One of them was a man on crutches. The *pousada* was only a few blocks away—and most of the visitors agreed that the walk might do them good. The owner of the *Pousada das Rosas* had sent a car to meet the bus; but as it turned out, the driver only had a couple of people to ferry over to the place. The rest of the group put their bags in the car and walked.

A block down the road, they passed by a little pizzeria, which Dawn explained had just opened, possibly to cater to some of the foreign visitors. As they passed by the open door, the fragrance of fresh-baked bread, scorched cheese, and spices wafted out. Elizabeth salivated, though she wasn't actually homesick for American food yet . . . *I think we'll have to give them some business, while we're here—maybe even tonight* . . . She noticed Nate looking into the little, dark restaurant . . . *I think it will be tonight* . . .

The Pousada das Rosas was appropriately named, a two-story building with a number of white and red rose bushes out front, the building's stucco painted a coral pink. As Dawn had guessed, there was a room available for Nate and Elizabeth. Dawn assured them that the pousadas on this street, nearby to the Joseph of God center, were all priced similarly. The woman who ran the place, Ana, looked to be a local Brazilian, with olive complexion—and seemed very cheerful and friendly as she spoke in her halting English.

They lugged their bags up the staircase. In the upstairs hallway Elizabeth noticed a placard on the wall, with Portuguese words and underneath them an English translation—*Don't Believe Everything You Think.* They found their room, small but pleasant, with white plaster walls and white curtains. Elizabeth felt exhausted and with the remnants of jet lag—and threw herself on the bed. Nate said he would go downstairs to look for some bottled water. He bought a bottle from the hostess, Ana—who had a refrigerator stocked with a few such amenities for the guests—though she assured him, also, that the tap water was perfectly safe.

When Nate returned, Elizabeth lay there with her eyes closed. He glanced at her, while moving their travel bag to a place on the floor where they were less likely to trip over it. She was actually asleep, now, snoring softly. He gazed at her for a couple of minutes, her face looking older than her years in the late-afternoon light. He unbuttoned his short-sleeve shirt, which stuck to him a bit with the stuffiness in the room. There was a ceiling fan, and he found the switch for it—clicking it on and   then   curling   up   beside   her   on   the   bed.

4.

***". . . he's a powerful 'trance medium'—and these
Entities use his body to access this world,
in order to help relieve peoples' suffering."***

At some point during the night they both must have awakened—they were under the sheets when a rooster crowing nearby woke them at dawn. A screened window had been left open overnight. And otherwise it was quiet outside, though with the distant melodic sounds of a few songbirds stirring from sleep in the bushes and trees around the village. There was an unusual chuckling bird sound from a tree in a neighbor's yard—possibly a parrot.

Nate went down the hallway to use one of the shared bathrooms, while Elizabeth, standing only in an oversized t-shirt, gazed out the window at the morning unfolding. The sun peeked through a bank of low clouds to the east, scattering sunbeams here and there—some distant hills were sunlit while the town of Adelândia was still in early-morning darkness. A cloud hung low in a lush green valley to the northeast, like it had just lifted from the moist earth. It felt to Elizabeth like they'd awoken in a mountain town, above the clouds . . . *But it can't be very high, here, in this part of the Highlands . . . maybe just two or three thousand feet. But I guess that's high, for Brazil . . .* The valley that the town was nestled in had a light, cheerful feeling to it, dimly lit though it was . . . *Something ethereal about it . . .* But she suspected it was just this curious daybreak moment—and herself being unfamiliar with the tropics.

The bedroom door opened—Nate returning from the bathroom—and he joined her at the window. They had turned the fan off sometime during the night, and a slightly cool, moist breeze came in at the window. He put his arm around her waist as they gazed at the brightening landscape. "Far *out.* Beautiful morning."

After leisurely washing up and dressing, they went downstairs and served themselves some breakfast in the little dining room. The owner of the house, Ana, had set out a plate of fresh bread and butter, and a coffeepot hissed on a hot plate. A couple from the West Coast group came down and joined them, introducing themselves. Elizabeth munched on buttered bread, flipping through a new book about Brazil that they'd picked up in the city. Nate had a bowl of some kind of hot cereal that Ana brought out, in a pot. After Ana had left the room he said, in a low voice, "Tastes like corn. I don't really know how to ask her what it is, though. . . . But it tastes pretty good."

Elizabeth looked over at him while sipping her coffee. "Maybe they eat *grits*, here—like I did, growing up in North Cackalacky, I mean Carolina."

"I think it is. Grits, I mean. Tastes like it."

"Hmm. Come to think of it, I read that they make a corn cereal that's popular here in Brazil . . . I think it's called *mingau*." Ana came into the room again, smiling, and bustled about, freshening peoples' coffee cups. Elizabeth tried out some of her Portuguese on Ana, and pointed at the coffeepot, *"Café . . . do Brasil?"*

"Yes, yes," Ana said. *"Com certeza!* (Of course.) From Brazil. From Espirito Santo—in the East."

"Very good coffee. *Café . . . Café é excelente.*"

"Yes," Ana said, "thank you."

Elizabeth glanced at Nate. *"Really* fresh coffee. From somewhere nearby—"

"Cool," he said. "It *is* good coffee."

Dawn came downstairs and into the dining room, wearing a conservative, loose-fitting white dress. She greeted Nate and Elizabeth with a "Good Morning," mentioning that a few of the others from the group were sleeping late. Ana came into the room and asked her, in Portuguese, some sort of question. Dawn smiled at her and answered with some rapid-fire Portuguese. Apparently Ana understood her perfectly—she just smiled, and said, "OK. *Só um minuto.*"

Elizabeth met Nate's glance and raised her eyebrows with a sly smile. She turned to Dawn, *"Boy,* I think you're someone we should tag along with, while we're here. You speak the language *very* well."

"Yeah, I've gotten pretty fluent with it. This is my fifth trip here, to visit Joseph—José. The last four times, I've come with a group."

"Well . . . you must have your hands full, I bet. With—what is it—

eight people who came with you?"

"Seven," Dawn said. "Eight, *including* me. No, really . . . I'll help you guys any way I can. This is a perfect-sized group that I have with me this time. I don't mind a bit, and I'm sure none of the group members will. People help each other out around here—as you'll find out. That's really what the whole thing is about . . . here in Adelândia."

"That would be *awesome,*" Nate said. "We're a little like fish out o' water, here."

"Right. . . . The town is pretty quiet today—so it's a good day to get acclimated. It'll be crowded tomorrow. I guess you guys probably know that Joseph—José—only does the healing work here on Wednesday, Thursday, and Friday. The other days of the week, he goes home to his farm to recharge."

"Yes," Elizabeth said. "We've heard that."

"So," Dawn continued, "today's a good day to get acquainted with the town. And look around, a bit, at the *Casa*—you know, the place where José does his healing work. Get a feel for the place."

Elizabeth nodded. "Yeah, we thought it might be good day to poke around town. Are you going over to the *Casa* today? 'Cause if you are, we'd love to join you."

"That'll be fine. We're gonna be heading over there, about an hour from now. It's just about five blocks from here. I'll knock on your door, before we go."

"That would be *won*derful." Elizabeth sipped the last of her coffee. She suggested to Nate that they take a quick walk down the street—back toward the "downtown" area.

They stepped out into the morning light, and it was mild already. A warm, humid breeze blowing from the north. They walked the few blocks over toward where the bus had dropped them off, the day before—the main crossroad in town—and explored a couple of shops that sold fruits and vegetables. Businesses that had been closed the previous afternoon. They bought a cluster of fresh-looking bananas from one of the greengrocers and walked back to their room at the pousada, where Elizabeth wanted to lie down for a few minutes before they went out again with the group.

A while later, mid-morning, they were walking up the narrow street with Dawn and her group. The street led north, up a slight incline, toward the outskirts of town and the surrounding countryside. There was only the occasional car rolling down the street. Once in a while, a farm truck. Dawn began to explain a little about the *Casa de Dom Francisco,* or the *Casa,* as it was called—where José did the majority of his healing work.

"Joseph—*José*—who's often called *Medium José* . . . well, he traveled around Brazil for many years, doing countless healings. But, eventually he was told by the spirits to build a healing center here, in Adelândia. So he did that. Bought the land, and everything. And started building the healing center here, in the '70s. He named it the *Casa de Dom Francisco*. Saint Francis Xavier was a Jesuit priest—and Francis is one of the spirits, or *Entities,* that incorporate into José's body—and perform the healings and surgeries. You see, José will tell you that he, himself, doesn't do the healing work at all. It's just that he's a powerful 'trance medium'—and these *Entities* use his body to access this world, in order to help relieve peoples' suffering. There are about thirty Entities that José incorporates, to do this work. José tells us that it's God's power—and love—that does the healing."

A gray-haired woman from the West Coast group shook her head slightly. "It's *amazing.*"

"It is," Dawn said. "All of us who've been here before would tell you to just keep an open mind . . . and suspend judgement, for a while, from your intellect. And you'll see some amazing things happening here. And hopefully, for you, yourselves."

The sun was beginning to feel hot, reflecting off the asphalt road. Elizabeth felt a trickle of sweat run down her lower back, as she glanced down the road. Ahead, the paved road appeared to give way into a rutted dirt road. Elizabeth looked at Dawn with a confused expression. "So, like . . . I'm having a little trouble with this—"

"That's normal."

"So I . . . well . . . I don't see how . . . I mean, if Joseph—José—can't actually *do* any of the healings, himself, then how do the spirits do it? Are they just, more or less using his body and hands?"

"Well," Dawn said, "yes and no. Because, you see, the majority of the healings here are what's called 'invisible surgery' . . . and they're mostly done in the three side rooms that we call the *current* rooms. There are only a few 'visible' or 'physical surgeries' that are done, each day—and they're usually done in the 'main hall,' the big room that has a sort of stage area. And José—or actually, the Entity (whichever one is incorporated in him, at the time)—will do a few 'visible' surgeries there. Sometimes the surgeries are on benign tumors. Also eye surgery, cancers. But people here will tell you that almost all of the healing takes place because of the *energy* of the Casa. This healing energy. *The Current.* Even when there's a physical surgery done, there's still a lot of the healing that's going on, invisibly. The assistants and helpers here will all tell you that—for most of the diseases and illnesses treated here— well, that the invisible surgeries and healings are just as effective, if not more effective, than the visible surgeries."

Elizabeth felt (as probably some others in the group did) something within her that couldn't fathom this. But another part of her mind—or maybe her heart, with the wide-eyed curiosity and innocence she had as a child—thought differently . . . *Yes. I think this might be true. Something about this sounds familiar . . . like I've heard this somewhere before . . .* After a few long moments contemplating this, all she could muster was a soft, "Huh."

"So it's really all energy," Dawn continued, "—energy work and energy healing—that's done here. Even when José is cutting someone open . . . they don't feel it, because of the spiritual energy, or spiritual anesthesia. And they usually don't bleed—because of the spiritual energy. And the rest of the healing is done, in the next few days or weeks, because of this energy. It all comes from God. Why wouldn't it?"

In a few more minutes they reached an entry gate to a fenced area enclosing a number of buildings. The buildings cheerfully painted in bright blue and white—but protected by fences around the perimeter as if it were some kind of cult compound. A tall, ruddy-faced man from the group spoke up, "So what do you tell people who suggest that Joseph of God is a charlatan? Or maybe *worse*—that he's using some kind of evil powers?" The gray-haired woman who commented earlier stood next to him, rolling her eyes . . . *Probably his wife . . .*

Dawn paused at the entry gate, smiling halfway. "Well, to be honest, I don't have any time for that. Whatever floats your boat. . . . The human mind has always been frightened—and often hysterical—about things it can't comprehend. For millenia. Probably from the beginning of time. Just look at the Old Testament in Christianity and Judaism, and the Torah. *Chock-full* of fear. Fear of God. Fear of evil. Fear of the Devil. Fear of death. Fear of most *everything.* Life, to me, is way too short to spend it fearing and hating something just because your fragile little ego can't figure it out. The human mind is so very limited."

The gate to the Casa buildings, with a masonry arch over it, was closed and locked. But Elizabeth noticed there was a side gate on one of the sidewalks leading into the compound—and that one stood wide open. She walked through it, glancing at Dawn as she did . . . *Hmm . . . a little testy, there, but I get what she's sayin' . . .*

The group walked onto the grounds, which were silent today except for the twittering of birds among the trees scattered over the brownish lawn. It was getting on toward midday, and several members of the group sat down on benches, which were for the most part placed in deep shade under the trees. Someone asked Dawn what kind of trees they were, and she answered that some were mangoes and a few were avocados. A couple of mimosas, and some kind of tropical locust trees.

A few people wanted to walk around, and as they meandered over the grounds Dawn described the layout of the buildings and their purpose. They poked their heads into the main hall of the central building—a sort of small auditorium that could hold a couple hundred people or so. Dawn pointed out how the *current rooms* were all off to the right side of the main hall, hidden from view but with doors leading to them.

Nate and Elizabeth peeled off from the group and wandered around the buildings on their own for a while. One small structure behind the central building had a back door that was unlocked. Curious, they walked inside. It was a large storeroom, separated off from a front room of the building. The front room seemed to be some kind of dispensary or pharmacy. This back room was a jumble of crutches, canes, wheelchairs, eyeglasses, and other personal items, which possibly were left by visitors who believed they no longer needed them. Rows of shelves along one wall, and in the center of the room, held jars and bottles filled with unsavory-looking human tissue—apparently growths and tumors—preserved in some pinkish liquid.

Nate peered into a jar, which contained some kind of pink sack-like organ with protruding tentacles. "Whew! Man. I wonder what they keep these things for? Maybe to whet peoples' appetite before lunch?"

"Boy," Elizabeth said, "I sure don't know. Maybe to convince some of the naysayers. You know, Barbara was telling me how there've been a few doctors who've tried to shut this place down. And the Catholic Church has tried to close 'em down a number of times."

"No shit."

"Yep. For different reasons. Barbara said that, lately, José often asks if there are any doctors in the room. . . . When he's doing the visible surgeries in the main hall. And he asks them to come up and watch the surgeries—so they can see that there's no sleight-of-hand going on."

"Huh," Nate said. "No kidding."

"Barbara heard that, once or twice José has asked to be blindfolded . . . while he's doing these surgeries. I guess . . . to show that it wasn't actually he, himself, who was doing the surgery."

Nate rubbed his chin, shaking his head slightly. "My God. *Unreal.* I'm havin' *just* a little trouble believing all this."

They made their way back outside again and found the group with Dawn. She was talking with a man who seemed to be an employee there. They talked comfortably in Portuguese while he leaned against a wet mop. When they finished talking, the man went back inside one of the buildings while the group rejoined the others who'd been resting on the benches. It was muggy and warm in the shade of the trees, now, hot in the sun. There was a peacefulness and calm about the place that seemed to affect the four that were seated—all of them looking somewhat drowsy. Dawn announced that several of the group members wanted to walk with her down to a nearby waterfall—quite beautiful, according to her. It was about a half mile to the waterfall, and everyone was welcome if they wanted to tag along. Otherwise, they could go their separate ways for the rest of the day—and meet up again around six, to figure out a place to have dinner.

Elizabeth felt she could manage a mile walk, so she tugged on Nate's hand to inform him of this. Dawn led the group onto a small red dirt track, which branched off of the street where the Casa was. Probably a road built to access someone's farm in the hills outside of town. The dry weather (common during the winter here) and the strong midday sun, made the red clay road dusty—in contrast to the deep green lushness of the vegetation on either side. Mimosa trees, with their fernlike leaves, and other tropical trees grew thicker on either side the further they went. The road crested a small rise, and then sank gradually into a moist valley. The shadows grew, across the road, as the trees got taller. And soon— toward the bottom of the valley—the trees had spread a solid canopy overhead. Just as the road began rising again to climb the far side of the valley, there appeared a gravel parking area on the left.

The parking area was empty, and Dawn led the group onto a trail in the thickening forest. For a couple hundred yards, it meandered down a gentle incline, as a vague roar of cascading water grew louder. Finally the trees parted overhead, and a pool about twenty feet across lay before them. A waterfall about ten feet high poured into the north end of the pool, and a stream left it on the east. Dawn pointed out several wild mango trees surrounding the pool, thirty to forty feet tall, spreading thick, gnarled branches over the water. "And a couple of these trees are *caju*—the trees that produce cashew nuts. They also bear a fruit that Brazilians make a juice out of. Good stuff. Both kinds of trees'll be covered with fruit, if you come here in the late summer." The waterfall, either because of the small volume of water, or because of the rocks beneath it, made a gentle, medium-pitched roar, unlike the earthshaking rumble of larger waterfalls. A shaft of afternoon sun lit up a brilliant patch of mist where the water hit the rocks.

"This is the *Cachoeira,* the waterfall," Dawn said, "and it's kind of a sacred place to many of the people who come to visit José. One of the townspeople sold the land to José—so it's become almost like an annex to the Casa de Dom Francisco. Many folks who come to the Casa have found that their healing work continues, here, at the *Cachoeira* . . . almost as if the healing spirits—the Entities—find that they can work on people easily at this spot. Maybe something to do with the energy of the place."

"It's *beautiful*," a woman said.

"I think so. And it's a powerful place. They always have someone who works at the Casa taking care of this area. They make sure that it stays clean and safe, here. They treat it like a shrine . . . like a holy place."

A few of the people in the group, including Elizabeth, took their shoes off and wet their feet in the pool, while others wandered around it. Several talked amongst themselves, doing so in hushed voices.

In the afternoon, Nate and Elizabeth rested for a while in their room at the pousada. Elizabeth was exhausted and fell asleep on the bed. In the early evening, they again went over to the "downtown" area. Part of their purpose, to look for a store that sold clothing. Their friend, Barbara, and Dawn, both had mentioned that it was suggested to wear white (or mostly white) when visiting José de Deus. When asked about it, Barbara had said that José—and the spirits that were working through him— could "see" a person's illness. And they could see changes in a person's energy field or aura more easily if that person was wearing white. Neither Nate nor Elizabeth argued about it or the necessity of it.

They found one of the stores Dawn mentioned, but the man who ran it was apparently just getting ready to close for the evening. He spoke some English, but not much. The prices were reasonable, and Elizabeth bought a soft white cotton dress. Nate, a short-sleeved white shirt. The shop also sold some groceries, and they bought a couple of bottles of tropical fruit juice—one of tamarind and the other of the local fruit juice Dawn had mentioned, caju.

Back at the pousada, the West Coast group had decided they were going out to eat at a local Brazilian restaurant. But Nate and Elizabeth decided on a quieter evening and walked the couple of blocks over to the pizzeria they'd seen the day before.

That night, even though she felt exhausted, Elizabeth had trouble sleeping. She'd only had a small cup of caffeinated tea at the pizza place, but felt a gnawing expectancy that wouldn't abate. Tomorrow would be a big day, with José de Deus in town and crowds of people coming to the place. She got up, twice—unable to sleep—so for a while she read a bit more in the book on Brazil. It was somewhat annoying, but Nate slept like a baby.

5.

. . . He doesn't have any gloves on.
Aren't they supposed to wear surgical gloves
when they do this kind of thing? . . .

In the morning, Dawn was already downstairs having breakfast when Nate and Elizabeth came down. As Elizabeth poured herself a cup of coffee, a bus rumbled down the street out front, heading toward the Casa. Dawn peeked out the window, her coffee cup in hand. "Probably an all-nighter bus, from Rio or São Paulo. Lots of people come here from those cities—sometimes even from places farther south. It's something like thirteen hours drive-time from Rio de Janeiro."

"My Lord," Nate said.

"Often," Dawn said, "there are more than five hundred people who come through the line to see José, on any given day. And some days, more than a thousand."

Nate raised his eyebrows, as he tried to picture the long lines of sick people . . . *Man, I had no idea. Sounds like this'll be fun . . .* When Ana came in she asked Nate what they'd like, and he said, in English, that they'd like scrambled eggs—though he looked at Elizabeth to make sure. They'd decided that eggs were probably the freshest thing available, since Ana had a chicken-house out back. As did some of her neighbors, also. Rooster and hen noises had wakened them this morning, as they had the day before.

Another bus rumbled by, maybe another all-nighter. Or an early-morning bus from Brasilia. Dawn was excited and chattered about some of the amazing occurrences she'd witnessed on her earlier trips to the

Casa. And she reiterated her offer of assistance to Nate and Elizabeth—that they should feel free to stay close to her and the group. She said she could translate anything that was spoken to them, and would advise them on anything they needed to know. "They've recently started using a volunteer—or maybe he's a paid worker for the Casa. Anyway, he translates any instructions or announcements into English. And anything that José says. Apparently there are enough visitors here—from either the States, or Europe—who speak English. So they decided it was worthwhile to have this guy help out. He's a good one, to keep an eye on and keep close to. A real nice guy, and very fluent with English. His name's Paulo. He'll probably be translating for you, when you're in the line to meet José. Or if he's too busy, then look for me—when it's getting close to your turn with José—and I'll help out. You pretty much need to have an interpreter with you."

"Sounds like it," Elizabeth said. "Guess we should have thought more seriously about going with a group—like what you're doing."

"Well, you know . . . it won't matter much. You'll find that people are very friendly and helpful here. And there's always people around—who work, or volunteer, for the Casa—who'll be glad to help out. A real community has grown up around the Casa."

Nate gulped a slug of the local coffee. "That is *awesome*." When he and Elizabeth finished their breakfast, they decided to go over, early, to the Casa de Dom Francisco. Not waiting for Dawn and her group, a few of whom seemed slow in getting organized. They went back upstairs, finished getting ready and dressed, and left the pousada. It was a bright and sunny outside, already over 70 degrees—and promising to be a hot day. With his hand, Nate brushed some damp hair away from his face . . . *Definitely hot, for winter . . .*

There were small groups of people walking down the street, looking like they were also headed toward the Casa. In the distance they could see the large white gate at the entrance to the place. A bus that had just passed by the gate turned into what looked like an unpaved parking lot across from the entrance—and a small cloud of reddish dust rose into the air. A horse-cart passing by startled them, heading in the same direction, and Nate wondered where the guy was going . . . *Maybe returning from delivering vegetables or fruit somewhere, to one of the farms outside of town . . .. Buses and cars. And horse-carts. What a fucking unusual place . . .*

When they reached the arched gateway, the gates stood wide open, and a large crowd of upwards of a hundred people already were within the grounds, milling around. Many of them crowding around the entrance to the main hall. The couple edged their way into this teeming horde—a human bottleneck around the door.

Most of the people around them seemed to be Brazilian, with olive complexion, dark eyes and hair. Some of the crowd looked to be Native American. Brazil, from what they'd experienced so far (and read about), seemed to be very much a melting pot of different ethnic groups. Some of the crowd had African features. Probably all of them would consider themselves to be either *Caboclo* or *Mestiço* background. There was the occasional European or Anglo person in the crowd, but many of them also seemed to be speaking Portuguese. The Portuguese chatter all around them, though not loud, felt overwhelming . . . *Much more guttural and different from Spanish* . . . Nate found he couldn't translate a single word being spoken around him . . . *And so far, not one American here—or any English-speaking types . . .*

Making their way into the already crowded room, Nate and Elizabeth were able to work their way up toward the front of the room. Many of the people hung back once they got through the doorway—perhaps because they'd been there before and wanted to make room for others to get close to the front. Or maybe because of a little fear, Nate thought . . . *But really, they all seem pretty relaxed and cheerful, considering . . .* He'd noticed that many of the people in the room were quite obviously ill or afflicted in some way. A few people nearby were wearing bandanas over the heads, covering baldness from illness or chemotherapy. A humid, sweaty human odor hit Nate's nostrils . . . *Man . . . many of these folks, packed in here like sardines, traveled all night by bus to get here . . .* The couple threaded their way close to the front of the room, where a small, jovial man was speaking to the crowd—in Portuguese—pointing this way and that. And pointing to the rooms alongside the main hall. He stood on a platform at the front of the room—a sort of makeshift stage.

As he finished speaking, he passed the baton to a man near him, pulling him up onto this stage as he himself stepped down. This other man, who looked to be of more direct European ancestry, spoke in English and introduced himself as Paulo. "Are there any people in the room who speak English? I will try to help you as good as I can. Please raise your hand if you need English—" When he saw Nate and Elizabeth's hands go up, he announced that any other English-speaking people could meet him over where they stood—and he gestured in their direction. Nate noticed a few people in the crowd looking at them with mild curiosity. A couple of people actually smiled.

This man, Paulo, hopped off the stage and threaded his way up to Nate and Elizabeth, introducing himself and asking their names. Before he could start to explain anything, another couple appeared—saying "hello," and that they were from Australia and also spoke English. Paulo went on to give instructions (as apparently the man before him had done), explaining how they did things at the Casa in order to keep things moving and organized. Newcomers like Nate and Elizabeth (and the Australians, who were also new to the Casa de Dom Francisco) would pick up a "first time" ticket. "It's called a *'primeira vez'* ticket—it will help you to go through the line into the current rooms first, so you can meet with José before the others."

He explained how other visitors, for whom today was a continuation of a previous treatment, would queue up after them. And many other patients who had serious maladies would go and sit, or lay down, in the third "current room," where their "invisible surgery" would continue all day. Paulo suggested that—since they were all newcomers—they might want to stand near the stage to be able to see clearly, for the morning's event. Because Medium José would be coming out soon to perform a few "visible" surgeries on the stage. Just as he was encouraging them to move forward in the room, a man and woman arrived, pushing a boy in a wheelchair who seemed to have some kind of palsy condition. They spoke English also—so it was obvious Paulo would have to explain things all over again. He smiled patiently, and said to the others that they should be able to find him when they went through the line in the current rooms. "I'll be helping José—in the second current room—and I can help translate for you, there."

They thanked him, and Nate grabbed Elizabeth's hand in order to keep her close while they made their way through the crush up to the stage area. He felt an expectant nervousness in the air . . . *Like a cross between a carnival and a Holy-Roller Christian revival. Or a rock concert, with Moses or Jesus singing lead vocals . . .* As they finally got close to the stage, Nate saw that it was really just a simple plywood platform raised about a foot higher than the rest of the floor, and it covered roughly twenty by thirty feet at the front of the main hall. Suddenly there was a commotion over at one of the doors at the far right corner of the room. A stocky middle-aged man, with unkempt longish black hair, who wore glasses and was dressed all in white, made his way over toward the stage area. He was followed by three women carrying something on metal trays. A few people near Nate made the sign of the cross as the man approached. Nate said softly, "Here comes the Grand Poobah." He didn't know why he said it that way. Elizabeth shot him an annoyed glance. It got quieter in the room, though the tension was palpable. Another group of three people, also dressed in white—two men and a woman—were led from one of the side doors to the stage by a male assistant.

Nate watched as the man with glasses, apparently Joseph of God—

José de Deus—stepped up onto the stage platform. He had a peaceful, maybe even tired look on his face, as they could see him clearly just ten feet away. He was barefooted. The three female assistants joined him on the stage, and José scanned the crowd while people were still entering from the back. The male assistant helped the other three people onto the stage—people who Nate decided must be those who had requested a "visible surgery." These three were led to stand at the rear of the stage against the back wall of the room.

José said something to his assistants, gesticulating about where to stand, near him. Then he crossed himself, closed his eyes, and spoke softly in Portuguese. A prayer. Nate became aware that Paulo had rejoined himself and Elizabeth, standing to Nate's right. After José completed the prayer, he brought two of the assistants up, to either side of him, holding their hands. In a louder voice, he spoke a couple of sentences in Portuguese. Paulo quietly translated, to Nate and Elizabeth, "He asks everyone to close their eyes and think of God."

Merely out of politeness, Nate closed his eyes, as it seemed most everyone else was doing. As soon as he had done so, he was startled by a rushing sound in the air overhead. He opened his eyes quickly and saw José stumble for a moment, as if losing his balance, or consciousness. The man released the hands of his assistants and stood up straight, taking off his glasses and gazing around the room. Nate thought his eyes looked different . . . *Kind of spaced-out, almost like he's stoned* . . . José finished scanning the room and turned, slowly, toward the assistants. He walked a few steps toward the rear of the stage. But slowly, as if moving underwater. It seemed as if he was getting his bearings. Then, acting more businesslike, he barked an order to the assistants—and they led the woman at the back of the room up toward the front of the stage. José put his hand on the woman's shoulder and said several words to her, paused—and then, more loudly, several sentences in Portuguese, to the audience.

"Ovarian cyst," Paulo whispered. "And José asks if there are any doctors in the room—he will be happy if they like to come forward, onto the stage. And he will be happy if they like to watch."

A gray-haired man, wearing thick glasses, threaded his way through the crowd to reach the stage. Appearing embarrassed, he clambered up onto the platform and said something to José. José smiled and pointed toward the woman's left side, after which the man moved to that location. José put his hand on the woman's right shoulder, while he waved over an assistant carrying a small tray in her hands, which held some kind of surgical instruments. José gently lifted the woman's partly-unbuttoned blouse and tucked it into her bra. Grabbing a scalpel off the tray, he pinched a fold of skin at her lower abdomen with his other hand, and quickly cut an incision about three inches long. The woman stood there with a gentle smile on her face.

Nate could see pinkish, sheath-like tissue sliced open by the incision, but it didn't bleed. José looked at the doctor standing next to the woman, said something, and then casually stuck two of his fingers into the incision, felt around for a moment, and then forced his thumb in also. He fished his fingers around in the woman's abdomen—and Nate noticed he seemed to be moving his fingers rhythmically, as if massaging something . . . *He doesn't have any gloves on. Aren't they supposed to wear surgical gloves when they do this kind of thing?* . . . The woman looked as if she was having a pleasant dream. After a couple minutes of this massaging motion in the woman's belly, José pulled his fingers out, grasping a shiny oval object, pinkish-purple and slippery wet. It was about two inches long and made a muffled thunk as he dropped it onto the assistant's tray. Standing next to Nate, Elizabeth made an audible exhale—as if she'd been holding her breath—but he didn't turn to look at her.

José wiped his hands on a towel, draping it over his shoulder—and picked up a suture needle off the tray, quickly tying off an internal suture. Then he tied off four more sutures to hold the woman's skin together. There hadn't been a drop of blood. José looked at a couple of strong-looking men standing at the back of the stage, made an imperceptible nod to them, and when they came forward he said something to them quickly. Gently grasping her arms, they guided the woman, who now seemed a bit wobbly, to the back of the stage, and helped her onto a gurney. They wheeled her through one of the doors behind the stage and into some back room.

Paulo glanced at Nate, who looked puzzled now. He put his hand on Nate's arm and said, "They will let her heal for a few hours in the third current room, and then she will be sent back to her room, in town. Or back home—to continue the healing."

Nate turned to Elizabeth, with eyebrows raised. "Wow. That was interesting." As José prepared for the next procedure, Nate turned back toward the stage, and said to Paulo, "I didn't see José using any antiseptic liquid, or anything. Aren't they afraid of somebody getting an infection—septicemia—or something? With him, uh, sticking his fingers in, like that?"

"No. I never see anyone getting an infection, here—in all the time I've been at the Casa."

"So, they give them antibiotics in the next room, right?"

"No," Paulo said. "Only the 'medicinal soup' and the 'medicinal tea' that's prescribed for everyone. Those things are blessed by the Spirits."

Nate muttered, "I'll be damned.". . . *Must be antibiotics in that stuff, then. No doubt . . .*

One of José's assistants led a wiry little man up to the front of the stage, where he would apparently be the next "visible surgery." It seemed the man was blind, or nearly so. José placed his hand on the man's shoulder and then looked around the crowd—giving the impression he was looking for someone in particular. He noticed someone standing near the stage, and motioned to him. A man at the opposite side of the room from Nate and Elizabeth. The man José pointed to looked behind him, with a confused expression, then turned back to José, pointing at himself. He asked, in English, "Me?"

José nodded, and the man made his way slowly up onto the stage. Nate recognized him as the man who was with Dawn's group—the man who had asked Dawn, the day before, some vague question about how some people thought José a charlatan. The man's face looked even ruddier than before, as he hopped up onto the stage. José said something to him but could immediately see there was a language issue. Paulo, without being cued, quickly came up onto the stage. Nate could hear him translating José's request to the man. Apparently José wanted him to assist with this surgery.

With a quizzical expression Nate glanced at Elizabeth, then back at the stage . . . *Well, this just keeps getting more and more interesting. That guy's even more of a skeptic than I am . . .*

José positioned a chair for the patient to sit in, and said something to the female assistant who'd brought over a tray of instruments. He asked a question of the man from Dawn's group. Paulo translated—and the man said in English that his name was Derek. José said a few more things, which were also translated, and Derek moved to the patient's left side while the man sat down quietly in the chair. Derek looked at José, then back at the patient, and then placed his hand on the man's left cheek. With his other hand under the man's chin, he stabilized his head. José said something to Derek, which again was translated by Paulo. Derek firmly pulled down on the man's cheek to expose his eye more fully. Paulo stepped down from the stage, and stood, again, next to Nate and Elizabeth.

José grabbed what looked like a kitchen knife off of the instrument tray, held the man's eyelids open wide, and began to scrape his eyeball with the knife. He must have been applying substantial pressure, because even from Nate's vantage point he could see the man's eyeball deforming and moving under the scraping process. Nate shivered . . . *Fuck . . . That's gotta hurt . . .*

José lifted the knife from the man's eyeball, scraped some debris off the blade with his fingernail, and then went back to work on the man's eye. Derek—the reluctant assistant from Dawn's group—seemed to be fully engaged with the procedure. But with a calm expression on his face. Nate, meanwhile, felt nauseous when he noticed the patient's eyeball being forcibly deformed again under the pressure of the knife. José cleaned the knife on his towel and motioned to Derek that he would begin on the man's right eye. Derek repositioned himself, stabilizing the man's head, and José went back to work, spending a few more minutes on the patient's right eye.

Nate wondered how such a maneuver could be performed, in such a rude, unprofessional setting, without actually tearing the man's cornea completely off the eyeball. Or at least damaging it. He muttered softly, "This is *terrible.*" The patient, though, was remarkably composed, his hands folded in his lap. Sitting quietly with no stress showing on his face, aside from the fact that his eyeball was being very nearly torn apart with a knife . . . *Man . . . there's no way this could be done, without some kind of heavy-duty sedatives or anesthesia . . .*

José finished what he was doing and dropped the knife onto the assistant's tray, wiping his hands on the towel. He thanked Derek for helping him and, gripping the patient's hands, helped him to stand up. José asked the man something, in Portuguese. Paulo quietly translated, for Nate and Elizabeth, "He asks if the man feels any pain."

The man smiled slightly and shook his head. *"Não."* (No.)

José asked him another question, which Paulo also translated, "Did anyone give you a painkiller?"

With a placid expression, the man shook his head. *"Não, nada."* (No, nothing.)

The hefty-looking guys came up, again, from the back of the stage. They helped the man into a wheelchair and then over to the rear doorway.

The third of the trio receiving visible surgeries that morning was led up to where José stood. José looked at the man for a long moment, put his hand on his shoulder and turned toward the crowd. He said something to the audience—and Paulo said, quietly, "Leukemia." José picked up a hemostat off of an assistant's tray. The stainless steel glistened as he held it up for a moment, maybe for the audience to see. From what Nate could tell, the long, clamp-like jaws of the instrument were about seven inches long, from the scissor-type handles to the pointed, curved end of the clamp . . . *Now, what does that thing have to do with treating leukemia? What in the hell? . . .*

José tilted the man's head back, causing his mouth to gape wide open.

José put the tip of the hemostat into the man's left nostril—and suddenly, forcefully, jammed the instrument in, until the two finger holes of the handle were against the man's nostril. The force of the maneuver made his head jerk back, and the man wavered on his feet slightly. Nate's jaw dropped involuntarily . . . *My God. Oh my fucking God* . . . José turned away, and proceeded to casually wipe his hands on a damp towel while he talked with the woman holding the instrument tray.

There was a dull thump in the crowd behind Nate and some whispering. He turned around to see that a man had fallen onto the floor—possibly fainted—while some people cleared a space around him. A couple more helpers, or orderlies, made their way through the crowd and reached the man behind Nate. A minute later, they were carrying him toward one of the doors on the right side of the room. Nate, a confused frown on his face, turned to Paulo. Paulo blew his nose into a handkerchief and sniffed. "Sometimes," he said, "the Spirits—or Entities—will begin to do "invisible surgery" on someone in the crowd . . . and it makes them to black out. They will put him into the third current room, while he is worked on."

Nate, a frown still on his face, nodded mechanically and returned to watching José, who had now turned back to the patient. The healer reached for the handle of the hemostat, still in the man's nostril, grabbed it and twisted it roughly, several times, before slowly removing it. Nate idly speculated that the curved end of the instrument should surely have shredded brain tissue—or at least deep sinus tissue and bone . . . *Or else it's a trick gadget, with springs or something . . . So that it doesn't go in all the way* . . . A small trickle of blood oozed from the patient's nose, as he was led away. Nate felt a mild headache coming on, and closed his eyes for a moment as if for relief. Turning to Elizabeth, his eyes still halfway closed, he said, "You okay?"

She nodded absently, watching as José—Joseph of God—walked slowly over to his assistants, where he spoke with them for a moment. Then he left the stage area, the others following behind, and disappeared into a doorway on the right—a door which apparently led to the so-called current rooms.

Paulo turned toward the couple, and spoke in a normal conversational tone. "So, you will want to get two of the first-time tickets—*primeira vez* tickets. And then you will want to get on line to go into the first current room. The medium, José, will be in the second current room. And you will meet him there."

"Paulo? . . ." Elizabeth asked, "so this was one of the Spirits—the Entities—that was using José this morning? Incorporating into him?"

"Yes. This was Dr. Augusto. Augusto de Almeida. He was a doctor in

Brazil, who died in 1908—and he comes here many times—to use José, to help the people. We . . . we who work here or volunteer here much . . . we can see which one is here, using José. Some of the Entities come and use José just once a week. Yes, this is Dr. Augusto. A very good surgeon. All of the Entities are good at some things—but maybe not another. They are all different. Sometimes José will use different Entities, in the same day."

Nate had a feeling that his headache might continue for a while and sighed audibly as he and Elizabeth made their way outside into the sunshine. They went over to the little annex building that Paulo told them was the place to get their *primeira vez* tickets. They found Dawn and her group over at this building, on line. She was curious to hear of the couple's impression of the visible surgeries. Nate was silent, while Elizabeth was almost chatty. As it came to be their turn to pick up tickets, at the counter, Nate got his wallet out. And started pulling out a few Brazilian *Real* (Brazilian currency). But Elizabeth put her hand on his wallet. "Oh, I don't think there's any charge for these tickets." Nate turned to look at Dawn.

"No, that's true," she said. "José doesn't charge anything for the healing, here. In fact, he's not allowed to. The Entities told him this. The 'medicinal soup' that's offered at lunchtime is also free. There *is* a charge for the herbal 'prescriptions'—but that's about it."

Nate picked up the tickets from a woman at the counter and turned back to the group. "Well . . . how do they, uh . . . how do they fund all this?"

"I guess," Dawn said, "that some people must donate to the Casa. To keep it going. And quite a few people donate their time—people who act as assistants or helpers. And people who act as mediums in the current rooms."

"Really? And so . . . do you mean that there are other mediums here? Besides José?"

"Oh yes. There are lots of people who come here for their own healing—or invisible surgery. And they sometimes stay in town for a while longer. They sit, every day, in the current rooms, acting as mediums and helping to channel the spiritual energy from the Entities. Some people have even moved to Adelândia, from other places—just to be a part of this, and to continue their own healing."

"Man," Nate said. He mumbled, almost to himself, "What an unusual place."

"It is. Actually," Dawn continued, "I think it's safe to say that we are *all* mediums—or can be. We *can* be mediums, I mean. This is something the Entities have told José. This is a place that awakens the spiritual side of us—the part that's dormant a lot of the time in our day-to-day lives."

"Uh-huh," Nate muttered. His facial expression seemed to be a confused half smile, half sneer . . . *This place is so fucking bizarre. It's killin' me* . . .

6.

***She felt a sudden rush of love flow into her—unconditional love
that had nothing to do with any human concept
of worthiness or unworthiness.***

Members of Dawn's group were already getting into the line at the right-
hand side of the main building—the *primeira vez* line, leading into the
current rooms. Elizabeth felt a bit jittery as she and Nate joined them in
line. After they discussed it, though, Nate decided not to go through the
current room line, this morning—he would wait outside while Elizabeth
went in to meet José. "Maybe it's important," he said, "for you to meet
him alone, Liz. After all, it's *your* healing that's the important thing,
here. Right? . . . And I can go through the line in the afternoon." He
kissed her forehead and turned away to walk over to a bench in the
shade. She smiled, as he sat down on the bench and looked back at her.
She waved at him nervously, with a funny feeling in her stomach—like a
little girl at a carnival trying to drum up her confidence to go on the
roller-coaster.

Elizabeth talked with a couple of the women from the West Coast
group, mostly about their impressions of the morning's visible surgeries,
and again she noticed a touch of butterflies in her stomach. Dawn
explained to the group members around her that the first of the current
rooms would be where they would experience a sort of spiritual
cleansing—and the healing spirits, or Entities, would be evaluating their
condition, learning about what each person needed. The second current
room would be where they would meet with José, who would be
incorporated by one of the Entities. "He'll give each of you some

instructions and probably a prescription for one of the herbal medicines. I'll be there, to help translate for you. And Paulo will most likely be there, also, to help.

"You'll want to keep in mind that the current rooms—even more so than the main hall—are like an electrical circuit. And the Entities send this healing energy through everyone here. It's God's energy. God's love. Anyone here will tell you that. It'll probably feel a little scary, at first. And there's something within each of us that resonates with this energy . . . and actually amplifies it. So it's always suggested that—especially here in the current rooms—that you don't cross your arms or legs. Whether you're *sitting* in the rooms, as part of the *current,* or standing in the line. It somehow disrupts the flow of the current—like the way crossed wires affect an electrical circuit. This might not make sense . . . but you'll experience it. And you'll know what I'm talking about."

When Elizabeth's part of the line finally entered the doorway of the first current room, she noticed several dozens of people—men and women—sitting in a row of chairs and benches along the walls. It was a long, narrow room, and the *primeira vez* line filed down the middle of it. The people along each side seemed to be in a meditative state, with relaxed faces and eyes closed. Elizabeth became aware of a slight humming or hissing sound, just on the edge of perception. It wasn't frightening. But when she closed her eyes it seemed to get louder with a pleasant pulsating effect. It made her sleepy. Dawn whispered to her, "I don't think I told you, but it's best not to close your eyes while you're standing in the current line. The Entities may start working on you—and you can lose your balance. Or pass out."

"Okay," Elizabeth whispered back . . . *Hmm. That seems like a pretty important thing to know about . . .* Though the line was moving at a snail's pace, and frequently stopped in place for a few minutes, Elizabeth labored to keep her eyes open. Several times, though, when she did close them for a few moments, she felt a euphoric, relaxed and peaceful state. As if something loving and warm was enveloping her.

Most of the people seated along the walls in the room were motionless and looked to be in a deeply relaxed state, like the hypnotic state before sleep. For the most part, they had their hands resting in their laps or on their thighs. A couple of women, though—perhaps unknown to them—were moving their hands rhythmically in front of them. One man's hands, resting on his thighs with palms upward, were vibrating noticeably though he had a placid expression on his face. Some of the people in this room, Elizabeth guessed, were probably volunteer mediums . . . *But I bet a lot of them are like me . . . looking to be healed from one thing or another . . .*

Even when her eyes were open, now, Elizabeth felt a warm, benevolent energy flowing through her. And she felt prodded to contemplate what she was there for. There was an awareness, now, of the tumor in her breast. And *the* question came to her . . . *Can it be arrested? Or healed? Eradicated? So that I can be around, to help my sons grow up?* . . . She felt a sudden rush of love flow into her—unconditional love that had nothing to do with any human concept of worthiness or unworthiness. Tears welled up in her eyes, as she accepted this love and let it wash through her. She was only vaguely aware of the people around her on line, but they all seemed humbled and calmed by the palpable energy in the room, now. There was no talking between them, the way there had been outside of the building.

As the line reached the doorway into the second current room, and Elizabeth passed through it, there seemed to be a more reverent hush in this room. But still with the slight background humming sound. And the occasionally audible voice of José, as he spoke with the people passing before him in the line. The people sitting on the benches along the sides of this room appeared to be even more calm and deeply entranced than those in the first current room. As if each one of them was completely unaware of the goings-on around them. The warm flow of energy felt even more pronounced here. Elizabeth was aware of it all around her now, and she felt joy that she hadn't experienced in a long while.

The line slowly inched toward José, and Elizabeth felt a pleasant prickly feeling on the crown of her head. A memory came to her of how her grandmother used to brush her hair, when she was little. She remembered having a similar sensation at that time, long ago . . . *Grandma had unconditional love for me. I miss that* . . . She felt tears welling up again, and closed her eyes. It made her extremely sleepy, so she opened her eyes again, trying to focus her attention on the room and the people around her on line. Some of the people nearby were from Dawn's group, but everyone seemed preoccupied. Either immersed in the warm, loving embrace that Elizabeth was experiencing or praying for their own healing. Some may have been praying for the healing of a loved one.

When Dawn, on line ahead of her, reached the chair in which José was sitting, Elizabeth felt a moist blushing heat come over her—her hands clammy with sweat. All her mind could summon was . . . *They could use air-conditioning in here* . . . Dawn spoke to José, and then handed him several photographs of people, apparently asking that there be some sort of healing for them. José looked at the photos, quickly, and placed them on a low table next to his chair. Dawn then led a woman from their group up to him—and explained, in Portuguese, why she was there. After José gave the woman some instructions and handed her a piece of paper, he looked toward Elizabeth. She found herself walking up to him unsteadily. Paulo, who was standing nearby, smiled and came to her side. José—José de Deus, as the people called him—sat in a simple wooden chair with a cushion under him. His black hair looked damp from the warmth in the room. He flashed Elizabeth a penetrating look while he took her hand, but instantly his eye seemed to be focusing on something else. As if someone was speaking into his ear.

Dawn had told her to look directly into José's eyes, so that he could learn as much as possible about her condition. So she steadied her gaze at him, though at this point it was obvious he was looking through her at something or someone else. While she kept her eyes on José, Elizabeth whispered to Paulo why she was there—why she was seeking help. And Paulo translated. José scribbled something on a piece of paper, handed it to her, and barked some instructions to Paulo, who led Elizabeth away from the medium and onto another line leading into the next room.

Dawn was there, in line, and whispered to Paulo for a few moments, in Portuguese. She turned to face Elizabeth, and whispered, "I'll help you to understand this, when we get outside of the third current room. I've got to help a couple more people in line, here." Paulo looked at Elizabeth, smiled, and both he and Dawn went back to stand near José.

Soon the line moved through a doorway into the third current room— a larger rectangular room, which must have been behind the stage area of the main hall. The room had dozens of portable cots at one end, with eight or ten people resting in them at the moment. After a short while, Elizabeth's part of the line was seated in folding chairs, in a circle. The cheerful Brazilian man, who had made the announcements first thing in the morning, was there. He said that his name was Miguel. And he asked the people—first in Portuguese and then in halting English—to hold hands, while a prayer would be said for their healing. Elizabeth still felt the warm embrace she'd been experiencing. And she honestly felt kinship and that she loved these people—who were all suffering in some way, as she was. After the blessing, they were guided outside into the bright sunshine.

It was hot in the sun, now, nearly noon. Several of Dawn's group were heading over to the refectory building, a roofed open-air structure behind the main building. The lunch of "medicinal" vegetable soup was being served there, and there were a number of benches and tables where people could sit. It was next to the small building she and Nate had explored just the day before. Dawn caught up with them on the way over to this refectory and checked in with everybody from her group. After encouraging them to take lunch there—saying it was essentially part of the spiritual treatment of the Casa—several of them got on line to be served.

Dawn stopped to speak with Elizabeth privately. "How was it for you, Elizabeth?"

"Well . . . quite amazing. Kind of a powerful experience. But I guess I was a little surprised at how quickly my meeting with José went."

Dawn smiled. "Right. He has to deal with a lot of visitors. But you see, the Entities have already assessed your condition. And will treat you accordingly. Medium José told Paulo that they are working on you. For the rest of this week, you'll need to sit in the second current room—where you'll get preliminary healing and cleansing. And you'll want to pick up the herbal prescription that José handed you. . . . That piece of paper he wrote on. You can pick it up, anytime, at the pharmacy counter. There's a small charge for it."

"Okay," Elizabeth said. "But I guess I was expecting more of a structured treatment plan—"

"This is totally normal . . . most treatments are like this. The Entities will be working on you the rest of the week. And preparing you for surgery."

"Surgery?"

"Yes. Medium José wants you to come back on Wednesday morning of next week. And you can choose either a visible surgery, or invisible."

"Oh. Okay." There were the beginnings of a concerned furrow in Elizabeth's brow. "I guess I'll know which one to do?"

"Yes. You will. José only requires visible surgery for certain people. They seem to need the physical surgery, for some reason . . . maybe having something to do with the degree of their faith. The degree of their belief—or lack thereof. The invisible surgeries are just as effective, for most of us. If not more so. You'll know."

"Okay."

"Are you joining us for lunch?"

"I think," Elizabeth said, "I'd better find Nate first. He's probably around front. We'll catch up with you in a bit."

Part II

7.

"Honey, we have to talk about something."

Nate sat on the bench out front of the main hall, watching people mill around, and watching the *primeira vez* line as Elizabeth and the others slowly made their way into the current rooms. The bench felt comfortable, in the shade of some leafy trees. But after the events they'd witnessed that morning in the main hall, his mind felt decidedly less than comfortable, confused thoughts circling around. After some few minutes, Elizabeth's part of the queue had gone through the doorway into the first room, while he gazed at the odd mixture of people standing around the yard of the Casa. A few of them in wheelchairs, some using crutches—an odd cast of characters for sure, most of whom appeared to be ill in one way or another. Feeling almost dissociated from himself, for some reason Nate thought of the lyrics from a Leon Russell song. *Stranger in a Strange Land.* At his feet, he watched as a couple of ants fought over a crumb of food in the parched grass. He thought about Elizabeth—and the long, slow road of struggle and illness that she'd been dealing with. And that he'd been dealing with vicariously . . . *How in the hell did we get here? Maybe this all started way back when we were building the earthship. Things were hard for Liz, then . . . maybe too hard . . .* Their life in New Mexico felt far away now—even though this was just their third day away from home—and he found himself lost in thought about the past few years.

Way back while they were still living in Santa Fe, he and Elizabeth had decided to build an environmentally-friendly home of the "earthship" style that was being experimented with in northern New Mexico, mostly in the Taos area. An architect there had come up with this unusual "earthship" design—a sustainable type of house construction—and he and his construction crew had made improvements on these home designs since the mid-1970s. Nate had worked, for several years in the 1980s, for a small construction company in Santa Fe that specialized in sustainable, environmentally-friendly home construction. But of his boss's clients, people who desired these new experimental types of houses were few and far between. And the building codes in Santa Fe were still decidedly less than friendly toward unconventional or experimental construction. The building codes in Taos county being much more lenient, in fact almost non-existent. Nate did have the chance, though, to work on one of these earthship-style homes in Glorieta—a town in the mountains east of Santa Fe.

And although the earthships were built using an unusual construction method—and fairly labor-intensive—he and Elizabeth both loved the idea of a home that could be built using a large number of recycled materials. For instance, using salvaged auto and truck tires, packed with earth, for the exterior walls. And they were homes that could be heated in the wintertime, for the most part, with just the sun's energy. Likewise, the idea of living "off the grid"—and not depending on the future benevolence of the utility companies—appealed to them greatly. These unusual houses looked something like an oblong Star Wars spaceship that had crash-landed into the ground. When finished, they looked sleek and futuristic from the outside—with a long, slanted window-wall of glass on the south-facing side and entry doors at each end of the structure. But were rounded, smooth, and organic on the inside, having adobe mud-plaster covering the tire-walls.

When Nate and Elizabeth decided that the city environment in Santa Fe wasn't where they wanted to live and raise their kids, southern New Mexico—and Silver City in particular—seemed like a good choice. The Twin Sisters community, outside of Silver City, seemed pretty much what they were looking for. They liked the land that was available there—many of the building lots perched on a south-facing flank of Twin Sisters Mountain and were prime for passive-solar construction. The place was an "intentional community," with most of its residents sharing a common goal of living in harmony with nature. In the Twin Sisters community, environmentally-friendly and "off-the-grid" homes were the norm—not an oddity.

Silver City was nearby, to the south. It was a small city on the edge of the mountains, a little over 6,000 feet in elevation, and had a laid-back feel to it. A college town—with some of the culture and amenities that came with that—and yet it still had some of the charm of an Old West mining town. Silver City also had a vibrant artists' community, and Elizabeth would be able to sell her jewelry in town. So before they knew it—in the early spring of 1987—Nate and Elizabeth owned a mountainside building lot at Twin Sisters community. And were endeavoring to build an earthship—quickly, and on a budget.

By the end of April, a year later, Nate had at last gotten the interior walls of the earthship to a stage where he was applying the final coats of adobe plaster to the walls in the living room and kitchen areas. On this day, he was troweling the next to the last coat onto the walls in the kitchen—part of the large westernmost "U"-shaped room, which also contained the dining area, the living room, and the main entrance door. The earthship had been built (as most of them were) with a series of three large "U"-shaped rooms, side by side, the walls of which were built with the rammed-earth tires. And a long corridor, along the south side window-wall, connected the three "U"s. The north, east, and west sides of the exterior were backfilled with mounded earth, so that these homes sat partway buried underground.

In many respects, Elizabeth found Nate easier to be in relationship with, lately, since he'd started going back to his AA meetings on a regular basis. And their marriage felt more solid and honest, actually, than it had before his relapse fiasco—six months earlier, in the fall. Nate hadn't had a drop of alcohol, as far as she could tell, since that time. And he seemed to have quit smoking weed. She'd been aware of it, before, of course—and sometimes noticed when he was stoned—but his marijuana use wasn't ever a major concern for her.

Lately, though, Nate did seem to be a bit more obsessive. More perfectionistic, especially with the construction of the house. But that wasn't much of an issue for her, either—being obsessively careful with construction of the house might mean they'd have fewer problems with it later on. Elizabeth did want to see the house get finished, though. Couldn't wait, in fact, to get moved out of the trailer next door.

In the afternoon Elizabeth came over after working at her shared studio at the community house. With the kids in tow, carrying a few playthings to keep them occupied. She still wanted to finish a few more silver pieces for the Cinco de Mayo Festival—but also desperately wanted to see the house get finished. And thought maybe she could help with some of the plastering work. She watched Nate for some several minutes, as he scooped the adobe plaster out of a wheelbarrow nearby, troweling it on. Then used a large float to smooth it out. She had an uneasy thought of the boys scratching pencils and crayons into what would most likely be soft adobe walls. Luke was five years old now, Joseph four . . . *Hmm . . . mud walls. The more I think about it . . .* "So," she said, "the walls here will get one more coat of adobe plaster? What's that going to look like?"

"Oh, it'll look good, Liz. You'll be happy with it. I've seen some adobe houses, with the last plaster coat having some mica flakes mixed into it . . . and it looks *awesome."*

Elizabeth thought again of how the boys were reaching that mindlessly destructive age. "And it'll be durable?"

"Yeah . . . well, you know . . . you can't go banging things against it. But you can always patch it, actually. Maybe we should paint the middle "U", though, I'm thinkin'. Where the boys' room will be."

"Huh!" she said. "Just what I was wondering. Because these guys'll un*doubtedly* be banging things up against the walls."

"You know it. And painting the walls will make 'em tougher—so they'll stand up to scratches and stains better. We can use oil paint. Pretty durable."

"Well, that sounds good," Elizabeth said. "So what can I do to help today, Hon'? Should I get to mixin' up another batch of plaster for you? You know, I screened another pile of that dirt, yesterday—so it's pretty fine and free of pebbles." She looked at Nate, sweaty with the afternoon warmth in the earthship . . . *Hmm . . . I wonder if I can mix it up good enough for him—he's such a darned perfectionist about certain things. But it's just glorified mud, after all . . .*

"Yeah. That'd be way cool. I'll just put this last bit, here, into a bucket. And you can take the wheelbarrow out to that dirt pile . . . and mix it up with just enough water so it's the same consistency as this." He nodded his head toward the wheelbarrow, while he shoveled the adobe plaster out of it and into a bucket. As he was shoveling he paused, raising his eyebrows. "Actually, you can mix it in here—'cause I'll still need the hose in here, to dampen the walls. Ha! That way, I can keep an eye on you, too."

"Okay . . . I wouldn't want to mix up your mud-pies all wrong."

"No worries," Nate said. "I'll just want to be more careful, mainly when I'm doing the last coat. Got to add the right amount of mica to it. And do it the same, for each batch . . . . So it'll all look the same, I mean."

"Sure." Elizabeth pursed her lips, as she grabbed the wheelbarrow to wheel it outside . . . *Yep. I don't think I'll get involved with that last coat unless he's really desperate for help. I 'spect he'd better mix that one himself . . .*

In May, they had sold well at the Cinco de Mayo Festival in Albuquerque. Elizabeth thought they might do well to try the Ruidoso Arts show, in June. It was a small show there—but Ruidoso had a vibrant little artist community, and her jewelry would likely be a good fit there. People from southeast New Mexico around Roswell often drove up to the mountains around Ruidoso and Cloudcroft to escape the summertime heat of the low country. And many of the wealthier oil company people from Roswell and Texas had second homes in the mountains around there.

Nate often went to these craft shows alone, to sell Elizabeth's jewelry and honey from his beehives. And a few items from other artist friends of theirs—like hand-painted t-shirts. He did in fact make a lot of sales of Elizabeth's jewelry at the Ruidoso show. And Nate was in a good, positive mood on this fine, early-summer day near the middle of June, when he drove the Winnebago back from Ruidoso.

The next day, he went back to work on some of the final plastering coats in the earthship. The family had already, to a large extent, moved in. They still used the bathrooms in the trailer—"*way* inconvenient," as Elizabeth called it. The boys, though—and Nate—would just pee in the sagebrush outside.

Nate did conventional stud-wall framing for the bathroom, situated partway along the window-wall, along the passageway connecting the three main "U"-shaped rooms. He and Elizabeth had decided to apply a stucco coat to the bathroom walls—but painted—to make it blend with the rest of the house. And with their neighbor Tom's help—if he was available the next day—a priority would be to install the composting toilet. Rather large and built like an alabaster throne, it would hopefully meet their bathroom needs. And wouldn't require plumbing or septic. Nate finished with the first stucco coat on the bathroom walls and, after a short lunch break in the trailer, began on some final plaster work in the living room.

The boys' old bedroom in the trailer had now become their new homeschooling classroom. In the early afternoon, Elizabeth had finished tutoring Luke and spent some time teaching Joseph his first lessons of the alphabet. She walked into the earthship alone. Both main doors were wide open, as was one of the skylights, and the strong June sun beat through the glass window-wall. It was hot inside. And humid, with the moist, muddy smell of adobe plaster.

To Elizabeth, inside it felt like a Carolina day in mid-summer, and the smell reminded her of the air just after a thunderstorm. She had dropped the kids off at Jean's house—their neighbor who would often baby-sit the boys, certain days of the week. Elizabeth intended to go back over to her studio at the community house. But instead had come over here. She wore a serious expression, a worried furrow in her normally smooth forehead. "Honey, we have to talk about something."

There was gravity to this statement, so Nate stopped what he was doing and set down the float he was using. "Sure. Yeah."

"You know . . . they got the phone bill for the mobile phone at the community house a couple days ago. Jean passed it on to me yesterday—and I looked at it last night. You know how that goes . . . all of us who use that phone, we're supposed to check the phone log we keep, there, and add up all our calls. And pay Aaron our share, for the use of the phone." Nate turned over an empty bucket, and sat down on it, his eyes darting back and forth between Elizabeth and the wall he was working on.

"Well," she continued, "I brought the bill with me over to the workshop today. You know . . . it's like pages and pages of calls. And I looked at it again. There were a couple of calls we made in early May, to a number in Albuquerque—I think it was Mike's number, the guy who organizes Cinco de Mayo. And there was another call to a number I didn't recognize—in Placitas. You know, the little town north of Albuquerque? And a call back from that number, like, ten minutes later. A *long* call—a lot of air-time. And I thought, *huh, we don't know anyone in Placitas*. We'd already worked out most of the details regarding the show, with Mike. So I thought maybe it was a mistake on the phone bill—though it was on the log that you'd called somebody there. Anyway, a couple of hours ago I just thought I'd call the number. Well, this woman answered . . . and when I asked her if we knew her she sounded very odd. . . . But then she said it was probably a mistake on the phone bill. The call I'm talkin' about was from the day before the Cinco de Mayo show. Do you know someone there . . . from Placitas?"

Nate stood up, turning to the wheelbarrow, and lifted the trowel, mixing the adobe plaster as if it were important to do so. "I, uh . . . no, I don't, really."

"You don't, *really?* What does that *mean?* Nathan . . ." Elizabeth looked at him, while a nauseating butterfly worked its way into her stomach. "Nathan, there's something you're not telling me . . ." There was a longish pause while she studied him. "Are you having an affair?"

Nate looked down at the newly-painted concrete floor. "Well, I, uh . . ." and he said, in a softer voice, "Maybe you should sit down."

Elizabeth wobbled and staggered back slightly. "Oh, God! Sit *down?*" She eyed Nate as she slumped down onto the edge of one of the chairs they'd placed around the new kitchen table. "*Oh, SHIT!*" She smacked her hand against the table—the table Nate had built just the week before, before the show in Ruidoso. He shriveled, at the sound of the word coming from her.

Nate stayed where he was, a good eight feet away from Elizabeth, and sort of crouched on the floor as he began to speak. "Liz," he said, sighing loudly and staring at the floor. "I've got to be honest with you . . ." His words sounded weak, with the sound-deadening walls of the earthship absorbing his voice. He exhaled loudly with his cheeks puffed out, like he'd been holding his breath. "I did have a brief fling . . . while I was drunk, last fall. She's someone I knew from the old days, at the commune. Morningstar Ranch—years ago. And she was at the Las Cruces show. I probably mentioned her to you, once, in the past. She was an old girlfriend—we'd been involved. I wasn't thinking clearly, and I was drunk. I know it's no excuse. I'm so sorry—I just wasn't even thinking that I might hurt my family . . . and especially you.

"I called her before the Cinco de Mayo show to tell her that I couldn't see her again." Nate looked at Elizabeth, with what might have been a concerned expression. Maybe even slightly relieved. "This is the truth."

She was silent, hunched over and staring down at the floor between her feet, for a long couple of minutes . . . *I knew something wasn't right, last fall. You bastard . . .* She rested the side of her face in her hand, shielding her eyes. Her eyes burned, as she began rubbing them with the fingers of her other hand. Sobbing quietly, her breath coming in gasps, she tried to steady her voice. At last, she said, "Oh, God." There was a long silence, while vicious thoughts of retaliation crisscrossed her mind. In a weak voice came the words, "Is it over?"

A hunted look in his brow, Nate glanced at her, then away. *"Yes. . . .* It is. I told her that. And I apologized to her, also, and—"

"You're *damned* right, it's over—maybe you and I are over. . . . And you apologized to *her? Her?*"

"I had to. It was selfish of me, in every respect. And my sponsor in AA thought I owed her an apology, too. Believe me, if there was anything I could do to make it right, I would. But . . . I can't change it. It's past. But I *am* very sorry about it . . . and it won't happen again."

"You're damned right, it ain't gonna happen again." Elizabeth tried to straighten up, and to compose herself enough to continue, while the churning of angry butterflies in her stomach continued. "Well . . . I wondered if something like this happened. It seemed like you weren't real straight with me—when you talked about going to the hot springs after Las Cruces. It didn't fit. Even if you were *plastered* . . . I couldn't understand your not calling me, for days."

Nate was sniffling, himself, now—and finally rubbed his eyes, snorting nasally. "I am so sorry, Liz."

Elizabeth got up unsteadily from the chair, wobbling a bit and holding onto the table. She glanced at Nate, sizing him up instantly. She turned toward the newly-painted door. "I think you need to leave, for a while. Go to Mac's place. Or your girlfriend's house—I don't care. Get your shit together and get outta here." She walked out the door, back toward the trailer. Nate got up to peer after her through the doorway. She walked away, staring at the dusty earth, with arms folded across her chest as if protecting a fresh wound. Her gray corduroy pants wrinkled sadly.

Stepping quickly up the makeshift wooden stairs to the trailer door, Elizabeth went in, grabbed some Kleenex and her keys, and left, slamming the door. She got into the Volvo and started it, wanting to be away while Nate packed up his things . . . *The bastard . . .* She drove over to the community house, hoping no one would be there.

8.

"Nate'll be gone for a while—if I have anything to say about it.
Or gone for good. . . ."

About an hour later, Elizabeth drove down the driveway with the boys in the back seat. Nate's pickup was still there, and a minute later he came around the corner of the trailer with an armload of clothes and tools. He leaned into the open door of his truck, putting things behind the seat and onto the passenger seat, while Elizabeth got the boys down out of the car. Luke made an effort to go over to where Nate was, but Elizabeth quickly grabbed his hand and ushered the boys toward the trailer. "Daddy's just going away for a while."

Luke dragged behind his mother, turning to look at his dad. "Where?"

"Oh, he's going up to see Mac." She corralled the kids inside and got them into their old bedroom, giving them each a project to work on before supper. When the boys had gotten busy, Elizabeth walked into the half-empty main bedroom, closed the door and perched on the edge of the now empty, rusty, angle-iron bed frame. Uncomfortable—but there wasn't anywhere else to sit. Through the thin walls of the trailer, she heard Nate's truck start up, outside, and the crunching gravel as he drove up the driveway. And she cried quietly for more than half an hour, stopping only once or twice to listen to the muffled talking from the other room. The faded curtains were drawn back, and late afternoon sun streamed in through the window. It had, after all, been a beautiful day.

Finally, she felt no more tears coming and could breathe again almost normally. Elizabeth noticed she was grinding her teeth. She wanted to break something. Preferably something of Nate's. Something he'd built, a tool or a gadget—or any object precious to him . . . *The bastard. I don't care if he was drunk . . . he knew what he was doing. Damn him!* . . . She felt doubly betrayed. The earthship was finally getting finished; they were at last able to move out of the trailer after being cramped in there for more than a year. And with Nate's seeming newfound commitment to sobriety, things had seemed to be smoothing out, for them, in their marriage—after his drunken debacle of the past fall. . . . *The nerve of that guy. Coming back here—and back into my bed—after pulling that kind of crap. I wonder if it's the first time? . . . Damn, I need to talk to somebody! Wonder if Bev's home? . . .*

Gathering up the kids—and picking up their crayons, pens and paper—Elizabeth drove over to the community house to use the phone. She and Beverly had talked at Christmas, so Beverly was somewhat up to date on happenings in New Mexico. She was one of Elizabeth's oldest friends—they'd known each other since childhood in North Carolina. And had been even closer friends in high school. They could read each other like a book, though their lives had certainly turned in different directions. Beverly had gone to school in cosmetology and was a hair stylist at a trendy, high-dollar salon in Asheville.

Elizabeth dialed her, but had almost hung up when Beverly finally answered the phone on the fifth ring. Apparently she had just walked in, home from work with a bag of groceries. Beverly consoled her as best she could, mostly by listening. While Elizabeth spewed out as much as she was able to, at this point. After listening quietly for almost ten minutes, Beverly finally said, "Well, Honey, at least you two *talked* about it . . . and he admitted it. Right? And he said he ended it?"

Elizabeth was nearly out of breath from talking nonstop amid sobbing. "Yup. For what it's worth."

"Well, it *is* worth something. You know . . . when my crummy ex, Tyler, and I separated, he never admitted to a *damned* thing. I only found out later that he'd been screwing around on me. The prick. And he had the nerve to blame *me* for things that weren't right with our marriage. I thought maybe it *was* about me—because of my having gained a few pounds, you know—and not being into it, anymore. He didn't seem to be, you know, as horny as he used to be. I thought—at least a few times—that maybe something was going on with him. You know . . . an affair."

"Aww. I'm sorry, Bev. I know you went through the wringer, with that."

"Uh, don't worry. I am *over* that one. And I'm better for it."

"And here I am," Elizabeth said, "vomiting my guts out, to you. And reminding you all about this kind o' stuff."

"Vomit away, girl. It ain't gonna bother me. And you'll feel better." There was a pause for a few moments, on Beverly's end of the line. "But, uh, can I ask you? I'm just curious. . . . Did you sense something was going on with him—before this business?"

"No, I didn't. Not before last fall. And when he messed up—last fall—and went on that drinking spree . . . well, he just seemed so torn up afterward, when he came home. . . . And I just thought it was because he felt so screwed-up, about his drinking and all. After being sober for a bunch of years. No. I just thought he felt guilty about the drinking—and for going AWOL."

"Well," Beverly said, "I bet he *did* feel screwed-up. Or like *he* screwed up. I don't know. I have a girlfriend who's an alcoholic, I guess. She must be. She goes to those AA meetings—and, I mean, who'd even *go* to those meetings if they didn't *have* to? But they *do* get weird about booze. Alcoholics do, I mean. She gets, like, really *guilty*, whenever she gets drunk. And I'm like—what's the big deal, get over it. So I can imagine Nate would, too, if he's an alkie. . . . Feel guilty, and screwed-up and stuff, I mean."

The knot in Elizabeth's stomach unraveled a bit, and her breathing became more relaxed. "Damn, it's good to talk to you, Bev. I wish you could get your butt out here, again."

"Me too, Hon'."

"I guess, you know . . . all his drinking, and careening around the darn countryside . . . doesn't hurt near so much as the fact that he chose to be with this woman."

"Sure," Beverly said. "Of course."

Elizabeth was aware of the knot in her stomach, again. "It sounds kind of retarded, and childish, maybe—but I just needed to hear myself say that. It's such a damned betrayal."

"I know, Hon'. It *is* a betrayal. Major betrayal. I guess, about all I can say is that. . . . Well . . . if the marriage is worth saving—and don't get me wrong, the pain won't ever go away completely—it will get easier. And it'll hurt less. If you want it to."

Elizabeth twisted her fingers into the springy phone cord. "I guess."

"You're not unique, in this, you know. I hate to say it—but it's true. Men are *pigs*. They think with their dicks more than with their brains . . . God help 'em. *Especially* if they're drinking. Know what I mean? Look . . . alcohol lowers people's inhibitions, right? I mean, it's a scientific fact. And I'm not defending Nate, at all, but—think about it. How many women do you and I know who've gone out drinking . . . and wound up getting involved with—or going to bed with—a guy they wouldn't look at *twice* if they were stone-cold sober? Why do you think so many people go to bars, thinkin' they'll find somebody to hook up with? It's more likely to happen if they're both drinking. Right?"

"I don't know. I never went to bars, much. But I know what you're sayin'."

"Well," Beverly said, "I'm not defending it. But it seems to be true. Men *are* pigs, though—no doubt about it. And unless they're some kind of damned *saint,* they usually won't mind wetting their whistle—if some woman acts willing. Maybe they're *all* built that way, I don't know. But it can go both ways, too, you know. I've known a couple of girls who fooled around—intentionally—after they found out their guys had." She chuckled. "One of my girlfriends is a little bit sleazy . . . she calls it a 'grudge-fuck.'"

"Oh, my God," Elizabeth giggled. I can't even think of that. . . . I'm so old-fashioned, I guess." She paused for a moment. "Besides, I don't even *know* any guys that might be available. Ha! Not that I *would,* you know."

Beverly laughed. "See, girlfriend . . . you're feelin' better already!"

The two talked for a while longer, on the topic of men. Beverly had more experience with men, on the dating scene. She had always dated more than Elizabeth, in high school and in the years following. And seemed to take matters of the heart a lot less seriously than Elizabeth did. Talking to her felt like a breath of fresh air from home—and the knot in Elizabeth's stomach gradually unraveled. Her thoughts grew less angry, lonely, and desperate.

"Damn it," Beverly said. "I should try and get over there to see you. I know we talk a lot on the phone . . . but we haven't got together since y'all's wedding. Too long!"

"Darn right! I really think you should get your butt out here. I could use the company, right about now."

"Well, seriously . . . let me look at my schedule, and see if it'll work. I've been makin' some pretty good money—and I haven't taken any real vacation time in God knows how long. We've got a new girl working at the salon—that I've been helping to train—and maybe she could take up the slack for me, next week."

"Oh, see if you can, Bev. It'd be *great* to see ya."

"Yeah," Beverly said. "It'd be fun. I haven't ever seen much of New Mexico, you know, except for the short time around y'all's wedding. I might even be able to find a cheap flight."

"Well, we've got plenty of *room,* now. Nate'll be gone for a while—if I have anything to say about it. Or gone for good. . . . I haven't decided on that one, yet. Maybe you can help me make up my mind on that—"

"Oh, Hon', I don't know. . . . That's your call, Liz."

"'Cause, for right now, I really couldn't tell ya what I'm gonna do about all this."

They talked for a while longer on lighter topics: how their parents were doing, the boys, Beverly's job, and her latest dating escapades. When they finally said their goodbyes, the phone clicked to a dial tone. For some reason Elizabeth listened to it for a while, as if it might reveal something. It sounded normal. Almost cheerful.

She looked in on the boys, who'd been relatively quiet, playing in the large living room area of the community house. "C'mon, guys. Let's go home and get some supper."

9.

... *Almost anything you do will be insignificant.*
But it's very important that you do it ...*

Nate watched his wife walking away, disappearing around the corner of
the trailer, and heaved a heavy sigh ... *That didn't go very well. Shit!* ...
Moving from one place to another like a zombie, he cleaned up his tools,
putting them away into the storage closet, at the back of the boys'
bedroom in the middle "U". Elizabeth's car started up, in the driveway,
and he heard her leave. He stood for a minute staring at the low
worktable he'd made for the boys, in their bedroom, already covered
with their drawings.

In a daze, he walked to the main bedroom, in the far easternmost "U",
where they'd put their mattress on the floor till they could find a better
bed frame. He found his travel bag and packed some clothes into it ...
How do you pack for something like this? I don't know ... Nate felt
completely different than he had a half hour earlier—as if suffering again
from a hangover, with the dissociation and desperation that sometimes
attended it. He mulled over his tools for a few minutes and decided to
bring a few of them, in case Mac might have some work he could do, in
Santa Fe. Especially if his eviction became prolonged—or permanent.
He decided to bring along some camping gear, a warm jacket, and his
sleeping bag, in case he did some camping in the high country. Those
things were in the trailer, so he made a trip over there and loaded the
stuff into his truck. He walked back into the earthship, drifting like a
ghost around the rooms, and vaguely contemplated what items still
needed to be finished, should he return any time soon ... *Maybe I won't*

ever be returning. No way to know . . . Somehow, thinking about the house construction lent some sense of normalcy to the situation.

A car came into the driveway—Elizabeth's Volvo. Nate grabbed the few items remaining to put into his truck, and carried them over to the little parking area. He looked at Elizabeth, but she wouldn't return the favor. She helped the boys down out of the back seat and, out of the corner of his eye Nate noticed her grabbing Luke's hand. And saying something about how his daddy was "just going away for a while." As he started the truck and drove up the driveway, he repeated to himself the words he'd overheard her saying. And said it again, out loud. "A while. Huh." . . . *Not 'a few days' or something—but 'a while.' What does that even mean? . . . A couple of days? A couple of years?. . .* "Whew! Damn it! . . . And so, the shit hits the fan."

As Nate headed down the highway in the late afternoon, away from Silver City and toward the interstate at Truth or Consequences, he worked out a muddled plan about spending some time in the northern part of the state. And stopping in at Mac's place to get some guidance and brain adjustment. If that was at all possible. He stopped at a gas station in Bayard to fill up on gas and use a pay phone. Mac answered his phone, and Nate asked if he could stay there for the night, though he'd be getting there fairly late. He said only that he and Elizabeth had an argument—and they needed some time apart. Mac said he'd leave a key under the doormat—and that he didn't have to be on the job early, the next morning—so they could talk a little, then.

After a long, boring drive on the interstate—mindlessly following other vehicles' taillights and the dotted line—Nate started to nod off at the wheel on the long incline between Albuquerque and Santa Fe. He'd run out of cassette-tapes to play and was exhausted by the broken record of dismal thoughts that circled in his mind. He rolled the window down and felt awakened by the crisp, chilly air of the Santa Fe night. At the top of the hill, the lights of Santa Fe sparkled down below, different from the endless carpet of lights sprawling over Albuquerque. Lights also flickered in the distance—on the looming, black mountainsides of the Sangre de Cristos to the east. He pulled the truck to the side of the highway and stepped out for a break and some fresh air . . . *Far out. The city always seems to sparkle, at night, from the top of this hill. Must be the altitude or something . . .*

Next morning, the clattering sound of dishes and the gurgling of a coffee-maker, coming from the kitchen, reached Nate's ears. And for a moment he shut his eyes again. But he extricated himself from his sleeping bag, on Mac's couch, noticing a new crick in his neck. Putting on a pair of army surplus pants, and throwing a towel that he'd used as a pillow over his shoulder, he made his way to the kitchen and greeted Mac with the voice and tone of a narcoleptic. Mac seemed way too cheerful as he greeted Nate and handed him a mug of coffee . . . *God. Like a doctor ministering to a patient in a psych-ward . . .*

Mac looked into Nate's face. And his next words were, "So. Elizabeth found out, huh? And kicked you out?"

Nate nodded his head slowly, focusing on a cracked linoleum tile. "Your powers of perception continue to amaze me. Yes, and yes. You were right, as usual—she did figure it out. Maybe it's just as well."

"Well, I hope you weren't too surprised. Women often know about this kind o' thing."

"Yeah," Nate said, slouching into a chair at the kitchen table. "You mentioned that, before. When we talked, last fall, I mean."

Mac tugged at his moustache and glanced at Nate. "Well . . . I'm not right all that often, about relationships. And every relationship's a little different. What did your AA sponsor in Silver City think . . . about making amends to Elizabeth, I mean? Oh, never mind—it's really none of my business."

"Uh, well . . . he thought I should sit her down and talk to her about it, right away. And face the consequences. But he left it up to me. And he did say that sometimes it's more hurtful to talk about all the details . . . if they don't know about it, I mean. I wish I had, now—told her, I mean. She's probably even *more* convinced that I'm a scumbag, now. Like I was trying to hide it from her."

Mac walked over to the refrigerator and came back to the table with a carton of milk. "Oh, she doesn't think you're a scumbag. I know Elizabeth. Maybe a bit of a *weasel,*" he said, thumping Nate on the shoulder. "But definitely not a *scum*bag."

"Thanks, buddy. Boy, you're in a good mood."

"Ah, hell—I'm just messin' with ya. It'll work itself out. Whatever God's will is—in this business—is what's gonna happen."

"Yeah, right," Nate said. "I guess I should find *that* reassuring."

"But it *is*. Reassuring, I mean. It's at least *some*what in God's hands. You can do your part . . . make amends and apologize, I mean. And see that it doesn't happen again. If you value your marriage, that is. That's a part of making amends, you know—to people we've harmed—is to not continue the hurtful behavior. If the relationship is strong . . . and you both value it . . . well, it'll work itself out. We can't re-live the past. What's done is done. The present is all that really exists. But we *aim* for a better future—and better *behavior*, in the future."

Nate looked at Mac, and then down at the table between them . . . *Yep. Looks like I'm the Prodigal Son, again. Showing up here at Mac's place, all messed up . . .* He tapped his fingers absently, on the table. "Yeah. I really don't want to lose her. She's an *amazing* woman."

"She is."

"For real, man. I can't even imagine living without her in my life."

"Well," Mac said, "then maybe you'll be willing to do a little more work . . . to keep her. Working on *yourself,* I mean. We can only really work on *ourselves*—and try to change our own behavior. Trying the change anyone else is pointless. And actually, impossible. Relationships *are* work."

"Seems to be the case."

"And a good bit of your work, obviously, is to stay *sober*. And not have this kind of craziness happen again. I'm guessin' this stuff wouldn't have happened, if you'd stayed sober. . . . Am I right?"

"No," Nate said. "It wouldn't. I mean, I'll *flirt* with a chick—I guess I always will—but that's as far as it'll go." Nate set down his coffee and went to the living room to get a bag of granola he brought. Mac refilled both their coffee mugs and got a few things out of the refrigerator to take with him to work. In Mac's kitchen cabinet Nate found a bowl and sat down, pouring some of the granola into it. He put his hand to the side of his face, as if he had a sudden toothache . . . *Liz's special granola mix . .* .

Mac looked at Nate, studying him for a moment. "How's your spiritual life going, lately? Your connection with a Higher Power, whatever you want to call it. . . . Have you kept working on that, like I suggested?"

"Yeah, I have. Gotten back into some semblance of a morning meditation and prayer time. And I guess I've told you—I've gotten into going to 'sweat-lodge,' on a pretty regular basis. It seems to help. It's a good way to pray. For me it is, anyway."

"That's great. Really good. You know, Bill W. says, in the Big Book, something about alcohol being a subtle enemy. And he says, 'We are not *cured* of alcoholism. What we really have is a daily reprieve, contingent on the *maintenance* of our spiritual condition.' It's all about working on it—on our spiritual condition. Maintaining it. Continuing to improve it."

"Gotcha," Nate said. "Yeah, I think you and I talked about that also, last fall, after my drunk. I've been trying to take that to heart."

"Excellent." Mac fixed a fried egg for himself. And they talked about less serious things. Mac's carpentry crew was finishing the roof framing on a house they were building in the Old Pecos Trail area of Santa Fe. And he mentioned about having trouble lining up a roofing contractor to do the tile roof on the job.

At some point on the drive up, the night before, Nate had decided to spend a few days up north, possibly doing some hiking in southern Colorado. He figured it was way too soon to even think about calling Elizabeth. "So, Mac? . . . would it be okay if I stopped by, again, early next week? And . . . if Elizabeth doesn't want me back, yet—and I don't imagine she *will*—would you maybe have any work you could put me on to? Carpentry? Labor? Whatever . . ."

"I probably could," Mac said, putting a couple of things into a small cooler. "Line up some work for ya, I mean. We'll be doing the roofing plywood, ourselves. And we might have to do the tile roofing, too—if I can't get that worked out, with a contractor. Kind of a priority, 'cause we could be getting some rains in a couple weeks, if the summer monsoon comes early. I could sure use an extra hand, if we wind up doing that, ourselves. Hard, tedious work, with a lot of lifting, though."

"I'm game for it, man. I do have a few muscles."

After an unhurried breakfast, Mac left for work. And Nate left his house shortly after, steering his pickup onto the highway heading for Española and points north. The radio station from Santa Fe that he was tuned in to forecast dry, sunny weather for the next few days.

By the time Nate drove into Taos, shortly after noon, he had settled on hiking in the Blanca Peak area. About an hour and a half north of Taos, in the Sangre de Cristos of southern Colorado. Since he had some time away from the family, he had a hankering to do something worthwhile with it. He felt drawn to climb Blanca—and also felt like he needed some introspective time alone. Outdoor-type people he'd known always said it was an impressive peak, one of the highest of the "Fourteeners" in Colorado (peaks over 14,000 feet). A friend once told him that, although it was easily accessible from the roads, it had the steepest elevation gain of any of the Fourteener trails. You couldn't drive very far up the jeep trail without an ATV. So you had to park your vehicle around 8,000 feet—and hike up to 14,300 feet in something like seven miles of trail. Steep.

He'd never climbed a "Fourteener" before. He had only minimal backpacking gear with him—a good sleeping bag, mediocre backpack, and a tarpaulin for shelter. But he could make do. At a sporting-goods store in Taos, he picked up a trail map of the Blanca Peak region, looking it over in the parking lot before he left town. And stopped at a grocery store for some lightweight food to bring. It would probably be a day-and-a-half or two-day excursion. He left town and drove up the two-lane highway from Taos up to Fort Garland, Colorado. The highway snaking over high-desert ranch land that skirted the western edge of the long mountain chain known as the Sangre de Cristo Range. North of Fort Garland he found the unmarked jeep trail leaving the highway, which wound up into the foothills and eventually became the trail up Blanca.

On the jeep trail, washed-out and rocky, Nate could finally drive no further. By the time he parked his truck along a straight stretch, in this sagebrush boulder country of the foothills, the sun was lowering in the sky . . . *Dude, I've got to get a move on. Gotta get partway up there . . . or I'll never make it up to the top and back tomorrow . . .* Slinging on his overloaded backpack, he started up the trail. The arid foothills of piñon pine and sagebrush gave way to forested slopes, and he hiked up this steep section into the valley of a rushing stream. Slogging up this valley for the better part of an hour, it seemed he was getting up close to timberline. The trees on the mountainsides becoming mostly alpine species, stunted and sparse.

It was chilly dusk when the trail came to a seldom-used campsite . . . *This looks like the place. Can't go further, anyway—I'm toast . . .* After catching his breath while the last of the sunlight left the sky, he quickly set up his lean-to and scouted around for firewood.

As the mountains darkened under the blanket of night, lights in the valley below delineated the highways and small towns in the San Luis Valley—Mosca, Hooper, and the distant city lights of Alamosa. The ridges and mountains around him stood silent, imposing and black. It was the first time he'd been alone, really, in a long time. And though he never thought himself a solitary type, this felt like a necessary balm to his soul. For a few minutes, it did. The immensity and dark silence of the surrounding mountains had a humbling effect, though—and an edgy fear crept in. He abandoned his contemplation of the scene and felt chilled all of a sudden, his clothes damp and clammy from the exertion of the climb. A search for firewood became more urgent . . . *Whew! I must be at around ten thousand feet, here—it's gonna be cold here, by dawn. No warm bed for me, tonight. I hope that sleeping bag'll be warm . . .*

Next morning, Nate explored around his camp area, finding a rock outcrop where he could survey the surrounding mountains and check his progress. He hit the trail mid-morning, leaving his lean-to, sleeping bag, and a few heavy food items. The sun came up slowly over the high peaks, here, though when it did it warmed the air quickly. It soon became rocky alpine country—the trail wending its way through alpine basins scattered with stunted trees and circling several turquoise lakes with patches of snow strewn about.

At last, by early afternoon the trail clambered onto a knife-edge ridge and wound around immense boulders and rocky spires as it climbed toward the summit of Blanca. He passed two couples—on their way back down. One of the men said, "Enjoy the day!". . . *Probably smart, those folks. Best to get off of the summit by afternoon, I think, this time of year. Never know when a thunderstorm might come up out o' nowhere and light up the summits. And that would be interesting* . . . Nate had the mountain to himself, now, though for all he knew there could have been climbers on the other peaks nearby. Reaching the top of Blanca, the view was immense. And still. The narrow spine of the Sangre de Cristos was no more than ten or fifteen miles wide here—but with cliffs, pinnacles, and ridiculously jagged peaks of bad-ass rock. Lower hill country lay to the east of the mountains. And to the west, the pancake-flat San Luis valley—from where he'd come—stretched to the limit of visibility where the blue serration of the San Juan Mountains arose on the far horizon.

Within a half hour of arriving at the top, a wind gradually picked up and became a nuisance. Nate crouched down behind some rocks that had been piled up, making a windbreak wall. He remembered an article he read somewhere about how there was evidence the Ute Indians used Blanca Peak as a lookout. Maybe these very rocks were piled up by Ute scouts . . . *And how many hundreds of years ago? Why? Maybe to locate herds of buffalo? Or to keep an eye out for enemy tribes?* . . . He pulled a jacket out of his pack and put it on. Out of the wind, he sat down and leaned back against a boulder—finding a place where the rock surface cradled him. And gazed into a deep blue sky patchy with clouds both above him and below.

Time crawled to a stop, and it seemed he was an infinitesimally small part in the big picture. His thoughts wandered—he envisioned camping with his boys once they were older, and bringing them up here. Maybe they would get a kick out of backpacking and hiking, as he did . . . *Liz would love this. The view here. We'll have to hike up here, sometime. If we . . . if we stay together* . . . His family seemed small, and far away, from up here in this immensity. But important. He thought of a quote, in a meditation book he used sometimes. A quote from Mahatma Gandhi . . . *Almost anything you do will be insignificant. But it's very important that you do it* . . .

He thought of Elizabeth. And of how he'd hurt her . . . *Boy, I sure screwed up, and now I might lose her* . . . He sighed and wished he could predict the future, regarding her and the boys. But since he didn't have that ability, he prayed to some amorphous concept of a Higher Power— or God—that he be given the strength and grace to accept whatever transpired with the family. Exhausted with his thoughts, and with the climb, Nate closed his eyes and dozed off for a moment. It must have been longer, though, because when he opened his eyes again he was chilled. And the sun shone at a lower angle in the afternoon sky . . . *Whew. I better get booking on down. A lot of mountain, between here and my truck* . . . He stood up, shivering a little, got a water bottle out of his pack and drank. He shouldered his pack and began down the winding trail—seeing spots in front of his eyes for the first few minutes but then getting his feet firmly beneath him again.

It was dusk by the time he reached his little campsite of the night before, but he decided to push on down toward where he'd parked the truck. So he packed up his lean-to and gear quickly. And continued down the trail, hiking the last mile down to his truck wearing a headlamp, not seeing the trail clearly at all. Wanting to avoid an accident—a sprained ankle or worse—every step made with the bouncing headlamp beam had to be more deliberate and attentive. And was exhausting. The moon, just a sliver in the western sky, offered no assistance at all, and he almost passed by his truck before he saw it parked in the sagebrush. Exhausted, he wolfed down a sandwich, unrolled his sleeping bag and slept in the bed of his truck.

10.

Hindu Sanskrit signs and a Jewish Shabbat service

The next day, it clouded up shortly after dawn and was overcast for a few hours—maybe the beginnings of the summer monsoon moisture moving in. Driving south, back into New Mexico and toward Taos, Nate decided on the spur of the moment to stop at the Lama Foundation to see what went on there. He'd always been curious about the place. The Lama Foundation was a spiritually-based community, a half hour north of Taos, and in the past he'd heard interesting things about it. He'd been told that they welcomed visitors, and you could usually camp there overnight unless they were busy with one of the workshops that were held there during the summer. Spiritual teachers from all over the country—and in fact other parts of the world—came there during the summer to lead these workshops and retreats.

It was early afternoon as Nate turned off the highway and onto the gravel road leading up to Lama. Tibetan prayer-flags fluttered in the breeze on both sides of the road. The road climbed uphill over a tilted, sagebrush-covered plateau of ancient sediment that had washed down from the high reaches of the Sangre de Cristos to the east. Here and there a small road branched off, leading up to houses that the permanent residents had built. There was only one power line, he noticed—and the houses seemed to be mostly of sustainable-type construction. One of these, which he could see from the road, appeared to be an adobe house with a large glass wall on its south side . . . *A lot like an earthship* . . . Another was a straw-bale house, a type of construction, which (like the earthships), was still somewhat experimental. The road continued up the slope, and as the land gained elevation the vegetation changed—sagebrush and piñon pine transitioned into ponderosa pine and aspen groves.

The road dead-ended into a parking area amid a scattering of small homes and cottages, a couple of large garden plots, and several large buildings. A young couple were walking down to the nearer of the garden plots—carrying gardening tools—and Nate asked them who he needed to talk to about camping, for the night. The man, who sported a large black beard, said, "Oh, no worries, man. There isn't any retreat or anything going on this weekend. You're welcome to camp at one of the campsites . . . down that trail there, below the dome." He pointed down the hill, toward a large stand of aspens. "Nobody else is camping there, tonight—or at least, not yet—so help yourself." The man paused for a moment. "And why don't you come and join us tonight? We're having Shabbat—like we do, every Friday. Folks'll be bringing some food over. We light the candles, and pray and sing and stuff . . . it's nice. Starts around sunset. I hope we see ya there."

"Excellent!" Nate said. "Thanks. I'll try to be there. Where do you do this?"

"Oh . . . over at the dome, there," the man said, pointing to a large, circular building with a geodesic dome roof.

"Nice. I'll see you guys later." Nate leaned into the pickup, pulling some of his camping gear out from behind the seat, and wandered down to the trail he'd been directed to. He gazed around at the scattered buildings, a network of stone pathways connecting them. By the side of the walkway leading up to the dome building, there was a large hand-carved wooden sign saying, "Welcome," with a red *Om* symbol below it. He shook his head, a slight smile on his face . . . *Wild. Interesting place. Hindu Sanskrit signs and a Jewish Shabbat service* . . . He passed a little shrine, set beneath some aspen trees—that featured a laughing Buddha sculpted out of stone, surrounded by several voluptuous goddesses who looked like Greek wood nymphs.

Later, after Nate had set up his lean-to, he looked around and found out where the bathroom was—which turned out to be a pit-toilet outhouse. After spending some time walking around the grounds as the western sky gradually turned a streaky red, he made his way over to the dome building, where a few people were starting to show up.

The Shabbat service reminded Nate of his Jewish upbringing—and of his parents, who used to observe at least some of the Jewish holidays. Also reminding him of how his father took him to temple, sometimes, when he was a boy. But in many ways it was quite different from any traditional Sabbath service he'd ever attended. The people there seemed to enjoy being together for the service, though Nate would have said most of them didn't look to be of Jewish descent, at all—many appearing to be of Anglo or Celtic background. Most everyone in the room joined hands in a twenty-foot-wide circle, while a woman in the center of the circle lit the two Shabbat candles. A man next to her spoke in Hebrew, blessing the wine with the Kiddush prayer. The woman blessed the Challah—the traditional braided bread—and it was passed around, from which people tore off pieces and ate, while her partner sang a psalm in English that spoke about peace and brotherhood.

After the man's song, everyone in the circle welcomed those standing next to them, and some low-key conversation and fellowship followed. An older woman standing to his right, with streaks of white in her dark hair, welcomed Nate—and a young, dreadlock-wearing guy on his other side introduced himself also. They asked if he was visiting. The group around Nate felt warm and completely genuine in welcoming him, as if they'd all agreed to leave their egos at the door and be neighbors. Meanwhile, a few people—probably residents, there—set about arranging bowls of food on a table. A couple of young men got out their guitars and began playing softly. And a few minutes later, the woman who stood next to Nate in the circle joined them, playing a Navajo-style wooden flute.

At the table, it was all vegetarian food that people brought. Which was fine with Nate. Lentil salad, hummus, a tofu Indian curry, different rice dishes, and green salads. After filling his plate, Nate sat down on the floor next to the man and woman he'd talked to, earlier, near the garden. The man's name was Joshua, and his wife was Susanna. They spoke a bit about Lama and their life there in the past year. They'd become permanent residents recently and were planning on building a small home on an adjoining property.

Joshua tried to address some of Nate's confusion about the spiritual basis of the community and the variety of religious philosophies welcomed there. "You see, we think of Lama as an experiment in community . . . like a microcosm of what community *could* be like, all over the world. The founders of the Lama Foundation were brought up in different faiths, and they based the community on certain other spiritual communities where there's been, like, a melding of beliefs and practices. We feel like there's no real reason why the different religions and spiritual paths can't coexist and be mutually respectful of each other. We believe that all religions have—at their core—the same practices of God-consciousness, love, and being in harmony with others and with nature."

"Huh," Nate said. "Yeah. . . . Nice idea."

Joshua and Susanna looked to be a very happy people, but the thought crossed Nate's mind that there was more than a little naiveté and idealism in what the man was saying . . . *Probably smokes a little too much weed . . .*

"But then," Nate said, "why is there so much strife—let alone warfare—that've been based on religious differences? . . . That kind of stuff seems to have infected *every* society, all down through history. Ever since the first religions *began.* And it drives me *nuts,* to be honest with ya."

Susanna stood up, with her plate, and went over to talk to another woman. Joshua looked at Nate with intense eyes. "But think of it," he said. "Is it really the core *belief*—in any religion—that causes that? Or is it what people, and their societies, have *done* to that core belief? In making it an organized religion, I mean. *Fear,* which I think we could all agree is a human emotion that was necessary for human survival— especially during the evolution of the species—is also absolutely detrimental to community in the larger sense. Fear—and the survival instinct—have always been the driving forces in forming the small groups, or collectives, of people . . . the tribe, if you will. But it's always *fear*—in one of its numerous disguises—that spawns the concept of the 'other.' The idea of 'us and them.' 'Superior and inferior.' 'Good and evil.' 'Black and White.' We have to get *beyond* this thinking if we're ever gonna survive, here."

"Yeah. I know what you mean." And though not convinced by Joshua's ideas on the cause and effect, he could agree completely on the seriousness of the problem. "Totally. We damned sure have our work cut out for us." Joshua scrambled up from his seat on the floor, and as he did so put his hand on Nate's arm. "I'll be right back." He walked over to where his wife was talking with the other woman, probably a neighbor.

Nate absently looked around the room as he finished the last bit of food on his plate. The people in the room—probably most of them residents, maybe a few visitors—appeared to be some of the warmest and happiest people he'd seen in a long time. He thought about what Joshua had said . . . *What if it is just that simple? But how do you get 'beyond' the fearful thinking? That's the trick. It's hard-wired into us. A product of the mind, and the ego. And of our evolution . . .*

Later, Nate went back to his campsite. And slept well, under a canopy of sparkling stars, enveloped by what felt like a harmonious silence. The next day was fair weather again, and he spent the early part of the day just talking with a few of the residents. He volunteered to do a couple hours of weeding work in the gardens. While he worked there, a middle-aged couple came over to speak with him. They were from Massachusetts, the Boston area, and were "Summer Stewards" at

Lama—people who would be doing service work and odd jobs around the place in exchange for room and board over the summer. Apparently there were usually five to ten of these people, at any given time—most of them folks who had been to the Lama Foundation before and found it worthwhile to spend part of the summer there. Helping the organization to function and thrive.

There were trails skirting the upper edge of the Lama property, where it bordered Kit Carson National Forest land. And in the afternoon, Nate hiked along a couple of these trails, his legs still aching from Blanca Peak. There was protected public land in the national forest to the east, which encompassed the high peaks of the Sangre de Cristos here. Lobo Peak was up there, and Lama Peak—both around 12,000 feet. At this upper edge of the Lama property it was partly cleared—maybe originally had been pastureland—and offered sweeping views down the sloping tableland toward the Taos Valley. In the distance Nate could see a section of that great crack in the earth—the Rio Grande Gorge—cutting across the high desert of Taos Valley. And a couple of solitary, high mountains (which were ancient volcanoes, actually). These were Ute Mountain and San Antonio Peak, in the hazy distance.

11.

. . . Like a universal aurora borealis. Everywhere.
And with this wonderful humming music . . .

A couple had arrived at Lama, mid-afternoon—and apparently would also be camping in the aspen grove, as they had already set up a tent there. Nate moseyed over to their campsite to introduce himself. The man, Keith, appeared to be in his late forties or early fifties and had accompanied his wife down from Denver. She was there to participate in a "Women's Circle" retreat during the next week. When they had gotten the campsite mostly set up to their liking, the man's wife went off to make arrangements for her stay there. It seemed that Keith would be staying no more than a day or so—his wife would later be sharing one of the retreat cottages, during the week. They had lived in Taos for several years, before moving to Denver for work, and had been to Lama a number of times when they lived nearby. So he was able to speak knowledgeably about the history of the place, and they talked for a few minutes.

"Well," Nate said. "I'll let you finish setting up your camp. I imagine I'll run into you again—it's not that big of a place."

"No, it isn't," Keith said. "But there's a great feeling of space, here, isn't there?"

"Totally. Feels like you can see forever, from the grounds, here."

"You know, if you want to learn more about the Lama Foundation, there's a good little library, here, in the small building right next to the dome. It has all kinds of books, and tapes—and transcriptions of all the people who've given spiritual talks or teachings here."

"No kiddin'. I'll have to check it out." A while later, Nate did wander up to this library room, in a separate building attached to the dome structure. The library was somewhat of an archive of many of the people who'd been to Lama. Some of them well-known spiritual teachers, some of them traditional group facilitators—from all the various workshops, spiritual enquiry and self-help groups that had taken place at Lama over the past few years. Chogyam Trungpa (the Tibetan Rinpoche) had taught Buddhist dharma there. Ram Das had been there a number of times, as he had in fact helped in starting the Lama Foundation. And shared his understanding of Hindu philosophy and spiritual concepts. Several Zen Buddhist teachers and Christian theologians had also led groups and spiritual retreats there . . . *Man, there's a little of everything, here. Eclectic, for sure . . .* Nate thought about it for a moment . . . *And not just a mish-mash of spiritual stuff, but more like all embracing. Welcoming. Like: 'All Roads lead to Rome.' Huh . . . I've got to get Liz up here someday . . .*

Nate heaved a heavy sigh—and wondered what she was doing on this Saturday afternoon. And wondered how the boys were . . . *Uh . . . too soon to call her, now. Shit . . .* Nate closed the door to the library and walked into the dome building, sitting empty and quiet. The night before, with the large group there for Shabbat, the room had an almost chaotic acoustic quality, with sound reverberating off the inside surfaces of the geodesic dome. But when he was alone in the room it manifested an immense silence. A little like the silence one could experience in the massive, sound-deadening walls of an earthship. He sat for a while near a window through which afternoon sun was streaming. He closed his eyes and tried to quiet his mind, longing to incorporate some of the peace and quiet of the place.

After ten or fifteen minutes of sitting in meditation, Nate heard the sound of footsteps. Someone walking through the entrance hall and into the dome. He slowly opened his eyes and turned to see who it was. Keith, the man from Denver. He came into the room and sat a respectful distance away, seeming to also want some quiet time. Nate sat quietly but didn't close his eyes again—only gazed, without focusing, at the floor. After a while, Keith broke the silence by talking a little about himself—about some difficulties he was going through with a couple of health problems and as a man reaching his middle-age years. Nate looked over at him . . . *Why the hell is he telling me all this? He doesn't know me from Adam . . .*

Keith looked at Nate, and then past him at the wall behind him. "I guess I'm talking about this, because . . . from just talking with you earlier, I'm guessing you're going through some kind of troubled time, yourself."

"It's that obvious, huh?"

"Well, yeah. It is. I mean, it seems like something about you is looking for answers. As if . . . some part of you is a seeker. Maybe I'm way off base, here—maybe not."

Nate felt a little tightness in his chest. A bit uneasy. He never liked it, when people assumed they could easily read him . . . *They always think they got me figured. Like a dime-store novel* . . . "Well, yeah . . . I've been going through some shit. And it's hard to say how it'll turn out."

"Well," Keith said, "I didn't mean to pry. It just seemed like you were at loose ends . . . about something—"

"Yep, you're right. I *am*."

"and I just thought, well . . . that I would just talk to you about something that might help. Part of the reason I came down here this weekend—aside from helping Sue to drive down from Denver—is that I heard from an old friend about something that's going on this weekend, nearby. These friends of mine, and some other folks, are getting together for peyote ceremony. We're doing the ceremony where an old friend of mine lives. In that old hippie commune—though it's not really a commune anymore. You know . . . the New Dawn community? Near Taos. Maybe you've heard of it? Anyway . . . a 'Road Man' from one of the Apache tribes is leading it."

"No kiddin'," Nate said. "Wow. . . . I haven't thought, lately, about doing that kind of thing."

"Anyway . . . I just thought I'd invite you. If you want to go. Anyone is welcome . . . if they're invited. And if they feel drawn to it."

"Well, I, uh . . . there's surely been times when I was curious about the heavy-duty hallucinogens, like peyote. But to tell you the truth, I, uh . . . I don't know. I've been feeling so screwed up lately . . . that I wonder if maybe it would turn out bad. You know . . . a bad trip. And maybe I'd make it lousy for everyone else there, too."

Keith looked at Nate with a concerned expression, but smiled. "I pretty much doubt that would happen. From what little I know about peyote . . . I 'spect it will show you what you need. Or give you some answers. Nobody I know has actually had a bad experience with it— except for maybe puking a lot. I'm sure it *can* happen, though . . . a bad trip, I mean. But this is pretty much a traditional peyote ceremony . . . a *mitote*. And I know the guy who'll be the peyote leader. He'll pretty much keep things in order. With no bullshit. If someone's acting like they're off the hook—or being a nuisance to others in the circle—he'll talk them down and get them back on track. It's best to do peyote with the traditional ceremony, I think. Keeps it under control. There're no guarantees, of course. But it's up to you. . . . I just thought I'd invite you—if you feel like you want to go."

"Huh. Well, thanks, man . . . I appreciate the offer. I'll have to think about it. I should probably take you up on it—you only live once, huh? But, uh . . . peyote's a pretty hard-hitting trip, isn't it? More so, than acid?"

"It's *definitely* different from acid. Yeah . . . you'll see things that aren't really there at all. Or, no . . . that's not quite right . . . most folks who're familiar with it would say that you'll see things that just aren't visible in ordinary consciousness. Like peyote is a doorway into another reality that's just as real and valid as this one—we're just not aware of it. I've just done it twice, before . . . and I've had a good relationship with peyote both times. It's shown me things that I needed to learn. A good vision . . . to help me with my life."

Nate was taken aback, somewhat, by this offer. And rubbed his neck, which seemed to be sore . . . *Maybe from the camping* . . . He looked at Keith and then back at the patches of sunlight on the floor. "So, like, do you need to know right now? Or can I let you know in a little while? After I think about it a bit. What time are you guys doing this?"

"Oh, we're gonna meet over there around six. New Dawn is over in Arroyo Hondo, you know. Won't take long to get there. But yeah . . . think about it. It's not something that anyone should take lightly. And *we* don't. We don't take it lightly, you know. I don't just do it for kicks—or just to get stoned. But, yeah, if you want to come, you could just meet me at the parking lot around five-thirty. I have the little dark blue Toyota four-door, there."

"Cool. Let me get back to you, on that. Thanks for asking."

"You bet," Keith said, getting up from the floor. "And if you decide *not* to . . . well, that's totally cool, too. It's not for everyone. Oh, but . . . if you *do* decide to go, you probably shouldn't eat any food, for the rest of the day. And quit drinking water."

"Otherwise, it'll make you puke, huh?"

"Yeah. It can make you puke a *lot,* if you've eaten or drunk much. The old-timers used to fast all day, before a *mitote* . . . but that was partly tribal tradition, I think."

"Good to know," Nate said. "I had a real small lunch, though—so I'd probably be all right, in that respect. *Bueno.* If I'm going, I'll meet you at your car."

"Okay. See ya."

Nate watched him leave, and then turned his gaze upward, looking at the intricate structure of the geodesic dome . . . *Huh. Wild* . . . A faint, nervous butterfly made itself known, in his stomach . . . *Peyote. That's heavy-duty stuff. And why's this guy want me to go? I barely know him. And I won't know anyone else there. Seems like a good guy, though. Maybe he just really feels like it's a good thing—and wants to share it. I'll be damned . . .* He got up and walked outside into the afternoon sun.

After the silence of the dome, the whispering of the wind and the birdsong in the trees sounded amplified, alive. Nate walked down the stone pathway to the parking lot and then continued down the entrance road. A woman, fortyish, was walking up the road, and asked him if his overnight at the camping area was okay. She had seen Nate at Shabbat, the night before. They talked for a few minutes about Lama—she was one of the full-time residents there. She was on her way up to the main building to fix some food, ahead of time, for the women's group that would be arriving. Nate continued down the road till the large trees petered out, and the sagebrush and piñon pines took over, with more wide-open views.

His thoughts meandered back to his conversation with Keith. He couldn't help thinking that it probably wasn't a good idea for him to participate in the peyote ceremony . . . *I think I know what most AA folks would say about it . . .* He knew it would be best to talk about it with Mac. Or Gary, his AA sponsor in Silver City. But he was reluctant to use the phone in the main building for a long-distance call . . . *And it's probably not a private phone . . .*

While he ruminated, Nate remembered a time when he'd asked Mac's opinion, once, on this same topic. Mac said he'd known a guy—a recovering alcoholic—who went to a peyote ceremony. And it was okay. The guy didn't feel a compulsion to drink, or anything. And stayed sober. At the time, Mac had said something like, "It depends on what your motives are. If you're honestly doing it for what you believe is a legitimate reason—like to gain some insight into your life, or to improve your spiritual life or your connection to God—then it's probably okay. But you know, in AA we generally believe in total abstinence from all mood-altering substances. If you're doing it just to get stoned—or to escape some uncomfortable feelings, like the way you abused alcohol—then you'll most likely drink again. Relapse. Myself . . . I wouldn't mess with those things." . . . *Yep. That's pretty much what Mac said. 'Course, I'm not him . . . But if I was to start drinking again, Liz would never take me back. My life there will be history . . .*

Still undecided, nervous and restless, he walked at a faster pace down the gravel road, as he took in the wide views of the valley below, slashed by the Gorge and its ancient river.

~ ~ ~ ~ ~

Nate listened quietly as Keith talked, driving down the highway to Arroyo Hondo. He spoke for a few minutes about how the *mitote* was organized. And more or less what to expect. "Since you've done sweat-lodge a few times, things probably won't seem so strange. I've been to this kind of peyote ceremony two other times. I don't think I'd *ever* do peyote alone. Or in a casual way. There's something about the structure of the ceremony that protects everyone."

. . . *Protects everyone?* . . . *From what? What? From losing our minds?* . . .

Evening shadows were growing long in the quaint old village of Arroyo Hondo, as they drove through it to the New Dawn community on the outskirts of town. The houses at New Dawn were certainly different from the adobe and cinder-block houses of the town. An eclectic air to them. One of the homes was adobe, but had a large stained-glass star built into the wall. Another had white Christmas lights strung along the eaves. In June.

They pulled into the driveway of a small adobe house at the end of a side road. The property had a large back yard butting up against a shallow rock cliff. A tipi stood in the sagebrush, facing east, with people standing nearby. Keith parked the car, and he and Nate walked over. A couple of men who looked to be full-blooded Indian stood near the door-flap of the tipi. Keith introduced Nate to the older of the two, a man named Manuel. Nate guessed that he was the peyote leader—the *Peyotero*—since Keith introduced him first and offered him a gift of a woven red blanket. The man might have been in his fifties, though something about his eyes made it impossible to guess his age. His hair was light gray, shiny, and braided back. Keith had given Nate a couple of pouches of tobacco to present as a gift, since he really didn't have anything suitable. As Nate handed him the tobacco—pouches of "Bugle" tobacco—Manuel smiled as if he'd won the lottery. And looked intently into Nate's eyes. The other man was introduced as Juan, who grinned shyly and immediately went back to work gathering up and sawing firewood.

A small group of people stood a respectful distance away, and Keith walked up to them, Nate trailing behind. An unusual mix of people. Keith introduced Nate to his friend, Larry—a local Hispanic from the Hondo valley. Keith greeted a few other people that he knew, and Larry introduced both of them to some new people. Three of the new people were from the Taos Pueblo, two men and a woman. Another man looked to be Native American but didn't say where he was from. The group numbered twelve all together—two women and ten men, including Manuel and Juan. Nate wore a pasted-on, nervous smile. Larry—maybe noticing his angst—looked at him with sympathetic eyes. "Is this your first time with peyote?"

"Yeah. Yes, it is."

"Well, I guess you're the only newcomer to it, tonight. But we've all been there. . . . It's a little scary, at first. Hope it goes well for you."

"Thanks," Nate said. "I hope so, too." Out of the corner of his eye, he noticed Manuel and Juan disappearing into the tipi. A few minutes later, while the people were talking quietly, smoke could be seen rising into the darkening sky from the smoke-flap on the tipi. From within, an odd drumming sound began. Very fast tempo, almost staccato, and changing in pitch from high to low, to high again. Unlike any Native American drumming that Nate had ever heard, it had a nervous yet mesmerizing effect. "Wow," Nate murmured to Keith, "That's some interesting drumming."

"It's called a 'water drum.'. . . "Used specifically for peyote ceremony. It's made out of a gourd with water in it." The drumming continued for a good five minutes or so, and then Manuel came out of the tipi and motioned for the others to come over.

A fire blazed in a fire pit in the center of the floor. There at the door, Manuel asked the women to sit on one side of the circle, near the door, and the men on the other side. Nate sat near the middle of the group of men, with Keith next to him. After everyone was seated, Manuel and Juan took their place at the west side of the circle, opposite the door. The floor of the tipi looked clean and was covered with soft, fragrant sagebrush branches. Nate noticed that a peculiar object—looking almost like a hairy, mummified arm—lay on the ground behind Manuel . . . *What is that? Some kind of dried plant?* . . . And next to it sat a half-filled burlap sack.

Manuel, with a half-smile on his face, asked the people to roll a cigarette out of some cornhusks and tobacco he was handing them—instructing them to light them in the fire and blow smoke toward the large plant behind him. He nodded deferentially to the plant, saying, "This is the 'Chief Peyote,' and he will be watching over things tonight."

Though the cornhusks didn't make for an easy time rolling a cigarette, Nate did what he was asked to do, as did the others . . . *Huh. A dead cactus plant, supervising things. Now that's something you don't see every day . . .*

Manuel asked the woman on his left—the woman from the Pueblo—how many of the peyote buttons she wanted, to start with. And handed her the burlap bag. After taking two of the light-green bulging discs, she put one into her mouth and began chewing it. She closed her eyes while chewing it and immediately passed the bag to the woman on her left. The burlap bag made its way around the circle and, one at a time they each took one or two of the peyote buttons and popped them into their mouths. Some of the people grimaced as they did so. When the bag was passed to Nate, Manuel held up his hand to stop. The man stood up and removed a button from his mouth that he'd been chewing. He stepped over to Nate, and held it out in his hand. Nate looked at the fibrous green mush in Manuel's hand . . . *What the hell? Is this a test or something? . . .* He glanced at Keith sitting next to him, who motioned, with his hand, to put it in his mouth. Manuel, after handing the green mush to Nate, sat down again across the circle from him. The *Peyotero* looked at him with a smile, but with questioning eyes. Nate looked at the mush in his hand again, and popped it into his mouth. It was very bitter, but he chewed it slowly, trying not to think about Manuel's already having chewed it . . . *Whew. Man, I'm about to hurl, already . . .*

When the bag came around to Juan, sitting next to Manuel, he picked a couple of buttons out and began chewing them. He picked up a drum, made out of a large, hollow gourd with a skin stretched over the top. He began drumming, rapidly, with a stick. The same odd, hypnotic drumming Nate heard earlier. He tilted the drum this way and that, and the pitch changed. Manuel put another button in his mouth, and a couple of minutes later began to chant, in what was probably some dialect of Apache.

The next time the bag was passed around, Nate was allowed to choose his own peyote buttons. The second and third ones were no less bitter . . . *Man. Unbelievably bitter . . .* The bag was passed around the circle once more, and then Manuel handed a long stick decorated with beadwork to the Pueblo woman seated next to him. He picked up the water drum and began drumming. The woman closed her eyes and started to sing, with the drumbeat in the background. Nate's vision became much sharper, as if seeing things in their true clarity for the first time. And he found himself smiling at this beautiful woman with such depth and soul to her voice. The fire suddenly blazed much brighter and more colorful, too bright to look at. He looked away. The people sitting in the circle had skin that glowed from within, most of them with eyes closed or partway closed. They were talking to Nate—each one—as he looked at them. Telling him their secrets, their sadness, their brokenness, their joy. He knew their stories to be true . . . *They're not moving their lips . . .* It didn't seem unusual—just a new telepathic talent he'd acquired. So he continued to question them by looking at them, one at a time, around the circle. The burlap bag—suddenly beautiful in its simplicity of form and function, and in its ingenious craftsmanship—was in front of him again. He took another couple of buttons, popping one of them into his mouth.

A muffled roaring sound, like a distant waterfall, grew steadily louder until it was over Nate's head, as he popped the other button into his mouth. And he was aware of a blinding, pulsating light above him . . . *A helicopter! What the fuck?* . . . He laughed at the absurdity of it—a helicopter, over the tipi, shining its searchlight down through the smoke-flap. Spying on him . . . *Crazy fuckers!* . . . He didn't dare to look up, though . . . *That would be a dead giveaway—and show them that I know they're looking for me. Just stay cool, now . . . Man, those jokers need to get a life!* . . . Nate laughed—a deep belly-laugh that shook his entire body violently and made him dizzy. He sensed now that the light and roaring sound was just above his head . . . *It's not a helicopter* . . . Genuine terror gripped him, and he found himself unable to move or to look up at whatever it was hovering over him. Darting his eyes from one person to the next around the circle, his gaze finally landed on Juan, who seemed to be staring at something just above Nate's head . . . *Maybe that's where the light is coming from. Right above me. But I can't look at it . . . Oh God . . .*

Juan lowered his gaze and met Nate's eyes, smiling. *"Peyote likes you,"* he said, without moving his lips . . . *He's playing with you, tonight . . .*

Nate stared into Juan's eyes. He felt nothing but kindness and understanding from the man . . . *He is? That's what this is? Whew! I'm glad . . .* The fear evaporated.

Sparks from the fire began to move with their own volition, in slow-motion, circling, hovering around Nate's head. He knew he could safely look up now, and he studied the dance of the sparks. Soon the tipi was filled with these sparks—they circled especially over the peoples' heads. It seemed dangerous, but nobody was complaining about them. Or even seemed aware of them. A man, sitting near the door, for some reason put another log on the fire—and with a roar a new mass of sparks joined the others, becoming too much to look at . . . *So, so bright* . . . Nate fell backward onto the ground. He closed his eyes, but the sparks were still there. Talking to him. Telling him of where they came from—how they brought light and heat from the sun. From the sun, through the trees, through the trees to the firewood. How they were very old and wise. And would not hurt him. The sparks sang to him, and he lost track of time in the melody.

Nate found himself lying in the sagebrush outside and, though there was no moon this night, the dark o' the moon wasn't dark at all. The earth and everything on it glowed from within. The sparks still moved around him like an endless cloud of fireflies. But now he realized they were flickering stars, surrounding him, above him and beneath him—all around. They began to move toward him, and soon were flying past him at great speed. Or maybe he flew past the stars, himself. He soon was rocketing so fast—between the stars—that they became streaks of light. With their own distinct color and sound vibration that wove itself into a flashing linear pattern of light, in a musical code he now understood. He sang with them. Their individual voices blended into a profound harmony—a soft roar like a distant, ever-crashing wave—and Nate cried with the beauty of the sound. The star-streaks continued to race by him and gradually slowed down until he was aware of a large glowing object. A softly-glowing orange pyramid, with an achingly beautiful music emanating from within . . . *Oh . . . the tipi* . . . Nate felt his body sitting down, inside. He was seated in the circle again, though the thought crossed his mind that maybe he'd never left. Instantly, he knew his body was an illusion and was in fact also traveling through time and space with a joyous energy. The people sitting in the circle were all luminous forms made up of glowing fibers, and Nate could tell who they were from the color and vibration of the music coming from them. One of the glowing forms was drumming again—another humming a beautiful melody.

Some time later—seconds or hours—Nate was again aware of himself, and now he appeared to be walking outside, normally. A network of light fibers spanned the sky, the earth, everything. It took some time before he could focus on anything. The stars were motionless now, awaiting something—but were blindingly bright, with light fibers streaming out from all of them. Of different hues . . . *What's that humming sound? Oh, it's just their light, again . . .*

Two other luminous human forms also were outside, and he knew them. Threads of light were attached to them—to the belly area—and these also were connected to everything else in the network. Threads of light emanated from the humans, the trees, the sagebrush. A distant neighbor's house. All connected, crisscrossing, pulsing with energy and different hues, and woven into a Great Pattern. Nate himself had no luminous threads attached to him—he was the Observer, now, and didn't need a body. These pulsing neon fibers—connecting all that was and all that would be—made up a woven undulating fabric across the sky and earth, of a heartbreaking beauty and texture . . . *Like a universal aurora borealis. Everywhere. And with this wonderful humming music . . .*

As Nate watched and became one with this fabric, a subtle movement began, and the fibers of light were slowly changing orientation until finally most of them seemed to converge on a point beyond the mountains to the east. The convergence point brightened from the increasing mass of glowing threads. As more fibers focused on this Convergence, it got brighter still, until there was a sentient critical mass of energy there. And at that moment it became a Source instead of a random convergence point. Energy and light began moving away from this spot, surging back toward everything within the fabric—the sagebrush, the trees, the stars. And the human forms. A third human form was in front of him now—made of glowing fibers like the others but different in hue and vibration. A pulse of energy from the Source beyond the mountains wove more fibers into it and caused the form to solidify and dim momentarily. It was a woman standing naked in front of him. A beautiful woman.

There came another pulse of energy from the Source in the east, and that became the first streak of light in the dawning sky. In the instant Nate realized that it was in fact the pre-dawn sun beginning to brighten the sky—from behind the mountains—the woman's form pulled back with instantaneous speed toward the source. And as she disappeared, he recognized her . . . *Elizabeth . . . And now she's gone . . .* More streaks of morning light streamed from over the mountains to the east. For an instant, Nate felt cheered about the coming dawn—and then an immense emptiness, sadness, and exhaustion settled down onto him. But something told him this was part of the beautiful fabric, too. And it would pass. In the dim early-morning half-light, he found a spot on the ground that felt warm and safe, lay down, and fell asleep in the sagebrush.

12.

"It'll be over in no time, for you—or it'll last an eternity."

The distinctive resinous smell of burning piñon pine rose from the fire pit at the sweat-lodge near Silver City, this day. And the fragrant wood smoke reminded Nate of the peyote ceremony. They had also burned piñon in the fire that evening at the *mitote*. It was almost two years later, now—June of 1990—and Mac was down for the weekend, visiting from Santa Fe.

He and Nate went back down the driveway to Nate's pickup, having forgotten to grab a few water-bottles they'd brought—while Elizabeth walked up to the circle around the fire pit, carrying a covered paper plate with fried chicken she'd fixed that morning. Since it was Mac's first sweat-lodge, Nate explained to his friend some basics about how the ceremony would typically proceed. Mac sounded ambivalent about participating. "I don't know, buddy. I have my own way of praying. And meditating. I don't see how sitting in a hut with people I don't know— and getting heat-stroke—can improve my spiritual life."

Nate snickered. "Ah, c'mon . . . don't be a pussy. You'll be fine. It's just like a sauna."

The lodge stood behind a cabin on someone's property in the ranch country west of Silver City, near the picturesque crossroads town of Riverside. The men walked back up the hill to the fire pit, carrying their towels and water. A small group of people stood around the fire, talking quietly.

Elizabeth and Nate had gotten back together and had returned to some semblance of an even keel in their marriage, with a new commitment and a new degree of communication and trust. Elizabeth had gone with Nate to the first few sweat-lodges he participated in—but stopped going after a while. She said something about how it felt like she was "a white girl trying to play Indian." Even though she *was* part Cherokee. She said the Cherokee never really had a tradition of sweat-lodge, anyway—so it wasn't even a part of her ancestry. She did decide to tag along today, though, maybe because Mac was visiting.

Nate appreciated the sweat-lodge tradition, though, and had found it to be helpful in his life. And he participated most every time they held a lodge at this place in Riverside—the sweat-lodge that had come to be known as "the People's Lodge." Gary (Nate's sponsor in AA) was almost always *Water-Pourer* at the lodges, and usually several other regulars from Silver City came. Quite often there'd be a newcomer or two—some of them people who were genuinely interested in Native American spiritual path, or new-age type people just wanting to try something 'new.' A few attendees had heard about it and were just plain curious. If nothing else, for Nate it was at least a place to pray, with some degree of forced humility. The heat and steam of the lodge had a way of humbling even the most arrogant types.

Nate, Elizabeth, and the boys had been living in the earthship now for almost two years, though there were still construction details that Nate was ironing out. The kids were growing like weeds—Luke was seven, Joey six. Nate kept fairly busy, as there was some semblance of a housing boom in the Silver City area. With a friend of his from town, he'd started a small construction company, doing mostly trim- and finish-carpentry jobs. Elizabeth continued with her jewelry work, successful as ever in her craft, though now she sold most of her work only through a couple of galleries in town.

The earthship they'd built—once it was completed and livable—was an environmentally-friendly kind of home and inexpensive to maintain. They were pleased at not having any monthly heating or electric bills. It was relatively warm throughout the winter, just from the passive-solar effect and thermal mass of the walls. And they needed a fire in the fireplace on only the coldest nights of the winter. The solar panels on the roof provided enough electricity to charge the bank of batteries, so that they had power for most of their appliances—unless there were several cloudy days in a row. There were of course other expenses. They'd finally gotten their own phone—a mobile "bag-phone" type, and *that* wasn't cheap at all if they had to make many calls. An LP gas tank had been installed, the LP gas being used to run the kitchen stove and the refrigerator. Aside from those amenities, they were "off the grid" and only minimally dependent on the utility companies and fossil-fuel.

Mac visited a few times a year—maybe to get a breather away from the city as much as for any other reason. He had, though, become an extension of the family again. Elizabeth had gotten over her temporary distrust of him—when it seemed to her that he had sided with Nate after his relapse fiasco and infidelity. Mac was one of the few people from Santa Fe that they kept in contact with, and he kept them up to date on happenings around their old stomping grounds.

The men walked toward the twenty-foot-wide circle—delineated with small rocks—which surrounded the fire pit. At one side of the circle sat a dome-shaped rough structure, built of bent saplings covered with blankets and canvas. A large blanket, acting as a makeshift doorway, was folded up on top of the dome, revealing a pitch-black interior.

As they stepped into the circle, Nate shook hands with a tough-looking guy who was splitting some firewood, and introduced him to Mac. Rocky was often *Fire-man,* and was again on this occasion. "Hey, brother," he said, "you know the drill—you've gotta be smudged before you come into the circle." He stood in front of Nate, passing a smoldering stick of burning sage around the contours of his body. Then did the same with Mac.

Nate walked over to a heavy-set guy standing, in shorts, next to the sweat-lodge. "Hey, brother!" He hugged him and introduced Mac. "Mac, I think you've met Gary once before. He's gonna be *Water-Pourer* today."

Back around the fire, Nate said hello to a couple other people he recognized. Elizabeth stood in the circle there, chatting with a woman whom Nate knew only vaguely. Another woman, unfamiliar to him and with long blonde hair tied back, stood off to one side of the circle beating on a drum nestled in her arm. She pivoted on her feet from time to time, so that the drumming was eventually done into all the directions of the compass.

While most of the others stood near the fire, Gary was crouching, in front of the lodge, doing something with a five-gallon bucket of water. Mac walked over to him. "What'cha up to, Gary?"

"Oh . . . just putting some Osha root into the water. It's traditional—and a healthy, cleansing herb. Good for the lungs."

"Huh. No kidding. Smells kinda like celery." Mac nodded toward the lodge. "So, uh . . . how hot does it usually get in here?"

"Oh," Gary said, "it'll get *hot*. But it's funny—sometimes you feel like the heat is gonna *kill* you, like you just can't take it anymore. And other times . . . well, the heat just feels good—and familiar, somehow—so that you don't even want to come out of there. See, the sweat-lodge, what the Sioux call the *Inipé* . . . is meant to symbolize being within

Mother Earth. With Mother Earth's heat and darkness. After each round—of hot stones and steam—we open up the door to cool it off a bit. There'll be four rounds. Rocky'll bring in new stones from the fire pit for each round. It'll be over in no time, for you—or it'll last an eternity. Depending on where you're at, or what you need from the lodge." Gary gazed vaguely up the hillside above, with its piñon and ponderosa pine. "And maybe how it goes for you depends on how honest and humble your prayers are. . . ."

"Huh. Interesting. Well, this'll be a new experience for me . . . so I hope I'll do okay with it."

About half an hour after they arrived, Rocky announced that the fire had done its work. The rocks were ready. The socializing and chatter died down to a murmur. Gary motioned for folks to gather up in a circle, where he explained a few things about the lodge—mentioning that there were a couple of new people at the lodge that day. He said that he would be Water-Pourer that day. That he was neither a "Road Man" nor a Medicine man. And he briefly described how the ceremony would proceed. Two people had brought drums with them—wide, hollowed-out logs with leather stretched tight over them—and they asked permission to bring them in to the lodge. People with metal jewelry, or watches, were asked to take them off and leave them outside.

Gary went into the lodge first, and could be heard saying some kind of prayer inside. The others followed him one at a time. At the doorway, each person crouched, saying a quiet prayer. As they entered, each had to crawl into the lodge—it being a low structure, less than five feet tall—and they circled around a pit in the middle of the floor. Planting themselves on some musty blankets covering the ground. Finally everyone except Rocky was settled into the dingy structure, some sitting cross-legged, some crouching. Some bits of colored cloth seemed to be tied, overhead, to the sapling structure of the lodge. Gary mentioned—apparently to allay any newcomer's fear—that if anyone felt overcome by the heat they could leave at any time. Others in the lodge could squeeze back towards the outer wall to let them pass. But if they went outside, he asked that they stay out for that round and stand near the fire. Another way to cool down, without leaving, was to press one's forehead down onto the bare ground near the outer wall. People were welcome to step outside for a break after each round when the door blanket was raised. To Nate, it felt stuffy in the lodge and cramped with all the people participating—the room permeated with an oddly familiar odor of wood smoke, burning herbs, and human sweat.

Gary must have signaled Rocky, because the man fished a large stone out of the fire pit and carried it over the lodge with a long-tined pitchfork. As he dropped the glowing red rock onto the ground at the entrance, he said a few words loudly to the group inside. In Lakota Sioux. "Ah-Hoh! Meh-tah-kwee-AH-sin." A friend of Nate's sat near the door and echoed back, "Ah-Hoh!"—and hoisted the rock, using a pair of deer antlers, into the pit in the middle. Gary said a few words in the Sioux language and sprinkled some sort of piney incense onto the stone. Rocky brought in, one at a time, six more stones—and they were placed, in some sort of sequence, around the points of the compass. The stones, when set at the doorway, glowed bright red like lava, and continued to have a dull hot glow to them as they were laid in the pit. At a sign from Gary, the man near the door pulled the blanket down over the doorway. The lodge immediately felt like a warm, dark womb, enveloping the people within.

Nate always found it a pleasant warmth, at the start—even in the summertime. Elizabeth sat next to him, on his right, a little closer to the door. It was pitch-black except for the dull glow of the stones in the center. Gary said a few words—thanking the "stone people" for bringing the sun's heat to the people in the lodge. In the darkness he must have started pouring water on the stones, because a loud hissing filled the place and it immediately became hot. A song was started, with Gary singing and someone accompanying him with drumming. Nate, along with several others, knew at least some of the verses and sang along. In the Lakota Sioux language.

After the song, Gary sloshed more hissing water on the stones, and soon Nate felt physically challenged, sweating profusely. There was an eagle feather being passed around—and while each person held it they could pray out loud, share about their lives. Explain why they were asking for help. As the feather was passed around, people spoke—and after a couple of people had shared or prayed, the feather must have been passed to Elizabeth. She began speaking about her family back East. She asked for help for her parents, her sister. And for her own young family and her husband. She sounded very different than when they talked at home.

When Elizabeth finished, she said, "A-Hoh," and a moment later Nate felt a soft object—the eagle feather—being pressed against his arm. He couldn't think of anything to say, feeling tongue-tied for some reason and preoccupied with fighting the heat. Gary had always said that praying out loud was optional, so he just held onto the feather for a couple of minutes while some of his neighbors in the lodge seemed to be breathing hard with the heat. Nate passed the feather to the next person. After the feather had made its way around the circle—Gary began another song, with someone drumming. This one Cheyenne, he said.

When the song was ended and the drumbeat stopped, the lodge was silent in the warm darkness for a minute or two. Gary said, "HOH-kah-hey!"—and the door blanket was raised with a blast of cool air.

Most everyone got up—crawling in a circle around the pit—and out the doorway. The woman who'd been drumming around the fire, earlier, stayed inside. In the dim light within the lodge, she seemed not to be affected by the heat. Elizabeth followed Nate out the door, and the gentle breeze cooled the sweat on their skin. There was very little talking around the fire. A few people gulped water during the short break. Nate felt relaxed and gazed into the fierce embers in the fire, as Mac sidled up to him. He muttered, "Well, that wasn't too bad . . . I might just enjoy this."

"Good! Hope you do."

Soon they were back in the lodge, and seven more red-hot rocks were added to the pit. This second round was hotter and was intended to be a silent round, with people murmuring their own prayers quietly. A woman on the other side of the circle began to cry in a soft, muffled way. The round ended with Gary quietly singing some unintelligible song, while others accompanied him with soft drumming and the sound of a rattle.

After another short break, outside, they were back in the lodge, and more glowing rocks were brought in. In the dense darkness after the door blanket was dropped, Gary sloshed more water on the stones—making a dull roar as the water hit the stones. Nate thought the heat a bit intense, now, in this third round—his cut-off shorts were soaking wet now, his skin felt on fire and the sweat wept out of every pore of his skin . . . *Dude . . . please go easy on the water—yeah—for Mac's sake . . .* The woman on the other side resumed her muffled crying, gasping with either shortness of breath or intensity of her sorrow. Her weeping became even more dampened and faint . . . *She must be pressing her forehead into the ground . . .*

While the eagle feather was being passed, and people prayed in turn, Nate found his thoughts racing in worry and desperation. He was having trouble breathing, which seldom happened to him in lodge. The woman on the other side continued crying with even more abandon. Nate felt a stifled rage building inside him . . . *Jeez, this feels hotter than usual, in here. Shit! . . .*

He squirmed around, and on hands and knees faced the outside wall of the lodge, jamming his forehead into the dampened earth. Some embarrassment and a vestige of anger remained, but he found his thoughts slowing down. For some unknown reason, he thought of his father . . . *Yeah. Dad always had 'anger issues' . . . He was an unhappy, angry man . . .* The thought came to him of the times his dad ridiculed him in front of company or relatives. Thought of the day his mother took him—and they left his father, staying with a friend of hers until she could find a place to rent. He had never liked his father, hated him in fact. With a deep hatred. But he missed him, too . . . *Why now? Why am I thinking of this? He's been dead more than four years, now . . .*

A curious, humble strength rose up in him—he wasn't fighting the heat anymore nor fighting something within himself. He was vaguely aware of Elizabeth's voice, next to him, but hadn't been listening. The eagle feather was pressed into his side, and he reached and grasped it.

He turned around slowly, facing the circle again, and started to speak, his voice cracking a bit. "Please help me to let go of this . . . this hatred. This hatred for my father. Creator, God, whatever you are . . . please help me to let go of this anger. And find forgiveness for this man. It's only hurting *me*. He was probably just doing the best he could. Please help me to heal. . . ." His eyes stung, and he couldn't find any more words to express the feelings. He passed the feather to the man sitting next to him. "Ah-Hoh."

Instead of getting a second wind, he began to cry silently. Soon his entire body shook with convulsive sobs. It always seemed okay to cry out loud in lodge, so he did. The tears flowed out of him and had little to do with the smoke in the air. As the others in the lodge shared and prayed in turn, he became less aware of them, and confused thoughts of his father crowded in. A slide-show of memories visited, uninvited. His father teaching him how to fish. At the lake . . . *Lake Tahoe. But there was something, something else . . . that happened there at the lake . . .* A distant memory—like a bubble from the depths—expanded as it rose to the surface.

Nate was nine or ten, and they were at the summerhouse on Lake Tahoe, where they'd sometimes go to get away for a weekend. He and his parents were down on the lakeshore, having a picnic with his father's business partner and his wife. For some reason, Nate remembered her being a redhead, and pretty. She told the others that she wanted to get potato chips and drinks from the store down the road. Nate's dad volunteered to go with her to get some beer, while the other grown-ups set up lunch things on the picnic table. Mom waded into the shallows of the sparkly lake.

They'd only had the summerhouse for a year or so, but Nate loved coming up here and getting away from the city. A few minutes later, he was bored and told his mother he wanted to get his fishing rod from the house. He walked through the woods up to the house and went into the basement. In the storage closet he found his new fishing rod that his dad gave him the year before. It was a shiny black rod, and he rubbed the slick surface, where it said "Fiber-Flex." He admired it as he carefully put together the two sections, when he thought he heard a noise upstairs. Carefully, so as not to poke the rod into the walls, he padded up the stairs. "Dad?" His parents' bedroom door was ajar, and he walked toward it and stood in the doorway with his fishing rod. His father was on the bed, lying on top of the redheaded woman. Her legs were spread apart, her dress hiked up high. His dad moved in a funny way on top of her. Groaning. . . . Nate backed up, silently finding his way to the kitchen and the back door, knowing somehow that he'd seen something he shouldn't have. He closed the door quietly. Heading back down to the lakeside, he tied a lure onto the fishing line and cast it out a few times. It was fun though he didn't catch anything. The rest of the weekend felt odd—and his parents seemed to be arguing more than usual.

This was the first time, since his childhood, that he consciously remembered that weekend . . . *Must've blocked it out of my memory . . . The bastard!* . . . Anger welled up in him. He was hot. And exhausted. Angry and sad. When there was a break at the end of the third round of the sweat-lodge, Nate stayed in the lodge with a couple of other people. The exhaustion he felt was oddly mixed with some relief, and he sprawled out on the blankets for a few minutes.

After the fourth (and final) round of the sweat-lodge was finished, everyone was asked to clear out of the lodge. People, for the most part, started setting out the food they brought, talking quietly amongst themselves. With a comradery similar to that of survivors of a shipwreck or other near-disaster. After standing in front of the fire a few minutes, Nate felt like he wanted to be alone, and he asked Elizabeth if she wanted to go or stay. She said she also was tired, but was feeling more sociable and wanted to stay for the food. Mac seemed to be enjoying talking with a woman in the group. So they stayed for a while and joined in with the communal potluck meal and small talk.

The sun sank behind a ridge, and the sky darkened into a deeper cobalt blue. When they'd finished eating, Nate was ready to leave while Elizabeth talked with one of the women. He stood near the fire, staring into the large mound of flickering embers. Gary came over and put a couple of small logs on it to keep it going. He smiled, thumping Nate on the shoulder playfully. Feeling exhausted and slightly confused, Nate said, "I think I'll need to talk to you about something, Gary. But not right now . . ."

13.

... Ha! I used to see country folks doing this ... out the car window. On those sweltering summer days in Carolina, when I was a young 'un ...

The following weekend it was sunny and very hot, as it often is in June in the Southwest before the summer monsoon moisture moves in. May had been a windy month, but the wind had settled down now. Saturday seemed like a good day to be outdoors, and the family piled into the Volvo for a day trip up into the Gila Wilderness area to the north. The boys were old enough now to where they could manage the trail up to the Gila Cliff Dwellings—some Anasazi-period ruins from the ancestors of local Indian tribes. Elizabeth and Nate had never taken the kids to the ruins before, and they had a hard time keeping up with them on the trail—the boys being excited and several times racing ahead. Luke, especially, was curious about the ancients who'd built the cliff dwellings and asked a litany of questions about them. He was first to begin climbing the ladder up to the cave where the stone and adobe ruins were—Elizabeth watching him like a hawk, from below. Apparently ready to catch him if he missed a step.

In the afternoon they meandered back home and stopped along the Gila River, parking the car in the shade of some Ponderosa pines. Although the sun was high—and there was scant hope of catching any fish—Nate attempted to show the boys how to use a fly-rod to fish for trout. Elizabeth leaned back, in a grassy spot up away from the river's edge, and rolled up the bottom of her tank top shirt to get some sun on her midriff. A half hour later, Nate walked up to where she was sitting, a resigned look on his face.

Elizabeth smiled. "I guess they're not ready to learn fly-fishing yet, huh, Hon'?"

"No. Not *nearly*. Do you think you could keep the guys away from the river, Liz? For a little while? Maybe give 'em something to do? I won't have a chance at catching *any*thing, with them mucking around in the water."

"Sure. Yeah, I can. Maybe I'll get them hunting for pretty stones. Or arrowheads. . . . In the other direction, upstream from where you're at."

"Excellent. That would be wonderful." He walked back down to the water and headed downstream toward a quieter, more promising pool.

On the drive back to the house, the boys were making a ruckus in the back seat, vying over who found the best stones, or something. And wondering if any of them were arrowheads from the Indians. Nate drove the winding road back toward town, concentrating on his driving but smirking as he listened to their chatter. He hadn't caught any trout, but at least the kids enjoyed themselves along the river. And the fish would still be there another day. Nate thought Elizabeth seemed a little distracted, chewing gum and quietly looking at the road ahead, ignoring the boys.

After dinner that night, Elizabeth washed a couple of dishes and turned in early. Nate, a short while later, got the kids into their room for their quiet reading time, before lights-out. And with a mug of coffee walked back to the far "U", where the main bedroom was. It was a mild night, and the earthship felt close. Elizabeth was lying on top of the bed sheets, in pajamas, reading a book. *Watership Down.*

Nate glanced at the book-cover. "Nice story, huh, Liz? . . . Yeah, I remember it."

"Yep. I've always loved it. Read it before, of course—but I just wanted to read it again. Kind of beautiful. A feel-good story, I guess you'd call it."

"Yeah. A good one." Nate sat down next to her, setting his coffee mug on the night table, and put his hand on her flannel pant leg, rubbing it softly. "Well that was fun, today, up in the mountains. But is everything okay, Sweetie? You seemed a little quiet."

"Yeah. Well . . . just tired."

"You want to talk about anything? Something going on?" he asked, with eyebrows slightly raised.

Elizabeth looked up at him, then back at the book. She sighed. "Well, yep . . . I guess so. I 'spect you *could* say I have something goin' on. . . . You know, I went to the doctor's, on Thursday—"

"Yeah," Nate nodded.

"and I asked her to check on what I thought might be a lump in my breast . . . my right breast. Well, she looked at it. . . . Checked it out, and wasn't real happy about it. She thinks I need to have a mammogram done—get it checked out, further. She wants me to make an appointment at the Women's Health Clinic in Las Cruces, where they're used to dealing with women's health issues and stuff. I *could* have it done at the hospital here, but they're a little too small. And only do mammograms certain days of the week. They're a little more expert, down there in Las Cruces."

"I 'spect they are. . . . Well, damn," Nate said. "I'm *sorry,* Liz. I hadn't noticed it. Yeah . . . let's make an appointment down there. The place in Las Cruces, I mean. I can drive you down."

"No, that's okay. I can drive myself. The doc wants to refer me right away, though—so it'll probably be this coming week."

"Okay. Good, let's get it done."

It was less than two weeks later that a receptionist called, from the Women's Health Clinic—Elizabeth needed to come in for a second appointment. During her first appointment, a medical oncologist had interpreted her mammogram—and had ordered (the same day) ultrasound imaging and a fine needle aspiration for biopsy. The tissue sample was sent to Albuquerque. And now the biopsy results were in.

Nate said he wanted to accompany Elizabeth for her consult with this doctor, so on that Thursday afternoon they drove down to Las Cruces for her appointment. Elizabeth felt optimistic, thinking it was most likely a cyst. And she relaxed, on the drive down in Nate's pickup. It was a hot and sunny day, near the end of June, now—and as she sat on the passenger side, from time to time she reached her arm out the window of the pickup. She curved her hand upward, and wind lifted her arm up. Curved her hand down, and it pushed her arm down. Letting the wind float her arm up and down like a bird's wing in the breeze . . . *Ha! I used to see country folks doing this . . . out the car window. On those sweltering summer days in Carolina, when I was a young 'un . . .* It was fun. And cooled the sweat on her arm and armpit.

~ ~ ~ ~ ~

The examination room smelled of ether and disinfectants, and Elizabeth soon had a queasy feeling in her stomach. While the doctor met with them, she only halfway heard him while he described the tissue as being undoubtedly "ductal carcinoma." An image of Luke and Joey playing in the dirt played across her mind—as she vaguely heard the doctor using terms like "very possibly invasive, or infiltrating." Something to do with the appearance of the cells. The nauseating feeling of a fast elevator drop sank into her stomach.

Elizabeth closed her eyes briefly, desperately wanting to appear composed. She looked at the doctor, focusing on his nametag. *Jacob Mossman MD*. She hesitated. Gulped. And then spoke with a quavering voice. "So. . . . What's the outlook? What do you suggest?"

The doctor looked at his clipboard and then focused on her with shrunken eyes through his glasses. "Well, Mrs. Lewis, this kind of tumor is *never* a good thing to have. But if we can get surgery done as quickly as possible—either a lumpectomy, or a quadrectomy (if the cancer has spread more than we think) . . . and if we follow it with radiation and chemotherapy, I think there's a very good chance we'll nip it in the bud. With complete remission. There's no guarantee of that, though, I would have to say. But we shouldn't drag our feet on this. . . ."

Elizabeth closed her eyes slowly, pursing her lips and letting out a long, whistling exhale. The leaden lump in her stomach would not dissolve and, blinking her eyes she looked around the room for a non-existent window to the outdoors. "Are there any alternative treatments that we could try? Like changing my diet? Doing things to stimulate my immune system? Anti-cancer herbs and supplements?". . . *Rhetorical question. He's not gonna agree to this* . . .

"No. I can't recommend that. What I mean is—not as a substitute for what I've suggested. You can *do* those things, of course—and it probably can't hurt—but this tumor is most probably at an invasive stage. The treatment *has* to be aggressive."

Nate stared fixedly at something on the wall over the doctor's shoulder, and glanced quickly over at his wife. "Well . . . do you mind if we get a second opinion? . . . And, if we opt for the surgery, how soon should it be done?"

"No," the doctor said. "It's up to you. I don't mind a bit—I mean, as for getting a second opinion. The lab results are pretty definitive, though.

And I don't think you should waste much time—it'd be best to have this surgery within the month. I can make arrangements for this at the UNM Cancer Research and Treatment Center. It's really the best hospital around for having this done. The Center, there, has a quality oncology department—with some excellent surgical oncologists. I'm familiar with several of them."

Elizabeth looked at Nate, both of them leaning back against an examination table. Their eyes met, and he reached over and took her hand.

The doctor studied them for a second. "Well, I'm afraid I've got another patient that I have to see. I'm sorry about this news. Please feel free to call me, if you have any more questions. But if I were you, I'd move right along on this. Don't waste any time." He stood up from the vinyl-covered swivel-stool he'd been using, Elizabeth's chart in his hand. He nodded to them and turned to leave.

Elizabeth chewed momentarily on the inside of her cheek, and watched his back as he left the room. It felt like a job interview that hadn't gone well—and now it was time to slink out of the office . . . *Move 'em in, and move 'em out. They treat us like cattle, here* . . . She felt dissociated from her body as they walked out to the parking lot.

As they drove one of the arrow-straight stretches of highway back toward Silver City, some part of Elizabeth wanted to cry. But she held it at bay until they were near Bayard, not far from home, when the burning in her eyes finally overwhelmed her . . . *I don't want the boys to see me crying. We've got to pull over* . . . She gestured toward the side of the highway, and Nate complied. He pulled onto the gravelly shoulder, smelling of hot asphalt, crunched to a halt, and turned the engine off. He slid over on the seat and put his arms around her, heaving a big sigh. The tears began to flow, for her. And as they hugged, Nate rubbed his eyes a bit, too.

After sobbing for a few minutes, Elizabeth took a deep breath, trying to get her breathing back to normal. She felt somewhat relieved, a while later, and with reddened eyes she began to think rationally about a few options she could consider. The thought crossed her mind of going to a doctor she'd used before, at a holistic medicine practice in Santa Fe. The doctors at the Complementary Medicine Center, there, were fully trained MDs. But also incorporated alternative medicine methods, whenever possible, into their treatment of illness and disease. "You know," Elizabeth said, "I really trusted Andi Sheaffer, there—and the way she helped me when I was pregnant with Joey."

Nate nodded. "I know. I was pretty impressed with her, too."

"And I sure think more highly of her than I do, of *this* bozo. This guy's like a *mortician*, or something—just dying to carve me up."

"Yeah. I wasn't thrilled with him, either. Pretty cold . . . and mechanical or something."

"Yep." Elizabeth wiped the tears off her cheeks with the palm of her hand. "I don't want him touching me anymore." She blew her nose, and Nate kissed her on her dampened cheek. They talked for a while longer, by the side of the road, before Nate started up the truck and drove the rest of the way back home.

14.

***. . . At least I'm a little bit more in control of my own destiny.
For better or worse . . .***

They stayed at the Old Pecos Motel, two weeks later, after driving up to Santa Fe and having dinner out with Mac. The room had that distinctive old motel-room smell to it—stale cigarette smoke and ambiguous body odors. But the place was clean, and the desk clerk told them the beds were new. The kids were staying over with their neighbor, Jean—which the boys seemed to regard as somewhat of an adventure or safari. Along with their sleeping bags, Luke brought his compass and map, which he'd gotten from Santa the previous Christmas.

Elizabeth's appointment with Andrea Sheaffer would be early the next morning, and she was nervous about it. "I really don't know what to say to her . . . Andi Sheaffer. She might very well want me to go the conventional medicine route. Entirely. And heck, that might be the best plan." The thought of herself—with one deformed breast, sunken eyes, and shocks of her hair falling out—flashed through her mind briefly. Not for the first time. "I just hate that it's such a darned drastic approach that most doctors recommend. It's like 'slash and burn'—like some kind of primitive warfare. And I guess it is, really. *Damn.*"

"I know," Nate said, as he scootched over to Elizabeth's side of the bed and threaded his arm behind her neck. He put his other hand on her belly and leaned over, kissing her forehead. "This sucks. It seems, so far, to be just crappy options to choose from. But maybe Andi will have some ideas."

"Hope so. I'm countin' on that girl."

Nate reached over to turn off the bedside lamp, and they fell asleep in each other's arms.

The doctor's examination room didn't have the same cold chemical smell that the clinic in Las Cruces had. In fact, Elizabeth noticed an odor of a burning herb in the air . . . *Nice. Maybe sage or sweetgrass? Or maybe it's that herb they burn when they're doing some kind of acupuncture work* . . . At first, Elizabeth's appointment with Andi Sheaffer didn't go as well as she had hoped. The doctor had received all of the previous radiology and cytopathology results, and came to the same conclusion that the practitioner in Las Cruces had. Doctor Sheaffer looked at Elizabeth kindly, but suggested the same breast cancer protocol that Dr. Mossman had.

Elizabeth pleaded, with her eyes. "Isn't there *some*thing I can do, besides all the radiation and chemotherapy? What about if I were to get the surgery done—lumpectomy, or quadrectomy—and then use diet and herbal supplements to boost my immune system and make sure the cancer's gone? . . . I just hate the thought of going for months or even years, feeling sick from the radiation and chemo. And maybe never even being the same again . . . after all those toxins and damage and stuff. I was reading in a science magazine about some research being done in China and Japan, about Shiitake and Maitake mushrooms, for instance. . . . That those mushrooms might actually have anti-cancer properties?"

Doctor Sheaffer sat down in a chair and crossed her legs, looking at a folder with Elizabeth's information in it. She cleared her throat. "Yes. There is really promising research on those two fungi. And there are a few other tumor-fighting plants and extracts, that we know of. But a lot of this is still experimental. There may be hope for these things, in the future. . . . But I think this tumor is showing signs of being invasive— and the conventional breast cancer treatment is really the best protocol to follow, at this point. Sure—there are dietary changes you can make. And herbal supplements you can use—to help your body fight the cancer. But these are things that, I think, could be done in *addition* to the conventional treatment: surgery, radiation, and chemotherapy. I'm sorry, but this is really what I'd have to recommend . . . for your best chances of beating this thing."

Elizabeth stared at the floor, some part of her feeling stubborn when it came to her health and her desire to live a simple life—in harmony, as much as possible, with nature . . . *I wonder if she'll still treat me, if I decide not to go the conventional-medicine route, entirely. She might just hand me my walking papers* . . . Elizabeth exhaled a long, slow breath. "Andi . . . would you continue to treat me—and give me your medical and healthcare advice—if I choose not to follow up the surgery with the radiation and chemotherapy? I just really have some reservations, about the status quo treatment of cancer. Burning and poisoning my body in the hope of killing more of the cancer than killing my body. You know?"

Andi Sheaffer clicked her pen a couple times as she glanced through paperwork in the folder. And then looked steadily into Elizabeth's eyes. "Yes. I would. I understand your concerns. But this would be against my medical advice. And I would have to have you sign a waiver, to that effect . . ."

"I understand."

"I *would* continue to treat you, though. I've always felt that the patient should be able to make his or her own decisions, regarding their own healthcare and what they're most comfortable with. As long as everyone involved is made aware of the risks that those decisions might incur. And sometimes, after all, it *is* the quality of life that also has to be considered. The radiation and chemo protocol is nothing to sneeze at. It's rough on the body. And a person's attitude and positive thinking may in fact be almost as important, in dealing with illness. Many people *do* go through these treatments—with extensive radiation treatment, and chemo—and the cancer is *still* not eliminated. Or there's only temporary remission. There's a lot of evidence suggesting that mind and attitude have a large part to play in our well-being."

With Elizabeth's input, the doctor further discussed the risks involved, in dealing with her cancer using a more "holistic" treatment. Pointing out the fact that, without radiation and chemo there was a greater chance that they wouldn't knock out all cancerous cells that might remain after the surgery. And that cancerous cells such as those could develop into additional tumors, in the future.

"For right now," Andi said, "we need to get you set up for an appointment with another medical oncologist. And I think we might as well have that done at UNM Cancer Treatment Center. Less of a drive, for you—and probably where we'll elect to have the surgery done, also. They'll do another fine needle aspiration of the tumor, there, and test it for hormonal receptors. And if the tumor turns out to be estrogen-dependant, then we can get you started on Tamoxifen, right away. I would say Tamoxifen would be *required,* if the tumor turns out to be of that type. No 'ifs, ands, or buts' about it. As long as you tolerate it well. Tamoxifen blocks estrogen and will slow the growth of this kind of tumor. Will you agree to that? I feel like I can't treat you, otherwise."

Elizabeth raised her eyebrows a bit. "Yes," she said. "I'd be okay with that. I've read about that drug, and it sounds fairly benign."

"Good. . . . Yep, most women tolerate it well. Once in a while it can cause nausea or depression, but many women are able to be on it for years with no ill effects."

"Okay."

"And the oncologist will schedule the surgery, soon after. I'm familiar with one of the surgeons there, and I think I'll recommend that he be involved with your case."

"Okay."

Later that day, as she and Nate drove back down to Silver City, Elizabeth was aware of a diminishing of the shadow haunting her steps for the past few weeks. She gazed at the mountainous horizon to the west, darkening into dusky blue . . . *At least I'm a little bit more in control of my own destiny. For better or worse. I can do as much research as I'm able. And talk to Andi about any new treatment options there might be . . .* In the next few weeks, she did do plenty of research, on her own. Reading through scientific journals and periodicals at the local library and at the campus library at New Mexico State-Las Cruces. She ordered books from booksellers: one on current medical understanding of cancer and its treatment, and two books about complimentary and alternative medicine.

Around the middle of July, Elizabeth drove up to Santa Fe again to meet with Andi Sheaffer for a second consult, before her surgery at the end of the month. Elizabeth's appointment with the oncologist in Albuquerque had gone well, in Dr. Sheaffer's estimation, because the tumor was found to be estrogen-dependant and could be treated with Tamoxifen. Elizabeth had already started on the drug and seemed to be tolerating it without side-effects. The doctor sat her down in a comfortable chair in an informal consult room at the practice, explaining some changes she wanted Elizabeth to make in her diet. She glanced at her clipboard and put her hand on Elizabeth's wrist for a moment. "Now,

Elizabeth . . . I'm going to ask that you make a few changes, here. And you can start on this now, before the surgery. Firstly, with your diet. I want you to eliminate *all* red meat—"

"Well, that shouldn't ought to be a problem. We sometimes cook vegetarian, for a day or two."

"but I still want you to get plenty of protein," Andi continued. "Lean protein . . . beans, tofu, eggs, poultry, and fish. Little or *no* animal fats. And no deep-fried foods."

"Okay."

"No *sugar.* No added sugar, in your diet. We've got a society that's addicted to sugar . . . and sugar, along with other refined carbohydrates, does *nothing* good for us—and actually encourages the growth of tumors.

"Echinacea. Do you ever take Echinacea? When you're catching a cold, or something?"

"Yep. I've got some."

"Well, I want you to be taking 900 milligrams, three times a day, with food. And use the kind made out of the root complex—it's more potent. You can find it at any good health-food store. . . . I've written these things down for you."

"Okay," Elizabeth said. "That'll help."

"And I've written down the quantities, and time of day, to take them . . . these herbs and supplements. Vitamin C, three times a day. Get the more natural kind—with Rose Hips . . . I'll write down a couple of brands I recommend. Pau D'Arco, also, three times a day. And Spirulina algae. It's in a dry powder form. All of these things you can find at good health-food stores—and let me know if you have any trouble locating them. The Spirulina takes a little getting used to—but you can actually make it into a pretty tolerable milkshake. All of these things will *really* strengthen your immune system—increase your T-cells, natural-killer cells, and antibody production. The Spirulina can inhibit tumor growth and helps your normal cells. There's a study that's been done, in China, on an Asian herb called Astragalus—also used in Indian Ayurvedic Medicine. It boosts natural-killer cells, and I want you to start taking it. I'll find out about sourcing it—it's not readily available here, yet. And I'm going to start you on a Maitake mushroom extract. It's also been studied in China, and in Japan . . . and seems to be especially effective at enhancing immune cells for breast cancer. It's also not readily available here, so I'll help you with getting that. . . . All of these can be used, safely, with conventional breast cancer treatment—"

"That's great."

"and they can be used long-term," Dr. Sheaffer said. "I think, that, after about a year or a year and a half, though, I'll want you to taper down on the Echinacea. It functions a little like a steroid—sort of artificially boosts your immune response. The other items, though, you can stay on for as long as we want."

"Okay. Are we talking, like . . . for *years,* then?"

"Yes. I'd say so. Cancers have a nasty habit of returning. There *have* to be lifestyle changes made, in order for there to be permanent remission. And again . . . since we're not going to the typical protocol of radiation and chemo, long-term use of these medicinal herbs will improve our chances."

Elizabeth exhaled a long sigh, blinking a few times and looking thoughtful. "Do you think I'm making a mistake?"

Andi smiled, pursing her lips a little, and patted Elizabeth's arm. "No, let's not even go there. Sometimes a person's first intuition on these things is the right one. Let's not have any more second-guessing . . . but focus on wellness, and kicking this thing. And one more thing . . . last, but definitely not least. I know you get regular exercise, but I'm strongly suggesting a regular meditation practice. Do you do any type of meditation? Transcendental meditation? Yoga? Tai Ch'i or Ch'i Gong? Or something similar?"

"Not really. No. Though I sometimes get into sort of a meditative state while I'm working—doing the jewelry-making."

Andi smiled. "Well, that's great, but not exactly what I'm talking about. Part of my prescription is going to be: that I want you to get into a daily meditation practice. Start with half an hour a day, and work up toward three-quarters or one hour a day. Buddhist groups are really good, for learning about this—about the type of meditation I'm talking about. Sometimes called 'mindfulness meditation.' It can have a *great* stress-reducing effect. Rest and stress-reduction are going to be your best friends, here. I'm entirely serious about this."

"Gotcha," Elizabeth said. "I'll look into it, and I'll do it."

"In Traditional Chinese Medicine, it's believed that there's almost always a spiritual or emotional cause for disease. And even American medical-school studies—researching stress—have supported this view of stress often being a cause of illness. In Chinese Medicine, there's a long-held belief that an excess of negative emotions—like worry, jealousy, fear—are usually the cause of breast cancer. And often, negative emotions regarding a partner, or a primary relationship. In fact, several European doctors who've incorporated Traditional Chinese Medicine into their medical practice have gone so far as to say that cancer in the *right* breast is nearly always related to conflict with a partner or spouse. . . . Based on data they compiled."

Elizabeth blinked her eyes a few times and noticed a peculiar feeling like a hunger-pang in her stomach. "*Oh?*"

"From my own experience, this often seems to be the case. Though I'm not so sure about the left-breast or right-breast aspect of those studies."

"Huh. Is that for real?"

"Well," Andi said, "we don't know for sure, but . . . can I ask you? Does this apply in your case? Have you and your husband had any relationship problems?"

Elizabeth twitched her shoulders a bit and sat up a little straighter in her chair. "Yep," she said, trying to sound casual. ". . . Yes, we have. We've had some difficulties. I found out—about two years ago, now—that he'd been unfaithful. I think it was just the once, that he cheated on me. And we separated for a while."

"Uh-huh. I see." Andi smiled at Elizabeth as a sister would, and patted her arm again. "Well, that's the past. It's *forward*, from here . . . okay? But actually, all the more reason for you to practice meditation, now. Not only will it decrease your *stress*—and give you another rest period during the day—but you might even find a permanent forgiveness toward your husband, through a meditation practice."

"Yep. I get it. But I think I *have* forgiven him." Elizabeth paused, and then twisted her face into a fake smile for an instant. "But . . . maybe I haven't."

15.

"But doesn't it seem weird to you—that the treatments they give you make you terribly ill? . . . With the goal of trying to make you better?"

From home in Silver City, Nate and Elizabeth worked out a payment plan with the hospital in Albuquerque, since her health insurance policy was minimal and didn't cover much in the way of daily hospital expenses. And Elizabeth's surgery would be costly. Through the hospital financial aid office, they were able to set up a monthly payment plan with no interest. It would tax their resources to the point where Nate needed to access more of the money in the trust fund his father had set up, but it was all doable.

As the date for her surgery approached, Elizabeth felt the need for more moral support—more than she could get from Nate. Or from her friends in the area, apparently. She called her old best girlfriend from back East, Beverly. Unbeknownst to Elizabeth, Beverly had decided (after their last phone chat) that she would take a week off from work and fly out to Albuquerque to be with the family and hopefully be of some help.

Elizabeth's eyes sparkled when she heard this, standing by the phone and doodling on a note pad. "Oh, that's *so* great, Bev . . . that you can get out here, for a bit. It'll be great to see you—though I wish it was under better circumstances."

"Yeah, well don't you worry, Hon'. It'll be great to see ya—under *any* circumstances. I only hope I can help out a bit. Nate's probably gonna have *his* hands full, too—stayin' up there with you in

117

Albuquerque, and all. I don't want you, or him, to worry about a thing. I can help with taking care of the kids. . . . And keeping 'em out of your hair and all, when you get back."

"*Girl*. . ." Elizabeth said. "That'd be *won*derful."

She talked for a while with her friend about the lumpectomy procedure and how long the recovery from that might take. Beverly asked her, again, if she still planned on saying "no" to the radiation therapy and chemo that would usually follow.

"Yep. I mean, yes, I'll be using alternatives. I don't really think of it as saying 'no' to all conventional treatments—but more like saying 'yes' to more natural alternatives. You know, Bev . . . I just don't want to feel halfway *sick* for the next couple of years. I've already been changing my diet—and been taking supplements—so that my body and immune system will be a lot less hospitable to cancer. There's lots of evidence showing that the herbs, vitamins, and fungus extract I'm taking have very real cancer-fighting properties."

There was a pause on the other end of the line, and Beverly spoke in a subdued voice, "You're takin' a risk, aren't you, Hon'?"

"Well, I guess I am. Yeah. But, *darn* it, Bev . . . the radiation treatments and chemotherapy aren't a sure thing, either. Not nearly. Radiation . . . burning the crap out of you—and hoping that you kill more of the cancer than you do of the healthy tissue. And chemotherapy . . . poisoning yourself to try and hurt the bad stuff without hurting a lot of the good stuff? It seems *crazy*—the way we deal with this illness. Something's wrong with the *picture,* here."

"Yeah," Beverly said. "It *is* kind of a screwed-up picture. But, well . . . I still think the doctors *do* know best."

"I'm not so sure, Bev . . . they don't even know what *causes* the cancer, half the time. They don't really understand the disease. Sure, it sounds like it *can* be genetic—or at least partly so. And it may be environmental—like exposure to radiation or carcinogenic chemicals. And it may be from the effects of hormones. And it might even be due to stress. Or *all* of these things combined. I guess it's true, that cancer research is still in its infancy. But doesn't it seem *weird* to you—that the treatments they give you make you terribly *ill?* . . . With the goal of trying to make you better? Does that really even make *sense?* How can you get better—when you're actually feeling even *worse?* "

"No. It doesn't totally make sense. It *is* weird—I hear what you're sayin'. But this is the best they can do, so far. Right? . . . Hey, when you're feelin' better—after the surgery and all—maybe I can pick your brain a bit, and you can give *me* some advice. I mean, about how to avoid getting cancer, and stuff. You know, having a healthy diet and all that.

Since you've been doing so much research, and reading about it and everything—you're the girl to talk to."

"Sure," Elizabeth said. "You bet. I wish I'd known a lot more about this stuff, before now—but you don't think about it much until you're in my situation. Or something similar."

"Yep. It's just the way it is. We go on our merry way, without thinking much about this kind o' shit."

"Yeah. Like I wish I'd given up red meat years ago. I'd *thought* about it, in the past. That maybe it wasn't too healthy. There's something about . . . about saturated animal fats, and other saturated fats, that can lead to cancer. *Especially* breast cancers."

"No kiddin'."

"For real. Quite a bit of research evidence, showing that. And there's something about fermented soy foods—like tofu, and tempeh, and miso, and even soy sauce . . . that has an *anti*-cancer effect. Especially for breast cancer."

"Huh," Beverly said. "I guess I should be eatin' more Chinese food."

"I wish I'd learned a lot of this stuff sooner. You know, my aunt—my father's sister—had breast cancer. And my grandmother, on my mother's side. I may be, like, genetically-predisposed, for it. I could've been taking better care of myself, all along, if I'd thought much about it."

"But we *don't,* Hon'. We're too busy tryin' to make it in this world . . . to care much about our health."

"Yep," Elizabeth said, and she paused. "You know, another thing I found out, is how certain metal compounds—especially heavy metals—can really tax our immune system. And damage it. . . . I might have been hurting myself, all these years of doing silver work. I read somewhere that a lot of the old silver solders had *cadmium* in them. My teacher, John—you know, the old Navajo silversmith that I apprenticed with? Well . . . he gave me a bunch of old silver solder once, that he'd gotten somewhere on the Rez—and I've been using it all along, for years. It's probably cadmium-silver solder. *Carcinogenic.* If you breathe the fumes all day long. And even the copper that's in sterling silver isn't good for ya. Heck, sometimes . . . when I'd been doing a lot of silver work, day after day, I'd wind up with a sort of metallic taste in my mouth. For *days.* And it wouldn't go away till I quit doing jewelry work for a while."

"*Damn.* That doesn't sound too good."

"*No.* And you know, Bev . . . I was gonna mention this to you. I've read so many darned things . . . but, seems like I read something about cosmetics and hair dye. Your workin' in a beauty salon kind of worries me. I'm pretty sure it said, somewhere, that hair dyes often have carcinogenic chemicals in them—either for color, or as a fixative."

"Oh, holy crap!"

"Yes," Elizabeth said. "I'm serious. The cosmetics industry isn't really regulated. See . . . cosmetics aren't considered food. Or drugs. So they're not controlled by the FDA. They can put *anything* into those products they want. So there're some unsafe chemicals in there, sometimes. You should really wear gloves, most all the time."

"Shit. *Wonderful.* I've only been working in a hair salon for like, nine *years,* now."

"I know. I'm sorry, Bev. I'm only saying this be—"

"Well, you're *right,* damn it—I know you're right about this. None of us pays any damned attention to this stuff. I even read, once, about how the chemicals we use in hair styling aren't all that safe. But did I *do* anything about it? *Hell* no. I *should* be more careful. I know it. And I will be, from now on."

"Yeah? You promise me?"

"Girl Scouts' honor."

Elizabeth smirked. "You were never a Girl Scout."

"I know. But I *wanted* to be. Mama couldn't afford the uniform, for it."

"Well, it's way cool that you're coming here. It'll be great to see ya."

The two friends talked for a while longer about lighter things. Beverly said that the heat and humidity in Asheville was *awful*, that summer. And she'd be glad to get out to where it was drier and cooler. She had firmed up her travel plans, she said—flying into Albuquerque two days before the surgery, and renting a car at the airport. She would hopefully get to their home in time to help Elizabeth with dinner, that night.

The 30th of July—a Monday, and the day of Elizabeth's surgery—dawned brightly with a clear sky. But if it was anything like the day before, it would shower by early afternoon. The summer monsoon weather had arrived, and it was a good thing because they were just getting into the hottest part of the summer. And—typical of the monsoon weather pattern—the hottest time of the day was late morning. By midday, the thunderstorms would start to build and it would cool off in the afternoon.

Beverly was up before the others, which was just as well since she was sleeping on the couch in the living room / dining area. She started some coffee and got breakfast going. Elizabeth was allowed to only drink liquids first thing in the morning—her surgery scheduled for mid-afternoon. Beverly fried an egg for Nate, but when he got to the table he said he couldn't stomach it. He settled on a bowl of oatmeal, saying something about having an upset stomach overnight. Luke and Joey straggled in, both in the habit of sleeping later, now, with vacation from their homeschooling. Nate and Elizabeth slumped in their chairs at the table, side by side. As it got closer to seven o' clock, Beverly, like an athletic coach, put her hands on their shoulders. "We need to get it in gear, now, you two."

Nate rubbed one eye, which seemed to be bothering him. "Yeah. I know. Gotta leave soon."

Soon, Beverly was more insistent, hurrying them along. And finally said, "C'mon. Y'all get going, now. Everything'll be fine, here."

Elizabeth pasted on a brave smile. "I know. Yeah, we don't wanna be late, for the pre-op party."

Beverly practically pushed them out the door, with a suitcase Nate had packed the night before. "The kids'll be fine. Everything's cool." She kissed them both, gazing for a long moment at Elizabeth as she did so. Beverly pinched her in the side. "It's gonna go fine."

They were on the road early enough so that the traffic was light, and got to the hospital in Albuquerque with time to spare. At the appointed time for the surgery, Elizabeth was ready—but apparently the hospital was not. A nurse said something about the afternoon surgeries often running a little behind schedule. They waited in the pre-op room, the air smelling strongly of alcohol and other disinfectant chemicals. Elizabeth lay uncomfortably on a hospital gurney. She was chilly—naked except for the run-of-the-mill hospital gown, apparently made specifically for Jane Doe. A nurse administered some kind of sedative and soon Elizabeth was too loaded to feel chilled anymore. She looked up at Nate, who seemed to be standing far above her, with the room in the background swimming in and out of focus . . . *Hmm. He looks pretty darn tense. And worried* . . . She slurred some words, "It's gonna be fine, Honey." She reached her hand out toward him, but forgot what she was intending to do and clumsily bumped him in the stomach.

The worry-lines on his forehead softened, and he gently took her hand. He winked at her. "Yeah. It *will* be fine."

Part III

16.

*". . . and I think it has something to do with breaking
the control that our minds have—over us.
Over our bodies. And our hearts. "*

At the Casa de Dom Francisco, in Brazil, Elizabeth made her way
through the clusters of people milling around outside the rear of the main
building. A number of them sitting on the lawn in the hot sun. With a
peaceful expression returning to her face, she walked down the concrete
sidewalk which snaked around the building to the front of the main hall.
It had been somewhere around an hour or an hour and a half that she was
in the current rooms, and as she rounded the corner of the building, she
looked over in the direction where Nate had sat on a bench out front,
earlier. Nate actually was still sitting on the same bench, a couple other
people next to him talking quietly. There was a book open in his lap—the
book on Brazil that he'd held onto, for her, while she'd gone inside.
Elizabeth halfway smiled as she came up to him. "Hey, you."

Nate looked up and for a moment seemed not to recognize her. He
blinked, consciously, and she came into focus. "Hey, Sweetie. . . . How
was it?"

"Oh, it's pretty darned amazing. You'll see. Or I reckon I should say
you'll *feel* it."

≈   ≈   ≈   ≈   ≈

125

After about an hour's noontime break, a crowd was again assembling in the main hall. As they had in the morning, Nate and Elizabeth found a spot close to the stage, to see clearly. The medium, José, with his assistants, entered the room after awhile. Nate wondered what kind of bizarre surgery they could expect this afternoon, and he murmured, "Do you think this is still Dr. Augusto, that the guy's incorporating? . . . The doctor they said he was using, this morning?"

"I don't know," Elizabeth said.

Without further ado, a man was led out, his shirt was taken off, and an assistant held his right arm up. José said something in Portuguese. Nate thought it possible that the man had cancer, as there were two large lumps in his armpit . . . *Right where some of those lymph glands are, I think* . . . José used a scalpel, cut the man's armpit open and removed these tumors one at a time, dropping them with a thunk onto the assistant's metal tray. One of them, the size of a hen's egg. The man didn't bleed a drop, from what they could see, and he was stitched up with the surgery completed in less than five minutes. José asked him a question, which they guessed was the same one that he had asked at the morning session—had he felt any pain? The man just shook his head.

Nate glanced at Elizabeth. "Weird, huh?"

She nodded.

The way they did these dramatic surgeries, in the open, in front of a crowd, struck Nate again as odd . . . *Like some kind of medical carnival. And no sterile conditions, no sterile surgical gloves? No anesthetic?* . . . He said, quietly, "Why do they do this? . . . I mean, who's this for? Couldn't this just as easily be done behind closed doors?"

Elizabeth turned to look at him, with something resembling patience on her face. "It has something to do with faith. Which . . . I think, has a lot to do with the healing that goes on here—"

"Yeah? Is that really the reason?"

"and I think it has something to do with breaking the control that our minds have—over us. Over our bodies. And our hearts. I think it's intended to break the trance we're all in."

Nate looked at his wife, baffled . . . *Trance? We're all in a trance?* . . .

Elizabeth seemed to notice his expression. "Yes. *Trance.* I said trance."

"And here I thought maybe they were doing this stuff . . . to like, put *us* in a trance. Or some kind of altered state . . . of consciousness."

"No. I think it's closer to the opposite. That these things are done—on this stage, in front of everybody—to help us snap out of it. To wake us up to some things that our minds can't comprehend and don't want us to see. Or won't let us see. Like . . . the possibility of miraculous healing. Here and now."

Nate muttered, "Wow, I want some of whatever it is *you've* been smoking."

Elizabeth looked at him with an expression close to disdain, rolling her eyes toward the ceiling. And sighed.

Nate frowned, in confusion . . . *Shit. Why do I say that?* . . . He himself sighed. "Well, I guess I'll have to go through this current line thing, this afternoon."

Elizabeth focused back on the stage, watching José clean up from the surgery. "You can do whatever the heck you want."

Nate pursed his lips, frowning . . . *All right. Quit with the cynical shit, man. Now!* . . .

When José had left the stage, a man stepped onto the platform—the same cheerful man, Miguel, who had given instructions to the crowd in the morning. He again explained things, in Portuguese, while people began milling around to get into the proper lines. Nate and Elizabeth again got on line at the annex building outside, to pick up tickets—Nate, to get a *primeira vez* ticket, and Elizabeth a ticket for sitting in the current rooms.

Elizabeth stood in line with a number of people who would be sitting in the current rooms—either volunteering as mediums, or as in her case, sitting in *the current* to allow the Entities to work on her. Nate watched her go into the first current room, with her line of people, who appeared to be noticeably quieter than the line he was in. But—similar to Elizabeth's experience with the current room in the morning—most all chatter between the people in Nate's line ceased as soon as they entered the first of the current rooms.

By the time he reached the second current room, Nate felt an inescapable feeling of wellness, even joy. And of being cared for, by some power much larger than himself. It resonated with a certain metaphysical aspect within him, as if coaxing or prying something loose. Like there was a stunted flower bud within him, which was being nourished and strengthened for eventual blooming. And like Elizabeth had, he felt a groggy, pleasant sleepiness whenever he closed his eyes for a while. In the second current room he noticed Elizabeth sitting at the far end of the oblong room—but he consciously tried to ignore her, somehow knowing that thinking about her could be disruptive, perhaps both to her and to himself. Or be disruptive to *the current*. It just didn't seem necessary to concern himself with her—she was being well cared for without his interference.

The *primeira vez* line had moved to where only a few people stood between himself and José. And Nate could now hear the man clearly as he spoke to the people coming by his chair, one at a time. The medium José somehow looked substantially different than he had in the main hall only an hour earlier. Nate noticed a fierceness in his eyes that wasn't there earlier. His eyes actually seemed to be a different color, now—the man had dark blue eyes when they'd seen him in the morning, but now they were brown, almost black . . . *Other than that, he looks like the same guy. I wonder if this is one of the other "Entities" . . . that he's channeling? What the hell? . . .* As before, when José moved around—scribbling on a pad of paper, holding each person's hand as they came before him—he moved almost in slow-motion, underwater . . . *Huh. A little like a marionette . . . with somebody else pulling the strings . . .*

From a doorway at the far end of the room, two women and a man—all dressed in white—came bustling into the room. Looking businesslike or as if they worked there. And they brought with them a young, cheerful girl, maybe nine or ten years old. She had medium length black hair tied into pigtails and wore a long white dress. Another man came into the room with a tray of instruments. One of the women seemed to be explaining something to José, as he looked intently at the girl. He stood up, put his hand on her shoulder, and asked her a few questions—to which she smiled and nodded her head. Gently grasping her jaw, José pulled her lips away from her teeth and peered into her mouth. Then put his forefinger into her mouth and felt around a bit. From Nate's vantage point, her teeth looked very crooked and possibly there was some deformity of her lower jaw. José again put his hand on her shoulder and asked her something, to which she nodded. The girl seemed to have a cheerful nervousness about her when she came into the room, but now she appeared calm, almost sleepy. José fired out a couple of orders to the assistants, and the man with the tray came forward, while one of the women went into the other room to get something.

Nate felt mildly confused by this activity in the room, but was more than happy to hold his place in line to witness some new, peculiar occurrence . . . *Huh. I didn't think they did surgeries in these rooms. Or at least not the "visible" ones . . .*

The medium José cradled the girl's jaw in his hand while she stood there, her eyes sleepy and half-closed. He felt around in her mouth again. He said something, and a male assistant came up behind the girl and placed a hand on either side of the back of her head, stabilizing it. Then, after José said something else, the man extended his fingers to support the girl's lower jaw. José picked up some sort of mallet off of the tray, and a chisel—and began hammering on one of the girl's lower left teeth. Nate began to pay attention, as if he'd been dozing off and needed to wake up now. The girl's head jerked back with each hammer blow. José then began hammering on a tooth on the other side of the girl's mouth, picked up a pair of pliers and began wiggling and twisting the tooth. There was a crackling sound and part of her tooth popped out onto the floor. Nate squinted, as if to see better. The girl's face was placid, as if she was simply having a pleasant dream. That tooth came out, in several pieces, as far as Nate could tell. José then used the pliers again to remove a tooth on the opposite side, this time without breaking it. He picked up the chisel again and began hammering away at the girl's teeth, this way and that.

The force of the hammer blows jerked the girl's head from side to side. It occurred to Nate that, if the man behind the girl wasn't holding her head tightly, the hammering would surely break her jaw. Or break her neck . . . *My God. This is terrible! How can they do this?* . . . José probed his finger into her mouth again, and then continued this hammering, doing it at an even faster pace, like some sort of dental jackhammer. Spittle flew out of the girl's mouth every few seconds while her head was knocked around spastically . . . *Terrible! Where the hell are her parents? This isn't right!* . . .

Agitated and nervous, Nate wondered what José was trying to do. Possibly make more room in her mouth—so her teeth would straighten out? . . . *It's not possible! A person's jaw just isn't pliable, like that. I'm no dentist, but* . . . Feeling truly anxious, now—and real concern for the girl's safety—Nate looked around the room for support . . . *Something has to be done about this* . . . But most everyone in the room seemed oblivious to the girl's plight, with calm, entranced faces. Even Elizabeth. He turned to the man behind him in line—who was also watching this spectacle—but he also looked unperturbed. A feeling of angry panic swept over Nate . . . *What the hell should I—* . . . Suddenly, the hammering sound stopped, and Nate whipped around to see that José was running his finger along the girl's teeth. There was a little blood, which he wiped off her mouth with a towel. And off his fingers.

The man behind the girl relaxed his hold on her and stepped away, while José said something to him. José placed his hand on the girl's shoulder, kissed her forehead, and said something to her in a questioning tone. She opened her mouth a little and seemed to be moving her tongue around, feeling her teeth—after which she nodded and smiled at José. He said something to his assistants, and two men escorted the girl back toward the third current room. She walked out on her own, though a little wobbly on her legs.

Feeling utterly confused for a couple of minutes, a thought that crossed Nate's mind was that nothing like this would ever be allowed to

happen in the States . . . *Child Protective Services would definitely hear about this. Lawsuits. And lawyers . . . Their asses would be in jail . . .* He wondered if anyone had ever sued the Casa de Dom Francisco. Or José. And why hadn't he and Elizabeth considered these contingencies? Then—like somebody flipped a switch—his mind stopped racing and he felt calm and contented again. He wished nothing but the best for the little girl. And for everyone else in the room . . . *What is going on here? .
. .* He knew he didn't really want to leave, now—though just a few minutes ago the thought came up repeatedly. He needed to find out what this creature named Joseph of God was all about . . . *Besides, I'm feeling so mellow, again. Huh. Maybe we're all stoned on something . . . Shut up . . .* And he closed his eyes.

In the late afternoon the buses had all left, as had much of the crowd that was there all day. Nate and Elizabeth intended to walk back to the Pousada das Rosas. Nate suspected that he had a dumb half-smile on his face, but felt curiously energized by the day's events. Elizabeth seemed also to be content but said she was exhausted. As they sat on one of the benches in the shade, on the Casa grounds, she complained that she was too weak and wobbly to walk back to the pousada just yet. Nate thought maybe they should get a taxi, but she said she'd be all right after a short rest.

As they sat on the bench, Nate noticed a few people sitting on another bench, this one in the full afternoon sun. A gentle breeze was blowing, the sunshine pleasant at this time of day. He thought he recognized the woman he'd seen at the morning healing session. "I'll be back in a minute, Liz."

He walked over to the other bench and recognized her as the woman from the morning's visible surgeries, on the stage. The woman who supposedly had an ovarian cyst. There was a cane next to her leaning against the bench, and she was sitting in a relaxed way, talking to a man standing in front of her. Speaking Portuguese. Nate was curious about something, so—looking at her, he tried out his pidgin-English, "Hi. *Olá.* How *are* you?"

"*Olá,*" she said, though apparently not understanding the rest—and she looked curiously at the man she'd been speaking to. Nate recognized him as being the doctor who'd come up on stage when José asked if there were any doctors in the room. The man smiled at Nate—and seemed to know some English—so he translated to her. She replied back to him, and the man turned to Nate, speaking in heavily accented English, "She says she is doing very well."

Glancing at the man, Nate said, "Please ask her if she's feeling any pain, now? And how well she's recovering?"

The man translated this to her, and he returned with her response, "I had a lot of pain in the recovery room. But it is gone now. José, the spirits, and God, have healed me."

Nate didn't want to ask anything inappropriate—or to appear as if he was interested in her. So he put on his best innocent face, and asked, "Is it okay if I see where the incision was made? What it looks like now?"

The man posed this question to her. Apparently she thought Nate's request to see an incision was perfectly normal. And the other man must have been equally curious, because he immediately adjusted his glasses and stooped down as she loosened up her blouse. She leaned to one side a bit, stretching down her waistband to expose the area. The doctor leaned in and looked at the site, asked her something, then touched the area. Then he moved aside, taking his glasses off and wiping them with a handkerchief, while Nate stooped down to look at the spot. The site of the incision was no longer an incision—the skin already knitting together in a slightly raised scar, pinkish-purple compared to her tanned skin. It looked as if the sutures could be removed already. Nate smiled at the woman. "Thank you. *Obrigada.*" He straightened up and looked at the man, who slipped his glasses back on, shaking his head.

The man shook his head again, almost imperceptibly, like an afterthought. In English, he said, "I have never seen anyone heal so fast from a surgery like this."

Nate nodded. "So, you're a doctor?"

"Yes. In Brasilia. I'm a doctor, for children . . . how do you say, Ped-i-a . . . Pediatrics?"

"Yes. That's what we call it in America."

"She should be in *much* pain . . . from a surgery like this. She should be in bed, in pain, for days. I can't believe it."

Nate talked with them for a couple more minutes, asking the woman where she was from and how long she'd been ill. He thanked them both, with "*Obrigado,*" and walked back over to where Elizabeth was resting in the shade.

An exhausted expression rested on his face, now—as if this last occurrence was just the last straw. After explaining his conversation with the couple, he rubbed Elizabeth's hand and asked how she was feeling. A few minutes later, the two walked silently the quarter-mile back to the pousada. The late afternoon sun quite comfortable now. The only thing breaking the silence was a group of people who passed them by going the opposite direction. It looked like maybe they were a local family, just taking an evening walk. They smiled at the group, and Nate said *"Olá."*

17.

"The skeptic is a lot quieter this evening.
I think the cat's got his tongue. The poor bastard
keeps trying to explain things . . . and he just gets tired of it."

When they got back to the pousada, Elizabeth went straight upstairs. The stairway seemed to use up the last of her energy—exhausted, she threw herself on the bed. Meanwhile Nate went downstairs to see if Ana could provide some semblance of dinner, perhaps just bread and cheese. When he got back to their room Elizabeth was already sound asleep. So he closed the door and, lying down beside her, dozed off, himself.

It was dark when he awoke—late evening, with a comfortable breeze wafting in through the half-open window. Mild, but a bit close with the humidity. Elizabeth was still asleep and didn't rouse when he got up to go downstairs to see if Ana had rustled up anything in the way of dinner. She had in fact set aside a tray for him, on the kitchen table—with what he asked for—so he left five Brazilian *Real* for her. When he got back to the room Elizabeth was awake, still lying on the bed. They had their dinner of bread and cheese while she talked about her experience in the current room.

For the first half hour or so, she'd had trouble calming her mind—her thoughts drifting all over the place. She remembered that a friend of hers, a woman who practiced Buddhist meditation, described this as "monkey mind." After a while she felt a narrowing down of her scattered thoughts—as if some force greater than she channeled her thoughts until there was only silence. She was completely relaxed and groggy but not asleep, and felt a surge of warmth flowing into and through her. "It was like what I had felt in the morning—almost like pure, unconditional love. And this time, sitting there in the *current,* I just totally let it have its way with me.

"I knew there were many other people in the room—and people sitting to either side of me. And I could see them all, like I was watching from above. And I could see myself, sitting there with my eyes closed. It was the *darnedest* thing. It felt like total bliss." She figured that she must have been in that state for hours—until the session was over, José left the room, and somebody roused them. "And it felt like I'd only just sat down, there, for a minute. The *darnedest* thing. When I stood up, though, it was almost like my feet were glued to the floor. And when we left the room, some of us could hardly walk. I was totally spaced-out. Exhausted. But happy, too."

She wanted to hear about Nate's experience going through the current line, and he told her the gist of it. "Before I got up to where José was, I'd thought about it and knew what I was asking for help with. Your well-being, of course. But also, for myself I knew that what I needed most was comfort and peace of mind . . . and *that,* without alcohol or drugs. José—or the 'Entity'—said that they would help me . . . at least, that's what Paulo told me afterward. And he told me that I need to sit in the current room—the first room—for the rest of the week. So it looks like we'll both be doing that, this week."

"Nice. I mean, that *will* be nice, right? Unless you're still thinking this is some kind of new age scam?"

"Uh, no," Nate said. "The skeptic is a lot quieter this evening. I think the cat's got his tongue. The poor bastard keeps trying to explain things . . . and he just gets tired of it. And gets a headache. Literally."

"I know the feeling."

"I mean . . . that crazy dentistry procedure that I saw in there—you know, the thing I told you about, when we were sitting on the bench, afterwards? . . ."

"Yeah," Elizabeth said, "I was in the room, but I wasn't really aware of that going on."

"I just keep coming back to that. It damned near blew my mind. It makes no damned sense. He was breaking teeth—and probably breaking her jaw bones—and afterwards, she was *fine.* Actually *smiling!* . . . And José wasn't even the same guy that he was this morning. He looked completely different. It was a different Entity he was using, this afternoon. Paulo told me, afterward, that it was Saint Francis Xavier— some Jesuit dude from the 1500s, that they named the Casa after. This place is a mind-fuck. I just can't argue with this stuff anymore—it's way beyond me. There's just no explaining it."

They woke next morning to the sound of a rooster crowing nearby, and like their first morning in Adelândia, a low cloud hung in the valleys to the northeast. The sun peeked over a distant plateau to the east. Elizabeth stood at the window, tying her hair back while she listened to the countryside waking up. The peculiar bird sound she'd heard the other morning was clearer this time—a low chuckling and then a rising-pitch call . . . *Definitely a parrot. Maybe a wild one, roosting in a neighbor's tree . . .*

After a quick shower before their housemates were up, they headed downstairs for breakfast. In the morning session at the Casa, events unfolded this day—Thursday—much as they had the day before: with three visible surgeries being done in the main hall. The entire group from the Pousada das Rosas stood together near the stage. And as before, the surgeries were for the most part mind-boggling. No anesthesia, no sterile operating room—and José barefooted, not even wearing sterile gloves or a mask. One of the patients bled, during her surgery—she stood there with a calm expression as her white skirt got soaked with a rivulet of blood. Nate asked Dawn about this. "Is there something wrong, this time?"

"Oh, no," she said. "Sometimes the patient bleeds. I'm not sure why some do and some don't. It seems as if the Entities slow down the circulation in the area where the work is being done. Sometimes it works better than other times . . ."

"Huh. That's wild."

"Yep." Dawn watched as José began stitching up the woman's belly. She said, in a casual tone, "Yep. This is Dr. Augusto, who's incorporated in José again this morning. He's a good surgeon."

"Uh-huh," Nate said, in a monotone. He sighed. "So, when José is working on someone . . . the Entities, like, slow down the circulation to the area that's being worked on? And somehow anesthetize the area?"

"Yes. A few people here call it 'spiritual anesthesia,' but it's not always a sure thing that it'll work. Sometimes the patient feels a little pain—sometimes none at all."

"Uh-huh."

The rest of the day—in fact, the next two days—passed similarly to their first day at the Casa. With varying numbers of people receiving visible surgeries in the main hall, and Elizabeth and Nate both spending time sitting in the current rooms. Elizabeth felt exhausted, both days, by late afternoon when the last session was over. While Nate claimed that he felt energized. She couldn't explain why she felt so tired—except that possibly there was work being done on her while she sat in the current. Nate found that he had to ask for help in getting her back to the pousada, both times. Derek, the man from Dawn's group, helped on Thursday—he and Nate supporting her on each side while she walked back to the house on unsteady legs. On Friday, Nate got Ana's taxi man to give them a ride back to the pousada.

There was a feeling of community surrounding the Casa, though it wasn't evident when one first arrived. The town looked poor, the roads hot and dusty, occasional smoke billowing from the brick factory at the other end of town. And the frequent arrival of buses spewing out their ill and suffering passengers from all over Brazil. But with time one became aware of an air of benevolence and compassion that permeated the place.

People who were total strangers, and lived thousands of miles apart, smiled at and talked with each other like neighbors. And people spoke about their illnesses without shame or fear of judgement. As if all was welcome and accepted in Adelândia. Old age, cancers, infections, organ failure, AIDS, mental illness—it all belonged in the big picture, here.

Many of the patients visitors from Brazil and other parts of South America already had a working faith that allowed for miraculous healing—and these people simply acknowledged healing as evidence of a benevolent Grace, or Purpose, behind it all. God's love for Creation. And the healing happened in partnership *with* God and Creation. Many of the simplest and poorest provincial people—from the little-known backwaters of South America—had in fact the most profound healings at the Casa de Dom Francisco. Possibly because their belief systems and religion were not a hindrance. And actually allowed for it. In fact, their lack of higher education and lack of scientific knowledge allowed for greater latitude when it came to possibilities. So they were able to tap into their own potential for healing—assisting in healing themselves through their faith in God, faith which ultimately was love for themselves and for all of Creation.

There was a sense of community and comradery in Adelândia—a communal experience similar to that found in survivors of a hurricane or other natural disaster. Elizabeth was aware of this sooner than Nate was—possibly because of her dire situation and her awareness of having nothing to lose, literally. And maybe female intuition. Nate was afforded the luxury of intellectually debating the veracity and/or the methods behind the healings and surgeries he'd seen. At least for a while. But even the most hard-boiled skeptics—and scientifically-minded academic or medical types—eventually had to concede that something beyond the ordinary was happening here at the Casa, in Adelândia. And couldn't be explained away in normal language—or with "normal" scientific precepts.

On Saturday morning Elizabeth still felt worn out and tired, though she'd slept well enough the night before. They barely managed to get up and moving (and downstairs) in time for a late breakfast. Dawn was there, with several from her group. She was telling a story about how she'd been visiting a friend of hers from California who was staying at a pousada on the other side of the street, the night before. Medium José showed up around 9 p.m., with a couple of assistants from the Casa, to see a man who was bedridden there at the pousada. The owner fixed dinner for them, first, and then José went upstairs to visit the patient. "José was still incorporated with one of the Entities. When they came back down to the dining room, a half hour later, the man looked like himself again—like José da Silva, the ordinary farmer. It was a Friday night—after days of working at the Casa—and he looked *very* tired. He had a cup of coffee and left. Saying that he was driving back, last night, to his farm. . . . He's got this farm, you see, outside of Anápolis. About forty-five minutes away."

"My God," a woman from Dawn's group said. "That man is a work-horse."

"Yes, he is. But there's probably a good bit of payoff, too. Not only does he have the reward of playing a part in a vast number of healings . . . but from what I've heard, he says he feels an overwhelming sense of peace when he's incorporated by the Entities."

Elizabeth listened, chewing on a piece of bread. "Still . . . it's got to be hard on the man."

"No doubt. But José says he wants to keep doing this work as long as his body will let him. He also says that he's constantly aware, because of the work he does and his contact with the Entities . . . that there *is* no death. . . . That death is not *real*."

Elizabeth stared at the tablecloth for a long moment . . . *No kidding. Wow* . . . She coughed, choking on a breadcrumb, and took a sip of her coffee. "Too bad, that more of us don't have that kind of awareness."

"It'd be nice, wouldn't it?" Dawn said. "Most of us don't seem to have that kind of belief. Or faith. Or maybe we only have it fitfully. And death, to us, seems dreadful—like the end of everything we know."

"So . . . he's gone for the weekend, and'll be back on Wednesday?"

"Yes. Wednesday morning."

"So, meanwhile . . ." Elizabeth said, "I should keep taking the herbal prescription? The herb tea? . . . Or infusion, I guess you call it?"

"Yep. It's part of the treatment they require, here."

"It's not bad. But it doesn't taste *great,* either."

"No," Dawn said. "But it's a beneficial herb mixture, mostly Passion Flower. *Passiflora.* I guess the main thing is, it's been blessed— energized—by the Entities. So, it has something to do with the healing work that goes on. It somehow *maintains* the healing work that they're doing, with you. Or the *connection* they have with you."

"*Really,*" Elizabeth said. "That's how it works?"

"Yep. This is totally true. A woman I'd taken with us—on an earlier trip here—went back to her home in Oregon. And somehow she stopped taking the herbal prescription. Anyway, her chronic-pain condition returned within a day or two. She was shocked at how quickly her condition deteriorated. So, yes. Definitely. Keep using the herb tea mix. And spend time, every day, in meditation. I think I talked to you about the diet . . . didn't I?"

"Well, no . . . I don't think you did."

"Oh, crap. I'm sorry. I guess I've talked to everyone in my group about these things. The diet, that they *strongly* suggest we follow—if we're having healing work done—is basically this: no alcohol, no pork, no fertilized eggs, and no red pepper or black pepper."

"Anything else?"

"Yes," Dawn said. "Actually, there is. No sex, also . . . for a period of time. It's usually suggested to stay celibate for thirty days. It has something to do with conserving our energy, for our healing. That's about it. But they're serious about these things. We have to participate in our own healing. So, if *you're* serious about getting well—and you're having healing work that needs to continue after you get back home— well, you need to keep up with every one of these things. The herbal prescription, the diet restrictions, the sex restriction . . . and meditation time every day."

The others sitting at the dining table were for the most part quiet, during breakfast, listening to Dawn. Nate and Elizabeth talked quietly and decided they would spend a low-key weekend there in town. But might possibly take the bus over to Anápolis—on Monday or Tuesday— just to see what the city was like. As they got up from the table,

Elizabeth felt woozy and staggered up onto her feet.

Dawn smiled at her. "I'm so glad you came here, girl. I really think this place will make all the difference, for you."

"I hope so," Elizabeth said, smiling weakly . . . *But not feelin' too hot right now* . . .

Saturday and Sunday were quiet days—the highlight on Saturday being a call they made, home, in the late afternoon. They used the phone at the pousada, trying out the long-distance phone card that Nate had found at a local store. The call went through perfectly, and Nate talked with his mother, Janie, for a while—to find out how things were going with her babysitting job at the earthship. Elizabeth's eyes sparkled as she waited her turn to get on the phone—wanting mostly to talk with her boys. She could hear, in Joey's voice, that he missed her. But Luke tried to sound tough. "Luke," she said, "you know . . . you're the man of the house, now. You be nice to your little brother, now. And Grandma."

"I *know*," he said. "Everything's *fine*, here. I helped Grandma plant some peas in the garden, today."

"Wonderful!" Elizabeth said. She brushed away a tear. "Remember to water 'em, now. They need lots of water, for the first two weeks."

"Okay. I will. When are you coming home?"

"Probably the end of next week." She talked with Luke a while longer, then put Nate back on to talk with him. While Nate talked with his son—and then spoke again for a few more minutes with Janie—Elizabeth felt tears welling up. And wasn't sure if the tears were mostly joy, or sadness. Or both. She sighed, loudly, and wiped her eyes. Later she felt much more relaxed and normal—for the first time since leaving the States.

They went to the *Cachoeira*—the waterfall—on Sunday, accompanied by a few people from Dawn's group who wanted to walk down there also. Elizabeth wore a bright azure blue one-piece bathing suit, which she brought for just such an occasion. She felt her exhaustion draining out of her as she stood under the cool stream of the pummeling waterfall. And felt an energized contentment for several hours afterward. For the first time in days. Maybe months. They turned in early, Sunday evening, after reading for a while—Elizabeth with her book about Brazil, and Nate with a book of various writers' discussions on the topic of existentialism.

Elizabeth slept well enough—that is, until the early morning hours. It was probably two or three in the morning when she awakened to a tingling sensation on the surface of her chest. It was just on the edge of perception—but it awoke her abruptly. She wondered for a moment if there were bedbugs in the sheets. It was, after all, the tropics, and probably not the cleanest house in Brazil. She sat up in bed and rustled the t-shirt she was wearing, in case some insect had gotten trapped under it. But the tingling, ticklish feeling continued, working its way into her breasts—and then she felt it in only within her left breast. The location of her tumor. Even though it was warm in the room, the chill of goose bumps rolled down her neck. She wondered if she was imagining it—or even having a nervous breakdown. Maybe the stress had been too much, lately . . . *Or could it be some kind of healing, going on . . . here in my bed?* . . . It felt as if tiny, warm fingers were working on her—or tiny butterflies fluttered within her breast . . . *Weird. It's giving me the creeps. Should I wake up Nate? . . . He'll think I'm losin' it . . .* She breathed deeply—calmed the defensive, watchful part of her—and just gave in to the sensation. It wasn't unpleasant. But was startling and peculiar. Elizabeth noticed a faint scent of flowers in the air . . . *What is that? Roses?* . . . After a few more minutes, the sensation and the fragrance faded away, till she wondered if it was only her imagination. And sleep overtook her again.

18.

". . . Seriously. You're not in Kansas anymore."

After they awoke on Monday morning, Elizabeth mentioned the night's occurrence to Nate in as much detail as she was able. And he felt genuinely curious about it. "That's interesting, Sweetie. Maybe we should ask Dawn about it." . . . *Bizarre . . . I wonder if she's losing it . . .*

At breakfast, downstairs, they lingered for a while after they'd finished eating—waiting to see if Dawn would show up. She did. The woman had hardly sat down—was reaching for the coffeepot—when Elizabeth, with a pensive expression, mentioned the night's odd occurrence. Dawn, still looking sleepy, listened with interest but didn't seem surprised.

"Oh that's great," she said, in a tone much like chatting about the weather. "And, no . . . nothing at all to worry about. It's actually very common, here. That people, you know . . . people have this sort of thing happen. That folks can feel some healing going on—or that the Entities are working on them—at their home or at the pousada where they're staying. Or even at the Cachoeira. It's really common. I'd say you've just experienced an invisible surgery—or at least *part* of what the Entities feel they need to do, to help you. Some people have noticed that the Entities are working on them, even when they've traveled back home—like back to the States, for instance."

"No foolin'," Elizabeth said. "Wow. You mean—if there's still more work to be done?"

"Yep."

Nate was listening attentively, a half-chewed piece of bread in his mouth . . . *Weird* . . . "Persistent little buggers, aren't they?" He cracked a half-smile, but thought better of it and the smile faded.

Dawn raised her eyebrows in a patient expression, though she did have a sort of pursed smile on her lips. "I, ah . . . I don't think 'little buggers' is quite the way I would refer to the Entities. But, yes, they *are* determined to help us—if we *want* that help. This group of Entities comes here to help us . . . knowing that we're all here for some desperate reasons. Suffering in some major way. And this place—the Casa—is one place where they can do this work."

With a penitent look in his eyes now, Nate stared at his plate. "Sorry. I didn't mean anything by that, you know. I just have to joke about things . . . things that I don't understand, I mean."

"I know. Don't worry about it. It's just your way of processing things."

"Yeah," he said. "*That's* the ticket. It my way of *processing* things." Finishing his bread and butter quietly, Nate sipped at his coffee and glanced at Elizabeth. He vowed to himself—again—to not make light of the peculiar events that went on regularly around the Casa, and Adelândia. Or at least not to verbalize it . . . *God damn it. Liz needs for me to be at least halfway serious about this stuff* . . .

Elizabeth listened in idly while Nate chatted with Dawn, mostly about California. And about having grown up there—something they both had in common. The state had grown, of course, and numerous changes had occurred, since the time when he left California in the late '70s. Nate circled around, with the conversation, coming back to something she'd said. "I, uh . . . I was wondering about what you said a few minutes ago. You know, about how this is one place the Entities can work on us. I mean, why *is* that? That they can do this work, here? In Adelândia? Why not in *Podunk,* Tennessee, for instance?"

"Maybe it could be done in Podunk, Tennessee," Dawn said, "and probably none of us knows the answer to that. Maybe it's partly because it's a culture, here, that doesn't have a major problem with miraculous healing. It's also a society that doesn't have much of a problem with 'spiritism'—or the use of mediums—in channeling spiritual energy. Maybe it's partly because of the geophysical energy of the place. . . . They've found out, for instance, that there are large quartz deposits—underground—in this part of the Brazilian Highlands. Crystal rock formations that may even create some kind of energy field we're not aware of. Maybe—for any number of these reasons—it's become a sort of portal between dimensions, or something. . . . Or the veil between dimensions is thinner, here."

"Huh. And these spirits just come here willingly to help ease people's suffering . . ."

"Yes. The Entities must be well aware that we humans, in many ways, suffer more than most any other sentient beings. It's because of our highly-developed ego—or psyche—and the feelings of separation and loneliness caused by that."

"Huh," was all Nate said . . . *Yep, Dawn's pretty sharp. And I thought she was just some new-agey California chick—and into the woo-woo stuff. She's deeper than I thought . . .*

The folks sat, late into the morning, at the dining table, not needing to be anywhere in a hurry. Nate and Elizabeth got to know a few more of the members of Dawn's group. When they got around to talking over their plans for the day, Elizabeth said she wasn't feeling up to going over to Anápolis, that day. She didn't feel strong enough to deal with the bus ride. Or with walking around a strange city.

Dawn overheard them talking and took Elizabeth's side immediately. "You know, Elizabeth . . . you should really get plenty of rest. You've just had invisible surgery done—or some kind of internal spiritual work—and we need to recuperate after this sort of thing. Just the same as if it was a regular, hospital surgery. It's best not to push yourself. Or you can actually do harm, to the work that's been done. Some people have to sleep all day, after having had some major invisible surgery."

"Sounds about right," Elizabeth said. "I feel *totally* pooped—even after just waking up and having breakfast."

The day passed quietly, with Nate spending time wandering around the Casa, ruminating about his wife's condition. In the early afternoon he checked on Elizabeth, back at the room. She was sound asleep, despite the fact that the room was bright with sunshine and had no shades to darken it. After making himself a sandwich, he found himself back at the Casa, sitting on a bench in the deep shade of a mango tree. A man—who either worked for the Casa or was a volunteer—had the doors wide open to the main building and was cleaning the floors in the main hall and the current rooms. Though he spoke only a little English, Nate could see it was hard work in the heat and humidity, so he asked—mostly with gestures—if he could help. The man, sweat dampening his shirt, nodded and seemed glad to have help. He said his name was Tomás. Nate helped him move aside numerous chairs and benches—so that the floors could be swept and mopped. And was glad for having something to do.

143

Tuesday started out as another quiet day. Elizabeth slept late, and felt exhausted again, as there had been another odd late-night or early-morning visitation. Similar to the night before, she'd had the sensation of something working on her—a fluttering, ticklish feeling within her breasts and armpits. She mentioned to Nate—and later, to Dawn—that it was actually a peaceful, pleasant sensation once she settled into it and allowed it. But she was tired, again, even after getting up late and having a late breakfast.

Back in their room, she put her oversized t-shirt back on and flopped onto the bed. Her face nestling into the pillow, she mumbled to Nate, "Why don't you go ahead and catch the morning bus, Hon'? . . . and go over to Anápolis today? Might be an interesting city."

"No. I don't think so, Liz. I think I'll just stay around town again, today. Tomorrow's gonna be really busy around here, again . . . with José coming back into town. Maybe today I can help, again, over at the Casa. It kind of feels good to help around there."

Elizabeth closed her eyes, gently, feeling tired but oddly contented. "I bet. . . . That can't be a bad thing to do."

"Nope. Kind of makes me feel like less of an outsider here."

The next morning, the sun peeked over a fog bank to the east, and a gentle, mild breeze rustled the curtains at the window. Elizabeth felt rested this morning—Wednesday—had slept well and wasn't awakened by any late-night weirdness. They were up earlier than the other houseguests, so she took a quick shower in one of the bathrooms. As Elizabeth came out of the bathroom mist and into the cooler air of their room, Nate surveyed her from head to foot. "You look *wonder*ful, Sweetie. Looks like you're really feelin' better."

"Yes. For real. And I'm kind of excited to see what all's gonna happen over at the Casa today."

"Yeah. Totally. . . . It's never *boring* around there."

Nate took a quick shower while Elizabeth dressed, putting on the cleaner of her two white dresses. She brushed and then braided her hair back into a quick French braid, fastening it with a turquoise blue barrette. Looking at herself in the small mirror on the wall, she debated putting on her lip-gloss . . . *Hmm. I'm supposed to be having surgery today. Why am I wanting to get dressed up? Huh? . . . I'm pretty sure it's gonna be invisible surgery. . . . I hope so . . .*

They left the pousada before the others had even come down for breakfast, thanking Ana for another solid breakfast. Since they were early getting over to the Casa—and Elizabeth felt rejuvenated—she suggested they go for a walk down the road to the waterfall. The dirt road had been dampened by the dew overnight, and their feet made the only marks in the moistened red-powder surface of the road. The morning sun felt good on Elizabeth's face, with the lush green depths of the tropical forest on either side feeling like moist balm, with a verdant, fertile odor permeating the air. Passing just overhead, a small flock of chattering and chuckling parrots surprised them, with a flash of green and scarlet. This morning, Elizabeth thought they didn't look at all gaudy—but sparkling and fresh. And happy. A few billowy cumulous clouds had appeared to the north that maybe foretold of rain in the afternoon . . . *It's the dry season, though. So probably not . . .* Though it was pleasant walking down the road, at a certain point Elizabeth felt it was time to turn around. "We probably ought to head back, Hon'—to make sure we get to the Casa on time." They turned and ambled back toward the village.

Nate looked for a few moments at Elizabeth, and paused before he spoke. "So, José, last week . . . he asked you to come in for surgery, today?"

"Yes. Today. This morning. I'm pretty sure it'll be invisible surgery—in the current rooms. Probably that third current room . . . where they do the more serious work."

"Uh-huh. You feelin' okay about this?"

"Oh, yeah," Elizabeth said. "Of course. I really wanna get done with it . . . this healing, I mean. I feel a *lot* better, already. But I've still got cancer . . . as far as I know. And I sure want to be done with it. *"*

"Yeah. I can see you're feeling better already, Liz. And I'm so glad. But, hell yeah—let's get *done* with the damned stuff!"

By the time they found their way back to the gates of the Casa, a crowd already halfway filled the yard, and another bus had just arrived. They worked their way into the main hall amid the spiritual carnival atmosphere, which they'd become somewhat accustomed to. To Elizabeth, it seemed very loud in the room, this morning, after the quiet of the previous days. But was a cheerful cacophony. José was nowhere to be seen. But they didn't expect to see him out in the main hall yet—he was most likely busy preparing for another long day. Nate led Elizabeth toward the front of the room, holding her hand as they threaded their way between the numerous groups of people already assembled. The small, jovial man, Miguel, who'd been there last week, was again standing on the stage speaking to the crowd in Portuguese.

Elizabeth slowed down as if dragging her feet. And tugged on Nate's hand. "I think this is where I need to go—to get permission to go into the third current room." She nodded her head toward a door behind the stage, on the right. "I wish Paulo, or Dawn, was here . . . but I'm pretty sure it's that doorway there."

"Okay, Sweetie. You go, girl. . . . I'll be prayin' for ya."

She glanced quickly but intently into his eyes. "You *will?*"

"Of course."

With a half-smile on her lips, Elizabeth kissed him, then turned and left. Nate watched her as she walked over to the door leading into the current room. The mother of their sons—sturdy, but feminine and attractive, even from behind—looking angelic in her long white dress. She spoke with someone at the door for a moment, waved at Nate, and disappeared into the room beyond.

A few moments later, Nate turned and wandered the room to see if there was anyone around that he recognized. And then walked outside, over to the annex building, to get a ticket for the current rooms. He had decided that he would again spend time sitting in the first current room, as José had suggested the previous week. As he walked outside into the bright morning sun, he spotted an Anglo couple who stood out from the crowd, looking a bit lost . . . *Huh . . . I'm pretty sure we looked like that. Just last week. That deer-in-the-headlights look . . .*

Walking over, he introduced himself and found they were Americans—which he'd already surmised—and they'd just arrived in Adelândia that morning. A young couple, probably both in their late-20s, Nate was amazed to hear that they were also from New Mexico. "My *God!* That's *amazing.* . . ."

"Yeah," the man said, "we live outside of Taos—on the west side of the Gorge. . . . We're in the Two Peaks area, west of the bridge."

"Jeez," Nate said. "We know Taos. We used to live in Santa Fe a few years ago. And we've built an earthship—near Silver City—that's a lot like the earthships up around you."

"Nice. . . . Yeah, we live right near the main earthship community, there—right across the highway from them." The man introduced himself to Nate and said his name was Jonathan. His wife's name was Alison.

"Awesome!"

Even though they looked to be a hippyish couple, and probably open minded, Nate sensed they were in culture shock here amid the carnival of the Casa de Dom Francisco. So, trying to help them feel at ease, he explained why he and Elizabeth were there. And suggested they sit for a minute on one of the benches. He pointed out the different buildings, describing what they were called and their purpose at the Casa.

Jonathan and Alison were staying in Brasilia until they could find a place nearby. And had rented a car in the city—so there would be a lot of driving back and forth, for the time being. He asked where Nate and Elizabeth were staying, and Nate told them about the pousada. "I believe she's all filled up—at the Pousada das Rosas—but there are several others around town where you can probably find a room. They're really very reasonable. And that drive is gonna wind up wearin' you out."

"Yeah, I 'spect it will. We'll need to find a place around here. . . ."

When Nate asked the reason they were there, Jonathan was reticent about it—something to do, he said, with a "female health issue." His wife, who looked stressed-out and tired, didn't elaborate. During their conversation, Nate pointed out Paulo among the people milling around outside. "Now, *that* guy, Paulo, is a godsend for us English-speaking visitors. Just look for him, if you have any questions. And he can translate for you. And there's another person here, from California—Dawn—I'll point her out if I see her. She's a great help, too. . . . Speaks Portuguese like nobody's business." After they chatted for a few minutes, Nate walked them over to the annex building, to get them their first-time *primeira vez* tickets—and to get a ticket, for himself, for the current rooms.

In some ways they seemed to know a fair amount about the place—probably from long-distance research and reading—but they nonetheless clung onto Nate like newfound gold. He led them into the main hall, where he predicted that soon there would be a few of the visible surgeries happening. In fact, José was already there on the stage—the morning session had begun. Apparently wanting the newcomers to experience the full effect of the visible surgeries, Nate tried to squeeze all three of them up close to the stage—barely remembering that he'd been an almost absolute "Doubting Thomas" just the week before. He pointed out to the couple which man on the stage was Joseph of God—José—and waved his arm like a game-show host over toward the small group of patients standing at the back of the stage. With a conspiratorial tone, Nate whispered that they would be the ones receiving visible surgeries during this morning's session. He began to explain the purpose of the current rooms, and was pointing over to that side of the main hall, when his eyes rested again on the four patients waiting at the back of the stage. His voice dropped to barely audible. With a confused stammer, he said, "Uh . . . Oh, my God." Near the middle of the group of patients stood Elizabeth.

The woman, Alison, glanced over at him. "What is it?"

"That's my *wife*. Over there near the middle . . . I mean, in the middle of that group at the back of the stage. Standing against the wall. Oh, my *God!*"

"What's wrong?" Jonathan asked.

"Well . . . nothing. I mean . . . I just didn't think they were going to *do* this. I thought she was going to get an invisible surgery in the current rooms. José—or *whoever* he is, now—he must've decided that she needed a visible surgery.". . . *Shit* . . . "I mean, I, uh . . . I don't know. I guess this'll be okay."

Jonathan looked at Nate with some genuine concern. "Why wouldn't it be? Is there something wrong?"

Nate answered the man, muttering mechanically, "You guys haven't seen what goes on here."

"Well, should we *stop* them?"

"Uh . . . no. No, no, I don't think so. But I'm not sure I can *watch* this. Oh, my *Lord!*"

Jonathan looked at him closely, his eyes darting back and forth between Nate and what was happening on the stage. "Are you *okay?*"

Elizabeth stood quietly with the other patients who were there for visible surgeries—her eyes open and a calm, uncomplaining expression on her face. There was the trace of a smile on her lips. But Nate couldn't help wondering what they'd said to talk her into this. José was already working on one man, doing the bizarre hemostat maneuver, inserting the instrument deep into the man's nostril . . . *My God . . . they're doing this again* . . . He stared intently at the man's face. Nate had learned, in talking with Paulo, that this hemostat procedure was in fact done quite often, to treat several different illnesses. And similar to the last time he'd seen it—José left the instrument in the man's nostril for a couple of minutes, grabbed it again, giving it a couple of violent twists—then slowly pulled it out. Amazingly, this time the man's nose didn't bleed at all. A couple of attendants led the man off stage, staggering a bit.

Nate returned to the present, hearing Jonathan, next to him, clearing his throat. "Ah . . . that was really *interesting*. Good God! How odd. But, how did he—"

"You might as well quit asking the 'how' question, right about now," Nate said, curtly. His face had a pale, deadpan expression. "Because you won't get any of the answers you want to hear. . . . Seriously. You're not in Kansas anymore."

"New Mexico."

"Whatever." Nate sighed loudly, feeling as if he suddenly wasn't getting enough oxygen. He raised his hand up to his brow and nervously ran his fingers through his hair, pushing back some loose strands. His forehead felt clammy and damp.

A couple of assistants led Elizabeth up to where José was, at the front of the stage. Nate glanced furtively up at her and then back down to the floor again, tugging at his hair. He muttered to no one in particular, "Creator . . . please take good care of her. God . . . whatever you are, *please* help her through this." The recent convictions he'd come to—that metaphysical events and miracles *were* in fact happening here at the Casa—seemed to have gone out the window for the moment. And the only thought that came to mind was that his wife was going to be carved up here in front of all these gawking strangers. He felt as if he was at the top of a brutal roller-coaster hill—starting to hurl downward—with his stomach lurching forward.

José placed his hand on Elizabeth's shoulder, as he gestured to a woman with a tray of instruments who immediately came over to his side. He said something inaudible to Elizabeth. And she began to unbutton the top of her dress. Standing there calmly in front of the crowd, she seemed to focus her gaze on nothing in particular, wearing a tranquil half-smile.

The Taos woman, Alison—standing on the other side of her husband, away from Nate—was apparently unaware of Nate's emotional state. She leaned forward to peer around her husband at him. Whispering, she asked, "So . . . this would be one of the *Entities?* That Joseph of God is incorporating now?"

Nate seemed to be focusing on some sort of blemish on the floor, a frown on his face. He blurted out, "Yeah. Yeah. This is probably Dr. Augusto . . . Augusto something or other. A Brazilian surgeon who died a long time ago."

"Really? That's amazing."

He thought for an instant about the seeming absurdity of what he'd just said—about the dead doctor. And thought about how that must sound to someone unfamiliar with the Casa. "Right. *Amazing.*" Dazed, he looked up at the stage again. And his anxiety skyrocketed again . . . *Man, I can't deal with this . . .*

On the stage, José gently tugged at the shoulder of Elizabeth's dress and it slid down to her forearm, exposing her left breast. He picked up a scalpel off the tray, and, supporting her breast with his other hand he deftly made an incision at least two inches long, down the outside of her breast almost to the nipple. Nate looked at the incision and could see that she wasn't bleeding, even though reddish tissue within her breast was clearly visible. Elizabeth's face looked like she was having a pleasant dream—nothing more.

"My *God*," Jonathan whispered. His wife exhaled loudly as if she'd been holding her breath.

Nate felt a great wave of warmth come over him—insistent and powerful and benign. Washing over the clammy nervousness he'd been feeling. A profound peace enveloped him as he felt his body surrendering. Aware of his consciousness leaving, he fell out, backward, his legs buckling—seeming to do so in slow-motion while calmly observing one of the light fixtures on the ceiling. Then that too disappeared—his consciousness reverting to a gray static screen. A few minutes later he was vaguely aware of people lifting him and carrying him somewhere. But couldn't seem to awaken from what felt like a more preferable dream-state.

As he opened his eyes again a lake lay in front of him. A huge lake, surrounded by mountains patched with snow. He felt a warm peace blanketing him, even while a breeze ruffled his hair. He could hear his parents talking somewhere behind him—and when he turned around to look, they were moving a table into the new cottage. The cottage was set back fifty or sixty yards from the lakeshore . . . *Mom and Dad are here, together . . . Of course . . .* He turned back to the water and gazed at the deepest, bluest lake he'd ever seen or even heard of . . . *Lake Tahoe . . .* He was eight years old, the summer his parents finished building the vacation house. They'd just driven up from home in L.A., earlier in the day. And the air smelled cleaner and fresher here than anywhere around the city.

Yet some part of him knew that he was really thirty-five, and his wife was being operated on at some odd place in Brazil . . . *So maybe this is nothing but a memory, or a dream. But it seems so real . . .* Small waves rhythmically lapped at the shoreline, and he stuck his foot into the crystalline water, wetting his tennis shoe . . . *Cold water* . . . His warm, blissful mood continued as he slowly and dreamlike took in the scenery, as if seeing it for the first time . . . *Maybe I'm really back here . . .*

. . . There's the fragrance of pine trees in the air. The sunset sky is quickly turning orange and pink over the dark blue saw-blade of the Sierra Nevada Mountains to the west. It'll be nightfall soon. Dad and I walk through the trees down to the lake, with fishing rods . . . I'm holding my new fishing rod that Dad gave me yesterday, back at home. Boy! A brand new fishing rod! . . . Oh! that good, fresh smell of the pine trees here. Dad says they're called 'Ponderosa' pines . . . It's a funny word, 'Ponderosa.' We step over rounded rocks to the water's edge. We put the tackle box down, and Dad shows me how to put a worm on the hook. But I don't like this part much . . . The lake is calm now. And Dad is showing me how to cast the line out into the water—the hook with the worm on it. And a bobber. After we get my line out into a good spot on the water, he casts his line out, too . . . And I feel good. Dad loves me— and he's showing me how to fish . . . We wait for a long time, as the sky is darkening and a cool gossamer breeze wafts off of the lake.

The bobber on my line is hard to see now, floating on the cobalt blue water, the ripples reflecting a sky of lavender and mauve. Suddenly it starts to bounce up and down on the surface and then goes under. I'm scared and excited . . . Dad! Look! I got one! . . . But I don't know where Dad went. He's nearby, though, and I hear his voice. He tells me how to gently pull the fish in to shore. I reel the fish in, and it splashes around in the shallows. Dad's voice, behind me, tells me how to gently remove the hook and release the fish—if that's what I want to do . . . Yeah. That's what I want to do. I want to release him . . . and let him swim away again . . . I can't see Dad, for some reason—I guess he's standing behind me. And he's still telling me how to remove the hook. It's a small lake trout. A beautiful, silvery fish with a long pink stripe down its side, in the dimming light. After I hold it in my hands for a moment, under the water, I release the fish . . . It makes one strong flip of its tail, and it's gone— back to deeper, safer water . . . Maybe to talk to his fish friends about this funny experience . . . Oh, that was fun!

I'm so glad to be here—just plain happy—and I sit down on a big, flattish rock near the water's edge . . . I'm so happy that I feel it in the top of my head—that same old happy ticklish feeling, on the top of my head . . . Like the way I used to feel when I was younger, and Dad would cut my hair with his electric hair-trimmer. I knew that he loved me, then—he was always careful not to nick me, and not to cut my hair too short . . . It's almost dark now. The sun went down a while ago, but the sky is still illuminated in deep amber darkening into purple.

I hear Dad's voice again, but it's all around me now . . . Maybe it's inside me . . . "I've always loved you, Natey," he says, "but sometimes I just didn't know how to show it. I will always love you—and you can feel this love anytime you need to. It's always here . . . and I'm always here, with you . . ."

It's very strange, because it feels like a memory from the past, but Dad's voice sounds like he's talking to me now. In the present . . . I'm crying now . . . but I'm happy at the same time. I don't understand it. Dad tells me that sometimes it's good to cry. And I cry harder . . . But I miss you, Dad . . .

He says, "When you go back—"

But I don't want to go back, and where to?

"you can always remember that my love for you is here—by the lake. Or wherever you are, really. And it's real. It's God's love . . . I know that, now. It's all the same love. You don't need to feel alone anymore . . . It's all around you—and flowing through you. And always will be . . ."

. . . I cry so hard—even though I'm happy here—that I just give in to the feeling. My body shakes with my sobbing, and I close my eyes . . .

When I open my eyes again, it's a bright, sunny day—though it was dimly lit dusk just a moment ago. There's a low-pitched wooden ceiling above me, made with light brown tongue-and-groove boards—and it gives a warm feeling to the room that I'm in. I figure that I must be leaving some sort of dream-state, and as I come back to consciousness realize I'm lying on some kind of cot. Someone is sitting beside me in a chair. It's this man, Paulo, who I remember from a while back. He seems like a kind man—as I've thought before. And I don't feel embarrassed that he's been sitting next to me while I was asleep . . .

Nate rubbed his eyes with his fingertips, as the room came better into focus. His eyes were burning and wet with tears. Opening his eyes wide, he shook his head, trying to shake off the sleep—or whatever it was.

Paulo smiled and patted him on the shoulder. "Some of us," he said, "were worried about you, a little, when you were sleeping. You cried much. But I see that you are better, now. Sometimes . . . crying is good."

"Funny, that you would say that."

"Many people cry much when they find their healing, here."

Nate felt a bit more cognizant of his surroundings—though still in a peaceful state, almost bliss. "Where am I? I remember watching Elizabeth, with her surgery."

"Yes," Paulo said. "The Entities started to work on you, I think. And . . . some people brought you in here. You are here in the third current room—the recovery room. You were here for a few hours."

"And *Elizabeth?*" Nate asked. "Where is *she?*"

"She is here, too, but she sleeps, now. She will be better in the afternoon." He pointed over toward a cot near the window, and the bright afternoon sun splashed on an attractive woman partly covered with a sheet.

Nate leaned up on his elbow, looking more closely . . . *Yeah. It's her. Wow . . .* "Can I go over, and talk with her?"

"No . . . best not to, now. She is having work done."

Nate's eyes lingered on her. "You mean . . . she's still having invisible surgery, *now*? Even after the surgery she had this morning?"

"Yes. Invisible surgery, now. Sometimes both are needed. She was very sick."

"I know . . ."

Paulo got up from the folding chair he was sitting in and stretched a bit, leaning back and gazing up at the ceiling. "I need to get lunch . . . and help get ready for the afternoon healings. I wanted to be sure you were okay."

Nate felt embarrassed, now, considering how many other people were there at the Casa with much more serious issues—many of them life-threatening. "Well . . . thank you very much. Sorry to take up so much of your time. *Obrigado.*"

"Yes," he said, as he turned to walk away. "No worries."

. . . *Huh! Wonder where he got that from? There must be a few Aussies who come here . . .*

Before he left, Paulo spoke with a woman who worked in the recovery room—and a couple of minutes later she came over to Nate and asked him if he'd like any soup from the kitchen.

"That would be wonderful. I mean, *yes. Obrigado.*"

He still felt something near to a state of bliss—and the same odd but pleasant ticklish feeling on the top of his scalp—as he slowly looked around the room at the patients lying in cots or sitting in chairs with their eyes closed . . . *Some of them must be recovering from treatment or surgery . . .* Perhaps for the first time in years, he felt a genuine kinship with people . . . *Even these strangers . . .* Around the room, Casa workers ministered to them . . . *God, there's so much kindness and love, here. In the way people treat each other. And the patients just accept— gratefully—whatever degree of healing that's offered to them. José gives so much of himself to this work. And the volunteers, the helpers, the mediums, all contributing, too . . . Wanting to be a part of this scene, I guess. Very cool . . .*

The woman returned with a bowl of vegetable soup, and Nate sat up on his cot, planting his feet back on the floor. After the soup had cooled, he sipped it and it tasted wonderful. Beans, onions, potatoes, and carrots.

Wholesome. When he finished, he walked over to Elizabeth's cot and watched her for a while, before pulling up an extra folding chair and sitting in it, beside her. He wasn't sure about whether or not to disturb her—but gave in and reached over to gently hold her hand. She opened her eyes for a moment, and then with a slight smile closed them again. With a calmness he hadn't experienced in a while, Nate watched her face for a few minutes and then quietly left the room.

After sitting outside for a while in the sun, Nate made his way back into the main hall, where the afternoon session had already begun. He looked for Paulo—and found him, again, up near the front of the audience, where he was speaking with one of the assistants. Nate asked him, in a whisper, if there was anything he could help with. Paulo thanked him and asked how he was feeling—whether or not he was feeling strong again.

"Yeah," Nate said. "I am. I'm feeling good."

"Excelente." Paulo suggested that he could try and help the other American couple that he'd been talking with, in the morning. Apparently, he'd seen the man sitting alone outside, and Paulo said he'd probably like someone to talk to. And if Nate saw any other Americans around—or other English-speaking people—he could help them to feel at home, also. "That will be very good," he said.

"Sure. I'll do that. Be glad to."

The sun was leaving the sky, its last rays alighting on the puffy cumulous clouds to the east, as Nate and Elizabeth gazed quietly out the window of their room at the pousada. They lay on the bed, both exhausted. Elizabeth, for the obvious reason of just having had an invasive surgery done earlier in the day—and Nate because, as best he could figure, there'd been some kind of major emotional displacement or healing that he experienced. They made another simple dinner of a plate of Ana's bread and cheese. Nate thought it tasted like manna.

19.

"Hell no. I don't think a place like this could even exist, in the States. They'd close it down . . . or turn it into a damned amusement park or something."

Elizabeth felt well enough to come down for breakfast in the morning. But after talking with several people at the table, Dawn reaffirmed what one of the nursing assistants had said to Elizabeth in the recovery room—she should rest for at least a day before even thinking about going back over to the Casa. So after breakfast she made her tea of the herbal prescription, in a coffee mug, and carried it with her upstairs. Nate followed her.

"Looks like I'm stayin' here, today," she said, changing back into her oversized t-shirt.

"Yeah, I 'spect it's for the best."

Elizabeth lay down in the bed, getting partway under the sheets. When she'd checked herself over—first thing in the morning—her breast area was still tender where the surgery had been done. The skin was knitting together quickly, though, and there didn't seem to be internal bleeding or discoloring. In the bed, she shifted herself onto her side, her right arm shielding the sore area. Nate studied her for a minute and climbed into bed, lying down beside her. He curled up alongside her, with his arms around her, spooning her. It was already a warm morning outside, though—and after a while it would be too warm to lie together comfortably.

He extricated himself and kissed the back of her neck. "I guess I'll go over to the Casa for a while and sit in the current room."

"Sure, Honey. I'm just gonna rest here. I'm tired. Haven't felt this way since I was a young 'un, with Chicken Pox. Today I'm stayin' home from school."

"Yep. You be a good girl and do that. I'll be back in the afternoon to see if you need anything."

"Sounds good, Hon'."

Nate got up and quietly let himself out of the room. Elizabeth began to doze off, while a niggling thought danced around in her head . . . *He's bein' a good boy. Odd, how this place rubs off on you. Before you know it, he'll be a saint . . .* She chuckled and a few minutes later dozed off.

On Friday, Elizabeth felt her energy returning. Felt like she could really move around again, comfortably. She and Nate walked over to the Casa—and at Paulo's suggestion, she spent the morning session in the recovery area of the third current room, resting on a cot. While Nate sat in the second current room. During the afternoon session she joined him there, though she insisted they sit apart from each other. As had been the case when she first sat in the current rooms, there was a rush of pleasant warmth and the sensation of being wrapped in unconditional love. Much of the afternoon, she sat in a meditative state, aware only of a silence inside her that seemed not to be empty but full of a nameless something.

This state was broken once by a long dream or vision of her grandmother. It was her father's mother—the one who was Cherokee (and her favorite grandparent when she was young). Her grandmother was showing her how to pick the medicinal herbs from the mountainside forests and hollows of the Great Smokies . . . *Grandma's here. And she wants me to get well . . .* Her grandmother's presence increased her feelings of well-being and love. Elizabeth let it flow in, and passed it on—back into the current. It made her feel well and whole. Not that she *could* be well and whole—but that she already was.

In the late afternoon, long after the last healing session was over and much of the crowd had left, the two walked down the dirt road to the Cachoeira. There were only a couple of people there at this time of day. Two women, wading in the pool. It was always quieter at the Cachoeira—with much less of human noise but more of the timeless sound of water splashing on rock. The town itself was starting to quiet down, with the bustling activity of the Casa grinding to a halt as it closed down for the weekend. Elizabeth was aware of a sense of wholeness and peace that she hadn't felt in a while—perhaps years . . . *Maybe, it's just because I'm getting used to the place now. But I'm pretty sure I'm getting better, too . . .*

They both sat down on a large mossy rock, and Elizabeth lay back on the soft green cushion. She looked up into the gnarled branches of a tree that spread a verdant canopy over them. The shiny leaves—almost foot-long leaves—allowed for only checkered patches of blue from the sky above . . . *I 'spect it's one of those mango trees that Dawn pointed out to us. Beautiful . . .*

The women who had been in the water were drying off at the water's edge, putting sandals back on their feet. Nate sat alongside Elizabeth, hunched over, hugging his knees. And seemed to be deep in thought as he gazed at the cascade. He said, almost to himself, "We could stay here, you know. I mean, stay here in Adelândia. . . . We could *move* here."

"Huh?"

"We could move here. I bet I could find work around town. And they're always doing repairs or renovations, at the Casa—they probably need a carpenter, sometimes."

"*Honey,*" Elizabeth said, "I don't know what you're *talking* about." She turned her head to look at him more closely . . . *What is going on with him? . . .* "And the kids? What about them? . . . They'd be *totally* out of place, here—having to learn a new language, and all. Are you serious?"

"Well," he said, reaching over and pinching her side, "yeah . . . kind of. I mean, we *could.* Just a thought. I mean, there's just something so amazing about this place. Don't ya think? The Casa . . . the town . . . this green countryside? There's a real feeling of community, here, too. You know? I've been thinking about it, the last couple of days. This is a freaking *special* place. There's something powerful going on here. And I mean—even aside from all the amazing healings and José de Deus stuff. There's just, like, naturally some kind of good mojo here, or something. Some kind of positive energy around here . . . maybe it even comes out of the earth. Like Dawn was saying—about there being some major crystal deposits underground, in this area. It's almost like heaven and earth meet here."

Elizabeth propped herself up on one elbow, looking at him . . . *Whoa . . . This boy's got to be reined in . . .* She looked past him at the waterfall—which they had all to themselves, now that the others had left. "No doubt, it *is* an amazing place here, Hon'. It's true. . . . I haven't seen any place like it, in the States."

"*Hell* no. I don't think a place like this could even *exist,* in the States. They'd close it down . . . or turn it into a damned *amusement* park or something. We're just too materialistic, back home."

"Maybe so," she said. "But what can you do?"

"Well," he said, halfway to himself, "we can *leave.* Leave that crap behind."

"Yeah, I guess we could. But you can't just totally buck the system . . . without becoming sort of an outcast."

"Screw the system," he muttered.

Elizabeth pinched him in the side, now, then tickled him. "You just keep your feet on the ground, here, buddy! We can always think about that in the future, you know."

Nate nodded his head and was silent for a few moments. "But you know, Liz . . . you're getting better, here. I can feel it. If we could stay here I'm sure you'd get completely well. I don't have any doubt of it now."

"Well, we can always come back, Hon'. If we can afford it. In fact, a lot of people *do* come back . . . sort of like a follow-up treatment. And some of the healing can still go on, back at home, meantime. At least that's what Dawn and some of the others say."

"I guess." Nate went back to gazing at the waterfall.

That evening they found themselves at the pizzeria down the street. Elizabeth felt her mood and energy level to be better than they'd been in a long while. Brazil, after all, had been a difficult couple of weeks—a blur of confusion, healing, and exhaustion . . . *Fact is, it's been a difficult couple of years* . . . The pizza tasted better than it did the first time they went to this place. Maybe because they were starting to miss American-style food. The restaurant workers looked to be Italian, but spoke Portuguese. And it occurred to Elizabeth—not for the first time—that Brazil was amazingly multi-ethnic, maybe more so than the States. As they walked back to the pousada, a band of puffy cumulous clouds over the hills to the west lit up from the setting sun in fluorescent hues of yellow, tangerine, and blue.

Later, as they lay in bed in the dark silence of their room, a high-topped thunderhead—probably from the rain forest areas to the north—

edged down toward their part of the Highlands. They watched as it lit up like a light bulb, repeatedly, from the inside. It was mesmerizing but didn't come any closer. And they soon fell asleep.

In the early morning hours, when the sky was just a little brighter before the dawn, Elizabeth awakened with the now-familiar but odd sensation of the Entities working on her . . . *Well . . . here it is again . . .* Tiny fingers or butterflies moving within her breasts and her chest. This time she relaxed into it . . . *I'm safe . . . and I'm being cared for . . .* It wasn't alarming anymore, so she dreamily allowed it and dozed off again.

At dawn, she fully awakened and stood up to look out the window at the misty sunrise. She touched the side of her breast, through her t-shirt, where the visible surgery had been done on Wednesday . . . *Hmm. It's smooth. And I don't feel the sutures. I wonder what . . .* She lifted up her shirt to look . . . *My Lord . . .* She darted back over to the bed, shaking Nate's shoulder roughly. "Nathan, look at this!"

He groaned and sat up, rubbing his eyes, and looked at her while she held her shirt up for him to see. "Okay, what is it? Ya tryin' to seduce me?"

"No . . . Look!" The sutures were gone on the side of her breast, and only a pinkish-purple raised area remained, where the incision had been made. It looked as though there wouldn't even be a scar as evidence of the work done there.

He squinted, looking more closely, and croaked, "My God. It's almost completely gone."

Before breakfast, Elizabeth looked under the sheets, to see if there were any traces of the sutures that had been embedded in her skin just the day before—little pieces of thread or suture material . . . *Nothing. Maybe they just fell out. Or I pulled them out. No, not possible . . .* She scoured the sheets, but couldn't find anything . . . *Well, now—that's not something you see every day . . .*

Their last week in Brazil was pleasant. And much more relaxed. On Monday, the Casa was closed as usual—and Elizabeth said she felt well enough to get around—so she and Nate took a bus over to Anápolis in the afternoon. The medium José supposedly had a farm or a small ranch, somewhere outside of the city. There was plenty of rural farmland outside of Anápolis, and a few forested areas, but the city itself was quite large with a modern downtown area that had a few skyscraper buildings. It was a tropical city—with scattered palm trees, parrots, and other signs of a sweltering climate—but Nate thought it could easily be mistaken for parts of downtown Miami or Los Angeles. Though smaller.

The Casa de Dom Francisco was busy as usual on Wednesday and Thursday, with what Nate now felt to be run-of-the-mill metaphysical events, there—major and minor miracles going on, depending on how one perceived them. Elizabeth met with José on Thursday, and explained (with Paulo's help) about how she had to go back home to America. José—with the Entity incorporating him—again held her hand while his eyes seemed to look straight through her. He said that he wanted her to continue with the herbs, the diet, and the meditation, every day. He also said that if at all possible she should come back in three months, to make sure the healing was completed.

She and Nate had arranged for a flight back to the States on Friday. So, after saying their goodbyes to Dawn, and Ana, and a few others they'd come to know—they caught a late bus back to Brasilia on Thursday evening. Brasilia felt very warm Friday morning, probably due to its lower elevation and being closer to the equator. The sun baked the surface of the concrete runway of the Brasilia International Airport—making shimmering heat mirages above it. Mid-morning, their plane left the tarmac. The jet was soon well above the popcorn cumulous clouds of this tropical country. With most of the clouds hovering close to the ground, apparently—little more than several hundred feet above the green landscape.

After twenty minutes or so, the jet had climbed to its cruising altitude. Far below the plane, Nate saw a vast green carpet dotted with clouds and their darker green shadows below. The lands below soon changed from the lighter greens and browns of the hilly country of the Brazilian Highlands—to the deeper, dense greens of the Amazon basin. He could make out tributary rivers leading toward the Amazon. The rivers glinted in the sun, shimmering veins of some vast green organism . . . *Man, I hate to be leaving this place. But maybe we'll be back here in a few months. I hope. It's so alive here. Maybe just 'cause it's the first time I've been here . . . Fucking incredible place . . .* He turned to Elizabeth. "We need to come back here, Liz. But it'll be good to get home, too, huh?"

Elizabeth was nodding off, her eyes closed. They hadn't slept well in the hotel room in the city, the night before—after having spent so many days in the quiet town of Adelândia. She opened her eyes momentarily.

"What? . . . Yep, it'll be good to get home."

It felt, to Nate, like they were leaving some kind of dreamworld behind . . . *Or are we heading back to a dreamworld? With just a different sort of dream?* . . . He sighed, and stared out the window for a long while at the endless green carpet below, so different from the arid and semi-arid lands of the Southwest. Elizabeth started her own quiet brand of snoring, in the seat next to him. He soon joined her, dozing off, himself.

20.

. . . For the Casa healings to work, it seems like
we've basically got to be more guided by spiritual concepts . . .
and be less infatuated with the material world . . .

During the layover in Atlanta, they made a phone call home and talked with Nate's mother. An hour and twenty minutes after their arrival in Atlanta, they boarded a connecting flight to New Mexico. It was late at night when the plane descended and banked over the Sandia Mountains outside Albuquerque. Elizabeth gazed out the window as the glow of the city spread below them in a carpet of myriad white and yellow lights—contrasting with the uninhabited darkness of the mountain range. She felt a vague knot in her stomach as she thought about having to deal with city traffic again. After a very long travel day . . . *Maybe Nate can do the city driving . . .* They had decided—while talking on the phone with Nate's mother—that they would tough it out and drive all the way back to Silver City. It was doable, but they wouldn't get home till the early morning hours . . . *Gosh. What were we thinking? It's a four-hour drive. We're gonna be toast . . .*

She rubbed Nate's shoulder briskly as he slung their bag, with a lurch, into the back of the Volvo station wagon. As it turned out—by the time they'd been shuttled to the parking area, where Elizabeth's car had been sitting for nearly three weeks—she was actually the more awake and animated of the two. "I'll drive first, Honey. No problem. I'm feelin' pretty alert."

"Awesome," Nate said. "Yeah, I don't know why I'm so tired."

"Well, I don't know why you *wouldn't* be. We've had a heck of a

162

long day. And we're probably feelin' some jet lag, too. But I'm good for a while. I can do this—drive for a bit. And then you can take over."

"Right on. . . . You're something, girl."

So they tossed their other bags into the Volvo, made a quick stop at a convenience store for some coffee, and hit the road. And though it was late in the evening—after ten—the highways around Albuquerque still radiated heat. They rolled the windows down. It must have been a hot day in the city—and it would be warm, driving, for a good while. Elizabeth figured, though, that by the time they got close to Silver City it would cool down. Being early morning, and at a higher elevation and distance from the warm valleys and cities. She felt fully awake and energized—looking forward to seeing her boys.

With a clicking sound, Nate leaned the passenger seat back, and said, mechanically, "I've got to sleep, Sweetie." He was soon snoring.

As they left the city lights behind them, the stars looked crystalline—brighter and clearer than in the humid night skies of Brazil. Elizabeth glanced up at the sky from time to time as they sped down the dark highway to home. The evening breeze smelled, intermittently, of warm sagebrush . . . *Gosh, I love New Mexico* . . . She chuckled . . . *And I can't wait to see the guys. Guess it'll have to be tomorrow morning, though* . . . She was hopeful, like she hadn't felt in a while. Hopeful that she really *was* on the mend—was in fact recovered from the cancer . . . *It's not just that I feel this* . . . *I know it. Or it feels like it's truth, already. The Casa—and Adelândia—what an amazing place. And José* . . . *God bless him. So much caring, there. And so much positive energy. Wonderful* . . . *I'm supposed to go back there in three months. A lot of traveling—but I'd better do it. And the diet, and the herbs* . . . *I really do want to stick around, here* . . .

She thought about the Casa, and the number of deathly-ill people she'd seen there. Many of them required to make even more profound sacrifices and spiritual commitment than she had, in order to get well . . . *Sometimes traveling for twelve or thirteen hours on a bus, for gosh sake. So many have had it much worse than me. I guess we're all required to lead more spiritual lives* . . . *in order for the healing to really work. How odd. Totally different from the way we approach it, here in America* . . . *with the purely scientific concept of illness* . . .

As a whiff of sagebrush wafted into the car again, she thought, further, about the spiritual type of healing in Adelândia . . . *For the Casa healings to work, it seems like we've basically got to be more guided by spiritual concepts* . . . *and be less infatuated with the material world* . . . Elizabeth thought of a song by George Harrison. From the '70s—"Living in the Material World" . . . *He knows about this stuff. Maybe that's our*

purpose here, anyway . . . In life. To move closer to God. Could be . . .
Elizabeth remembered how Dawn had said that most all of the illnesses
treated at the Casa were basically spiritual disorders. Spiritual illness.
And that the spiritual illness can manifest as a physical illness . . . *Wow.*
Certainly possible. Yes, it is possible—maybe even probable—though the
doctors here will tell you otherwise. But they don't know everything. Not
by a long shot . . .

The breeze coming in the cracked-open car windows felt cooler as the
evening passed, moving toward midnight. Nate snored softly in the
passenger seat. Something about him sleeping in the car reminded
Elizabeth of road trips with her family when she was a girl . . . *Gosh . . .*
I've got to call Mom and Dad. Haven't talked to them since our third day
in Brazil . . . They passed by the lights of the city of Socorro. But it
wasn't till the glow appeared on the horizon from the town of Truth or
Consequences that Elizabeth truly felt tired. She woke Nate as they
approached the town, and pulled into an all-night convenience store to
get coffee and fill up on gas. They switched places, with Nate planning
to drive the rest of the way home. Once they hit the road again, she fell
asleep and didn't wake till she heard the sound of crunching gravel in
their driveway.

Part IV

21.

"Kind of like Jesus, and God, and ancestral spirits,
all wrapped up together in the other world
—and just possibly trying to help us, in this world."

By mid-morning, Nate felt alert and awake enough to don his beekeeper's veil and begin checking the beehives. Though he was tired and feeling a touch of jet lag, it usually felt invigorating and yet meditative to check on his bees. He'd already spent some time with his mother, over coffee and breakfast. And horsed around with the boys for a while, after they'd gotten up. But Luke and Joey apparently decided they wanted to hang out more with their mother—so they dragged her out of bed. That being the case, next on Nate's checklist seemed to be looking in on the bees.

Taking care of his beekeeping work had more or less of an odd stabilizing effect on Nate. As if the welfare of his bees indicated a larger sense of well-being and of things being right with the world at large. Out of the fifteen hives he had now, most of them were doing well, the queens laying plenty of eggs and the worker bees beginning to store some honey in the comb. The monsoon showers had started, while they were gone—a little early, this year, this being the second week in June. And early summer wildflowers, which the honeybees could feed on, were beginning to bloom. The chokecherry trees in the valley had also been blooming. As Nate looked around, he noticed that the Yellow field clover was just starting . . . *Far out* . . . "You girls are going to have *plenty* of nectar, soon—as long as we keep getting some showers."

He would soon have to put honey supers on top of his stronger beehives so that the workers could start filling them. Three of his hives were doing poorly—struggling—but he figured if he put some brood frames into them from the stronger hives that they would soon get up to speed, also. "You girls are doing *great*. You know, I thought about you girls a lot, while we were gone." He shooed away a yellow jacket, trying to get into the hive he was working on. "I'm *so* glad you all are doin' well." The combined odors of fresh nectar, honey, pollen, and bee propolis produced a heady fragrance—at least, in Nate's opinion—and the odor had its tranquilizing effect on him. He always knew, though, that there was a chance that one or two of the beehives would be irritable and angry at being disturbed. And that maybe he'd get stung. "Yep. Some of you girls are temperamental—like some women I've known. Huh!". . . *And I sometimes can't tell which hive it's gonna be . . . But that's part of the thrill of it . . .*

To cool off for a minute, Nate took off his veil, and he gazed across the valley below, past the cottonwoods and over to the dry slope beyond scattered with junipers. The sun blazed on his face. With none of the cloying humidity of Brazil . . . *Yeah, I like it. The sun actually feels good, here. But maybe it won't, a month from now . . .*

While Elizabeth and the boys had a late breakfast—or by now it was graduating into brunch—Nate burst through the screen door, still wearing his blackish bee-veil over his face. He walked, stiff-legged, with his arms outstretched in a fair imitation of the monster from an old horror movie, *The Creature from the Black Lagoon*. He staggered over to the boys, who were perched at the table listening to their mother's stories from Brazil. Nate snarled some unintelligible monster noises and grabbed at the boys—at which they yelled and laughed. When they quieted down, Nate pulled off the veil and picked up a jar he'd left at the door. There were chunks of freshly cut honeycomb inside, and he handed Luke and Joey each a piece. Luke's eyes brightened, and he popped the sticky chunk into his mouth. "Yum! Thanks, Dad!"

Joey did likewise, using the exact same words, which instantly prompted Luke to frown at him.

Nate was screwing the lid back on the jar, enjoying the kids' reactions, when his mother, Janie, interrupted. With slight irritation in her voice. "Well, don't *we* get any?"

"Uh . . . I don't know. Have you been good?"

"I'm always good," Janie said. "What are you talking about? Have you heard something I'm not aware of? Besides, I've just taken care of these two hoodlums—I mean, boys—for the past two weeks and four days, not that anybody's counting."

"Yeah, yeah," Nate said. "And we sure appreciate it." He offered the jar, first to his mother and then Elizabeth. Soon everyone at the table was chewing on sweet, gooey honeycomb, as fresh as it gets. Nate handed some napkins around.

Janie looked her son over, as maybe only a mother can. His long hair tied back into a ponytail, but loose strands around his forehead looking wet and sweaty. No doubt from wearing the bee-veil and a long-sleeved shirt, out in the sun. From a short distance away, Janie Lewis could easily be mistaken for a young, carefree hippie girl. And was probably stunning when she was younger. She was still very attractive, but her long bleached-blonde hair might have looked better on a younger woman—it betrayed her as a woman not very comfortable with the idea of growing old. She looked over at Elizabeth, sitting next to her, and patted her arm. "So, Elizabeth's been telling me about all these amazing things that happened down there in Brazil. You weren't smoking some kind of killer *weed* down there, now, were you?"

Nate rolled his eyes and exhaled loudly. "Mom . . ." Nate said. "*No,* we weren't. It's kind of hard to talk about these things, I think, to someone who hasn't been there. And so much of what goes on there is just totally antithetical to western medicine. This stuff is just too peculiar, to even convey it."

"Well try me, anyway."

"Okay," Nate said. "Maybe later. I'll let Liz tell you the basics. And we can talk more about it this evening."

Janie was cooking dinner, that night, as she had said she would when they returned. She borrowed the Volvo to shop for some ingredients for her lasagna. It was part of the mother/son game they played every time she made one of her annual visits. She had to make lasagna. Apparently Nate had always liked her lasagna—and it was an unspoken expectation that she would make it. Elizabeth had long since gotten over being annoyed about it, and decided this dynamic between her husband and his mother was harmless—actually kind of cute. At least, for the short term . . . *He doesn't really even like lasagna all that much. Or, at least, huh . . . he never asks me to make it. Hmm . . . maybe I don't make it quite the way she does. Oh well, I won't have to cook tonight . . .*

At dinner, as a cool breeze drifted through the screen door, they sat around the table and let Janie hold forth, a bit—talking about friends of the family, and relatives, in California. People Nate had known growing up. Elizabeth made note of the fact that the boys polished their plates clean, and Luke asked for seconds on the lasagna . . . *That boy's got an appetite, tonight. Or maybe he's got worms . . . But I think I'll check with her, about that recipe . . .*

The plan was that Nate would drive his mother to Las Cruces, the following day, Sunday. They had a shuttle bus there—once a day—that would take her to the Albuquerque airport for her flight back to L.A. The adults sat up late into the night drinking coffee and tea, and talking. Janie seemed genuinely fascinated by their descriptions of Brazil and the healing work of Joseph of God. She looked at Nate. "I can only imagine what it's like, in Brazil. You know, your father and I made several trips down to Mexico—spent some time there—"

"Right," Nate said. "I know. I mean, I remember."

"and, well, this one trip we made—I think you stayed with Grandpa and Grandma that time—we stayed for a few days around San Miguel de Allende. And we visited some of the smaller towns in the Sierra Madre Mountains around there. They, uh . . . I really got the sense that—at least in the rural areas of Mexico, where the people are largely Mestizo or Indian background—that there's much less rigidity in their religious beliefs and practices. . . . And that the Catholic church had to make concessions, in other words, to allow a fair amount of freedom in the local people's belief system. I remember that, in the artwork and crafts of the country people there—and even in the artwork in the churches— there's a lot of imagery regarding the existence of a spirit-world. Or an alternate reality, coexisting with our world."

"It's like that, too, in Brazil," Elizabeth said.

"And most of the people don't have any issues reconciling their native belief system with Catholicism. Kind of like Jesus, and God, and ancestral spirits, all wrapped up together in the other world—and just possibly trying to help us, in this world. Maybe, in certain places, there's not even much of a barrier between the two worlds . . . it's more like a thin veil. And it's probably . . . at least partly dependent on the majority consensus, of the people living in that culture. I mean . . . as to whether or not there can be what we call miracles—or metaphysical phenomena—taking place."

Elizabeth looked at Janie, while the woman paused to sip at her tea. She thought, not for the first time, that Nate's mother was in fact highly intelligent and thoughtful. And a deeply spiritual person . . . *Different from the image she presents, sometimes—as a ditzy California blonde . . .* "I see, Janie, that your anthropology background's coming out."

"Yep." She wrinkled her nose for an instant. "I can't help it, sometimes. A year in grad school—and you'd think I was published, or something. And I guess I blend my cultural anthropology with my own brand of mysticism."

"No, really," Elizabeth said, "I wasn't discounting, at all, what you were saying. We know *exactly* what you're talkin' about."

"Well," Janie said. "I can only imagine that—in many places in South America—there's a lot of this cultural blending going on, with different belief systems and religion. Especially in the rural areas, where the indigenous belief systems can stay intact. Sometimes I think that America is one of the most materialistic societies on the planet, at this time. And that's not really a good thing. Not at all. And the farther away you get from that—physically, and culturally—the more likely you are to find bending of the 'rules.' Or, you could say . . . more allowance of events that don't fit into our neat, pigeonholed view of reality."

"Totally," Nate said, as he got up from the table to refill his coffee mug. "That's pretty much the case, in Brazil."

"Anyway," Janie continued, "from what I've heard about your time down there, this place, Ada . . ."

"Adelândia."

"yes, Adelândia. This place must be a pretty unusual, spiritually-based society—where the veil between the worlds is perceived to be very thin. And almost nonexistent, at times."

"Yes," Elizabeth said. "We've surely felt that to be the case, there. Almost anyone who goes to Adelândia—and spends any time there at all—can't help but believe that something *really* unusual is going on in that place. I'm sure it's no accident at all, that Joseph of God—José— showed up there. And apparently was told by these Entities that he should build the healing center in that town. In Adelândia."

Janie glanced at her son, and gazed, with perhaps more of feminine intuition, at Elizabeth. *"Anyway.* It sure seems like both of you guys benefited from being there." She patted Elizabeth's arm. "And Liz . . . I mean, you look spectacular. Like you've really *healed.* Are you okay, talking about this? I mean, only if you want to talk about it . . ."

Almost imperceptibly, Elizabeth sat up a little straighter in her chair. "Sure. Yeah."

"Do you *feel* like you're healed? . . . I mean, maybe you should still get checked out, with ultrasound, or radiology. You know?"

. . . *Good question. Yep, Janie doesn't pull any punches* . . . "Well, I s'pose I *do* feel healed. Like the cancer's gone. Or that I'm at least ninety percent of the way there. But I still feel like I need to continue with the protocol José wanted me to continue doing. . . . The diet, and the herb mixture, every day. And meditation. The man was quite clear about that. And we're supposed to go back there in a few months. But I *do* have an appointment with my doctor, here in Santa Fe, to have a checkup." She glanced over at her husband. "But I think Nate would say, too . . . that I'm a lot better."

"Oh, hell yeah. No doubt at *all.*"

Janie looked at Elizabeth with kind eyes. "Yes. No doubt. You know, I didn't want to say anything, before you guys left for Brazil . . . but, well, I felt like there was something about your eyes that looked tired. And I hate to say it, but, like . . . maybe you weren't going to be around here much longer."

Nate cleared his throat and squirmed in his chair, as if to get up. Elizabeth looked down at her hands and felt her eyes beginning to burn. Janie seemed to notice it, and she rubbed Elizabeth's hand. "But that look is *gone,* now, Sweetie," she said, with a smile. "I mean just gone. And I'm so happy about that. *Wonder*ful. Not only for you, but for this boy you call your husband." She nodded her head slightly in the direction of her son and winked at Elizabeth.

Elizabeth let go a long, sighing exhale, fidgeting a little. "Can I get you another cup of tea, Janie?"

She took her up on it, and they talked for quite a while longer about some of the peculiar things they'd witnessed at the Casa de Dom Francisco. Janie wanted to know more regarding some of the mundane things about small-town life in Brazil. About Adelândia, and Brazilian culture in general. At least, as much as they'd been able to gather.

And they spoke about lighter subjects. About how their earthship home was working for them—how it was, for them, living "off the grid." They talked for a long time about the boys, Janie's grandkids. Nate and Elizabeth were having to help the boys get more socialized, after growing up in a way that was relatively isolated from other children. Before they'd left for Brazil, it was decided that Luke would start attending public school in Silver City. Elizabeth had taken him over to talk with the assistant principal of the school—and Luke appeared to be genuinely excited about it. They would have to continue with some more homeschooling over the summer, to make sure he was up to speed with the class he'd be joining.

It was late by the time they were talked out, and tired. A chilly nighttime draft seeped through the screen door, and a half moon was low in the sky. Nate closed the door and wished his mother a good night. Janie helped Elizabeth do a last bit of kitchen cleanup. And they once again made up the living room sofa into a makeshift bed. She felt a tinge of embarrassment at having her mother-in-law sleep on the sofa, again, but Janie wouldn't have any of it. "No, no. Not to worry, Sweetie. I've slept in worse places before."

"Hmm. I bet there's a story, there."

"Yeah . . ." Janie said with a smirk, "but not for tonight. No, you guys get a good night's sleep, now. You're still recovering from all that traveling." When they'd gotten the bed made up, she hugged Elizabeth tightly. "It's so good to have you back, Sweetie. And I don't mean that the kids were trouble, or anything. They weren't. They were pretty damned good for me, actually. I mean . . . you're really *back*. We were starting to lose you, for a while, there."

Elizabeth could have laughed or cried, she wasn't sure which. Instead, she hugged Janie again. "Thanks, Mom."

22.

*"... Maybe I messed up. Sometimes, you know,
I just feel like I want to be on vacation from bein' sick."*

Life returned to some semblance of normalcy, at the Twin Sisters Community, U.S.A. Nate had scheduled some work that Steve could do while he and Elizabeth were away. Painting work—interior and exterior—on the addition they were finishing up for Jim and Barbara, in Pinos Altos. The couple had been very accommodating, allowing the guys to take a while longer in completing the job. But finally they were becoming impatient and wanted the job finished—apparently expecting a visit from their children over the summer. They were curious about Nate and Elizabeth's experience in Brazil, though. And demanded that they come over for dinner some evening, so that they could debrief them about the trip.

Elizabeth, over the past year or so, had cut way back on her silversmithing work, and now only did enough of it to keep some of her jewelry for sale in the co-op gallery in town. She had more time, now, to work in the garden and rest. And more time to help Luke, with additional schoolwork—to get him ready for the public school. Gradually, the magical reality they'd experienced in Adelândia faded more and more into the background, though Elizabeth was vigilant in following the protocol for healing that José had suggested.

One thing that broke the mundane daily routine that life had returned to, early in the summer, was a surprise visit from Beverly. She was now part owner of a modest beauty salon in Black Mountain, North Carolina. And Beverly had made plans, ahead of time, to fly out to New Mexico and surprise Elizabeth. Nate had been made aware of her visit, beforehand—she actually discussed it with him before the trip to Brazil. But Elizabeth only heard about it three days before her arrival. Beverly's flight landed in Albuquerque close to midday on the second of July, in time for the Fourth of July weekend. Not wanting to be any burden, she'd arranged for a rental car at the airport so she could show up right at their doorstep.

Late in the afternoon, Beverly drove her little rental car into the driveway, honking the horn (or rather, beeping it) a couple of times. Nobody was home. She unloaded her bags and lugged them over to the door of the earthship. A half hour later—while Beverly prowled around the garden to see what they were growing—Elizabeth drove up with the boys, back from town where she'd been running errands. Elizabeth noticed the car in the driveway and figured Beverly must have arrived . . . *Earlier than I thought* . . . She grabbed a shopping bag out of the back seat, when she glanced over at the garden. "Bev!"

Beverly clambered over a loosely stretched section of chicken-wire fence, smiling at the little group piling out of the Volvo. She muttered something and rubbed her leg, glancing back at the garden fence. Her smile returned as she reached the trio, and she hugged Elizabeth tightly. "*Hey,* girl!" She grabbed Joey next and gave him a bear hug. "Hey there, Baby! My God . . . look at these guys." She hugged Luke a bit more formally.

"Yep," Elizabeth said, "the young 'uns aren't so young anymore. Hey, are you okay? It looked like maybe our magnificent fence caught you, there. You all right?"

"Yeah. Nothing much. It didn't really catch me . . . just caught my nylons." She turned her leg to reveal a long run on her calf. "They were about done, anyway."

Elizabeth frowned for a second. "Oh, I'm sorry, Bev. That fence is a nuisance. It does more, for catching *us,* than it does for keepin' out the rabbits and pocket gophers. But why in the *world* are you wearing nylons to our place in New Mexico? What were you *thinking,* girl?"

"Well, I'm just a city girl, I guess. And I wanted to look nice—this morning—doing the airport and airline thing. Trying to look professional, or something. Ha!" Beverly grabbed one of the shopping bags, and they walked around the old trailer toward the earthship. As they walked through the shade of the large piñon pine, she remarked on how much cooler it felt, considering it was Fourth of July weekend.

"Yeah," Elizabeth said. "No kiddin'. I remember, for sure—about how hot and sticky the summers can be, back East. Even in Asheville. I don't miss *that* a bit. Here, when you step into the shade, you know it."

"For sure," Beverly said. As they reached the door of the earthship, she was saying something about a guy who sat next to her on the flight from Atlanta to Albuquerque. "Really cute guy. I might just look him up, while I'm here. I gave him your phone number, here—I hope you don't mind. He lives somewhere near Santa Fe. Some kind of engineer type. I didn't get all o' that . . . about what-all he *does*, I mean."

Elizabeth noticed a touch of her own southern drawl slipping back into her speech—making humid, lazy diphthongs out of simple vowels. "O-ka-ey. A hunky sorta guy, I s'pose? Huh?". . . *Boy, I slide right back into it like molasses, whenever she's around* . . . "We gotta get caught up on stuff, girl."

Earlier in the day, Nate had brought his trout fishing gear with him to work. He had a hunch he might be finished by mid-afternoon and thought it would do him good to get out on a stream . . . *If I can get done early enough* . . . Beverly would be arriving in the afternoon—no doubt she and Elizabeth would have plenty to talk about, and probably needed girl-time together.

The remodel job in Pinos Altos was essentially completed. Behind schedule, but finished—except for a few final details. Details that Jim and Barbara just might want to see finished, Nate thought . . . *Like getting these damn doors hung, for instance. People like to have doors in doorways. They're funny, that way* . . . That in itself was a minor operation—they were pre-hung doors that they'd taken off of the hinges in order to paint them. There were also the doorknobs and lock hardware to install, as well as hardware for the windows. And electrical switch and receptacle covers to install. Steve had taken a few days off, before the holiday, to visit some friends in Texas.

After Nate finished screwing the last switch cover into place, he looked around the rooms for anything he might have missed. And thought with satisfaction that the job was well done, and the customers would be happy . . . *It looks good. Damned good* . . . Jim and Barbara were out of town this weekend, but he knew they'd be pleased and would settle with him soon on the final payment. He wolfed down a sandwich he'd brought, and loaded up a few tools along with some leftover lumber into his pickup, humming a tune he'd listened to on the cassette player, earlier. Neil Young—*Everybody Knows This Is Nowhere*. He made sure every door at Jim's house was locked, and left.

It was half-past two as he drove on the curvy two-lane road—Highway 15—passing the entrance to Twin Sisters. He decided not to stop in at the house for anything, but continued on the winding highway as it snaked its way up into the Gila Wilderness. Where the road finally reached the east fork of the Gila River, Nate slowed down, not decided on where he wanted to fish. There were several spots on the river, near here, where, after scrambling a few hundred yards downstream—away from the road—one could get to a some good trout pools. He parked the truck at one of his favorite parking turnouts, munched on some potato chips from the bottom of a bag, and stepped out.

The sun was still high, and bright, as he padded through a springy blanket of pine needles in the shade of a cluster of ponderosas. The numerous ponderosa pines, though—as well as willows near the river's edge—offered little or no shade to the middle of the river. The air smelled fresh and clean . . . *Man, I love being on this river. Something about the air, here. Maybe it's true—what I've heard—about how there's negative ions near moving water. And it affects people's mood. Makes you feel good* . . . Though there was little shade on the water, and they weren't ideal conditions for trout fishing, Nate still felt optimistic about his chances . . . *They could be biting, if there's an insect hatch going on. Never can tell—at least I can't. But I'll damned sure give it a try* . . .

There wasn't any need to hurry, in getting back home. Nate suspected his culinary talents weren't going to be necessary that evening, unless the women wanted him to do some grilling in the barbeque pit they'd built. He was fly-fishing, today. His favorite kind of fishing, lately. Part of the satisfaction of it wasn't necessarily in catching fish, but in getting the fly to land on the surface in just the right spot. It took patience and skill to do this—and was somehow meditative, usually quieting his thoughts.

When the sun sank a little lower, finally there was a little feeding action going on at the surface of the river. He caught, and released, two trout, both fairly small. A brook trout, and a Rio Grande cutthroat. He was able to get the hook out easily, with both, and released them quickly. Though he felt satisfied with the fishing this afternoon, he sat down on a boulder at the water's edge and gazed at the river listlessly . . . *What the hell's wrong with me? Why am I feeling so crummy?* . . . Nate almost never kept the trout he caught, unless they were of a noteworthy size. And he never kept the cutthroats at all—since they were an endangered species, and if you kept one you could face a really hefty fine. He always felt good releasing the fish, so they could live another day. He felt good about the construction job, good about being finished with it, and good about the fishing this afternoon. But there was a nagging sadness in the background.

Nate gathered up his gear and trudged up a small knoll—a promontory on the ridge overlooking the water. And sat down beneath a large ponderosa. It was cool in the shade, no doubt due to the elevation being higher, here, than anywhere around town. Pleasant. He sat quietly and closed his eyes, trying to decipher, within himself, where the sad feelings were coming from. It eluded him. Life was good. Elizabeth seemed to love him, despite his character flaws and eccentricity. She seemed to be recovered from the cancer—he felt there was a very good chance it was gone entirely, now. The kids were great. Of course they made all the usual mistakes—in growing up—but seemed to be acquiring good values. And the fishing had been good. Everything it needed to be . . . *But, huh . . . something about the fishing . . .*

He remembered his experience at the Casa de Dom Francisco—and how his father had been showing him how to cast out his fishing line. During that odd dream—or vision—that he had after he blacked out. It came to him that he genuinely missed his father—or something about his father. Maybe it was just something as simple as what the psychology people referred to as "closure," on what felt like an unfinished relationship.

In his late teens, while Nate had gotten more heavily into smoking weed and drinking, he'd heard from his father's second wife about the man's illness. But he made no attempt to see him before his death. Granted, he didn't know at the time that his father's illness was terminal and that he wasn't long for this world. But now a tight, heavy knot grew in his stomach as he remembered how callous he'd been.

His father had always seemed aloof—absorbed in his work with the investment firm. But had always been generous with Nate, at least, in terms of providing him with material things. In fact, his parents had spoiled him, growing up as an only child, tending to give him most anything he wanted. And, as Nate got older—long after his parents' divorce—his father set up a trust fund to provide for him in the future. Maybe (like Mac had said once, when they'd been talking about it) Nate's father actually did love him, but just wasn't capable of showing it aside from helping him financially.

Nate's parents had divorced when he was a junior in high school, in L.A. And he felt—at that time—a vague sense of betrayal and anger toward his dad. Their divorce brought up for him a distant, fuzzy memory of something he'd seen his father doing with a woman who wasn't his mother. At the time it had happened, there were no words or comprehension in his eight-year-old mind to process what he'd seen. But it gradually gelled, later, into some vague feelings of resentment and betrayal. Betrayal toward his mother, betrayal toward the family.

Sitting under the pine trees near the Gila River, as the water murmured below him, Nate realized that—for all of his teenage years and all of his adult life—he had never liked his father. At some point, had decided he was a traitor. Hated him. And yet, something inside had shifted after that peculiar experience at the Casa in Brazil. He heard in his father's voice, there—and knew, with a body knowledge—that his father loved him. Loved him profoundly, though in this world it was in a bumbling, inept way. He had felt that love wash over him and flow through him. And Nate accepted—during that experience—that his dad was just another flawed man, another human being trying to make his way in a baffling world. And doing so without having the instruction manual and only a piss-poor map.

The water babbled merrily in the background, as Nate thought about his father dying alone in a hospital room. Maybe his stepchildren didn't even come to see him. And Nate, the man's only flesh and blood, had refused when he'd been asked to come visit. Nate felt the knot in his stomach unraveling as a searing heat came to his eyes. The tears welled up and overflowed. He cried for a few minutes. "I'm sorry, Dad. . . . I'm *sorry*." Nate cried more, sobbing for nearly ten minutes. And then knew it was enough. That somehow he was understood. That maybe his father understood—or even that God understood. And it was all okay . . . *That's what I went fishing for, today . . . And I can go home now . . .*

In the early dusk under the trees, Nate gathered up his fishing gear and walked slowly to where he'd parked the truck, in what seemed like many hours earlier. His father's love, which he'd felt undeniably during that odd dream experience at the Casa . . . *Or maybe it was a visitation? Is that possible? Huh . . . It feels like something's melted, inside of me. Some frozen, hard spot. I've been a sick puppy—but I'm getting better. I actually miss the guy . . .* He sat motionless in the truck for a couple of minutes, seeming to stare far past the dashboard in front of him. Then started it up and switched the headlights on. As he drove the winding, darkening highway down toward home, he recalled another time he and his father had gone fishing. When he was thirteen . . . *Yeah, that was fun, Dad. Good one . . . that day we went out to Catalina Island, off the coast. Ocean fishing. Man, that was way fun. Thanks for reminding me . . .*

It was completely dark by the time Nate pulled into the driveway, with stars out. He shut off the engine, gazing at the earthship. The window-wall of the earthship glowed with light from inside, its sparkling slanted glass wall looking like the outer wall of a Frank Lloyd Wright house on acid. But it felt like home. Through the screen door, Nate heard the muffled sound of laughter from within—Elizabeth and Beverly must be catching up on news and telling stories . . . *And hopefully not with me being the source of amusement . . .* When he walked into the kitchen, he hugged Beverly tightly. Elizabeth was doing something at the kitchen sink, and he draped his arms around her, kissing her on the back of the neck.

"I was telling Bev," she said, "about how freaked-out you were when José was cutting me open, on the stage at the Casa."

. . . Aha . . . they really were telling stories about me . . . He glanced at Beverly, whose face was shining. "Oh, I was freaked, all right. You must have heard that, from those folks from Taos?"

"Yes I did."

"Well, any guy in his right mind would've been a little perturbed, I think. . . . You—my wife—being cut open on the stage . . . with this odd smile on your face."

"I know," Elizabeth said, giggling, "and I'm not really poking fun at you, but—"

"Oh, yes you are. But I'm sure it did look a little funny—my reaction, I mean." He looked at Beverly, who smiled innocently, as she tipped up the bottle of beer she was drinking. Corona beer. "So how *are* ya, Bev? It's good to see you."

"Good to see you, too, Nate. I'm doin' good, thanks."

It didn't bother him, that she was drinking. She always appeared to be a normal drinker, and he'd never seen her drunk. Or maybe just once, at the party after their wedding. Nate found that he was often okay around social drinking. It was just being around hard-core drinking—drinking to get drunk—that made him uncomfortable. He glanced at Elizabeth and noticed that sitting on the counter next to her was a brown bottle. A look of confusion came over his face. *"Liz? Are you drinking?"*

"Well, yeah . . . I just thought I'd have a beer, with Bev." She turned back to what she was doing at the sink, washing some lettuce from the garden.

"But, I thought that, well . . . You know, it's part of the diet—that they wanted you to follow—was, uh, no *alcohol."*

Elizabeth glanced at him with what looked to him to be a phony smile. "Well, you know . . . I think they meant no, like, regular—or daily—drinking. I'm just havin' a brew with Bev, here, this evening."

Nate raised his eyebrows, looking at her solemnly. "Uh . . . *no,* Liz. I'm pretty damned sure they meant *no* alcohol. *Period.* That's the way I understood it, from Dawn. And Paulo said the same thing. About the diet."

"Well, I didn't think it was any big deal if I had a beer with Bev."

"I don't *know,* Liz. I don't think they were kiddin' around, when they said that stuff. . . . Something to do with the long-term healing process."

"I don't get it," Beverly said. "How can just having a little beer affect Liz's healing that much?"

Nate exhaled audibly. "You had to *be* there, Bev. To understand. I don't know. There's, like . . . some long-distance healing, that continues, when you go home. Isn't that right, Liz?" He gazed at Elizabeth with an almost pleading expression. "Didn't you *get* that? From talking with the people there? That the Entities continue to work on people, even after they've gone home?"

Elizabeth looked at him bashfully. "I don't know. Maybe you're right. But it's not like I'm drinking and smoking—or going out partying every night. But maybe I messed up."

"Well," Nate said, "I think it *is* a mistake, Liz. But it's *your* recovery—and your healing. . . . Seems like maybe you're being a little too casual about this."

Beverly cleared her throat—and Nate knew her well enough to know that she'd come to Elizabeth's defense in most anything they might argue about. He shot her an annoyed glance but she interrupted anyway. "Oh, come on, now, Nate. I just picked up a six-pack on my way here from town. I didn't think twice about it. It's a holiday weekend, for God's sake. We're only talking about a couple of beers."

"She's had a *couple* of beers?" Elizabeth had her back turned toward him. Nate realized, for a moment, how absurd and prudish this sounded—coming from someone who used to get tanked on a daily basis. And yet he was raising his voice in frustration. "I'm tellin' ya, you had to *be* there, Bev. To even know what I'm *talkin'* about. You can't possibly understand—without going down to Adelândia and experiencing it for yourself. See . . . the healing that the Entities, or spirits, do . . . well, it's often long-term healing that continues after you leave the Casa. Isn't that *right,* Liz?" Elizabeth didn't answer. "The diet, and the herb tea, and the meditation—is all about changing our habits and lifestyle. And living in a more spiritual, God-oriented way. Staying away from alcohol—and other drugs, too—is a part of that."

Beverly had a somewhat confused or surprised expression on her face, when Nate glanced at her . . . *I don't care what she thinks—if she thinks I've gone religious or something. Or if she's never heard me talk like this before. She's hearin' it now* . . . Then, apparently addressing Elizabeth's back, he said, "I just want the *best* for ya, Babe. It's all I've ever wanted. And I don't think this is gonna *help.*"

Elizabeth turned, with pursed lips, placing a salad bowl on the table—and looked for a few moments at Nate. "Sorry, Honey. Maybe you're right. Maybe I messed up. Sometimes, you know, I just feel like I want to be on vacation from bein' sick." Beverly gazed at the two of them in silence. And sipped the last of her beer.

Nate looked from his wife down to a spot on the floor. He sighed, and said, with a lowered tone to his voice, "I know, Liz. I know."

Dinner was subdued, for a while. At least it was till the boys started acting up, where they were sitting over on the couch. Joey was getting scolded by his older brother, for playing with his food—pushing it around on his plate, according to Luke's report. Beverly looked at the kids, halfway smiling. "Don't you boys be makin' a mess for your mama, now! And I've gotta sleep on that couch tonight, you know."

By the time the women were clearing off the table, they were happily chatting again—something to do with Beverly's trouble with local politics in the mountains of North Carolina. Nate took the boys outside into the cool evening air, where they set up a broken drainpipe, leaning it against the cement blocks of the barbeque pit. As soon as the women came outside, they used this to fire off a number of bottle-rockets and a couple of Roman candles.

Beverly's visit over the holiday weekend seemed a breath of fresh air to Elizabeth, if not quite so well received by Nate. Beverly was down to earth. There was nothing overly clever, intellectual, or flaky about her—the way Elizabeth felt sometimes about some of her female friends in New Mexico. And as usual she was sad to see her friend head back to Albuquerque to catch her flight back East.

23.

*"... Sometimes, the whole thing seems unbelievable
—almost like we were in a dream-world, there."*

Two weeks after Beverly left, Elizabeth had her scheduled appointment with Andi Sheaffer at the Complimentary Medicine Center in Santa Fe. Nate decided he would go up north with her and help with the driving. Ben, another old friend of theirs from Santa Fe, had offered to have them stay over at his house in town. Elizabeth's appointment was on Monday—and though she knew how Nate felt about churches (or temples, for that matter)—she wanted to hear Ben's sermon at the church where he was pastoring, now, in Santa Fe. So they drove up on Saturday, intending to visit Ben's church on Sunday morning. And see a couple other friends, before her doctor's appointment the following day.

At the ten o' clock morning service of Christ The Redeemer church, Ben's sermon was based on Paul's book, 1 Corinthians. Ben talked about love—and referred several times to a specific chapter in that book of the New Testament. Elizabeth had never—in their spiritual and religious conversations with him, in the past—heard him talk much at all about love. But this morning he did. In fact, most any religious discussion with him, whether referring to Old Testament or New, often sounded harsh. But that was actually familiar to Elizabeth—she had, after all, grown up as a girl in the southern Appalachians, regularly attending a southern Baptist church. This was one of the first times she realized that the Apostles might very well have felt compassion and love as she experienced it. Instead of fearfully harping on what the sinner needed to do in order to avoid being cast into some eternal "lake of fire."

After completing the sermon, Ben motioned to several elderly people who were sitting in the front rows, and Elizabeth was surprised when he led them over to the pew where she sat with Nate. The people sitting near them stood up, as if on cue, and moved aside to make room. And these four elderly, kind-looking people—two men and two women—came and stood with Ben next to Elizabeth. With a calm, affectionate look at Elizabeth, Ben motioned for her to stand up as he talked about healing—the way it was described in the book of James. One of the women dabbed something oily on Elizabeth's forehead. And then these four, with Ben, all held hands, encircling her, while they closed their eyes and prayed. For Elizabeth, and for her healing. She glanced at Nate, who sat on the bench looking somewhat ill at ease. She looked back to the elders, standing around her, praying—and she gently closed her eyes also, as she felt a warm sensation all over her body . . . *They really care about me. And they don't even know me . . .*

Ben's son, David, had been their eldest son Luke's best and oldest friend from way back in their Santa Fe pre-school days. Nate and Elizabeth hadn't seen either of them (or Ben's ex-wife Beth, for that matter) in several years. After having lunch with them both—at a small downtown eatery that Ben recommended—Nate and Elizabeth drove over to Mac's house. They hadn't been able to reach him by phone, the week before, but were hoping to drop by and see him. They knocked on the door a few times, with no answer, when Mac's neighbor (whom Nate had met once before) came over and told them that he'd gone overseas. In fact, was traveling in India.

Nate looked at the man with an deadpan expression. *"India?* Are you sure?"

The neighbor was certain of it. "Yeah, I'm not sure whereabouts he was going, though."

"India! I'll be damned. Never would've thunk it. Was he chasing some girl, there?"

"I don't know. Said he was going there for several weeks. Some couple—I don't know who they were—they came and picked him up to go to the airport."

"I'll be damned."

Later in the afternoon, they spent time with Elizabeth's silversmithing mentor. John—though she often referred to him, out of his earshot, as "Navajo John." He and his wife Maria lived off of the highway south of the city, near the old town of Cerrillos. Since Elizabeth hadn't seen him in nearly five years—and had at one time been very fond of him—they visited for a couple of hours. And then were talked into having dinner there.

When they arrived back at Ben's house, he seemed almost sloppy in his happiness to see them. They had called from Navajo John's house to say they wouldn't be back at Ben's for dinner. But it was apparent Ben had gone to some trouble to prepare a nice dinner, though they hadn't talked about it earlier. His wife Beth had left him two years earlier— though they hadn't divorced—and Elizabeth sensed that he was longing for some female company . . . *Or maybe any kind of company at all . . .* No doubt it had been hard caring for their son, David, though the boy did regularly spend weekends with his mother in Texas.

They sat down with Ben, having tea and coffee. And apple pie that he'd picked up somewhere. Ben had heard, through a mutual friend, of Nate and Elizabeth's trip to Brazil. And he listened attentively as they described a few events that they'd seen and experienced there. Elizabeth mentioned how Joseph of God was referred to—by himself and by others around him—as a medium. And about how the Entities, or spirits, actually performed most all of the healing work done at the Casa. As she spoke, it seemed as if a curtain came down over Ben's eyes, and his expression changed to one of patience and even concern.

Elizabeth took a sip of her tea. "You don't quite believe any of this, do you?"

"No, really . . . I'm listening," he said. "All ears! Actually, I've heard of this guy before."

As she spoke about her own experience—with the invisible surgeries, and then her visible surgery—Ben absently flipped through the pages of a book that was lying on the coffee-table, though his eyes rarely left Elizabeth. He wore a slight smile—maybe of sympathy, maybe of patience, it seemed to Elizabeth . . . *Huh. Almost like he doesn't want to hear what I'm saying. That's odd . . .* She continued describing about how the use of the herb mixture had to be maintained, and the diet—and that the Entities could continue working on a person long after they'd gone home.

Nate got up, stretched, and said he wanted to go see what David (Ben's son) was working on. Wanted to see what he was doing in the kitchen. After Nate left the room, there was a minute or two of silence, broken only by muffled conversation from the kitchen.

Ben spoke, with what now seemed to be a look of concern—his forehead furrowed and his eyes serious. "I see . . . Yeah, I've heard of this guy . . . who you call *Joseph of God.*" To Elizabeth's ears, his pronunciation of the man's name sounded a bit disdainful. "I've heard of him, in the clerical circles. I think the Catholic Church in Brazil has tried to shut him down, a few times."

"Yes," Elizabeth said. "So I've heard."

"And a few doctors—medical people—have also wanted to shut him down."

"Yep. Heard that, too. But, I think in both cases they're pretty much afraid of losing something. Like, I don't know . . . maybe they consider him a bit of a threat."

"Well," Ben said, "I can't imagine he's really that much of a threat to the Catholic Church." He grinned for a moment. "But who knows? The Catholic Church has, at times, felt some kind of a threat from us Pentecostal-Christian folks, too. For treading on their turf."

"I 'spect so."

It was quiet for a few moments, except for the sound of talking going on in the kitchen. Ben cleared his throat, "Ah, can I ask if—when this man, Joseph, was doing all these healing maneuvers—if he ever used the name of Christ? Or Jesus?"

Elizabeth smirked a bit, not noticing a serious intent behind Ben's questions. "Well, of course I don't really speak Portuguese. I mean, I don't speak it worth a darn . . . just a few basic words and sentences. But our friend, Dawn, who was there with us . . . she told me that at the end of each healing session, he usually says, 'By the power of Jesus Christ, and God's will, you are healed.' But I couldn't tell whether or not he always said that. Like I was sayin'—*muy poquito* Portuguese."

"Interesting. And this man has no real religious training or anything."

"No. Apparently not. He came from a very poor family—was brought up Catholic, I beleive. And he was a tailor, before he was called to do this healing work." Elizabeth didn't feel put off by Ben's questioning. Or feel any need to be defensive, in describing their experiences in Brazil. But she knew some people—her husband included—considered Ben very opinionated, especially regarding religious or spiritual topics.

Elizabeth, though, had always liked him—and respected his passion and training in Theology, Bible Study, and Christian philosophy. Maybe partly due to the fact that her father was an academic, teaching at the university in Asheville. And Ben was another product of academia, having earned a Masters in Bible Study. Maybe it came from childhood memories of frequently going to church on Sundays with her mother—and showing respect to the preacher. At any rate, the combination of the genteel southern accent from his upbringing in Georgia—and his ability to discuss in depth most any part of the Bible—never felt challenging or uncomfortable to her. Closer to the opposite, actually—talking with Ben felt like touching base with someone from home. A lot like her friendship with Beverly.

Once she got over her initial sense of Ben's skepticism—regarding Brazil—Elizabeth was comfortable again, and they talked at length about goings-on back home in the South. Nate came back into the den and joined them for a while, helping himself to another slice of pie. Later, Ben cleared away a few plates, saying he had to prod David to get ready for bed. When he came back, their conversation turned toward differences between the Southwest and the Southeast. And about difficulties in raising kids—with some semblance of a moral compass— in a society that often seemed to be more and more bereft of morals. Nate didn't seem to have much to add to the conversation and finally said he needed to turn in. He said his goodnights—glancing at Elizabeth for a moment—and disappeared down the hallway to the guest bedroom.

As they continued talking for a while, Ben steered the conversation back to Elizabeth's healing experiences in Brazil. Clearing his throat, he gazed at her with a serious expression and then stared down at his coffee mug. "I'm bein' straight up with you, Liz . . . I mean, this is some interesting stuff . . . but I'd have to say it *worries* me, a little. As a Christian—and as a Christian pastor. This talk about these 'Entities.'. . . And these 'Entities' being the spirits of dead people, helpin' this guy to do healing work. Certainly the Bible is full of stories of healings . . . especially those done by Christ and the Apostles. But there's also a lot of warning, in the Bible, about mediums—people who 'call up the dead.' The books of Moses, and Samuel, and Isaiah . . . well, they're chock-full of stories about sorcerers and mediums who used the spirits of the dead. What was called 'familiar spirits.'"

"Uh-huh."

"And God warns us—in these books—not to use these kinds of powers. Or have *anything* to do with the people who use them."

Elizabeth sighed and shifted herself on the couch. "Oh, come on now, Ben. This sounds a bit like Salem witchcraft-trial stuff. And isn't all of this pretty much Old Testament talk? . . . Really ancient, fearful stuff that has little or nothing to do with Christianity?"

"Well," he said, "there's no doubt it is old. *Ancient.* . . . but it *is* the word of God."

"Uh-huh. Well, I'd better call it a night, Ben. Gettin' kind of late— and I've got to get to my appointment tomorrow morning. Good talking with ya, tonight. And we enjoyed the church service today. I'll see you in the morning."

"Okay. Good night, Liz."

Carrying her half-cup of tepid tea with her, Elizabeth padded in stocking-feet down the hallway to the extra bedroom. She shook her head, almost imperceptibly . . . *Good Lord, he sounds a little negative, there. I don't really want to get him goin' on that topic. I think he misses Beth . . . Poor guy . . .*

The next morning, at her appointment with Andi Sheaffer, Elizabeth explained to her some of the events that had occurred at the Casa in Brazil. The doctor didn't express any opinion regarding the healing work being done there—said that she had only read an article once about Joseph of God.

"You know, Elizabeth, when you called me, a month and a half ago—to tell me you were going down to Brazil—I spoke with an associate of mine in the city here. One of his patients, you see, had gone down there to visit this same healer. My associate heard good things about the healing center in Brazil. But I don't know what the ultimate results were. And, for myself, I just haven't learned enough about it to have formed any real opinion . . ." The doctor felt it important to set up an appointment for Elizabeth to get the usual periodic imaging work done, at the Women's Health Clinic in Las Cruces.

A week later, Andi Sheaffer called Elizabeth at home. She'd been sent the results of the imaging she ordered. The doctor sounded excited, over the phone, explaining that the radiology and ultrasound reports didn't show any tumors at all, though the sonography showed some recent scar tissue. "It looks like you've been doing the right things, Elizabeth. I'm very pleased with these results—just keep doing what you've been doing. Let's stick with the diet you're following, and we'll keep you on the Tamoxifen, for the time being. I'm fairly optimistic about this—but I'll feel much better if we have the same results six months from now." As she hung up the phone, Elizabeth wiped away a tear . . . *My gosh, it's been a long haul . . . This. Maybe I can get back to living, now . . .*

That evening just before dinner, when Elizabeth talked to Nate, he grabbed her in a bear hug. "Oh, I'm so *glad,* Sweetie."

"It's great, isn't it? Maybe we can get back to a normal life, now."

"A *normal* life?"

She giggled, tickling his side. "Well, something akin to normal. It's all relative, isn't it? But I still don't feel like I'm strong enough to go back to doing my silver work, full-time."

"No," Nate said, "and I don't think you should. We're getting by, okay, on what Steve and I are doing. I think we still better plan on going back to the Casa. Brazil. Maybe in September? You think? Make sure the healing's completed, like José suggested? Mid-September might be a good time to go."

"Oh, Honey . . . I don't really think it's necessary. I feel like I'm completely healed. I mean, I'm so sure of it that I stopped taking the herb mixture from the Casa last week."

Nate frowned. "Huh?"

"Don't get me wrong . . . I think our trip down to Brazil was very helpful in my recovery, but I really think I'm all better now. . . . And besides, it'll be *so* expensive for us to go down there again."

"Well, shit, Liz . . . it's a small price to pay, in the big picture." Nate rubbed his forehead, as if he had a sudden headache. "I really think we *should* visit José, again. And certainly not just because he *said* so—you know I don't like being told what to do. I just think the healing work you did there was *critical*. It's not just a goddamn coincidence that your ultrasound came back negative, now. And I wish you hadn't quit, on using the herbs from the Casa—didn't you feel like that was still helping? Like some kind of healing work was still being done?"

"I don't know," Elizabeth said. "I haven't felt like there was any more healing work going on, for quite some time. Since we left Brazil, actually. For real. And, when I think about it, doesn't it seem kind of bizarre—that these Entities would continue working on me, after I'd come home from the Casa? Sometimes, the whole thing seems unbelievable—almost like we were in a dream-world, there."

"But," Nate continued, his eyes pleading now. "You saw the same miraculous stuff there, that I did. And you experienced it—for yourself—even more than I did. I don't get it. You know this stuff actually happened . . . and that it was real. *Don't you?*"

"Well, yeah," she said. Some part of her felt noncommittal about it, though. Ambivalent. "But, you know—since we've been back in the States—it sometimes seems like everything that happened down there was strange. Almost otherworldly. Like we were in a trance, you know?"

Nate looked at her, confusion and concern written all over his face. "I don't know, Liz. It seems like since we got back, you've been acting more and more casual about continuing your recovery. Like you just don't care anymore. Getting halfway tanked, with Beverly, a couple of times . . . quitting with the herb mixture. And I s'pose Ben scared you a bit, too—about Brazil—with some of his biblical crap. I'm sure *that* didn't help."

"Oh, come on. Leave him out of this."

"Really! I just don't know what's up with you lately, Liz. It's almost like you *want* to get sick again."

"*Fuck you,* Nathan. Fuck you. That is *not* fair."

"Well, I just don't get it. I mean, if I was as sick as you were . . . and had the same amazing recovery as you've had . . . and saw other miraculous shit, like we both did at the Casa—well, I'd just keep doing what worked. Even if it looked *weird,* to other people. Or if it didn't fit in with other people's understanding of the world—SO WHAT?! *Fuck* 'em! Why are you *doing* this?"

Elizabeth shoved him back a step. She turned away, her eyes beginning to burn. "What the hell do *you* know, anyway, about what I've been going through? For you, this has just been some kind of interesting metaphysical *adventure.* I'm the one who's had a tumor in my breasts—a cancer that's trying to eat me alive. You're a *bastard,* Nate!" She stormed out of the kitchen to their bedroom at the far end of the house . . . *The bastard. Why's he picking on me? He can't imagine . . .*

Nate finished up cooking up what Elizabeth had started, on the stove. The boys ate dinner with their father, at the kitchen table. Luke wondered why their mom wasn't eating with them.

"Your mom is mad at me, guys. We were arguing. She'll be all right. I'll bring some dinner in to her, later. She needs to be alone for a little while. You guys just finish up what's on your plate, now."

A while later, in stocking-feet, Nate quietly walked into their bedroom, carrying a plate. He cleared his throat. Elizabeth lay on the bed, on her side, in a fetal position. Nate sat on the bed beside her, setting the plate down, and gently put his hand on her hip. "I'm so sorry, Lizzie. I don't have any business talkin' like that."

"Damn right," she mumbled, without moving. Her face was reddened, damp with tears. And she was tired.

"I guess I'm just scared, Sweetie. But I'm *so* glad about the tests coming back negative. I'm just afraid of this shit coming back. I'm still scared of losing you."

"I know. I'm doing the best I can."

24.

. . . a likeable guy when he wasn't busy being a minister.

Elephant Butte Lake is the largest lake in New Mexico though it is
technically a reservoir—a dammed-up section of the Rio Grande. The
lake is usually impressive, but the waterline was low this week, lower
than the time when Ben had been there once before. On that previous
occasion it was springtime, when the Rio Grande runs high from the
melting snows in New Mexico's mountain ranges.

Ben thought it would be a great place to take a short father-and-son
vacation, at this time in mid-August, a couple of weeks before school
would start. His son David had never been there before and was
impressed with the place, never having seen a large lake before. Ben
reminded him that he and David's mom had taken him down to the South
Carolina coast once, when they were visiting family back East. But the
boy couldn't remember it.

Being a Protestant pastor from the Southwest, Ben had use of the
facilities at The Galilee Christian Retreat Center on the lake. They
camped there—the first time David had ever been camping—with Ben
showing him how to set up the two-man nylon tent he'd brought. They
pitched the tent under a couple of large piñon pines, set back from the
circular drive around the camping area. They had the campground—in
fact, the entire retreat center—to themselves, at this time around the
middle of the week. After a day and a half at Elephant Butte—and a dose
of sunburn—they drove down to visit Nate and Elizabeth and family. A
little further south, and west. David chattered in excitement about seeing
their new house for the first time and his old playmate, Luke.

≈   ≈   ≈   ≈   ≈

Nate pulled into the driveway, mid-afternoon. He'd been able to leave work early—and would have plenty of time to clean up a few tools he'd left lying around the house, as he'd promised. Elizabeth had said—that morning—that she'd need help getting the place ready for company. She was going to "clean up the house a bit." Nate suspected that this translated as "cleaning frenzy," and she'd be unhappy if he didn't do his share. She'd already begun cleaning—sweeping, using the vacuum cleaner, and mopping the floors—when he walked in.

When she saw him she smiled, in between mop strokes. "That's great, Honey," she said. "I was wonderin' if you'd get home in time." She motioned, with her head, toward the main bedroom. "It's still a mess in there. You and your never-ending projects!" Nate still hadn't finished the planter box along the window-wall in the main bedroom. The planter box—built of mortar and recycled aluminum cans—would eventually recycle "gray-water" from the shower and bathroom sink, using it to water plants in the long masonry box.

He'd already finished the planter box near the main entrance, on the west side of the earthship—the planter box that used "gray-water" reclaimed from the kitchen sink to water a few plants they'd put in. A couple of dwarf lemon trees, ferns, and an indoor trellis up next to the glass with jasmine and Bougainvillea vines climbing it—all of which thrived on the dirty sink water.

Nate gathered up most of the tools around the bedroom construction area and put them into the tool-shed outside. While Elizabeth mopped the floors, now working on the hallway and the bathroom, he came back in to sweep up around his dirty indoor masonry job. As he swept, an astringent odor of cement dust filled the air . . . *Ecchh . . . I'm not looking forward to this . . . this visit . . .*

He glanced at Elizabeth, "I know you like Ben, Sweetie—and God knows David was the best friend Luke ever had, for years—but I sorta hope they don't stay too long. Did Ben say whether or not he had to be back in Santa Fe for the Sunday service?"

"I don't think he said, for sure. He said he might have found someone to fill in for him."

"Uhh . . . that doesn't sound too definite."

"Oh, come on, Hon' . . . he's okay. I like Ben. I like hearin' him talk—he reminds me of some "good ol' boy" from back home."

"Yeah, I know." Nate sighed. "He just kind of rubs me the wrong way . . . a little too preachy. There's a bit of that 'holier than thou' thing, going on there."

"Holier than *you,* anyway, huh? . . . He make you feel guilty about something?"

. . . *Huh. Maybe so* . . . "No, not really. I'm sure some of the lousy things I've done, he's probably at least *thought* about doing."

"Well," Elizabeth said, "try to get along with him, okay? Even if it's only for Luke's sake. . . . Gosh, he and David were darned near inseparable when we lived up there."

"Yep. And, I mean, we *did* have some good times with those folks— Ben and Beth, and David. But man, now that Beth's gone . . . I realize I'm just not all that crazy about the guy."

"Yeah, I definitely miss Beth, too. Maybe she was, sort of, the better half of that relationship."

"Yep," Nate agreed, though not wanting to sound emphatic about it. "And I think he probably knows it. Poor guy." He glanced behind him at the window. "Oh, for God's sake, they're *here* already! They're here *early.*"

Ben stood in the yard on the south side, with arms folded, gazing at the earthship's window-wall. Elizabeth quickly put away her mop bucket. The screen door banged—David came rushing in and hugged Elizabeth. He asked where Luke and Joey were and then trotted back outside to look for them.

Nate finished what he was doing and strolled out of the side door. He met Ben and shook hands with him. "What? You look surprised. . . . You haven't seen an earthship house, before?"

"No. Believe it or not, I haven't. There aren't that many of 'em, around Santa Fe . . . and the few that there are, are tucked away in the hills outside of the city. And I hardly ever get up to Taos—to see them up there."

"Yeah. True. There aren't that many of 'em around, period. Mostly just Taos. Well, let me take you around on the house tour . . ."

Luke and Joey both were glad to have a familiar playmate around for a couple of days. They hadn't seen David in years, though, and it took a good half hour before they were yelling and laughing like old friends.

On Saturday, they all took a trip up into the mountains to visit the Gila Cliff Dwellings. Luke and David raced ahead of everyone to be the first to climb up to the ruins. Elizabeth yelled after them, "You guys be *careful,* now. And you wait till we get there, before you climb up that ladder. I mean it!"

Later, in the evening, they had a barbeque dinner, sitting outside, with chicken grilled in Nate's barbeque pit, potato salad, and cornbread Elizabeth baked in the oven. After dinner, Nate fired off some bottle-rockets for the benefit of the kids—though he admitted to Ben that he had a bit of a pyromaniac streak in him when it came to fireworks. After it was completely dark and the kids had gone inside to play in their bedroom, the three adults sat around the fire and talked. The resinous incense odor of piñon pine smoke filled the air, in the cleared "front yard" of the earthship. Ben tilted back in the lawn chair he was sitting in, remarking about how clear the skies were—the stars so much brighter and clearer than in the urban skies around Santa Fe.

"Yeah," Nate said. "They sure don't have any kind of 'dark skies' ordinance, do they? Around Santa Fe, I mean. *Thousands* of streetlights. They're talking about that, up in Taos, you know—about having a ban on outdoor lighting that shines upward, lighting up the sky. So at least some of these New Mexico cities won't have a bunch of light pollution, at night. Like Albuquerque or Santa Fe do."

"I've heard of that," Ben said. "It's not a bad idea. Y'all are *so* lucky, you know? And blessed. Living in a beautiful part of the state. Being able to find work, here—and being able to live a simple life, off the grid. What a wonderful place."

They all seemed to have a good weekend visit—Nate included. Maybe it was due to the fact that Ben was out of his element—visiting friends in a country home, off the grid. But he seemed very relaxed and comfortable. In a quiet moment when Nate and Elizabeth were alone, he confessed that Ben was actually a likeable guy when he wasn't busy being a minister.

25.

. . . Strange. I've never heard of such powerful healing work going on . . . and on such a regular, daily, and weekly basis, like this. I don't get it . . .

Summer was officially over. Labor Day weekend had come and gone. It was mid-September, now—the cottonwoods, and the aspens at the higher elevations—were starting to turn. Luke was beginning to like the public school in Silver City, though the first week was touch and go. Tense, and a major adjustment for the boy, who'd been homeschooled for years. Ben called again from Santa Fe, with a silversmithing project that he wanted to talk to Elizabeth about—a project for the church. So he and David came to visit again, this weekend in early fall.

The days were getting noticeably shorter, and they arrived at the Twin Sisters Community after dark. Elizabeth fed the boys first. After the boys had left the table and were horsing around in the other room, the adults sat down to a late dinner. They'd finished eating (though Nate was helping himself to some seconds), when Ben brought up the topic of the church project.

"I hope this'll be something you'll be interested in doing, for us, Elizabeth." It was a simple yet creative and artistic project, which he said might be "right up her alley." He and members of the church vestry were in the midst of changing the altar of the church so that it had a more Southwestern feel to it—and had settled on the idea of a silver and turquoise crucifix. As it was, they had a large polished brass cross at the center of the altar. Ben asked Elizabeth about the feasibility of soldering silver designs, and adding turquoise, to this cross—essentially using it as a base structure for a new crucifix. He'd brought a full-scale drawing of the cross, which was about twenty-five inches tall and two and a half inches across at the base. He'd drawn it on a piece of cardboard—suggesting that she could use it as a template for designing the cross, if she was interested in taking on the project.

"What do you *think,* Liz? Is this at all interesting to ya? I mentioned, to the vestry and the church elders, about your amazing work as a silversmith—and we'd really be pleased to have you do it. If you want to. You could just about name your own price, and we'd be okay with it. Well . . . I mean, within reason."

Elizabeth looked at the cardboard drawing . . . *Hmm. Might be fun . . .* "Well," she said, "it sounds interesting. Why *me,* though? . . . Aren't there plenty of other silversmiths or jewelers around Santa Fe who might be interested in doing this? Might be more practical, for y'all to find someone local."

"Well, possibly," Ben said. "When I mentioned that I knew someone who did wonderful silver work, they asked who you were. I told them that you'd been to our Sunday service a couple of months ago. That we'd prayed for you and your healing at that service, and, well . . . some of them remembered you. We all decided we'd really like to have you do it—if you're interested."

"Oh, huh . . . I hope they're not thinking of me as a charity case."

"No. Not by a long shot. . . . Really."

Elizabeth's eyes sparkled and she sat up a little straighter in her chair. This would be the first semblance of a creative challenge in her silver work that she'd had in more than a year. Her jewelry making had become stale and repetitive, lately—and she'd been doing much less of it since her illness. "Well, I *have* seen silver soldered onto brass—and it can look *really* great if it's done well. But unfortunately brass doesn't solder very well—in fact it's pretty darned difficult—so I guess I'd try to have it be a really minimal design with as few solder points as possible." She reached over and dragged the cardboard drawing across the table, in front of her, grabbed a pencil and sketched lightly on it.

"Maybe there could be a large turquoise set in the center of the cross, with a little silver wire-work around it." She thought out loud while sketching. "Huh, yeah . . . and maybe a series of smaller turquoise 'cabochons' down the center of the vertical and horizontal axes . . . of the cross. Probably one-inch 'cabs,' down the middle, would be about the right size for this surface. This could look pretty cool." She glanced at Ben, who seemed to have a questioning look on his face.

"*Cabs?*" he asked.

"Yep, '*cabs*'—or cabuchons—is the name used for the way stones like turquoise are usually cut and polished. Sort of dome-shaped, with a flat back. I think that oval cabs would look best, for this cross." Elizabeth held the cardboard at arm's length, to see the drawing better. "I would tend to keep it simple . . . but this could look *really* nice. You said the cross you have is polished brass?"

Ben was smiling, now, propping his chin in his hand with an elbow on the table and watching Elizabeth do her problem solving. "Ah . . . yeah. Yes, Ma'am. It is."

"*Solid* brass?"

"Yes it is."

"Good. It could be soldered, then. I'd probably want to dull the brass finish first, though. Use a fine wire-brush on it—or an abrasive. It'll look a lot better, that way."

"Gotcha," he said.

Nate seemed content, watching the two discuss the project, while he quietly sipped from a coffee mug. He smiled at Elizabeth and got up, carrying a few plates and glasses over to the sink. And running some water into one half of the sink, he added dishwashing liquid and began to wash dishes.

"But, you know," Elizabeth said, "umm . . . a turquoise and silver design could look really *great* on brass, like this, but it's gonna take a *lot* of turquoise. Could be five hundred to a *thousand* dollars—just for the turquoise. But, umm . . . well, we could probably use Tibetan turquoise—which can still look darned good, and it might only cost *half* as much as Arizona or Nevada stones." She wrinkled her nose for an instant as she glanced at Ben. "Turquoise ain't cheap."

A wry smile crossed Ben's face. "Well, this sounds great. I guess I wasn't thinking—about how expensive that part of it might be—but I 'spect it'll be fine, to use the cheaper turquoise. And I'm glad . . . I guess I won't have to twist your arm too much. To get you interested in doin' this, I mean."

"*No.* I reckon not. Sounds like it'll be an interesting project . . . and a mite bit of a challenge."

"*Excellent!* I know you'll make the right decisions—about the turquoise and stuff. This'll be *great.*"

Ben led the service at the church in Santa Fe, Sunday morning—and stood in front of the congregation, partway through the service. He planned to introduce his sermon this morning—which he was ready to begin—by reading a passage from the book of Revelation. It was a stormy autumn morning—a change in the weather coming—and outside, ominous clouds cluttered the sky. A salvo of hail rattled on the roof of the church. Aside from the weather, for some reason Ben felt uneasy. He took a deep breath . . . *Let's see if I can carry the message, here* . . . The congregation seemed listless. The air inside the church felt stuffy, with a couple of women in the crowd fanning themselves.

The wind must have picked up outside. And it tore the clouds apart as the sun shone through for a moment and illuminated the stained-glass window behind the altar—igniting it, in fact. The only fancy window in the otherwise plain church. Out of the corner of his eye, Ben was startled by a dark shadow flapping on the outside of the colored glass. He wheeled around to look more closely at the window and realized it was some kind of large bird trying to get in. But, judging from the shadow, it must have had monstrous wings, too large for any normal bird.

. . . *What in the world?* . . . The flapping of its wings became frantic, now, and it broke through the glass, raining colored shards onto the carpet. And Ben saw instantly that the creature had some sort of leathery wings, with a huge wingspan, seven or eight feet . . . *This is impossible! Like a pterodactyl—that I saw in a book, once* . . . The thing seemed to have curved horns on its head, though. A shroud of fog, or mist, made it only dimly visible . . . *This can't be happening* . . . The creature forced its way through the window with a splintering of wood and glass. Ben shut his eyes and turned, flinging his arm up to shield his face as glass fragments flew through the air, showering the altar. As he ran from the altar, the people in the first few rows reeled, staring in horror up at the window. The horns on the creature reminded him of something . . . the horned dragon from The Revelation . . . *Wait* . . . *this has gotta be a dream* . . .

The horned creature reminded him of something else. And suddenly he *was* somewhere else. In a clearing in the woods stood a young deer—a buck—twenty or thirty yards away. Though probably just a yearling, the buck must have fed well and had virile spikes on its head . . . . *I remember this . . . I've been here before. I was just a kid. I remember* . . . It was Ben's first hunting trip with his father—the stern Baptist preacher dad of his childhood. His father wanted him to shoot the deer . . . *But I don't want to. He's a beautiful animal* . . . His father snarled something at him, pointing to lines in a large black leather-bound book in his hand. Again, he knew his father wanted him to kill the deer. But he couldn't pull the trigger on the heavy cold-steel rifle in his hands. The gun went off anyway, though, startling him awake.

It was dark in the room where Ben awoke—he'd been asleep and dreaming. Some sound must have awakened him. He blinked a couple of times and saw that the room was very dimly lit. He remembered he was at Nate and Elizabeth's house—the earthship near Silver City. There was a soft light at the far side of the room, and as he got his bearings he realized he'd been sleeping on a couch. Their couch in the living room. A candle flickered—some distance away—where a woman's figure, in a nightgown, stood next to the stove.

"Elizabeth?" he said. "Is that you?"

In a hushed voice she said, "Oh. I'm so sorry, Ben. I didn't mean to wake you. . . . I was havin' a little trouble sleeping. Thought I'd make a cup of chamomile tea."

"Oh . . . no problem," he said, lowering his voice to match hers. After a few moments, he added, "Well . . . could you make me a cup, too?"

"You sure? I'll be done in just a minute, and then I'll be out o' here. And leave you in peace."

"No, really . . . make me a cup, too. If you don't mind?"

Ben roused himself and, throwing off the blanket and sheet, he grabbed his long-sleeved shirt that was draped over a nearby chair. Earlier, when he'd gotten his overnight bag out of the car, he noticed it was chilly outside. But it was quite warm, almost stuffy, in the earthship tonight. He had socks on his feet, and he padded, quietly, over to the kitchen table. The calming odor of the burning candle near the stove permeated the air. Elizabeth turned from what she was doing and looked at him. Ben offered a tired half-smile. "I wasn't sleeping very well, either . . . a cup of chamomile tea would probably do me good, too."

Elizabeth poured some boiling water into a teapot and dropped a metal tea ball into it. Ben quietly slid a chair out from the table. "While we're up, I'd love to hear some more about these healing experiences you had in Brazil. . . . If you're up to it."

She glanced at him, bringing the teapot to the table, and looked over in the direction of the hallway leading to the other end of the house. "Yep . . . I don't mind a bit," she said quietly. "The kids can't really hear us—with that curtain we've put up across the hallway, there. And Nate's fast asleep."

Ben felt he needed to know more about what she'd told him, at his house in Santa Fe a couple of months earlier. Question marks crowded his mind, regarding the physical surgeries—scalpel and knife—that Joseph of God did. And the invisible surgeries that Elizabeth also experienced. And other goings-on at the Casa in Brazil. Elizabeth began describing several of the visible surgeries she'd seen, that José performed on other visitors to the Casa.

Ben listened intently, though having trouble making sense of it. "And all of these surgeries seemed to be done without any anesthetic?"

"Yep," she said. "No anesthesia. Often—afterward—José would ask the patient if they'd felt any pain. And he'd ask if they were given an anesthetic. They always said no—to both questions."

"*Amazing*. But they seemed to be in a trance, or something?"

Elizabeth raised her eyebrows a bit, as if trying to remember something. "I don't think I'd call it a 'trance.' No. When I've tried to describe it to people . . . like when José did the visible surgery on me, in front of the crowd—it felt kind of like I was wrapped in a warm blanket. Like something warm and loving was taking care of me. Watching over me. I just had my regular clothes on. Or rather, I had on the clothes that *they* wanted us to wear—a long, white dress, in my case. And I knew where I was . . . and that José was going to operate on me. But it didn't seem like anything I needed to be worried about. The warmth got more intense when he started to cut me open, but it wasn't painful or even uncomfortable. And it felt sort of like, well . . . like a part of me was standing outside of myself, watching what he was doing. It was pretty strange but not unpleasant. I didn't feel any real pain at all—until a while later when I was in the recovery room. And even then, the pain wasn't much to complain about. I could still feel this great love and warmth."

Ben listened intently, though now feeling a bit tired. And baffled . . . *Strange. I've never heard of such powerful healing work going on . . . and on such a regular, daily, and weekly basis, like this. I don't get it . . .* "So, Liz. . . . You said, when we talked that other time, a couple months ago, that . . . well, that Joseph of God has said—when he talks to people about it in interviews and stuff—that it's *God's* power that does the healing? Is that . . . did I understand that right?"

Elizabeth poured a little more tea into her cup. "Yes. That's what I've heard that he always says, about this."

"But," Ben said, "if he's using God's power, then why does he need these 'Entities' to help him? These spirits of *dead* people? That's the part that I have a little trouble with. And it gives me the *creeps*, a little, to be honest with ya."

"I don't *know* why . . . but I never really felt afraid or worried about that."

"So," he said, with a little concern in his voice, "it didn't bother you—that these were dead people's *souls* that were working on you?"

Elizabeth grimaced for an instant. "I didn't think of them as dead people's *souls*, I guess. I mean . . . everybody there talks about them as being spirits—or 'the Entities.' And that they were there, voluntarily, to help people."

"Well," Ben said, "and I'm just kind of wondering out loud, here . . . but do you really think that, after somebody dies, they would want to stick around here—as a *ghost*—and help others still living in this world? Or would they tend to do that only if they were *forced* into it?"

Elizabeth stared at her teacup with a slightly furrowed brow. "I don't know. I guess I didn't worry about it that way. Or worry that they might have been ghosts that were *forced* into it. I just got the impression that these spirits were the souls—or consciousness—of people who had passed away. And that these Entities, or spirits, wanted to stay close to this world and *help* us, on this side of the veil. It just didn't seem like anything to *worry* about."

Ben looked at Elizabeth with some sympathy and concern, and then he gazed vaguely at the ceiling . . . *Yep. I guess there aren't many people down there in Brazil who 'worry' about it. Or worry about the fact that a lot of this goes against scripture—God's instructions—from the Bible. How can I say this, without offending her? . . .*

"I mean, don't get me wrong," he said. "Healing people who are sick and suffering is *great*. Wonderful. Folks in the church I grew up in—and in my current church . . . well, we believe that having the power to heal people is truly a gift from God. We call it a 'spiritual gift.' And it comes from the Holy Spirit. But that gift allows us to do healing work by using God's power . . . without using spirits of the *dead*."

Ben paused and exhaled, with a serious expression. "The New Testament, of course, is full of accounts of healing work. That Christ did. And Christ also gave that power to the Apostles, according to the accounts in the Gospels. And in the book of Acts—stories of where the Apostles performed amazing acts of healing and casting out of 'unclean spirits.' But they didn't use the spirits of the *dead*, to do this. There's a difference here . . . and it sounds like a very *big* difference, to me."

Elizabeth was silent, staring at her teacup with the beginnings of a frown. She stirred her tea, looking preoccupied.

"Am I bothering you, Liz . . . saying all this? I don't mean to be worryin' you about this. . . . You okay?"

"Yep, I'm okay. And it's *not* bothering me. Makin' me a little *uncomfortable*, I guess. But maybe I need to be hearing this."

He took a deep breath . . . *Maybe she is listening to me, after all . . .* "Well, I gotta say, ah . . . I'm just a little concerned about this guy in Brazil. After I talked with you guys, up in Santa Fe last time . . . well, I was just so darned curious, that I felt like I should read up on him, a bit. So I did. And I talked with a couple of guys I know who've done missionary work in South America. Those guys both said that 'spiritism'—believing in, and using, the spirits of the dead—is pretty widespread in many of the rural areas of South America. Especially in Brazil. And that 'mediums,' who channel and communicate with these spirits, are also real common. And often are highly respected in those societies. The Catholic Church, apparently, has had an ongoing battle, in trying to counteract the prevalence of spiritism. The church clergy has been worried that a lot of this stuff actually lures people away from God. And of course, away from the Catholic Church, too."

Elizabeth looked at him with a somewhat tired, perplexed expression. "So, I take it that you feel, Ben, that . . . well . . . using a medium is not a good thing?"

"No . . . in fact, I think it's a pretty dangerous thing. But I can only pass along what I know from what the Bible tells us. And . . . you might have guessed it," he said, with a wry smile, "but I have a Bible with me. Mind if I get it?"

Elizabeth sighed, a bit heavily. "No—go ahead. But it *is* getting pretty late. I know it's like your guidebook, though."

"It is," he said. "But I'll try not to take too much time, with this." Ben went over to his travel bag and fished out a fairly small but thick, dog-eared, and beaten-looking book—and walked back to the table while flipping through the pages. There seemed to be lots of bookmarks in it. "I'll just skip around, a bit—but you'll see what I'm talking about. Here's one, from one of the books of Moses. Deuteronomy. And this is what he transcribed, from God: 'There shall not be found among you anyone who practices witchcraft . . . or one who conjures spells, or a medium, or a spiritist, or one who calls up the dead. For all who do these things are an abomination to the Lord . . . and the Lord your God drives them out from before you.'"

"Hmm. What does that mean? . . . God 'drives them out'?"

"It means, sort of, that God separates them from the family and from the believers. Separates them from the 'Chosen.'

"In Leviticus—another book of Moses—He's a little more severe. Let's see . . . where is it? Oh, here. God told him that 'A man or a woman who is a medium, or who has familiar spirits, shall surely be put to death; they shall stone them with stones. Their blood shall be upon them.' . . ."

Elizabeth grimaced and took a deep breath. "Good *Lord*, Ben. Those people were vicious. *Savage* . . . I mean, the people who wrote that part of the book . . . with this talk about killing mediums."

"Well," Ben said, "it's widely attributed to Moses. And we believe it *was* the word of God, being given to Moses. These books were written more than 3,000 years ago. . . . But I think God was making it plain that He didn't want us fooling around with this stuff. With mediums—and 'calling up the dead.' And if you're thinkin' that the tribal people who were the early Israelites were savage . . .well, certainly by today's standards they'd be considered less 'civilized' than we are. But that point might be debatable. Look at all the nonsense that's going on around the world, now. The stuff that's going on in Iraq, now. Utter chaos, car-bombings, and slaughter. Genocide, in the Bosnian War. Crime in our inner cities. We are *still* uncivilized and savage."

With a confused furrow in her forehead, Elizabeth said she'd never heard this sort of talk when she'd gone to church as a young girl in Asheville. "We just never really heard any talk about spirits, or mediums. Except in ghost stories. . . . And I kind of quit going to church, when I was a teenager."

"Yep." Ben wasn't exactly listening, as he continued to flip through the pages. "Let's see . . . I know there's more mention of this, from Isaiah. . . . Here it is. . . . If it was suggested by someone to seek out a medium, for guidance, Isaiah says, 'Should not a people seek their *God*? Should they seek the *dead* on behalf of the *living*? To the law and to the testimony!' He means, here, to refer back to the law of Moses—to God's law that was given to Moses. Mosaic Law. Isaiah ends that passage by saying, 'They will see the gloom of anguish, and they will be driven into darkness.'"

Elizabeth sighed. "That doesn't sound real good."

"No. He means there will be no salvation for them . . . and they will be condemned to hell."

"Ben . . . I don't really *believe* in hell. I mean, I just don't believe it physically exists. Or *Satan*, for that matter. . . . I guess I believe that evil exists—in some kind of abstract sense—but I don't see the need to believe in hell, or the Devil."

"Well . . . a lot of people these days don't believe in hell. Or Satan. Of course, for that matter . . . a lot of people, now, don't believe in God either. Maybe, for people like you who doubt this, you could think of it another way. Very possibly, hell—damnation—is nothing more than being separated from God, after Judgement. And never being rejoined with Him again. No doubt, there are lots of references to hell as being darkness and 'unquenchable fire,' 'fire and smoke,' or a 'furnace of fire'—in the Old Testament as well as similar references in the New. But I think maybe these descriptions are metaphorical. And also are reiterations and reminders of what the earlier prophets had said."

Elizabeth looked both tired and distracted now. And began doodling with a pen on the cardboard cross template which they'd left on the table.

Ben was flipping pages quickly, now—he was in his element . . . *Where is that? There's another good mention of the concept of hell. Oh of course. It's in Luke* . . . "There's a lot I like about the Gospel of Luke. He was a close friend of Paul and had a *lot* to do with the early days of the Christian church. He says, here, 'There will be weeping and gnashing of teeth, when you see Abraham and Isaac and Jacob and all the prophets in the kingdom of God, and yourselves thrust out.' There, he's talking about being separated from your family and your tribe. Your people. And most of all, being separated from God. . . . Maybe hell doesn't need to be any more complicated than that."

"I see," Elizabeth said. "I guess I don't know what to say about all this. And about the healing stuff we did, in Brazil. I never was worried about it—at the time it all seemed *wonderful*. And amazing. And harmless."

"I know that's how it can seem, Liz. This stuff can be seductive."

She looked at Ben with a tired though serious expression on her face, as she gulped the last of the tea in her cup, and sighed. "I'll have to see how this all settles out, with me. I've actually pretty much discontinued the diet and herbs that they had me maintaining on—the people in Brazil, did, I mean. But I *have* gone back to the diet I was on before we went to Brazil. The diet my doctor suggested. Lots of vegetables, no red meat— and the mushroom extracts I was on. You know, physically I really feel better on a good diet like this, anyway. . . . And I don't think I can afford to be on a sloppy, greasy, junk-food diet like I did when I was younger— even if I *didn't* have cancer. I guess I don't need to tell ya, about Southern food. Like the kind you and I both grew up on? Ha! . . . Beans, or collard greens, with fatback? Or with 'streak o' lean'? Salty and greasy and overcooked? Good gracious, I don't think so! Not for me, anymore."

Ben smiled. "Not the world's most healthy diet. For sure. But sometimes I miss good old southern pork barbeque. With hush-puppies and slaw."

"God, me too. Well, I'm glad we talked tonight, Ben . . . or is it morning now?" Elizabeth rose from the table, returning the teapot and her cup to the counter. "I'd thought, before . . . that you were uncomfortable with what I said about Brazil. And it sure seems that you *are*. Uncomfortable about it. Well, I'm glad you've explained to me your reasons, and we've sorta cleared the air. But I'm pretty much tired out now—and I don't think I'll have the least bit o' trouble sleeping. Though some of the things you said to me don't set too well. . . . But I'll sleep just fine."

Ben got up from the table, and they said goodnight with a sort of formal arm's-length hug. "Sleep tight," Elizabeth said, "an' don't let the bedbugs bite." She chuckled.

26.

". . . And I don't see things the same way that people like him—
religious people—do. Black and white. Good and evil.
God and the Devil. Us and them."

It was a crisp Saturday morning, with the warm autumn sun chasing away the morning's chill. The kids were up early, helping themselves to some cereal while trying to be quiet in order not to awaken Ben, sleeping on the couch. Their attempts at stealth were in vain, though, and he awoke at the first bit of chattering. Ben dragged himself out of the makeshift couch bed and staggered to the bathroom to take care of business and dress in a change of clothes. Nate and Elizabeth were sleeping late.

Ben managed to keep the kids subdued, while he fixed himself some toast with butter and made a pot of coffee for whenever the others roused themselves. When it was obvious that they wouldn't be up for a while, he suggested that the boys get themselves dressed—quietly—and he would meet them outside to show them something.

The house was tranquil when Nate awoke. Elizabeth didn't want to get up when he did, so he dressed quietly and padded, barefoot, out to the kitchen, combing his hair back with his fingers. He thought it was unusually quiet—especially since it was already late and a Saturday. Stopping near the coffeepot, he looked out of the glass wall into the "front yard" area. Ben and the boys were crouching around some sort of sheet or tarpaulin on the ground . . . *What in the hell are they doing?* . . . His attention was drawn back by the smell of fresh coffee, and he was pleased to find coffee already made. He fixed himself a mug and sat down at the table. Not terribly curious about what was going on outside—and just enjoying the relative silence. The quiet broken only by the muffled conversation out in the yard. After he'd had a cup and a half of coffee—and his curiosity got the better of him—he put on his work boots and made his way out the door to see what they were up to.

It was the time of year when the warmth of the sun was beginning to feel welcome. Colder days lay ahead. Nate guessed that his honeybees would be active on a morning like this. A quick glance past Ben and the boys, downhill past the trailer, confirmed this—faint clouds of the bees could be seen buzzing around in front of the hives.

On the tarp that Ben crouched over, there were bright red objects in a pile. Nate strolled over, a curious smile on his face. "Oh . . . chilé peppers, huh? I was wondering what it was you all were workin' on."

"Yeah," Ben said. "Good morning. We picked 'em up yesterday. They're Hatch chilés . . . and I couldn't resist getting a bunch of 'em from a little stand along the highway. I thought I'd show these guys how to make a chilé *ristra* out of 'em."

"All *right!* They're beauties . . . such a bright red."

"Yep. It just don't seem like fall, if you don't have a ristra to hang outside—or in the kitchen or someplace. I didn't get any green chilés—figured you probably already had some, for cooking. But I got enough red ones to make a ristra for you guys, and one for us."

"Far out," Nate said. "We'd love one."

"I was showing these guys how to thread them onto the string, near the stem end of the peppers. That way, the pointed end of the peppers stick out more—and the ristras look better."

"Gotcha. Huh. . . . It *does* look better, that way . . . more like the ristras you see for sale."

Ben was using the only tools he had on hand, in the morning—without waking up the others. He was punching holes in the peppers and threading them on a string, using some kind of leather-punch tool on his Swiss Army knife. And threading the peppers onto some doubled-up fishing line.

It looked, to Nate, as if it was a little slower and more laborious than it needed to be. "Hey, Ben . . . you want a large sewing-needle for that? I'm sure I can find you one."

"No, it's okay. I'm makin' do. No *problemo.* "

"Okay, suit yourself. I just thought we could make it a little easier." Nate watched him thread another pepper onto the string . . . *Man, the kids are gonna have a hard time doing it like that . . . that is, if he intends to let them do any of it at all. Whatever. I guess he's having fun, anyway . . .*

"Pretty cool, man. You're like the, uh, Michelangelo of chilé ristras, buddy."

After the chilé-stringing workshop, the kids spent the rest of the morning down the hillside to the south—on a neighbor's property, actually. Clambering around the dried-up streambed, looking for arrowheads. Around midday—instead of calling the kids up to the house—the adults decided on having a quiet lunch without them. The urchins could be fed later, whenever they finally showed up. The three had a leisurely lunch with cold cut-and-cheese sandwiches, and salad.

Ben discussed with Elizabeth some last details about the church cross project—and said he could forward her a check, up front, so she could purchase the turquoise. Elizabeth told him she had no doubt that the actual work on the piece would only take a couple of days—once she had procured the turquoise. In fact, she could get all the turquoise pieces ready—with the silver wire-work and bezels—ahead of time. By simply using the cardboard template as a guide. Ben could bring the cross down, next time they visited—and she could solder all of the fastening points at once. In a few hours' time. So they could in fact have the cross back at the church the next day.

"A lot of traveling back and forth, for you, though," she said.

Ben finished chewing a large bite of his sandwich and sipped some iced tea. "Not a problem," he said. "David loves coming down here, too—and horsing around with your guys. I think he likes getting out of the city, too. There's just so much more fun for kids to get into, out in the country, here."

"No doubt," Elizabeth said. "But, Nate can tell you, also, that there's a whole lot more *trouble* they can get into, out in the country. Yep, it's great they still get along. Just like when they were young 'uns."

Nate added, "For better or worse, there's only a few kids here, in the neighborhood. So it gets kind of lonely for the guys. Luke's really glad to have David comin' down here, too."

After finishing his sandwich, and when the conversation had run thin, Ben steered it back to what he and Elizabeth had been discussing the night before. He looked at Nate. "I 'spect you heard us talkin' last night—didn't you, Nate? Me, and this most wonderful woman, here . . ."

"Yeah," Nate said, "I did notice you guys were up talking, pretty late. . . . When I'd got up to use the can, once. I didn't know what you all were talkin' about, though."

"Well, we were talking about Brazil. And, uh . . . I gotta say it, Nate. But the more I hear about this Joseph of God character, and what they do there, in Brazil . . . well, it's kind o' troubling to someone like me, looking at it from the viewpoint of a Christian minister."

. . . *Oh, Good Lord. This guy . . . Just can't leave well enough alone, with his religious dogma* . . . "What d'ya *mean?* What's troubling about it?"

Elizabeth glanced up from her salad bowl, a tired, hesitant look on her face. "Ben's concerned about their use of mediums—and the Entities. He thinks it's a bad idea."

"How can it be a *bad* idea?" Nate said, his face suddenly feeling hot. He exhaled loudly. "They're *healing* people, for God's sake. How can *that* be a bad thing?"

Ben drew in an extra deep breath. "All I can say is what I know, Nate. That God—in many places in the Bible—totally forbids the use of mediums. And using the spirits of the dead."

Nate couldn't keep his voice from raising a notch. "Oh, come *on,* now! This is bullshit. It's just all antiquated Old Testament *crap.*" He got his voice under control—to a more even keel. "And anyway, isn't it true . . . that in the New Testament, there's almost no mention of mediums? A guy in Brazil told me that. He was a visitor, and said that—at first—he was worried about the Joseph of God healings, because it went against some people's understanding of the Bible. But someone showed him how those caveats are really only in the Old Testament, when the early Israelites were a more tribal people, and very fearful—"

Ben interrupted, quietly, "There's plenty of mention, in the New Testament, about Satan."

"Satan!" Nate nearly yelled the word. "Why are we talking about *Satan?* Come on!" He paused for a few moments and stared down at the table, puffing his cheeks out with an exhale. "I'm sorry, man . . . I know I really need to chill out a bit, here. . . . I mean, I know I'm not any religious expert—in fact, I'm not religious at *all.* But this is *crap!* I was brought up a Jew, you know—us guys who *wrote* the Old Testament. But to me it's just an interesting book of historical stories mixed up with a bunch of colorful fiction and *allegory.* Some of you evangelical Christian guys believe in the Old Testament even more than we *Jews* believe it. And we *wrote* it! An interesting bunch of fables—nothing more. With a little wisdom, here and there."

Ben didn't appear rankled by Nate's outburst, but in fact wore a patient smile. "I know some people feel that way—but we believe it to be the word of God."

"Some people feel that way? How 'bout anyone with a brain? Anyone with critical thinking ability." Nate exhaled. "Damn . . . I'm sorry, man. But sometimes I just get so frustrated with you."

"I know. I'm sorry, too. We just see things differently."

"I'll say." Nate turned to look at Elizabeth for a moment. Her eyebrows were raised, and she looked uncomfortable with the arguing.

Nate continued, "But . . . why would you want to mess with this? Can't you see that Liz is a *whole* lot better? She may be cured. Permanently, for God's sake. What the *hell* can be wrong with *that?"*

"Well, it's true, I didn't see y'all, before you went down to Brazil. So I don't know how much better she is. All I'm saying is . . . there's a *reason* the Bible forbids us to use mediums. And spirits. From my studies—of other Bible scholars' research, and my own studies of the scripture—the reason for those warnings is probably because it's easy to be tricked. And deceived. By evil spirits . . . or Satan." Ben's countenance still had a patient look on it, but no smiling.

Nate appeared to be resigned and tired, and spoke in a lowered tone. "I don't know. . . . I never once had the sense there was anything *evil* going on there, at the Casa. Quite the opposite, in fact." He paused for a moment. "Did you, Liz?"

"No," she said. "Not really. I mean, *no.* But there sure were some unusual things going on there."

"Well, yeah," Nate said, "damn right, there were. Unusual things going on, there, I mean. . . . Doesn't mean it was *evil* crap going on there. For me, in fact, it was the closest I've ever been to feeling there really is some kind of God—or benevolent purpose—behind all of this. Inside, and outside of us. I don't know what else to say . . ."

Out in the yard, the kids were now audible, and they soon came bouncing through the screen door. All three were red-faced, after what must have been a race up the hill from the arroyo. Luke touched his mom's arm, panting, and—speaking for all three of them—said they were starving. Elizabeth got up from the table, with what Nate thought was a distracted, unhappy expression. After she inquired as to what they wanted in the way of a sandwich, she set about fixing their lunch.

Nate sat at the table, one elbow propped on the surface and shading his eyes while rubbing his forehead with his fingertips . . . *Man, this guy is really giving me a headache* . . . Ben sat across from him, leaning forward with arms folded in a relaxed way, resting on the table. To Nate, the man's expression was inscrutable, as he glanced at him again. Nate contemplated some blemish on the floor, out of the corner of his eye. With a scowl on his face.

Elizabeth finished making the boys their sandwiches, and they were allowed to take them outside on paper plates. The two men sat at the table wading through an uneasy silence. Finally, Nate got up from the table, noisily, to carry his plate over to the sink. And stopped partway there, next to Ben. He gave him a light squeeze on the shoulder. "Sorry for raising my voice, dude. I guess—sometimes—you and I just get along like oil and water. Maybe we can just agree to disagree."

"Yeah," Ben said. "It's true. I wish we got along well. Or that we got along well, more *often.* You know I care about you guys. That's the only reason I got concerned about this stuff. I love you both."

"I know. Likewise. And our kids just have so much fun together. Too bad we can't be more like them, I guess . . ." After getting to the sink, Nate changed his mind and brought his plate back to the table to make another sandwich from the cold cuts. He first offered the plate of meats to Ben, though, who took a slice of ham.

Later in the afternoon, everyone sat outside in the afternoon sun. Probably even the boys were aware that the days for sitting out in the sun were numbered—the sun on this day in September already noticeably weaker and lower in the sky. The tension evident just a short while ago had vanished. Nate, for his part, well aware that it mostly had to do with the topic of Joseph of God and the healings . . . *Or most anything having to do with organized religion, actually . . .*

The boys had helped, earlier, with completing the chilé ristras—and they wanted to see one of them hung up outside the house, now. So Ben and Nate, with the help of a stepladder, hung it near the main doorway, suspending it from one of the roof beams of a little pórtico that Nate had built there.

"That's it! That's the look." Ben said. "Now this looks more like a New Mexico house, in the fall."

Nate smirked. "Yep. Or maybe a New Mexico *hobbit-hole,* in the fall."

Ben chuckled. "Well, a futuristic one. I don't think hobbit-holes have a glass wall quite like this one does."

The boys admired the way the ristra looked, alongside the earthship. But David asked a question. "Dad? . . . What's a *hobbit-hole?*"

They left somewhere around four in the afternoon, Ben apparently wanting to get back to Santa Fe at a reasonable hour—and needing to do some work on his sermon for the next morning's service.

After dinner it was easy, for a change, to get the boys settled down for the night. As Elizabeth prodded them into getting ready for bed, she reflected on how good it must be to find such an innocent exhaustion from a simple day of just exploring the countryside and making strings of chilé peppers. Nate turned in early, after the boys had quieted down and lights were out. Half an hour later, when Elizabeth came to the darkened bedroom, she flicked on the small lamp on her dresser, softly illuminating the room.

Nate, not asleep yet, turned over in bed to look at her. "Hey there, Sweetie."

"Oh . . . hey, Hon'. I thought you'd gone to sleep and wouldn't notice the light."

"Uh, it's okay," he said. "I just couldn't drift off yet."

Elizabeth readied herself for bed, removing an elastic from her hair to let it down. Nate lay on his side, propping himself up on one elbow, his head resting in his palm as he sleepily surveyed his wife. "A little tense, today, with Ben. . . . Huh, Liz?"

"*Yep,*" she sighed.

Nate must not have been feeling all that tired, as it turned out. He spoke again, "I didn't know you guys were talking about all that stuff, last night. I really don't like him scaring you, with all that religious talk."

Elizabeth turned to look at him for a moment. "He wasn't scaring me."

"I mean . . . if he was such a great friend of ours, why's he want to make us feel bad—or worried—about the healing work we did, in Brazil? What gives him the damned authority to bad-mouth a healer like José? He's never even *been* there—to Brazil—or to any of these healers."

"Well, he knows some missionaries who *have* been there . . . and who're familiar with the mediums. And with spiritism, in Brazil."

"And? . . . So what?"

"Well," Elizabeth said, "these are religious people . . . And I respect Ben's familiarity with the Bible—and Christian teachings."

Nate mumbled, "You know, maybe I respect Ben's familiarity with the Bible, too."

"No, you *don't.*"

"How do you know? I *do,* actually . . . in a sort of abstract and historical sense. But I haven't been sold the same bill of goods that he has. And I don't see things the same way that people like him—religious people—do. Black and white. Good and evil. God and the Devil. Us and *them.* I just think he's got some nerve, getting you all worried about Joseph of God. And the Casa." He paused for a few moments. "And getting you *worried* about it, might even set back—or even *undo*—some of the healing work that *was* done there."

"Uh," Elizabeth said, "now it sounds like *you're* the one that's worried."

"I'm not *worried*. I'm just concerned about how this fearful crap could affect *you*. I just don't see the point in looking a gift-horse in the goddamn *mouth*. Amazing healing work is done there, at the Casa. You *know* this. What the *hell* can be wrong with healing being done? And people's suffering being relieved? I mean, really. Would Satan—if the fucker actually existed—really even *want* healing work to be taking place? I don't *think* so. It doesn't even, logically, make any sense."

Leaving the lamp on, Elizabeth came around to sit on the edge of her side of the bed. "I guess—with Ben—it's just the *way* that the healings are done, that bothers him."

"Oh, hell," Nate said, "I don't believe that for a second, Liz. That's not the *real* problem he has with it. I think it's just the fact that *he* can't do healings like that, himself—and also he can't comprehend this stuff. And who *can*, actually? . . . That's what *really* bugs him. He'd like to walk on water a bit, himself."

"Maybe so."

"I'm damned *sure* of it. Listen . . . do you honestly believe *evil* things were going on down there? At the Casa? That these are really evil spirits that're doing all this healing work down there? For some ulterior motive? *Come on!*"

"No," Elizabeth said. "I never felt like there was anything evil going on there. But I've thought about it sometimes . . . and wondered, well . . . like, if we were all really in our normal state of consciousness, or not. Sometimes it seems like we were all under some kind of enchantment. Like we were in a trance."

Nate's face crinkled up as if smelling a foul odor. "I don't believe this. A trance. A *trance?*" He exhaled. "If there's any goddamn trance going on it's the trance we're in, in this country. In this society. Tryin' to screw each other out of every penny we can get . . . chasin' the almighty dollar. Running around like chickens with their heads cut off, starting wars to make sure nobody stops us from getting what we want? Now, *that's* a trance. And it's rampant. All over this crazy world."

Elizabeth took her socks off and looked at Nate, not wanting to provoke him any further. Especially at this late hour . . . *Yeah, boy . . . Ben, and his talk about the Bible, really gets under his skin. Maybe he thinks I like Ben. A little jealousy . . .* "Honey, all I meant was that . . . after we were back in the States a couple o' weeks, it felt almost like it was all a dream. And like I was just waking up from it—startin' to feel normal again."

"Well, I guess we both just see it differently. I think you were starting to feel *normal* again, because you were finally starting to feel *well* again—after being sick for years. Personally, I think the only reason it seemed like a dream was because so many unusual things were happening there . . . things that the human mind just can't comprehend. Miracles. Honest-to-God miracles. Little miracles, and holy cow I don't fucking *believe* it miracles. You know all this—I don't need to tell ya. But it doesn't mean we were in a *dream,* or enchanted. Or in a trance or something. No . . . I don't believe *that* at all. Those things really happened."

27.

. . . a bit different from the church I went to,
when I was young . . .

It was nearly the end of October when Elizabeth's work on the crucifix
for the church was completed. Her best turquoise supplier worked out of
Tucson—and it took several weeks for Elizabeth to get a hold of the
stones that she wanted. Fifteen, altogether—fourteen medium-sized
turquoise "cabochons," and one larger one. She wanted them all to match
in color, and they were able to do that, providing her with stones from
the same quarry. Tibetan turquoise. And at a reasonable price, for
turquoise.

Elizabeth had called Ben earlier, around the middle of the month, and
explained the delay. But he didn't sound concerned. He said—if need
be—they had another smaller cross that they could use during the
interim, while she worked on the project. It just wasn't a problem. But he
did say that they were busy, lately—with his own work at the church and
with David's schoolwork—and he didn't feel they had the time to bring
the cross down to Silver City. Could he send it to her? And when it was
completed, she could either ship it back or bring it up to Santa Fe in
person. "Whatever you're comfortable with, Liz. I imagine you've had to
ship things, before . . . silver work, I mean. And it can probably be done
safely, right?"

"Oh, sure, I've shipped small pieces to customers before. But never
anything very large. And this piece will be kind of delicate—with the
wire-work. Maybe I'll plan on carrying it up with me. I bet Luke might
want to come, if it's on a weekend. He could hang out with David."

"Sure, that'd be great. And we'll be glad to pay for your gas expenses, driving up."

"That would be wonderful. I'll take some photos of it—in place, there, at the church. . . . Something nice for my resumé."

"Right . . . as if you really need something more for your resumé. Your work is *great.*"

On the afternoon that Elizabeth finished her work on the project, she pressed the remaining turquoise cabochons into place—into the silver bezels she'd soldered onto the cross. Her stomach lurched for a second . . . *Yep. Careful, now . . . this turquoise may be a little soft . . .* She burnished the edge of each bezel to hold the stones firmly in place. It was finished . . . *Yes! I like it. They'll be happy with this. A nice Southwestern feel to it. This'd look good in any church in the Southwest . . .*

Nate wasn't overjoyed at the idea of making a family trip up to Santa Fe that weekend, so Elizabeth decided she would make the trip up to the city and deliver the cross herself. Luke sounded like he was thrilled with the idea of going with her, it being Halloween on Saturday. They could bring up his Frankenstein mask, and he could trick-or-treat with David—probably really cash in on some major Halloween candy in the neighborhoods around Santa Fe. He had some homework to do for school, but he could bring his schoolbooks . . . *Anything, to spend a couple of days away from Joey, I guess . . .* And so—with Nate's blessing—they left Saturday morning to allow plenty of time for bringing the cross over to Ben's church.

In the afternoon, at the church in Santa Fe, they installed the cross in its place on the altar, Elizabeth taking a few photographs. Ben talked to her, at the church—and again later, back at his house where they had dinner—about how a friend of his ministered to a large congregation in Albuquerque. And wondered if she'd want to accompany him to the Sunday morning service, there.

At the dinner table, Ben, with excitement in his voice, spoke of this church. "You know, they've got a very strong, big congregation . . . and truly *filled* with the Holy Spirit. They're Pentecostal—like our church. But a good bit stronger, I'd have to say. I heard from Pastor John, this week—that this Sunday's service is a healing ceremony. It might be a really good service for you to experience . . . truly Christian healing. And I think it would help to keep you on track—in makin' sure you continue to get well."

Elizabeth felt a bit ambivalent about it, and it showed on her face. "Ah, you know, Ben . . . I'm really doin' pretty well as it is. I really think I'm in remission."

"Well, then, it couldn't hurt to keep it goin' in the right direction, now, could it? I think you should come—you'll find it's a powerful service they have there."

"Oh, I s'pose I *could*," Elizabeth said. "It wouldn't hurt me a bit—to go there. We might could stop in, for that service, tomorrow morning on our way heading back down south."

"Yeah," Ben said. "That'd put you part way down the road, as a matter of fact. Actually, I've got to be here in Santa Fe—for the service tomorrow—but I could drive down there with you, beforehand. John thought we could meet up with them for breakfast at their house. With him and his wife, Miriam."

Elizabeth looked at him for a long moment . . . *Hmm. Sounds like he's already cooked this up with this other pastor . . . Wonder what they said?* . . . "Uh, yeah. Okay. Sounds like it's doable—and that should get us back to Silver City pretty early tomorrow. *Meanwhile* . . . you know, it's getting close to trick-or-treating time, tonight. I know Luke is anxious to get out and try the neighborhoods around here. I'm gonna help him get his costume ready."

"Oh, okay. . . . You know, we've never really celebrated Halloween. Beth never thought it was a great idea to support this *'holiday.'* But . . . oh, well. I don't see why David can't go around with Luke . . . and have some fun with it. We don't really have a costume for him, though . . .'"

Elizabeth set about creating a makeshift costume for David . . . *Jeez, I hate that this poor boy hasn't ever been out on Halloween. Let's see . . . we'll need some makeup* . . . Elizabeth, herself, didn't use much in the way of cosmetics—but they found a few cosmetic items that Ben had still held onto, from the time he and Beth were together. With some dried-up eye shadow—and lipstick for blood—she transformed David into a really passable vampire. Or zombie, they weren't sure which.

Ben seemed to be getting into it, too, and—since the boys weren't old enough to go around alone—he said he would join Elizabeth in escorting them. They went trick-or-treating to fifteen or twenty houses in the neighborhood. Luke lost count, but was very pleased—gushing, in fact—about how much more candy he'd gotten than he ever would around Silver City.

≈ ≈ ≈ ≈ ≈

Next morning, after a cup of coffee for the adults, they all piled into the cars, early, for the drive down to Albuquerque. Elizabeth and Luke in her Volvo, following Ben. A dusting of early snow mantled the upper reaches of the Sandia Mountains to the east of Albuquerque, and the morning air was crisp. On the north side of the city, Ben found Pastor John's house—a sprawling ranch home—and pulled into the driveway, Elizabeth following.

Pastor John welcomed them at the door. A jovial, large man, he hugged Elizabeth as if he'd known her all his life, then hugged Ben and ushered the kids into the house. "The missus, here, she heard we were havin' a couple of *genuine* Southerners over for breakfast, so she's baked up some biscuits for us. Even made up some sausage gravy for 'em!"

Elizabeth grinned . . . *Well, this guy's sure from the South* . . . "All *right!*" she said. "You know, it's hard to find good biscuits around New Mexico—it's true. I miss 'em."

John walked them into the kitchen and introduced his wife. "Yeah. Miriam and I are both bona fide Texans. From east Texas. And you know how it is . . . people around here just don't much appreciate good down-home Southern cooking."

Elizabeth shook her head. "No indeed, they don't."

Miriam opined on how Southwestern cuisine had its merits, as did Tex-Mex, but in her opinion couldn't hold a candle to real Southern food. The breakfast table was soon set, complete with a bowl of steaming freshly made hominy grits. And sausage patties. Ben was smiling— perhaps glad that Elizabeth was feeling at home with his friends. When they sat down to the meal, John asked him to say grace. After they all started digging in, Ben quietly prodded David to eat quickly. "Hate to say it, y'all, but we have to hit the road, soon, for the drive back to Santa Fe." After they'd finished, said their goodbyes and left, the others had a lively but unhurried breakfast.

When everyone had gotten up from the table, Elizabeth helped Miriam with a small bit of cleaning up in the kitchen. And then they got in their separate cars—Elizabeth following them over to a large church on the east side of the city, near the Sandia foothills. Inside the modern-looking church, already over two hundred people had arrived, milling around and chattering like in a classroom before the bell. With a touch of nervousness, Elizabeth glanced around. She hadn't been in a large group of people since they'd visited the Casa in Brazil . . . *Boy . . . a bit different from the church I went to, when I was young* . . . She grabbed Luke's hand and sat themselves down next to Miriam, in the front row. Miriam introduced her to a few people while John talked with a couple of older men at the front of the church. He later disappeared into a side doorway to ready himself for the service.

A couple of young men, who looked to be in their late teens, sat in folding metal chairs at the front of the church near the altar, playing guitars next to a microphone—while a young woman with long black hair stood and sang into another mike. The trio's music sounded pleasant and relaxed, though unprofessional. Even so, the guitar accompaniment wove itself around the woman's vocals in a well-rehearsed manner. To Elizabeth, the lyrics of the song at times sounded corny and at other times beautiful—about the girl's search for Jesus.

As the trio's song ended there was scattered applause. And the service began a few minutes later. The service included some prayers, recited from a prayer book—prayers unfamiliar to Elizabeth. There were a few hymns, accompanied by the musical trio, in which the congregation joined them with enthusiasm. The trio also performed their own version of a gospel song that Elizabeth vaguely remembered from her childhood.

Pastor John sat to the side, while an elderly man came to the lectern and read the last couple of pages from the Gospel of Mark. It began with the description of Christ's crucifixion and led to the end of the gospel, where the risen Christ visited the disciples in Galilee. The elderly man finished his reading, sat down, and Pastor John returned to the lectern. To Elizabeth, John seemed as cheerful and relaxed as he had been earlier—like the huge crowd in the church was no different from the small group of people sitting around his kitchen table.

The topic of his sermon was faith—and the extraordinary powers that went hand in hand with that faith. John reiterated, for emphasis, a couple of long lines from the gospel that the other man had read. "These signs will follow those who believe: In My name they will cast out demons; they will speak with new tongues; they will take up serpents; and if they drink anything deadly, it will by no means hurt them; they will lay hands on the sick, and they will recover." John, smiling, scoured the room with his eyes, and continued about the powers given to "true believers." Powers that were "spiritual gifts" granted by the Holy Spirit. Elizabeth heard him mention the Book of Acts, a part of the New Testament that Ben also had brought to her attention. And something to do with the celebration of the Pentecost, in Jerusalem—where the apostles were filled with the Holy Spirit and began to speak in other languages . . . *Speaking in tongues, huh? I never did understand that . . .*

John's voice was rising in a more excited manner now, as he continued his discussion about the apostles—and about how they became more and more able to perform miracles. Miraculous healings of the ill and diseased. All in the name of Christ. Elizabeth remembered, then, that this was one of the church's healing services. John mentioned a couple of other books from the New Testament. In which those books described how the apostles—especially Paul, and Peter, and Luke—were able to travel to other parts of the world and perform miraculous healings in those far-off places. Meanwhile, spreading the word of Christ and increasing the membership of the new Christian church. John's voice had an infectious quality to it, his happy enthusiasm obvious. This wasn't lost on his audience—or on Elizabeth, for that matter—as she sat in the front row sandwiched between her son and Miriam. From time to time, someone in the congregation would shout, "Amen!" or "Amen, Brother!"

To a casual observer just entering the church, it would appear that John had worked himself into a frenzy as he—often in mid-sentence— pounded his beefy palms into the lectern for emphasis. But to those involved with the entire service, his body language was just another aspect of the electric excitement in the air. He expounded about the apostle Paul and the miracles he performed in his travels all over Asia Minor. He asked, in a smiling loud voice, "Do you *believe?*" A few people in the congregation yelled back an affirmation. And then he yelled, "I said, Do you BELIEVE?!!" Many more hollered back, "YES! Yes, Brother! Yes!"

Pastor John glared around the room, and proclaimed that those who truly believed—and felt called to—should come forward to "lay hands" on the sick, then and there. He waved to a woman who sat by the side aisle of the church, with a leg-brace on and crutches, motioning for her to come forward. Nine men and women—mostly middle-aged, a couple of them elderly—came forward to act as healers. The woman wearing the leg-brace came to the front of the church, next to John. The group surrounded her, with the pastor included, her head and upper body encircled by hands pressed to her. They all appeared to be moving their lips silently with eyes closed. Elizabeth watched the process intently— then for some reason reached down and squeezed Luke's hand, smiling at him. After several minutes of praying for the woman, John looked up and said in a loud voice, "By the power of Jesus Christ, you are *healed!*"

Elizabeth thought this sounded familiar . . . *Yep. That's what José says. During and after the healing events* . . . The woman with the brace walked back to her seat, still using crutches but seeming to walk with greater ease. Pastor John, beaming, looked straight at Elizabeth and waved for her to come forward. She felt a slight lurch in her stomach . . .

Oh, Lord. I never talked to him about how sick I've been . . . Ben must have . . .

Miriam, sitting next to her, nudged her and smiled. "Go ahead, Child." Elizabeth pasted on a brave smile, and, patting Luke's thigh, got up and walked the short distance to where the little group stood. In a similar fashion to what she'd seen with the other woman, the people surrounded her with calm, smiling faces. Pressed their palms and fingertips against her on all sides, with John placing his palm on her forehead. Elizabeth closed her eyes, feeling a warmth and love enveloping her . . . *Like when José de Deus touched me . . .*

≈   ≈   ≈   ≈   ≈

Back at home, the following week returned to a semblance of normalcy, with Luke going to school in Silver City and Joey having homeschooling lessons and study exercises. After having finished what she deemed to be a successful and artistically satisfying silver project—the cross for Ben's church—Elizabeth felt a void and longed to get back into more frequent jewelry making.

Ben called on Saturday and spoke with Elizabeth—to thank her again for her work. And to let her know that her rejuvenation of the church's crucifix was an overwhelming success. "Many of our church members gushed about how beautiful it is. Maybe this is your new calling. I'm serious. It could be a niche market—this style of cross you've made for us could be popular *all over* the Southwest. The style is perfect for this place! And I haven't seen many others like it. You could own the franchise, Liz!"

Elizabeth chuckled. And smiled inside, glad that her rather expensive modification of their cross was appreciated. "That's really great, Ben. Very good news."

They talked for a while about their kids. Luke was adjusting well to the public school system. According to Ben, David was thrilled—at long last, this year—to have gone out trick-or-treating on Halloween. Ben decided it was silly to forbid the boy from participating in that small guilty pleasure—even if it *was* a holiday celebration of which Ben's training and church could not approve. Near the end of their phone call, Ben said he hoped she didn't mind, but he'd given Pastor John their phone number in Silver City. "There's something John wants to discuss with you, Liz."

"Oh, okay. Not a problem, Ben . . . John's a great guy. And a pretty darned inspiring pastor."

"He is, isn't he?"

"Maybe he wants one of my crosses, too, huh? Ya think?"

"Maybe so, Sweetie. Maybe so."

28.

".... Well, how's this supposed to make me feel?
Of course it's makin' me feel uncomfortable, hearing this.
This is a little creepy, to be honest with ya."

Pastor John did in fact call, later that day. It was early evening, and Elizabeth had begun fixing dinner—Chicken Cacciatore, which the kids always seemed to enjoy. Wiping chicken slime off her hands, she answered the phone, where it sat on the kitchen counter. She told John she could talk, but needed to turn the burner off on the stove, first. After doing that, she wiped her hands more thoroughly and picked up the phone again. Elizabeth assured him it wasn't a problem—that she could continue what she was doing after a while. "Yeah, thanks, John, for inviting us to your church on Sunday. It's a pretty dynamic church you have there. I enjoyed the service—and I think Luke pretty much liked it, too. And thank you, for the laying on of hands. . . . I wasn't expecting that, but it was very nice. And powerful."

"Oh, you're most welcome, Elizabeth. We'd be very pleased to have you come to our church anytime you're up this way. And if you are, why don't you let us know, ahead of time—so we can have breakfast with y'all again."

"Oh, that's very sweet."

"You bet. We really felt very blessed to be able to do a laying on of hands, with you. And I hope you don't mind—that Ben told me a bit about your illness, and about how y'all went to this healer, in Brazil."

"No," she said, "Not at all. That didn't bother me."

"Well, we're glad to help any way we can. And I don't know if Ben told you, but we have a healing service at least once, every couple of months. Depending on the need for it. And we often have some remarkable healings happen, on those days. We've got a congregation that's filled with The Spirit . . . and a couple of our members, well, God has seen fit to give them the gift of healing.

"In fact, that's something I wanted to talk to you about. You see . . . when folks are baptized with the Holy Spirit, oftentimes they receive these spiritual gifts—for the good of the people and to show God's power and love. And it's like what's described in many places in the Bible—and Paul talks about it, in Corinthians—that there are many different gifts that are bestowed on folks, by The Spirit. To folks who have faith. Gifts for miraculous healing, gifts for speaking in tongues. And there's the spiritual gift for the 'discerning of spirits.' One of our church members has that gift . . . and she was there on Sunday, workin' with the others, laying on hands.

"People who have this gift are able to sense when spirits have become attached to people. Involved with them. Good spirits . . . and evil spirits—those that the Bible refers to as 'unclean spirits.' Well, Sweetie, ah . . . that woman talked with me after the service on Sunday and said she felt a strong presence of an 'unclean spirit,' in you. Now, I don't mean to scare you about this. I'm just tellin' you the truth, as I know it— and just tellin' you what our friend said she experienced. She's been doing this for a while—years—and this is only the second time she's felt this kind of presence."

Elizabeth, her brow furrowed, felt a slightly queasy feeling in her stomach. She moved the phone away from her face for a moment and looked down at it as if it smelled rank all of a sudden. She raised it to her ear again. "Well, I don't know what to say, John. This is kind of a strange conversation we're having."

"I know, Child. I wish I could've come down there to talk to you in person, but we've been pretty busy this weekend. Like I say—I'm not meanin' to scare you, about this. Or make you uncomfortable—"

"Well, how's this *supposed* to make me feel? Of course it's makin' me feel uncomfortable, hearing this. This is a little creepy, to be honest with ya."

"I understand."

Elizabeth pursed her lips, her face a definite frown, now. "I mean, if this is *true,* well, I mean . . . how could this even *happen?* I'm not even sure I believe in evil spirits—or what you call 'unclean spirits.'"

"I understand," John said. "Really, I do. It may seem hard to believe, in this day and age. Or easy to believe—depending on how you look at it—with all the craziness going on in the world, today. Jesus, Himself, you see—and, later, the apostles—did many healings and casting out of 'unclean spirits.'"

"This is startin' to give me the creeps, John."

"It might even be that an 'unclean spirit' was actually the cause of your cancer, in the first place. Or it could be that this healer in Brazil—who apparently uses spirits, from what I've heard about him—is a little careless. And unclean spirits are gaining a foothold, in people who go to that place."

Still with a frown on her face, Elizabeth was thinking—mostly—about how she could end this conversation and get off the phone, now . . . *Boy . . . I thought I liked this guy. And that he was really a good, nice man—and a good pastor. But he's makin' me feel really crummy now . . .* A few questions niggled at her, though—she didn't want to hang up just yet. She asked him about the evil spirits. "These 'unclean spirits' that you're talkin' about, John, uh . . . where do they come from?" There was silence for some moments on the other end of the line. "John? Uh . . ."

"The Enemy. They come from The Enemy."

"You mean Satan?" she asked. "The *Devil?*"

"Yep. They can be fallen angels—which we're told in the Bible can be all around us, on earth. Or they can be the disembodied spirits of wicked people. The Apostle Paul tells us that Satan, himself, can change his form into a being of light. To trick people."

"Well, if we believe all o' this . . . then, it sounds like *we're* in trouble from the get-go."

"We are, Child," John said. "Satan literally means 'adversary.' And we're told, a number of times in the Bible, that this whole world is under the *sway* of Satan. But there is hope for *all* of us—if we put our faith in God, and the Son of God, our Savior. Paul talked about 'godly sorrow' . . . for any of us who turn away from God. But he also tells us—if we confess this to Jesus, and believe in our hearts that God raised Him from the dead—that those who believe in Him will not perish but have eternal life. Same thing, in the gospels. . . . It's pretty simple, really—our salvation is through Christ. All we have to do is believe in Him with all our heart."

Elizabeth exhaled a long, pent-up breath. "Well, John, I have to say this has been pretty darned disturbing. But I have to go now and get supper going."

"I know . . . and I'm sorry, Elizabeth, that I couldn't call with better news. And I'm sorry I couldn't come down there and talk to you about this in person. But I still thought maybe it was best to talk to you about it right away . . . so's you can act on it as soon as possible. If you want to."

"And how would you *act* on this, John? I mean, what would *you* do?

If you were in my shoes. . . . And have you dealt with this sort of thing before?"

"Well, Sweetie . . . I haven't, myself. But, about five years ago—before I was pastoring at our church—well, the gentleman who was pastor here before me did what we call a 'Deliverance' ministry. These services are done only when it's been decided—by people who have the gift of discerning spirits—that The Enemy has gotten a foothold into someone's body and soul. Most of these cases are like that—just a *foothold,* mind you, that The Enemy has got. There's only a very few cases where there's total possession. Where Satan has gotten complete control over somebody's life. And I don't need to tell you, but that's certainly not the case with you. But I would say that this is definitely something to be concerned about."

"Well," she said, sighing, "you've surely got *me* a little concerned, now."

"If you want, I can call around, Elizabeth—and talk to some other pastors. I can find out where the best church or congregation is, to get a Deliverance ministry done . . . and which pastors have experience with this."

Elizabeth tried to picture dragging Nate to a church for this kind of service . . . *Can't picture it* . . . "Well, let me think on it, John."

"Okay. I'll make the calls anyway, Sweetie. I'm curious about it, myself."

"All right. Thanks, John. I'll talk to you soon." She hung up the phone with a prolonged, sighing exhale. And stared down at the counter where the phone lay.

Later, at the dinner table, Nate noticed that Elizabeth didn't finish the minute portion of spaghetti with Cacciatore she'd served herself, and seemed preoccupied. She snapped at the boys when they'd gotten noisy after leaving the table . . . *Huh. She wasn't this grouchy earlier today. I wonder who that was that called a couple hours ago* . . . After clearing the table, Nate helped her wash dishes, and pried a little. "Who was that you were talking to on the phone, a while ago?"

Elizabeth went on to describe some of her conversation with Pastor John.

"What?" Nate said, his eyes incredulous. He squinted at her, as if what she was saying was out of focus and could be cured visually. "You know . . . I didn't even want you going to that church. Between Ben—and now, this guy—what's his name, John? . . . I mean, this is *absurd.* Do you even realize that you were doing *well* when we got back from Brazil? Who *gives* a damn, if the healing they're doing there goes against some of the Old Testament verses? The book's as old as dirt. . . . And *meaningless.*"

Elizabeth put some leftover sauce into a Tupperware container, and into the refrigerator. She muttered, "Well, a lot of this stuff—about healing, and spirits—is in the New Testament, too."

"Huh?" Nate looked at her and rolled his eyes to the ceiling. It sounded, to him, as if she were halfway defending Ben's (and now John's) opinions. He looked back at Elizabeth and sighed. "Yeah? And? . . . I mean, so *what?* You know how I feel about this stuff. Why are you *doing* this? Most of the New Testament is written by God-only-knows who—no pun intended. And for what motives? A lot of it was written down decades after Christ's death—from what I understand. Who knows how much of it is even what the man *said?* Some of them—like Paul, I think—never even *met* Christ."

Nate rubbed the side of his face with his hand as if he suddenly had a toothache. He spoke again in a more moderate tone. "Liz, I just can't see getting worked up about this stuff. It all seems so *fearful*—so much of the writing from that damned book. Whether you're talkin' Old Testament or New. And you know what? I mean, look . . . obviously I'm no divinity-school graduate like Ben. But, from what I know about God—what I feel, deep down, to be truth about God—is that *fear,* or fearful teachings, have nothing to do with it . . . with God. Fear *always* comes from the human mind. From the human ego or the psyche. And it comes from one group of people or another, using fear to try and control their own people—or to control others. It's *always* from the minds of screwed-up humans. That shit doesn't come from *God!* What does God have to be afraid of? Come on! And why would God have the need to frighten us? *He,* or *It,* has gotta be much bigger than *that.* If He isn't, well—I got no use for him.

"You know, whenever somebody's tryin' to convince me of some religious or spiritual teaching—and there's fear involved with it . . . well, I can just guaran*tee* you that God has *very little* to do with it. And I pretty much stop listening. . . . Fear is *always* from the human mind. It's something we're stuck with—hell, we've inherited it, from the apes on down through time. Just a product of the damned ego! Nothing more. And this talk about Satan—and 'unclean spirits'—is only fear."

Leaning back against the edge of the kitchen counter, Elizabeth, her lips pursed, stared at the floor. Nate lowered his voice to a more reasonable tone. "Liz . . . I just don't think you should talk to these folks anymore. It's not doing you any good. And I mean Ben, too. This is simply negative, fearful crap they're trying to sell us on—and we just don't need it. You've already been through a hell of a lot, with this illness . . . and I think you just need to focus on keeping a positive attitude, and keeping your strength up. And falling into this fearful thinking is not gonna help."

Elizabeth looked at him and then raised her gaze toward the ceiling, exhaling, with her breath making a slight whistle through her lips. "I totally hear what you're saying, Honey . . . and part of me says you're right about this. But another part of me grew up goin' to church every Sunday, back home. And some of the best people I knew, growing up, were churchgoin' people. How can believers—for almost two thousand years—all be incorrect? Or misguided? I grew up hearing that the Scripture was the word of God. The Truth. My momma, at least, seemed to believe that. It's hard for me to let go of that . . ."

"I know. I know it is."

"Dad never really went to church. He was more of an academic type, more educated—teaching at the university and—"

"Yep," Nate said, "and what does *that* tell you?"

"Not sure it tells me anything."

"Well, Liz . . . I really think we should at least consider going back down to the Casa in Brazil. You know, José strongly suggested it—after about three months. I really think we should go."

"Uh-huh. We *could.*"

Nate looked at her, rubbing his face again. She sounded ambivalent. And was, unlike their first trip to Brazil, hesitant. He felt a vague sadness as he thought about her. Feminine, and old-fashioned as she was in many ways—she could also be willful and stubborn when her mind was made up about something. And part of him longed to return to Brazil. There was something vibrant and hopeful about the place—and about what they'd experienced there. He sighed . . . *I bet if I could get her back there, she'd change her mind about it. There's a heaviness, here, in this country. With all this fear and shit. It's like we're stuck in the mud . . .*

In the following weeks the weather got chilly and the nights cold, as the seasons shifted gears into late autumn. Elizabeth's work on the cross for Ben's church had in fact primed her creative juices, again—she was busy with her silversmithing work, making many more pieces of jewelry for the co-op gallery in town. Nate brought up the topic of Brazil several times, but apparently he was the only one wanting to go back there.

Elizabeth, it seemed, couldn't be persuaded to continue with the healing work they did at the Casa de Dom Francisco.

29.

"The Kingdom of Heaven is at Hand" –Matt. 10:7

Elizabeth sat, for the most part comfortably, in the passenger seat of the compact Buick that Ben had rented during his stay in Georgia. He'd been in Georgia for the past week, visiting his mother, and had just picked up Elizabeth at the arrivals area of the Hartsfield-Atlanta airport. It would be a little over an hour's drive north, he told her, from the airport to their destination—a small-town church in northern Georgia. It was a Sunday at the end of October. A year after Elizabeth had worked on the silver and turquoise crucifix for Ben's church. She looked out the car window at the beltway around Atlanta . . . *And it's Halloween again . . . how odd! This year, it's falling on a Sunday. And here I am, hangin' out with Ben, again.*

"Funny, huh, Ben?" she said, adjusting her seat. "We keep meeting up on Halloween."

"Yep. It is. Must be somethin' about this day, for you."

"I guess. I sure used to enjoy it, as a kid."

Traffic was light, it being Sunday. As the interstate circled around the downtown area, the north side of Atlanta still looked very much urban—city blocks jammed with small houses and apartment buildings. Elizabeth hadn't spent any time visiting Atlanta since she was a girl—except for time spent in the airport, catching connecting flights. Sunshine flashed into her eyes, the late afternoon sun reflecting off the glass of a large, modern building close to the highway. North Atlanta Regional Hospital, a large sign in front of it proclaimed. As she surveyed the glass and concrete of the imposing structure, Elizabeth felt a nervous flutter in her stomach—her usual unpleasant reaction to hospitals. Even now—a few weeks after her last surgery—she felt a twinge of pain in her armpit and some numbness in her right arm. It darkened her thoughts . . . *That surgery didn't go so good. They must have nicked the nerve, there, darn it . . .*

Otherwise, it was a pleasant enough drive once they left the metropolitan area. And relaxing, compared to the cramped tension of the plane flight from Albuquerque. After they left the city—and despite the season—it was still very green, only a few trees turning their fall colors. As was often the case whenever she traveled back East, Elizabeth thought the countryside almost painfully green compared to New Mexico.

Come sundown, Elizabeth's boys—back home—would be trick-or-treating around the neighborhood. As would millions of other kids, all over America. She hadn't been to Georgia since she was a girl, and felt some childlike excitement about it, smiling to herself. She wouldn't be dressing up for Halloween, though. But would soon be attending a Sunday evening service, with Ben, at his friend's church. A special service. A "Deliverance" ministry . . . *This'll be a different kind of Halloween, for sure . . .*

She also hadn't spent time with her parents in several years, and the plan was for her to catch a bus up to Asheville, North Carolina, the following day—where she would visit with them for a good part of the week before heading back to New Mexico. She frowned for an instant as that leg of the trip crossed her mind . . . *That part might be difficult. Yep. Momma and Daddy are kinda worried about me. Heck, they want me to move back to Asheville—to get cancer treatment there. But it'll be good to see 'em . . .*

The little town of Cumming, Georgia, though relatively close to Atlanta, still appeared to be remnant of the Old South. Small white houses with the mandatory front porches, where one could sit and cool off in the muggy summertime evenings. And the larger houses of the wealthy residents having wrap-around porches with rocking chairs. As they passed through the town, soon there were scattered groves of pine trees, interspersed with small farms, their crops of corn and silage now a brown stubble. In just these few miles north of Cumming, it felt like the first real countryside since they'd left the bustle of Atlanta. Elizabeth rolled her window down partway to smell the air. As they passed a side road, on the left, Ben pointed it out. "My momma lives down that road, there. We'll be staying at her house tonight . . . she's got plenty of room for ya."

"Oh, okay," Elizabeth said, "Huh. It's nice country around here."

A mile or so later, Ben turned right, onto a side road heading east. A large lake in the distance could be glimpsed from time to time through the trees. After a couple of miles, they pulled into a gravel parking area covered with pine needles, in front of a small white church set back from the road. Several pine trees, with huge trunks and thick, scaly bark overshadowed the church, and Elizabeth glimpsed a number of gigantic pinecones on the ground. A few of the pinecones eight or nine inches long.

"Wow. *Loblollies*."

"What's that?" Ben asked.

"Loblolly pines. I love them . . . and I haven't seen 'em since I was a girl. They don't grow near Asheville. And they *sure* don't grow in New Mexico."

"Yeah. They *are* kind o' beautiful, aren't they?"

Stationed near the front of the church was a white plywood sign with bold black letters. Cornerstone Full Gospel Church. There was also one of those temporary signs out closer to the road—the type of sign on which the words can be changed like religious Etch-A-Sketch. It stated a line of scripture: "The Kingdom of Heaven is at Hand" –Matt. 10:7."

While Ben parked the car, Elizabeth watched an elderly man, kneeling on the ground along the front wall of the church. He appeared to be poking around with a trowel, planting something. As they got out of the car, the man consciously—and in slow-motion—stood up, resting his hand on his lower back for a moment. If he was the pastor, Elizabeth already knew something about him—Ben, on the drive had related some stories to her about the man and his earlier life. A life of drunkenness, dissipation, and prison time—before his salvation through Christ and the church. He'd been a close friend of Ben's father when his father was ministering. All over northern Georgia, he was well known as a popular revival preacher.

They walked up to him and he greeted Elizabeth with a kind and genuine smile. "Jim Henson . . . and *not* the 'muppet' guy who plays with puppets! So glad you could come, Elizabeth. . . . We're gonna have a nice little service here tonight."

"Thank you. I'm glad to be here."

"You bet. . . . Now, I was tellin' Ben, here—this morning—that most everybody in the congregation knows this'll be a Deliverance ministry, this evening. We don't advertise it, but word gets around—and I wouldn't be surprised if a few extra people show up tonight. For Deliverance and healing. Or some of 'em may be bringin' somebody with 'em, for that. Another young lady will be comin' by here, any minute now, I believe. And what better evening—for a service like this—than *Halloween?* Ha ha! Like John says, '. . . the blood of Jesus Christ His son cleanses us from all sin.' Ha ha! Praise the Lord!"

While they chatted about her flight from Albuquerque, Pastor Jim complimented Elizabeth on a full, bursting, white carnation that she'd stuck into the breast pocket of her shirt. She liked it. And thought it symbolic of her intention to be healed of her breast cancer. He asked her if she'd gotten it at the airport.

"Ah . . . yes. I did, Jim. That was a good guess. I thought it looked nice."

The Pastor's smile appeared to dim somewhat. "Were they *Hare Krishnas,* who were selling them?"

"Well, I don't know. I guess they might have been Hindus. They were two women—just ordinary American-looking women—who were handing them out, for donations. But they *were* dressed in loose, white dresses, wrapped around them. Indian-style, maybe."

"Well, Child . . . I'm gonna ask you to leave *that* flower outside—and *not* bring it into the church."

Elizabeth looked into his face for some cue to see if he was joking . . . *What's he talking about? . . .* "What do you mean? What's wrong with it?"

"You see, Elizabeth, we have to be careful about these kinds of things . . . even though they look harmless enough. The Hare Krishnas—you see—they worship the Hindu god Krishna. And Krishna is a demon god. A fallen angel. It's also not safe to use certain kinds of Indian incense, either . . . for the same reason. They're manufactured by the Hare Krishnas, and that can be a sly way that evil spirits get a foothold into our bodies and souls."

"You're not *kidding* me, are you, Jim?"

"No. Not for one second. We're at *war,* here . . . and always *have* been. Spiritual warfare. Ever since Lucifer was cast out of the heavens. This kind of business is all about ensnaring souls. Collecting souls, on both sides. God's side—or Satan's. To be judged on the Day of the Lord. And, Honey, the only safety, and salvation, is through Christ, the Savior."

A cloud appeared to lift from his darkened eyes—the humor coming back to his face—as a small Datsun sedan with banged-up body panels pulled into the parking area. Jim chuckled as a thin young woman got out of the car. She looked to be in her late teens, with dyed raven-black hair. Her eyes scanned the yard quickly before she walked over to the trio standing near the door. Jim hugged her. And she introduced herself to the others as Jill. They all walked through the arched doorway into the church.

It was darkening toward dusk outside, a pink and apricot sunset visible through the windows, as Pastor Jim flipped a switch to brighten up the nave of the church. He led the women to the door of an adjoining room—sort of a pantry and living room annex to the building.

He gestured toward a teakettle on the stove. "Please, y'all make yourselves at home, with a cup of tea. Or there's a percolator you can get goin', if you have a mind to. Over there in that cabinet. Come to think of it, we probably need to get some coffee brewing, anyway. If you wouldn't mind gettin' it going? . . . Folks won't be here for a while, yet, but it'd be good to have some coffee ready for 'em. Ben and I are just goin' to talk for a bit, out here in the chapel."

"Sure," Elizabeth said. "Jill and I can get that started. It'll give us something to do." The sun must have set over the ridge of mountains to the west—it was dark in the annex—and Elizabeth turned on a set of flickering overhead fluorescent lights in the pantry area. She took it upon herself to set up the coffee percolator. A tinny, West Bend commercial percolator, the size of a 30-pound propane tank. "What do you *think,* Jill? Maybe twenty cups? Or twenty-five? . . . But that's probably not enough if they're a bunch of real coffee drinkers." She wanted to draw out a conversation with this woman, but it was easier said than done.

Jill had a dark, desolate look in her eye—no spark at all—and tapped her fingers nervously on the countertop. "I'm not sure." She eyed everything Elizabeth did but without any real interest.

Elizabeth looked at her with some genuine concern and smiled. "How's your day been, Jill? Everything *okay?*"

"Well . . . it's been a day, that's for sure." She bit at a hangnail but immediately quit.

"Yeah. You *do* seem kinda ill at ease. Feel like talkin' about it?"

"Uh, well. Yeah. I can talk about it. I just got out of the detox in Gainesville. . . . Been there ten days—tryin' to get clean. Clean and sober, I mean . . . off o' the dope."

"Oh, sorry. Dope habit, huh?"

"Yeah," Jill said, "I've had a pretty bad time, with it." She sighed. "Since I was a kid, really. Pills. And, lately, smack. . . . Heroin, I mean. I've been craving it today, for sure. My boyfriend's had to get off it, too. They've got *him* in the hospital at the jail, though. And it looks like he won't be comin' out from there, either—cause they've got charges up against him."

"Boy. I'm so sorry . . . I guess this *has* been a rough day for you." Elizabeth looked at the woman, up and down. She took the couple of steps over to where Jill stood and gave her a hug, squeezing her thin shoulders. "It's gonna be okay, Hon'."

Jill seemed unconvinced, though, and teared up a bit. She wiped her hand across her eyes. "Yeah. It will be." Turning away, she walked over to a window, wiping her eyes again. She looked out over the darkening front lawn of the churchyard. "I used to come to this church, sometimes, when I was little. Momma liked to come here. At least . . . a few times a year, anyway."

"Nice. I bet you've got some good memories of this place."

"Yeah. I've known Pastor Jim all my life, pretty much." She turned partway round and gave Elizabeth a sidelong glance. "What did *you* come here for, tonight?"

Elizabeth touched the edge of her armpit for an instant, unconsciously, as she plugged in the coffee percolator. "I've had cancer."

"Oh, Hey. I'm real sorry."

"It's a long story. But, yeah—the cancer's come back. It's been just over a month ago, now . . . that my doctor had me to get some surgery done. *Again.* They had to remove some lymph nodes in my armpit." Elizabeth stood with a somber expression for a few moments, staring at the percolator and listening for the first cheerful perking sounds. "It's kind of weird how it started out as breast cancer. And now I'm cancer-free, there . . . in my breasts. But they've found it in my lymph glands, this time. And that means it's more serious, I guess. Spreading. Looks like I can't win for losin'."

"*Shit.* I'm really sorry."

"Yeah," Elizabeth sighed. "Me too. I guess it might be I've made some mistakes. In getting the cancer treated, I mean. Well . . . *obviously.* I could *still* choose to have chemotherapy done. But I don't want to feel sick all the time. There's a good chance that chemo might not even work, now.

"Anyway, some friends of mine have thought that maybe a Deliverance service could help. . . . That maybe there's been some evil spirit—or bad mojo—that's been affecting me. Something like that. That's what Ben thinks—and he's a pastor, too."

"Whatever. I guess it's possible. . . . I mean, I *know* it's possible."

"Yeah," Elizabeth said, "I 'spect it *is* possible. My husband thinks this is a bunch of B-S . . . but he doesn't know everything—"

"No. You know, sometimes I think maybe the Devil is real . . . right here—and everywhere—alive and well."

"Yep," Elizabeth said. "You see, we went to a healer in Brazil . . . and they use spirits, there, to help heal people. They call them the 'Entities.'"

"No shit. Really?"

"Yes, really. See, the healer, there, is a medium—who uses these spirits. And so it's possible—according to Ben and some others—that I've let something into my life that I shouldn't have ought to. Oh *heck*, I don't know . . . I was sick *before* that. I don't know what I believe anymore. I thought I was doin' the right thing."

"Well," Jill said, "maybe the Deliverance ministry, tonight, will help you figure out what you really believe. Maybe things will get clear."

"That'd be real nice."

"And maybe you'll be healed."

30.

*. . . A little like a rock concert—with the same tribal feeling
of togetherness. And power . . .*

Only a couple of people who showed up for the service early helped
themselves to a cup of coffee. But Elizabeth was glad they'd made a
large pot anyway, guessing that many might want a cup afterward. A
crowd of about fifty or sixty had taken seats by the time the service
began at seven o' clock. Cars and pickup trucks filled the parking area
with a few spilling over onto the shoulder of the road. Elizabeth sat next
to Jill in the front pew, over on the left side of the chapel. Numerous
candles flickered at the front of the chapel: on the altar, on the
windowsills behind the altar, and on several tall tables. Elizabeth noticed
a musty odor saturating the air—perhaps the smell of old wood
combined with decades of human sweat from hot summer-morning
services. A choir of six women sat in wooden chairs on the left side of
the lectern and led the congregation in a couple of old hymns. *The Old
Rugged Cross,* and then *Amazing Grace.*

As the last strains of *Amazing Grace* dissipated into the expectant
silence, Ben walked up to the lectern. He cleared his throat. "Pastor Jim
has asked me to speak, a bit, tonight—" And he nodded over to where
Jim sat, beside the choir. "so I hope I can do him proud. You know,
we're meeting here, together, on Halloween night—and what better time
to talk about Jesus, our Savior! While other people are celebrating the
darkness, we will celebrate the *light.* The *light* that the disciples saw, on
Christ's face after His resurrection. And the *light* that blinded Paul, on
his way to Damascus!" Ben paused, flipping open a Bible he'd brought

with him to the lectern.

"As you may know, friends . . . the coming of Christ, the Messiah, was anticipated by many of the prophets. Isaiah called him 'despised and rejected by men, a Man of sorrows and acquainted with grief' . . . 'He was wounded for our transgressions, He was bruised for our iniquities. All we like sheep have gone astray; we have turned, everyone, to his own way; and the Lord has laid on Him the iniquity of us all.'

"This is what was foretold. That this Man of sorrows—with such great love and compassion for the suffering of mankind—would be led, like the Passover lamb, to slaughter. Now, Christ knew his fate, as He preached and healed people of all kinds of disease. Matthew tells us that 'He called His twelve disciples to Him, and He gave them power over 'unclean spirits,' to cast them out, and to heal all kinds of sickness and all kinds of disease.' Matthew names and describes the twelve disciples, and says that Jesus told them to go and preach that 'The kingdom of heaven is *at hand.* Heal the sick, cleanse the lepers, raise the dead, cast out demons. Freely you have received, freely give.' And so, the disciples began healing the sick and casting out demons.

"And our Savior reminded them again—after He was crucified and had risen from the dead. . . . Mark tells us in his gospel that a few days later He appeared before the disciples, in Galilee. He told them that those who believe would be saved from death—but those that don't believe would be condemned. And that signs would follow those who believe: In Christ's name they would cast out demons, they would speak with new tongues, and they would lay hands on the sick and they would recover.

"You see, by now Christ had exhorted the disciples, a couple of times—that they would have the power to heal. He did, while He was in the flesh, alive. And now, again, after He'd risen from the dead. But they still had a lack of faith, it seems . . . like all of us do, sometimes. But we're told, in the Book of Acts, that, finally—and I can tell you, the Lord was gettin' a *little* annoyed by now—finally the Holy Spirit came over the disciples while they were gathered in Jerusalem for the Day of Pentecost. We're told that It came upon them like a mighty wind—and the fire of the Holy Spirit anointed them. A new kind of baptism, you see—baptism by the Holy Spirit. And *now* the believers were able to speak in tongues, in foreign languages that they didn't know beforehand. Just as Christ had foretold. And within a short while, the disciples were healing people, left and right, all over the place. And the numbers of believers grew—many Judeans repented and were baptized into the new church.

"Now, friends, some people will tell you that it depends on the *strength* of our faith—that is, our faith and belief that God raised the

Lord Jesus from the dead, for our salvation. And that it's the *strength* of this faith that decides as to whether or not we can heal people, and cast out demons, and perform miracles. But I say, *No! Not so.* That's not what the Good Book tells us. These gifts are *freely* given, by God, to those who believe. And the giving is *not* based on the strength of our belief. It's only a matter of *knowing* that we can indeed do these miraculous things." Ben pounded the lectern with his fist. "Friends, we believers can *ALL* perform MIRACLES!!" Ben scanned the crowd, taking a long, deep breath. "I'm gonna turn it over to Brother Jim, now."

Pastor Jim stood up, and walked up to the lectern, his first few steps with a limp. With a smile, he shook Ben's hand, as Ben stepped over to sit down again next to the choir. Ben glanced at Elizabeth as he sat—and she smiled at him, giving him a discreet thumbs-up gesture. She felt genuine pride in knowing him. The atmosphere was pleasant and exciting. And the calming odor of burning candles had finally overcome the mustiness in the air. As Jim got behind the lectern, he gripped the sides of it, almost for balance. Then he seemed to grow stronger as he stood there—the lectern itself lending him vigor and strength. His eyes got more intense. "Thanks, Ben, for that inspiring reminder of the wonderful gifts we've been given, through our salvation.

"Now, tonight I might not sound quite so nice, as Ben just did. But that's just 'cause it's not my way. You see, we're in *trouble* here, friends. John says—in his first epistle—that we, here, who are Believers, are *of* God. . . . But that the whole *world* lies under the sway of the wicked one. The *Devil.* And he also says, in that book—I believe it's in John's Epistle—that this is the *last* hour. That the Antichrist is *coming.* And that other antichrists are already here. This is the *last hour!*

"Paul speaks more about this, in his letter to the Ephesians . . ." Pages rustled as the pastor flipped through his Bible, looking for the right passage. "Paul says, here, 'For we do not wrestle against flesh and blood, but against *countries,* against *powers,* against the rulers of the darkness of this age, against spiritual hosts of wickedness in the heavenly places.' This *is* the last hour, folks—make no mistake about it. We are wrestlin' with these dark powers, in this world today. Paul warns us to take up the shield of faith—which we can use to stop 'the fiery darts of the wicked one.' Now, what he's sayin' is symbolic, but it's not idle talk, friends. Paul had seen a lot of the world, by that time—in fact, he was in prison, in Rome, when he wrote this. Christians were being put to death in many parts of the Roman Empire. The world was under the sway of the 'wicked one' then—and we're even *more* under his sway *now.*"

Pastor Jim smiled, but with fierce eyes looked over the congregation as he flipped to another page. "I'm a-goin' to head back into the Gospel of Matthew, here, because I want y'all to get this part. Jesus said, 'Nation will rise against nation, and kingdom against kingdom. And there will be famines, pestilence, and earthquakes in various places. All these are the beginning of sorrows.' And I don't need to tell you, we got sorrows, now, friends. Sorrows. Nation rising against nation. Why, just earlier this month, China exploded another nuclear bomb—they broke the moratorium on nuclear bomb tests. The U.S., Russia, China, England, France, India, and Israel *all* have nuclear bombs now. And Iraq is workin' on getting one. *The last hour!* Nation rising against nation. The signs are all here, friends . . .

"Now Jesus, you see . . . He's sowing the good seed—His teachings. He told a parable, once—also in Matthew—about the good seed and the weeds. The seeds that sprout into weeds are from the evil one. The Devil. And at the end of the age—the Judgement—the reapers will be angels. Jesus said he will 'send out His angels, and they will gather out of His kingdom all things that offend—and those who practice lawlessness— and will cast them into the furnace of fire.' And there'll be 'wailing and gnashing of *teeth.*'" Jim looked over the congregation and slammed his hands down onto the lectern. "Do y'all want to find out what that furnace of fire *feels* like?!"

Several in the congregation yelled back at him, "No!"

"No, I don't want to feel it, either!" Jim lowered his voice a notch and continued. "Now, I'll say it again . . . John tells us that 'this is the last hour.' There ain't no more *time* to mess around, friends. The Day of the Lord is coming. Make no mistake. Even though Christ talked about this, and the apostles did also, almost two thousand years ago. . . . You see, time is imaginary—irrelevant—in God's kingdom. Two thousand years passes by in a blink of God's eye." He began to raise his voice again. "The Book of Revelation tells us that anyone not written in Christ's Book of Life—well, they'll be cast into the *lake of fire.* And they'll be *tormented,* day and night forever and ever. Y'all want to see what that lake of fire *feels* like?!"

A few people hollered, *"No!"*

The pastor slammed his hands down again on the lectern, making it shake, as he bellowed, "It's *unquenchable* fire, people! Hell is *that* place . . . where you're awake and conscious . . . but in never-ending darkness. In unquenchable fire! Without love and without God. With no *end* to it. Do y'all wanna end up THERE, for all ETERNITY?!!"

Many more yelled back, *"NO!!* No, Brother! NO!"

"Well, let's get right with the Lord, now . . . NOW! This is the LAST hour." A woman, somewhere behind Elizabeth, could be heard softly weeping. Several in the crowd started praying out loud. Pastor Jim smiled, his tone temporarily calm, again. "Now, friends, we've got a few people who've come here tonight for Deliverance . . . and if their hearts are pure, in asking for it, then the Holy Spirit will *give* them that Deliverance. You see, it's not surprising that many of us get deceived by The Enemy. After all . . . Paul says that, when Satan wants to, he can transform himself into an angel of light—and that his ministers can transform themselves into ministers of righteousness. Pretty *convenient,* huh? It's easy to get deceived here, friends.

"Now—coming back to what Matthew says here," Jim said, jabbing his forefinger into the page several times. "Jesus said to us that 'false christs and false prophets will rise and show great signs and wonders to deceive, if possible, even the elect.'. . . And when he says 'the elect'— He means even us *believers* here tonight. Now, we have a sister with us here, tonight—a friend of Ben's—who came all the way from out West to get Deliverance with us, tonight." He glanced at, and gestured with his hand, toward Elizabeth with a smile, then looked back to the rest of the congregation with a serious face. "And I hope she doesn't mind my sayin' so . . . but she was taken in by one of these false prophets. A medium, who uses spirits to heal people. This was through no fault of her own. You see, we live in a *dangerous* world, friends—and like I said before, the whole world lies under the sway of the wicked one. And time is runnin' out! Our only hope is with the Lamb of God who takes away the sins of the world! Can y'all hear what I'm *saying?*" A number of them in the crowd yelled back in agreement.

"And I'm a-gonna turn to the Gospel of John for a minute, now. You see, Jesus tells us that He's the *living bread,* which came down from heaven. He says, 'whoever eats My flesh and drinks My blood has eternal life, and I will raise him up at the last day.' Now, what He's talkin' about here, is simply about becoming *one* with Christ—and believing, in our hearts, that *He* was sacrificed for our salvation. 'For God so loved the world that He gave His only begotten Son, that whoever believes in Him should not perish but have everlasting life.' I know y'all have heard *that* passage before. Paul says about the same thing, in his epistle to the Romans—except, instead of 'everlasting life' he says that we will be saved. Now, I'm askin' you, Do we want to be *saved?"* A few people yelled back their agreement. Jim bellowed, now, with a smile but ferocious eyes. "I said, *Do we want to be* SAVED?!!"

Many in the crowd hollered back, "*YES!! Yes,* Brother!" Elizabeth, caught up in the moment, yelled back with them, "Yes!"

Jill, sitting next to her, didn't show much enthusiasm, but Elizabeth was excited and very much caught up in the enthusiasm of the moment . . . *Dynamic preachers and an excited congregation . . .* She chuckled . . .

A little like a rock concert—with the same tribal feeling of togetherness. And power . . . Childhood memories came to her of the occasional exciting church service when she was young. And she felt at home, here—with everyone's lazy southern accent having a soothing effect, though the words themselves sounded like a jittery lullaby.

Pastor Jim asked that all the elders of the church come forward to assist with the Deliverance. A group of men and women stood up from various places in the congregation, came to the front, and stood around Jim while he seemed to be giving them some sort of instruction. Most of the elders were in fact elderly—a couple of them possibly in their fifties, but the majority much older. The women of the choir sang some soothing gospel hymn, sotto voce. With a sparkle in her eye, Elizabeth nudged Jill. She leaned over and placed her hand over Jill's for a moment. "Are you gonna *do* this?"

"Oh yeah. I am. Nothing to lose, really—and maybe it'll help me."

"Good. I'm gonna do it, too." She felt a slightly nervous butterfly in her belly, as she watched Jim talking to the others. A couple of minutes passed—then Jim asked everyone who desired Deliverance to come forward. Six people did. Four men—and the two women. Jim assembled them in front of him, the elders standing close by.

"Now . . . first I want to do a prayer for Deliverance, with y'all. I'll say it slowly—line by line—and you folks can repeat it after me. . . . One of my favorite prayers for this kind of service, 'cause it covers all of what we're askin' for, here. It was channeled from the Spirit—and written down—by a powerful preacher named Derek Prince."

He looked at all six of them, one by one, with a serious face but a half-smile. He glanced at some kind of cue card in his hand. "And here we go—with y'all repeatin' it, after me: 'Lord Jesus Christ, I believe you died on the cross for my sins and rose again from the dead. . . .'" He waited for their reiteration. "You redeemed me by your blood and I belong to you, and I want to live for you. . . . I confess all my sins—known and unknown—I'm sorry for them all. . . . I forgive all others as I want you to forgive me. . . . Forgive me now and cleanse me with your blood. . . . I thank you for the blood of Jesus Christ which cleanses me now from all sin. . . . And I come to you now as my Deliverer. . . . You know my special needs—the thing that binds, that torments, that defiles; that evil spirit—that 'unclean spirit.'. . . I claim the promise of Your word, 'Whosoever that calleth on the name of the Lord shall be *delivered.*'. . . I call upon you now. In the name of the Lord Jesus Christ, deliver me and set me free. . . . Satan, I renounce you and all your works. . . . I loose myself from you, in the name of Jesus, and I command you to leave me right now in Jesus' name. . . . *Amen!"* A few moments later, the six finished repeating the Deliverance prayer.

"AMEN!" someone yelled from the congregation. The pastor paused, looking at the six again. He then raised his eyes heavenward in what seemed a humble supplication, raising his arms high. In a loud voice, he pleaded, *"Lord . . .* Lord Jesus, we ask that You send the gifts of the Holy Spirit that we need to minister to these people here, tonight. We ask these things in the blessed name of Jesus Christ, our Lord and Savior. *Jesus*—stir up the demons in our souls so that they can be identified and cast out. We take authority over Satan, NOW!"

He lowered his arms and stared at the six in front of him with faraway eyes. "Satan, we come against you—by the power and blood of Jesus Christ, by the name of *Jesus,* and by the authority of our Believers. *Satan*—because of our belief—we sit in heaven with Christ Jesus. . . . And we are OVER you, your demons, and all the forces of evil. We command you to come *out* of these people—quickly—in the name of JESUS!"

A man who was standing next to Elizabeth, and on whom she'd noticed an odor of alcohol—smelled like a distillery, in fact—began to shiver uncontrollably. The pastor reached for the man's shoulder and pulled him a few steps forward. He motioned to the elders standing by, and they surrounded the man. Elizabeth watched, as if from a dream, as Jim poured some kind of liquid out of a bottle into his hand and smeared it onto the man's forehead. He kept his hand there, while the elders pressed their hands on the man's head and chest, encircling him. They leaned in toward him, moving their lips with some inaudible prayers. Pastor Jim glanced upward and then down into the man's eyes. "We take authority over you *now,* Satan! We are *over* you. And we command you to come out of this man, *now,* in the name of Jesus Christ."

Elizabeth gazed at the man from a few feet away, aware of a struggle within him. Without intending to—and without thought—she found herself trembling. She felt love and sympathy for this man whom she'd never met before . . . *Please help this man surrender. Let it go . . .* The man's legs became wobbly and he collapsed to the floor, shivering. A couple of the elders crouched near him, keeping their hands on him and whispering into his ears.

Pastor Jim stepped forward and, putting a hand on Elizabeth's shoulder, guided her the few steps forward. They had to sidestep around the man, who was now immobile on the floor.

Someone yelled, from the congregation, *"Hallelujah!"*

"Praise Jesus!" a woman shrieked.

The pastor's palm felt hot and oily on her forehead, as the elders also laid hands on her and whispered different prayers into her ears. She felt love and kindness coming from these people, though some of their words were stern and harsh. As though standing outside of herself and watching the ministry from other eyes, she heard Jim saying, "We take authority over you *now,* Satan!" She saw his face close to her own and yet distant, looking skyward and then down into her eyes. He was utterly engaged in the process . . . *He almost looks like he's possessed by something . . . But I know he cares about me. They all do. And I want to be free. I've got to let it go. Let everything go . . .* A warmth and happiness came over her—it reminded her of being a little girl again, and of her grandmother's unconditional love. She'd felt this way, sometime recently . . . *Yep, that's right . . . At the Casa in Brazil . . .* Pastor Jim had finished his prayer, but the warmth still washed over her, cleansing her, as the elders' prayers continued. Some little part of her knew—on a conscious level—that she wanted to make these people happy. And give them what they wanted—give them some sort of profound surrender. Her legs felt quivery but she remained on her feet, as the pastor pulled another man to the front and began ministering to him.

It was a quiet morning, and they had a relaxed breakfast in the kitchen with Ben's mother. She had fixed country ham and biscuits. And Elizabeth knew she was really back in the South. Esther Smith was a country woman, having always lived either on a farm or in a small town in Georgia. And like many southern housewives, she served her biscuits with cups of Luzianne coffee, with its touch of aromatic chicory root . . . *All right! Haven't had a cup o' Luzianne in years . . .*

To Elizabeth, the events of the night before seemed almost dreamlike—and though Mrs. Smith had been at the service, she wanted to hear all about it from Elizabeth's perspective. So Elizabeth obliged. Later in the day, Ben would be driving her over to Gainesville, where she would catch the bus to Asheville and her parents. But for the time being, it was a restful morning with good southern cooking and company.

After breakfast, Elizabeth helped Mrs. Smith clean up the table. Ben attempted to help—but his mother scolded him as maybe only a southern mom could. Told him to clear out of the kitchen and let the women finish their work. He went outside, and a little while later could be seen in the front yard raking some early fall leaves. While they sat over one last cup of coffee, Mrs. Smith gleaned all she could of Elizabeth's experience at the church. Elizabeth rinsed out her cup and went to use the shower. A short while later she was toweling off in the bathroom and putting fresh clothes on, when the phone rang. Ben's mother could be heard, muffled through the bathroom door, speaking with someone—while Elizabeth dressed, quickly, slipping on some dark green denim slacks and a cotton turtleneck sweater.

Mrs. Smith knocked on the bathroom door. "Elizabeth? Honey . . . the preacher's on the phone. For you. Do you want that he should call you back?"

"No, that's fine . . . I can get it now." Elizabeth opened the door, with a puff of steam escaping.

With a quiet smile Mrs. Smith led her to where a private phone was, in the living room. "I'll hang up the phone in the kitchen, Honey. Y'all talk as long as you like."

Elizabeth picked up the phone and, after they'd greeted each other Pastor Jim asked how she was doing. He told her he was proud of her for following through with the service of the night before—and proud that she'd chosen his church to have her Deliverance. As she spoke with him, he sounded very curious to hear about any difference in the way she was feeling.

She finger-combed her damp hair back as she thought about it. "Well, I feel very peaceful, this morning, Jim."

"Very good. You know, Elizabeth . . . you have salvation, now. And we've beaten back The Enemy. But this is still more of a *process* than an event. . . . You see, this ain't like they way they show it in the movies— about exorcism. It's something we have to keep working on. It's very possible—even likely—that your illness had its origin with The Enemy. Through the presence of an unclean spirit. But Satan just had a foothold, in you—you see—and now you've got to fill that space with the Holy Spirit."

"I understand."

"I'm gonna ask you to continue with the good work you're doin' . . . and get yourself hooked up with a good church like ours—Pentecostal— back where you're livin' in New Mexico. Ben can help you find one, I'm sure . . . though I hear you're kind of a far drive from where he lives. If there isn't one close by . . . well, maybe you can find one that you can get to at least once or twice'd a month. And let that preacher know where you're *comin'* from . . . and that you've had Deliverance. He'll know how to keep helpin' you to stay close to the Lord."

"Okay. I'll do it."

"And, Elizabeth . . . it's important that we continue to confess our sins—and even the sins of our ancestors. Because without this confession . . . well, we never get the humility that it takes, to fully let the Spirit in and be absolved of these sins. Like I said last night, 'the blood of Jesus Christ cleanses us from *all* sin' . . . but we have to confess those sins . . . and let the Holy Spirit *in*. Our Savior's blood was shed for *you*, Child. And Jesus—the Lamb of God—*loves* you. And He wants you to come back to the fold. You hear what I'm sayin'?"

"Yes, Sir."

"Now, I know I talk a lot . . . but that's 'cause I'm sure that we're runnin' out of time, here. The Day of Reckoning is gonna be here a lot sooner than people think . . . and there's a lot of work to be done. And when that day comes, there's gonna be a lot of wailing and gnashing of teeth. Pure terror. I don't think you want to be on *that* side."

On her end of the line, Elizabeth was silent for a few long moments. "No. I'd just as soon not be. You know . . . I appreciate all the help you're trying to give me . . . and tryin' to help me with my illness."

"Well, it's the good work, Elizabeth. It's what we're born to do. Now, Child, ah . . . I'm gonna suggest one more thing. I'm askin' for you to clean out your house of anything that could be from the Evil One. Anything you might have around from the Hare Krishnas—the Hindus— like incense, or *Buddha* statues . . . get 'em out o' there. And any kind of cult things: dolls or puppets, good luck charms, crystals, toy dragons. Jewelry (if you don't know where it came from), five-pointed stars (especially with a circle around it). . . . Even horror-story books or movies. In fact, even the 'Peace sign'—that everybody thinks is so wonderful—is actually an ancient witchcraft symbol. It's all *around* us, Child. All these things can be ways that unclean spirits weaken us. And get a foothold back into our lives . . ."

Elizabeth massaged her forehead as she listened . . . *Wow. Is he for real about all this? Dolls and puppets? Toy dragons? Good Lord! . . .*

The pastor spoke again. "And *burn* those things! I'm not kiddin' about this, now."

"Really? Okay. I'll do it."

"I'll keep prayin' for you, Child. Jesus loves you . . . and I love you, too. You call me anytime you want, now. Okay?"

"Okay. Thanks, Jim. Love you, too. Bye-bye, now." Her ears were still ringing slightly, as she sighed and hung up the phone.

Part V

31.

... 'Scarlet Begonias'. ...

The cottonwood trees down in the cañon below the earthship had put on their springtime garment of translucent green. It was six months since Elizabeth's excursion to Georgia, for Deliverance. A Saturday morning, in mid-April of 1994. Their oldest son Luke was eleven now. Elizabeth watched him, from indoors at the kitchen sink, as he helped his father work on the beehives partway down the south-side hill. They were doing a springtime inspection of the hives . . . *Hard to believe. He's in the sixth grade, now* . . . Luke had taken an interest in learning about beekeeping, and they'd bought him a bee-veil hat so that he could safely help his dad. The hat looked comically large on the boy, but they figured he would grow into it if beekeeping continued to interest him. His brother Joey—on the other hand—had no use for bees and was playing at a friend's house near the other end of the community.

It looked hot out in the sun, though it was a comfortable temperature in the earthship. Elizabeth mused, as she took a break from her housecleaning, that they'd be having company this weekend. Ben and David were coming down from Santa Fe. It seemed that Ben felt obligated to continue helping Elizabeth ever since her trip to Georgia. He introduced her to a nearby church, in Deming, that was similar to his church in Santa Fe—and made certain she was able to get there at least once a month. She sometimes made it to the service twice a month. Though in fact it wasn't really nearby—Deming was almost forty miles from Silver City—though to get there it was on straight, level highway across the flatlands away from the mountains. A fast, easy drive.

Ben suggested to her, as Pastor Jim had also, that she regularly read certain books of the Old and New Testaments. And spend time each day in prayer—to ensure her being filled with the Holy Spirit. Elizabeth looked forward to Ben's visits much more than Nate did—Nate in fact seemed to merely tolerate Ben, for Elizabeth's sake. She maintained an untainted humble conviction that—through her cleansing with the Deliverance, and her faith in Jesus and the church—her healing from the cancer was entirely possible.

But as she watched Luke helping his dad outside, she leaned down onto the kitchen counter and cradled her chin in her hands, elbows propped on the counter. The earthship exuded an insulated silence that perhaps only a building surrounded by earth can foster. Dead silence. Her eyes felt hot and tired. She had trouble seeing down toward the beehives, now, her eyes misting up . . . *He'll be twelve soon. This fall . . . But I might not see him get much older . . .*

Elizabeth had brought Luke with her when she'd gone up to Santa Fe a couple of weeks earlier. She had an appointment with Andi Sheaffer, and figured it would be okay if Luke missed one day of school—a Monday. She figured he wouldn't mind missing school, and could hang out with David again. They stayed at Ben's house both Saturday and Sunday nights—going to his church service Sunday morning.

At a previous checkup with the doctor, Elizabeth had complained about some shortness of breath, which she thought might be allergies. Quite a few people she knew had developed allergies to pollen from the junipers—a very common allergy in New Mexico. The doctor started her on some long-acting antihistamines but also requested that new radiology be done at the clinic in Las Cruces.

At her appointment with Andi Sheaffer on this Monday, it seemed clear to Elizabeth that the doctor had something on her mind. The woman looked at her chart and reports, and seemed to be composing herself—which made Elizabeth a little nervous. Andi steadied her gaze at Elizabeth, and said that the radiology report showed, unmistakably, a tumor in the right lobe of her lungs. With an empty expression, Elizabeth listened, as the doctor discussed some options with conventional cancer treatment. She gazed at the doctor's white jacket and watched her lips as she enunciated words. Then looked into her eyes. In a broken voice, she said, "Well, what would the *point* be . . . in starting radiation and chemo now?"

"Uh, well, yes . . . Elizabeth . . . I'm afraid we *are* talking about metastasis, at this juncture. The cancer has spread to your lungs. It's common with metastatic breast cancer. Intervention with radiation and chemo are both still perfectly viable options, here. But I'm afraid this protocol will be helpful only in prolonging your life by some length of time . . . and in possibly making you more comfortable. I'm very sorry about this. The cancer, by all indications, is irreversible."

An icy lump in the pit of her stomach made Elizabeth feel nauseous, but for some very long moments she took deep, slow breaths—trying to calm the chatter in her mind. "I don't think, Andi, that I want to get into radiation and chemo, now. Besides—I've already passed the point where that's going to be of any *real* help. I've read, recently, about some pretty hopeful research showing that shark-cartilage has anti-cancer properties, and . . . Oh my *God,* what am I *talking* about? *Dammit!* I am just shit out o' luck. My time's *up,* isn't it?"

Elizabeth bit her lower lip, and frowned, holding back angry tears that wanted release. She tried to collect her thoughts. The room was silent, except for the muffled sound of music coming from an office next door. Maybe one of the other doctors at the practice—trying to relax, on his or her break time. And for some reason, it seemed important to try and make out what the music was. She focused on it . . . *'Scarlet Begonias'*. . . *My God, it's the Grateful Dead. Wish I could laugh . . .*

Andi asked her if she wanted a cup of water or tea. But Elizabeth said she was okay in that respect. The doctor patted her hand, gazed at her with sympathy in her eyes, and after a long moment, spoke. "If you *do* want to continue with alternative treatments . . . well, we can still go that route. We can work out a protocol that may be helpful . . . and may actually slow the progress of the cancer. The mushroom extracts you've been taking—Maitake and Shiitake—they'll still strengthen your immune system against the cancer. As well as the Astragulus. None of them will have any adverse effects, but they very possibly won't help—" and she hovered over the last word, "much."

"Uh-huh." Elizabeth felt a bone-weary exhaustion settling in.

"But I really think, though," Andi said, "that for intervening with the progression of the cancer—as well as possibly giving you a better quality of life—that I still have to suggest conventional cancer treatment, with a specialist. And I can refer you to a couple of good Medical and Radiation Oncologists at UNM. But, either way—whichever path you choose, from here—at some point we'll probably have to consider a regimen of standard cancer painkillers."

Almost to herself, Elizabeth responded, "I don't believe radiation and chemo are something that I want to mess around with. Not now. It's too late. I think I'd just rather continue with alternatives, Andi. Fewer side effects. And, I guess, the painkillers when it comes time for that."

Elizabeth and Luke left Santa Fe, for home, in the late afternoon. The old Volvo that they'd had for years still got them around but was starting to show its age. The blue paint on the car, no longer shiny, had faded to a blotchy pastel shade. The car chugged along, laboring up the long hill south of Santa Fe. Elizabeth mentioned to Nate—on a regular basis—that the engine often made audible complaints about needing some work done. A valve job, or at the very least a tune-up. Cars passed them by, on the hill, in heavy rush-hour traffic, some of them honking their annoyance.

An angry knot in her stomach, now, Elizabeth found everything irritating—the doctor's appointment, the late-afternoon sunshine glare, the Volvo, the traffic, and now Luke's complaining about not wanting to go to school the next day . . . *This damned car needs repair work, NOW! Nate keeps sayin' we'll get it done, but it never happens. Why are we always so strapped for money? And short on time? Shit!* . . . Elizabeth's rage over the vehicle's mechanical trouble at least seemed to be something she had control over—or *should* have control over.

The traffic was heavy all the way to Albuquerque. After driving more than an hour and a half in crowded, high-speed highway conditions, she felt like she couldn't take any more of it . . . *I've gotta pull over and take a break* . . . With some little relief, Elizabeth signaled and eased the car onto an exit ramp, on the south side of the city. Central Avenue, with its run-down urban neighborhoods—not the best part of the city in which to stop. But maybe stopping and getting an early dinner would improve her mood. She pulled the car into a McDonald's, which looked to be very possibly the oldest McDonald's in New Mexico.

Luke was thrilled, though—it looked as if he might get a bonus junk-food meal for the month. And there was no McDonald's in Silver City, so this was doubly exciting. He had a sly smile on his face. "Mom? Can I get a 'Big Mac?' Or a *'Double* Quarter-Pounder?'"

"You sure you can eat that much, Honey? That's a pretty big hamburger, you know."

"Yeah . . . but I'm gettin' big, too."

"Yes, you are. You are indeed." Elizabeth let go a long sigh and sat behind the wheel for a good minute, rubbing her shoulders with her fingertips to try and relax. "Okay. Let's get somethin' to eat."

It was crowded in the restaurant, so Elizabeth ordered the meal to go.

She asked for a Double Quarter-Pounder, for Luke, and ordered a burger for herself—definitely not caring, at the moment, to continue with her diet. She carried the couple of drinks out to the car. While Luke carried the greasy white bag of burgers and fries. To Elizabeth, he seemed to be holding the bag as if it were gold.

In the vacant parking space next to the Volvo, a homeless-looking man was sitting on the curb, leaning on a duffel bag. Elizabeth decided she wasn't going to make eye contact . . . *He'll only ask for money, anyway . . . if we so much as look at him* . . . She eyed him, quickly. An Anglo man, with a weathered face. He looked to be exhausted from walking around the city, and had the appearance of not having showered in a while . . . *And probably drunk* . . . She unlocked the car and slid in, unlocking the passenger side for Luke to get in. She turned on the radio and got the burgers and fries out of the bag. Luke started right in on his French fries.

Elizabeth started into her hamburger and realized she had to use the bathroom. "Honey . . . I'm gonna go back in and use the restroom, here. I should've gone, while we were in there. I'll be back in a minute. You just stay here . . . and keep the doors locked, okay?"

"Why?"

"Oh—just *do* it, Luke! It's because it's the city . . . and not a very good side of town. Okay?"

He fished out more of his French fries. "Okay."

While Elizabeth was back in the restaurant, Luke watched as two policemen walked up to where the homeless man was sitting—or slouching—on the curb. They were asking him about something and stood over him in an authoritative way. The man's face, through his wrinkles, had a haunted aspect to it. One of the policemen raised his voice a bit and, saying something, pointed to the street. They turned back toward the restaurant, snickering about something. The man slowly stood up—glancing in a dispirited way at Luke for a moment—and picked up his duffel bag. He turned to leave.

When Elizabeth walked back out to the parking lot a few minutes later, Luke was outside of the car, opening the car door to get back in. The man who'd been loitering there was walking away, lugging his duffel bag. Elizabeth frowned for a moment, and said in a low voice, "Luke . . . I asked you to keep the doors locked. And I sure didn't want you going out and talking with strangers. Didn't you hear me?" The boy got back into the car and reached over to unlock the driver's-side door for his mother. She got into the car and, with a confused expression, looked at her son. "Is that what you were doing? . . . Talking to that guy?"

"Yeah, Mom," Luke said. "I was. He looked sad. I gave him my hamburger."

She looked at him with a blank stare, and repeated in a monotone, "You gave him your hamburger."

"Yep. I did. I'm not all that hungry."

"Darn it, Luke!" Elizabeth gazed at him for a long moment, with fierce eyes that slowly softened. "Oh, *Luke* . . . I don't know if I should be mad at you . . . or give you a big hug."

"I wasn't trying to make you mad. I just felt sorry for him."

She looked at her son, incredulous, tears welling up in her eyes. Luke fidgeted in his seat, gave her a sidelong glance, and looked away again. Elizabeth leaned awkwardly over the parking brake in between the seats, and hugged him to her tightly. "Oh, Honey . . . I could never be mad at you for *that*. That was very sweet of you. If more people acted like that, the city here would be a much better place. I was just wantin' for you to be careful, while I was gone." She gave him most of her fries while she finished her hamburger in silence, glancing over at him a few times. Finally she giggled. "I'm gonna get you another burger. That be all right? . . . Would you eat it, if I did?"

A wry smile came to Luke's face. "I bet I would."

So Elizabeth went through the drive-thru window before they left the parking lot. As they drove back toward the interstate, they passed by a bus stop—where the homeless man was sitting on a bench, eating his hamburger. As they passed him by, Luke followed him with his eyes. And when he turned back around there was the trace of a smile on his face.

Elizabeth looked at her son for a moment, then back to the road . . . *What a great guy he's growin' up to be* . . . "That was a *really* nice thing to do, Luke—even though you disobeyed me. You know . . . that's really what Jesus wants us to do . . . to be kind to each other, even strangers. Even our enemies. It's called 'Charity.' Jesus loves you, Honey . . . and He loves that poor man there, too. Don't ever forget that."

As they drove south from Albuquerque, the sun got low in the western sky—one of those very clear and dry evenings of springtime in New Mexico. The strong sunshine, even at this low angle in the sky, illuminated the forested slopes of the Manzano Mountains to the east a day-glo green. Elizabeth thought of the magnificence of the New Mexico landscape—and how blessed she really was to be living here. And blessed to have such good kids, actually growing up with good values.

She returned from her reverie, shaking her head a bit and wiping her eyes. As Elizabeth came back to the moment she recognized Luke—again—in the morning sun. Wearing his oversized bee-veil hat. He had jumped back from the beehive they were working on, shaking his hand vigorously . . . *He must have got stung* . . . Nate was talking to him and rubbing something on his hand . . . *Yep* . . . *he's a really good kid* . . . After a couple of minutes, the two started on another beehive—Luke puffing the smoker into the hive while his father gingerly lifted the top off of it . . . *I'm so proud of him. I'm damned sure gonna miss him. And Joey . . . Maybe I'll still be able to keep an eye on them—after I'm gone. I hope it works that way . . .*

32.

As his wife began reading the first chapter of the book,
Nate listened to the tone of her voice.
A melodic love-song to their boys.

Elizabeth returned to her morning project of clean-up around the house before company arrived. Ben drove up—around midday—and he and David watched from a respectful distance while the guys finished up their work on the beehives. After Nate closed up the last beehive, he carried a toolbox over to a shed near the old trailer. There wouldn't be any honey at this time of year. But Nate thought that if the monsoon rains were good, in a couple of months, and if there was a healthy wildflower bloom . . . *Maybe, just maybe it'll be a good year for honey . .* .

While he was putting away the box of beekeeping tools, Ben asked him, in a lowered voice, about Elizabeth. "I was real sorry to hear that her doctor's appointment wasn't good news. How's she doing? I hope she's able to keep her spirits up?"

"Yeah," Nate sighed. "She's doin' pretty well . . . considering. Her arm bothers her a little bit—and it's swollen. I guess, due to the surgery last fall. But she's bearing up pretty well."

"Well, Liz has a heart o' gold. And she's a trooper."

Everyone seemed to come into the kitchen at once—everyone except Joey, still at his friend's house. And they looked ready for some kind of lunch. Nate and Luke were damp with sweat, and washed up at the kitchen sink. Elizabeth was resting on the couch in the living room, reading something, but got up to welcome Ben and David.

Nate was rubbing his "special" citrus cleaner onto his hands, to clean off the stickiness of the honey and bee propolis from the morning's activities. "Don't worry about lunch for us, Liz . . . we can get our own sandwiches." He turned to Ben, "We've got some cold-cuts and cheese, here . . . I'll get 'em out. And maybe the guys'll want peanut-butter and jelly—I'm not sure."

Once everyone was sitting down at the table, Elizabeth came over to the counter and made herself a sandwich also. She sat down, wearing a patient smile. Nate thought (as he had, several times in the past couple of weeks) that she looked more tired than usual. And he suspected she'd been losing weight, recently—her face drawn, a bit, with her cheekbones more prominent. But he hadn't asked her about it. Looking at Ben, he passed him a bag of potato chips. "So, how are things up there in Santa *Fake?*—I mean Santa Fe?"

"Oh . . . 'bout like usual. It is getting crowded around town, though. You guys know what I mean. Seriously . . . more crowded every year. It's a popular place to retire, and all that. But our church is growing, which is good. Liz can vouch for that, I think." Ben glanced at her. "You came to our service—what—a few weeks ago? Palm Sunday?"

"Yep," Elizabeth said, "just a couple weeks ago. It was a nice service—you're doin' well with the church, there, Ben."

"Thanks. Yeah, I think we're doing well. And we get new members on a pretty regular basis . . . helps, in spreading the Word."

"That's cool," Nate said. He'd been trying not to interfere with Elizabeth's renewed interest in the church and Christianity—and the Bible teachings that went along with it. He and Elizabeth had forged a cease-fire along that boundary. Her belief in Christ seemed to make her happy—or at least comforted. And Nate could find no fault with that. But it hadn't changed his own opinions . . . *Whatever floats your boat . . .*

He glanced at Ben. "So, I guess, all these new members . . . that means job security, huh?" At almost the instant he finished the remark, he grimaced and looked down at the table. "Sorry." With an impatient sigh, he added, "I don't know why I'm such an asshole, sometimes."

"Well . . ." Ben said, "we're saving a seat for you at our church."

"Good. Make sure it's an asshole seat." Nate smirked. "Liz—cover Luke's ears, will ya?"

Elizabeth chuckled. And to Nate, her laugh sounded like music. She'd been much quieter with him—and pensive—since she got back from Santa Fe those couple of weeks ago. And spending more time than usual with the kids. He watched her as she listened to Ben, who was talking now about the Easter service at his church on the previous Sunday. Elizabeth respected Ben and cared about him . . . *Maybe talking with*

*him, face to face, is just what she needs. She just loves hearing from him
. . . about God, and Jesus. Hey, whatever works. I just can't stand to see
her sad . . . I need to keep my damned mouth shut . . .*

In the afternoon they all piled into Ben's mini-van and drove into the mountains to hike up to the Gila Cliff Dwellings—just like they'd done a year and a half earlier, when Ben and David made their first visit to the Silver City area. The kids enjoyed it, as always. This time Luke was able to talk about the ruins halfway knowledgeably—his teacher at school had taken the kids on a class trip there. He described some details about the place that even the adults weren't aware of.

After dinner, the parents talked quietly in the living room, the lights down low and a few candles lit. The boys were settled down for the night in the other room, and talked in whispers—with occasional giggles—until after a while there was quiet. The conversation in the living room, after running the gamut, meandered back to religious and spiritual topics. Nate listened in for a bit, feeling no need to jump in. He grew tired, though, and got up to bid Ben goodnight. He kissed Elizabeth and went back to their room to turn in.

Next morning, Ben and Elizabeth both got up earlier than the others and, rousing David, they all three went down to the Sunday service at the church in Deming. Even Nate said, later, that he enjoyed the weekend—and Ben's visit. As usual, finding it best to just not open his mouth when the inevitable religious topics were brought up. And he couldn't deny that Elizabeth looked lighter and more content after spending time with Ben.

That evening, after their visitors had gone and things were settled down, they had a light dinner, and afterward Elizabeth helped Luke with his homework. Joey had also started attending the public school in Silver City now—since the previous fall. He found himself having a little more trouble than his brother did, with arithmetic. Since Nate had an aptitude for math the ball fell into his court, often, to work with him on it. After the kids finished their homework—and had a short play time, while Elizabeth washed the dishes—she coaxed them into brushing their teeth and getting ready for bed.

Elizabeth announced that there was enough time for a bedtime story.

Though Luke at first appeared reluctant to put up with this—probably thinking he was way too old for that, now—he caved in without much wheedling on her part. Elizabeth brought in an extra pillow from her bedroom and carried in her hand a hardcover book. She sat down on Luke's bed and nudged him in the side. "C'mon—scooch over."

Nate, in stocking-feet and on his way out of the main bedroom to take a shower, stopped at the doorway. It had been a windy day, as it often was in the springtime, and he could hear the muffled whistling of the wind as it buffeted the skylight on the roof and the piñon pines outside. There was only a small bedside lamp lit, now, in the boy's bedroom, and the room felt womb-like and warm. Elizabeth and the boys didn't seem to be aware of him standing at the doorway.

Joey squeezed onto the twin-size bed, also. With Elizabeth sandwiched between them. "You haven't read to us in a while, Mom," he said. "It's usually Dad."

"I know. I've missed doing this." She reached her arms around them both, squeezing them to her.

Luke grimaced for an instant. "*C'mon,* Mom. So . . . what are you reading us, anyway?"

"It's a book I ordered at the bookstore in town. I used to *love* this book, when I was a girl. And I think you guys'll like it. It's called 'My Side Of The Mountain' . . . and it's about a young guy—a guy who's a little older than Luke—who doesn't like living in the big city. New York City. So he runs away from home, to go live in the Catskill Mountains in upstate New York . . . and he learns how to survive in the woods there. It's a cool story. So this is how it starts . . ." Elizabeth cleared her throat. "you see . . . he buys a ticket for a bus ride up into the Catskill Mountains, to this little town, there, called Delhi—"

Joey squinted his eyes. "*Delhi?*"

"Yep. It's a real town. I looked it up once, on a map—when I was a girl and was reading this book. Maybe it's named after the city in India, I don't know . . . "

As his wife began reading the first chapter of the book, Nate listened to the tone of her voice. A melodic love-song to their boys. He could have listened in, longer, like a mesmerized fly on the wall. He could have listened forever . . . *Damn. I wish I could capture this on videotape or something . . .* A tightness in his chest felt like it was going to suffocate him. And he turned away . . . *How are these guys gonna make it without her? . . .* He glanced back at them and—not wanting to break the spell of the moment—like a petty thief he padded off quietly back into the main bedroom. And decided to skip the shower, thinking that the noise might be disruptive because of where the bathroom was located in the center of the house.

33.

*".. . Like I've been acting in a play, and it's not
being directed very well. Or the script is fucked-up . . ."*

Nate found it hard to believe, of his best friend, who'd always seemed to
be fairly staid and conservative . . . *Mac, of all people, spending time in
India! India? What's up with that?* . . . It was now early September, and
Mac had just returned from his second trip to India. This time, for a
much longer stay than he had a couple of years earlier. For the better part
of the past three months he'd been spending time with some spiritual
teacher named *Papaji,* in a city in northern India called Lucknow. Nate
always knew Mac had a spiritual bent—or some sort of spiritual yearning
similar to his own. But, India? And yet, why not, if the man had a
hankering to explore that part of the world? After all, he was divorced,
unattached, and didn't have the same obligations that Nate did.

While Elizabeth was out on one of her increasingly rare trips into
town, shopping, Nate talked with Mac on the phone. He of course had
spoken with him in the spring, after they'd heard the latest prognosis
about Elizabeth's illness. But things had only gone downhill since then.
Nate stood by the kitchen counter—where the phone was—and brought
Mac up to date. The tumor in Elizabeth's lung had progressed to where,
for the past few weeks, she'd been on a fairly strong painkiller,
oxycodone. The tumor was causing her a lot of discomfort and coughing,
and it seemed apparent that soon they'd have to consider a stronger
opiate or synthetic opioid drug. She was getting used to the painkiller,
now—though it caused her some degree of nausea and dizziness. And so
Nate also was concerned, lately, about her driving ability, especially with

the dizziness.

As he spoke with his friend, Nate ran his free hand through his hair, tugging at it slightly. He had to remind himself repeatedly not to grip the phone so tightly—his fingers getting pins and needles as he explained Elizabeth's condition. Mac listened in silence to this anxious soliloquy. After many minutes of this diatribe against the ignorance of the medical profession and the lack of scientific understanding regarding cancer—and a diatribe, in fact, against organized religion as well—there was silence on the other end. "Mac? . . . You there?"

"Yeah . . . I'm here, brother. I'm so sorry you guys are going through this. And, God . . . I just love Elizabeth. It's gonna be a very tough time, for both of you. . . . Might be a good time to double up on your AA meetings. Are you still *going* to meetings?"

"Yeah," Nate said. "I go once a week—to the meeting in Silver City. It helps."

"Right . . . I 'spect it will. You'll probably hear from at least a few people who've gone through difficult times . . . sober. And I guess I don't need to tell you, but if you start drinking again, now . . . well, it'd be like putting gas on the fire."

"No. Oh, *hell* no. I can't afford to do that. I'd *never* forgive myself . . . I mean, if I put Elizabeth through *that,* one more time. As ill as she is. I couldn't live with myself."

"You might at least want to double up on your spiritual work. Praying for help and guidance, I mean—from whatever concept of God or a Higher Power you're using, lately. And spend some time in meditation."

"Yeah," Nate said. "Totally. You're right. I *am* trying to pray for help, more often . . . 'cause I damn sure need it. But you know what sucks the worst about this? It's not really *me* I'm worried about, if Liz passes. It's the guys. Luke and Joey. It makes me want to rip my teeth out when I think about them without their mother. But it's damned likely that I'm in denial about that, too. . . . I'm probably gonna be one broken motherfucker if or when she dies."

"Maybe," Mac said. "Maybe not. Maybe you'll be completely at peace with it. It's not *here,* yet. A word of advice from a guy who used to be your sponsor in AA: Don't *project.* It's probably the worst thing that people do to themselves—projecting. And probably we alcoholics are worse about it than most people. . . . Trying—*today*—to deal with the wreckage of our future! . . . Pointless. Don't go there. There is *some* sense in preparing for the future. But only up to a point. If we're effectively dealing with the *present* . . . then it follows that we effectively deal with any possible future events, when they happen. And that's where meditation can help . . . in just being present in this moment."

Nate exhaled a long, pent-up sigh. Somehow, Mac's words felt like balm . . . *Like balm on a bee-sting* . . . "Right. That's what I needed to hear. . . . Makes total sense. I just want to be here . . . *here* . . . and not be thinking about the goddamn future. I want to be free of this suffering. I know it's my wife that's suffering—sick and dying, in fact—but I'm getting *my* ass kicked, too. Suffering like a som'bitch. It's like I'm sick and dying, too . . . right there along with her. Like something's being ripped out of my guts."

As if Mac hadn't heard what Nate said—or was listening to something else—he said quietly, "You see, the present is *all* there is . . . and that's where Consciousness, or Presence, or God, is. Nothing else is real. All of the awakened spiritual masters point to this. It sounds trite—or even *obvious*, when you think about it—but all events and phenomena can happen *only* in the present. In the Now. . . . The past, and the future—they exist only in our memory or in our imagination. In the gray matter in our brains. You know what I'm saying? . . . The past, the future—neither of these is *real* . . . and yet that's where most *all* of our suffering comes from. At least, our mental and emotional suffering. Physical pain or illness is a different animal . . . but often morphs into the mental suffering. And most humans spend their entire lives hoping for something in the future, just out of their grasp. . . . Some sense of security—or a pain free state—that might seem more pleasant than what's happening right now. While the present moment is actually all there is—and it's slipping past them. The present can be truly *awesome*. But only if I am 100 percent *here* . . . and not spinning my wheels over some other crap."

"Right," Nate said. "I think I get what you're sayin'. . . . I totally need to get back into a regular meditation practice. I've been letting it slide a lot, here, lately. At least, when I was practicing meditation . . . well, I'd have a few moments, or minutes, of being in the present. And didn't feel like I needed to change one damned thing. Peace. Silence, in my brain. And that was wonderful."

"Yeah. That's the stuff. That's where peace is. But you know . . . you can be there *all the time*. In the present. In Consciousness. This is what my teacher *Papaji* points to, over and over again. But the paradox is, you see, that meditation—as a continuing lifelong practice—can ultimately be a trap. Many of the other teachers, preachers, and gurus teach meditation almost as if it's an end in itself . . . with enlightenment or spiritual awakening being some future goal. At some future date. Or, sometimes they even suggest that enlightenment is in store for us only in a future lifetime. . . . *Bullshit.* That's one of the traps of spiritual practice. And meanwhile, they're overlooking what is here *right now*. Within us.

And all around us . . . all the time. Closer than close. Consciousness. Presence. The Self—with a capital 'S.' God. . . . You see . . . everything else changes. And anything that changes is ultimately not real."

"Huh?" Nate said. "Not *real?* What the heck do you mean?"

"Nothing that changes is real. You see, brother . . . we live in a world of constantly changing phenomena, which are essentially manifested by the mind. And similarly, the changing phenomena of our society—and of the world at large—are also manifested by the *collective* mind, the collective ego. We look for, and long for, stability and peace . . . in a constantly changing world. Where it *can't* be found. This is the origin of suffering. And that's exactly what the Buddha talked about, over two thousand years ago—attachment to the impermanent as being the basic cause of all suffering. It's like we're trying to take a meaningful photograph of a constantly changing scene—and with a camera that is also constantly changing and transforming. This is suffering. *Samsara . . . to use the Sanskrit word.

"The only thing that *is* real, in fact, is the *Self.* Find out who this Self is . . . the part of you that is observing and questioning all of this suffering and discomfort you're experiencing. The Seer. Consciousness. Enquire into this—as to who this Self, this Seer is—and you'll find the only thing that is unchanging. The only thing that is real. Unchanging and unmoved. The substratum from which all phenomena arise and fade back into. Some of us call it God. And it's right here under our noses— where we're all too stupid to look. Not on some lofty cloud or behind some heavenly gates. Here . . . now. Always present. But we're all in such a trance—and in such a state of constant confusion—that we can't see it. Can't experience it. And we can't realize it. . . . Actually, we *won't* realize it—out of ignorance and choice—not *can't.*"

Nate was quiet but with eyebrows raised, as he listened with the phone held more loosely to his cheek, now. Perplexed but uncomplaining. "Whew. . . . Man, you have *changed.* Not sure that I'm getting all that you're saying . . . but some part of me feels like this is true. And somehow familiar . . . like I've *heard* it before."

"Find out for yourself if it's true. Part of you knows it. But don't take my word for it . . . experience it for yourself. If you feel like you've heard it before maybe it's because you have. Somewhere along the way . . . or even in a previous life." There was a long pause. "I'm sorry, brother. I'm talking a *lot.*"

"No, it's okay," Nate said. "I'm interested in hearing about this stuff.". . . *I guess I must be interested, or I would've cut this conversation short a while ago . . .* "So, these things you're talking about—these concepts, these teachings . . . is this what you've learned from this guy,

Papaji? Is this, like, a kind of Buddhism?"

"Not Buddhism, no. There're a lot of similarities, though. No doubt, the Buddha was an awakened spiritual master. But this isn't really Buddhist. And not really Hindu either, for that matter—though you could say these teachings have always been one aspect of Hinduism. Papaji grew up in a Hindu family. And so did his teacher—his guru—a guy called *Ramana*. Ramana Maharshi. These concepts are basically one set of teachings from the Vedas—an ancient Hindu scripture. Hindus call it Advaita Vedanta. In the West, some of us call it 'nondualism.'

"Funny, because these teachings are often overlooked by Hindus, too. It's almost, like . . . way too simple for any organized religion. But yet, there are aspects of these teachings in all religions. Christian mysticism. Judaism. Sufism. Islam. I have no doubt that Christ was an awakened spiritual master—in his realization of the Self, and in his awareness of his underlying connection to God. Actually, it's in one of the gospels—I think it's Luke—where Christ said something like, 'Don't look here, and don't look there. For indeed, the kingdom of God is within you.' But I 'spect his teachings were almost completely misunderstood, from the start. And altered, for various reasons . . . as is most always the case, with organized religion."

"Huh," Nate said, "Yeah . . . I hear what you're sayin'. Interesting." His brow was furrowed as he looked down at the tiled countertop, running his finger along its edge . . . *But some of this, I'm not too sure about* . . . Barely noticeable, he shook his head. "I have a little trouble with what you were saying . . . about how things that change aren't *real*. What does that even *mean*? Like . . . our bodies change, right? So you're saying our bodies aren't real?"

"Ultimately, that's true. We are not our bodies. In Western society, especially, we can't even conceive of this possibility. We think of ourselves as our bodies. Period. End of discussion. . . . But the body is just a form that Consciousness is inhabiting. Forms—in this manifest world—come and go. We're so much more than just our bodies. Our form."

"Huh?" Nate was frowning now. "I mean, what are you saying? If our bodies aren't *real* . . . then . . . you're saying that *my* body isn't real, *Liz's* body isn't real? . . . That even Liz's illness is not real?"

"Our bodies are within the realm of phenomena and form. They come and go. Ramana once said to Papaji—during Papaji's awakening—that 'What appears and disappears is not real.' All forms that come and go— or appear and then disappear—are ultimately not real. *Cannot* be real. Our *bodies* come and go. . . . Elizabeth is not merely her body. She's so much more than that. We all are."

Nate repeated the words, mulling the words over as he did so, "Elizabeth is not her body. . . . Huh. Damn! I'm just not getting this."

"Let me put it this way—we all have a body that will die, right? Everything born into this manifest world will die. We all know this, intellectually. But still we can't fathom it. The ego cannot comprehend its own annihilation, so it constructs an imaginary world-view that it thinks will guarantee its own safety and survival. Even to the point where—on a cultural level—the collective ego creates organized religion. . . . Which is just an expansion of the individual ego's fear and desire for immortality."

"Huh. I can dig *that*. That's been, like, in the back of my head for a long time . . . what it is I don't get, about religion, I mean. There's some falsehood there—some kind of mental masturbation, about immortality—that I always thought was bullshit."

"Yep," Mac said. "And unfortunately, the ego, a creation of the mind—essentially just a bunch of thoughts and concepts, reinforced by those around us—is part of the body. And it dies when the body dies. The ego thinks that it alone is the part of us that will live forever . . . continue on in some form, after the body dies. Or even gain a pair of wings, and continue on in some heavenly realm. And yet this bundle of thoughts expires when the brain stops functioning, at death. It's not even *real*."

Nate gazed out the window at nothing in particular, nodding his head. "I think I can understand that part. Makes sense." As he looked over toward Elizabeth's flower garden, out front, he frowned again . . . *Huh. Yeah . . . I can see the ego dying along with the body. But, there's something else within us . . . Right? . . . Something at the core of the ego, at the core of the mind . . .*

Mac spoke again. "We think that the 'me'—the concept of self, separate from everything else—is all that there is, here. All that we are. . . . Because that's what we tell ourselves—and have been taught that by everyone else around us since childhood. It's all part of our conditioning. Our programming. But that's *not* all there is . . . and that's not who we really are.

"When we're able to take a step back from all the melodrama, acrobatics, and suffering created by the ego in its struggles . . . and sometimes we can achieve this through meditation, or through self-enquiry into where it is that the 'I' thought comes from . . . we can recognize something else there. In the background, at the core. The Self. The Seer. The silent observer who is unperturbed by the chaos surrounding us—and who gets us to laugh, sometimes, at the craziness of our own behavior. This Seer—Consciousness—exists both within us and outside of us, simultaneously. Everywhere, in fact. It's the source of all knowledge . . . or I should say, it *is* knowledge. This part of us—the Seer, the Self with a capital 'S'—is actually the only part of us that *is* real. It never changes. Unfathomable, endless, unchanging, and always present . . . it's the part of us that's not subject to the cycle of birth and death. In fact, birth and death—and all other forms and manifestations of *samsara*—arise from within this substrate. And dissolve back into it, when they're made unmanifest again.

"This Seer or the Self is the aspect of us that experiences bliss and reunion at the moment of death and—unlike the ego—isn't at all frightened of death. This is also the deep well that we are all capable of immersing ourselves in . . . always available, right here and right now. It's where we are all able to find lasting peace. And bliss. It's what we're all secretly looking for.

"The point is, with these Advaita Vedanta teachings . . . is that we all experience bliss and reunion—an end to suffering—at the moment of death. But we don't have to wait until death for this end to suffering. We can experience this while we're alive. Can in fact live all our lives in a state of bliss and contentment—without fear thoughts controlling our every activity. Without worry lying underneath everything we do.

"Some of us are *done* with samsara, in this lifetime. This time around. Exhausted with it. I know *I* am. Samsara, the word from Sanskrit, means literally 'repetition of desires.' It's a never-ending chain—of desires, the fulfilling of those desires, and then their replacement with new desires. And all of this causes suffering . . . what seems like endless suffering. But some of us—maybe we're old souls, who've been here many times before—become aware of something else. A way out of the suffering. Through awakening to our true Self. Consciousness.

"Others of us—inhabiting this world—are almost totally unaware of Consciousness. Unaware of the Self. And these people suffer almost continuously. Like it says, in the Bhagavad Gita, they are 'so strongly shaken, in the grip of the senses . . . Truly, the wind is no wilder.' There's no peace there, ever. We all know people like that. And we've all been there and done that, at times. Running from one distraction to another—anything to keep ourselves occupied and distracted from thinking about how much we suffer. We run around like chickens with their heads cut off. I don't know about you, but I'm *done* with that. Just done. Toast. . . . I've got no more time—or energy—to give, to that kind of life."

Nate recognized kindred thoughts, in himself, that had bothered him off and on for most of his life . . . *It's like I've never been able to put a finger on it—this discontent I've had, since I was a kid. Like I've been acting in a play, and it's not being directed very well. Or the script is fucked-up* . . . He sighed and said quietly, "I kind of feel like I'm exhausted with it, too. Or like, well . . . like a part of me sees through all the bullshit, here, and has no more energy to give it. I can't drum up even the slightest interest in politics, anymore. Or religion. Or even world events, for that matter."

"Right," Mac said, "Well, you've always been a bit of a seeker—like me—ever since I've known you. Maybe it's even some kind of trait common to alcoholics. Funny thing is . . . there's nothing to *seek!* Hah! A bit of a cosmic joke, there. 'Cause it's always *been* here, all along. Consciousness. God. An end to suffering, which is freedom—the freedom that everyone is looking for and the only *real* freedom there *is*. Papaji always says that he's not *giving* us anything. And that's why we can never lose it or have it taken away—as we can and will, with any number of other impermanent things. We already have it—it's *here*. All this teacher does for us is to point out, in a very precise way, what is already here but below the radar. Beneath our 'normal' perception."

"Cool. . . . I don't know *exactly* what you're referring to—maybe I'm not even close—but I wish I could meet this guy. . . . Your teacher, Papaji. I can tell you've found an answer, for yourself. And like you've found some real peace, with this stuff." On the other end of the phone line, there was silence. Mac had been on a roll and doing most of the talking. Nate had been listening intently—but after a few more long moments of silence, he wondered if they'd been disconnected. He squinted, as if to hear better. "Mac? . . . Hey, Mac, does Papaji ever come to the States?"

The silence continued for a few more moments. "Uh, yeah. Yep. I think he's been to *D.C.,* once. Washington, D.C. He's been to Europe a few times. And of course all over India. But he's getting well up in years, now—in his eighties—and has some health issues. He can't walk too well. So most of the time, now, he stays close to home in Lucknow. He's been starting to get a lot of visitors in the past couple of years. People from all over the world. Sometimes, in the winter—when it's cool in India—there'll be two or three hundred people coming to his satsang, every day."

"His what?"

"Satsang," Mac said. "Satsang translates, roughly, as a 'fellowship of truth.' In Papaji's satsang, people sit with him to meditate and hear his teachings. Though he himself would say that he's not really a teacher . . . and that there's nothing to teach. He *is* an awakened spiritual master, though, and he's perfectly adept at showing us—pointing out to us, precisely—the peace and stillness that is already a part of us. The Self . .

. Consciousness. Somehow, just being in the presence of a *satguru*—in the presence of someone like Papaji—helps us to realize our true nature. And awaken to the Self. Many of us have realized enlightenment in his presence. He holds satsang almost every weekday, there, at a house in Lucknow. And almost every day—with his guidance—people find spiritual awakening."

"Very cool. This sounds amazing. I hope I get to meet this guy someday. I *absolutely* want peace. And freedom. Freedom from this never-ending nuthouse. I don't mean this house, *here* . . . I mean this nuthouse of a human race."

"Gotcha. And this *is* a nuthouse. But this teacher tells us that—if we truly want freedom—to keep a fire burning for that, in our hearts. And that this fire for freedom will burn away everything that's obstructing us. He says, 'Pour a little *benzene* on it!'" There was a chuckle at the other end of the line. Mac said he had to get off the phone, but suggested Nate call him anytime he wanted.

"Yeah," Nate said, "I'd like to rap with you some more about this stuff. It almost sounds familiar to me. And hopeful, for some reason. I'd like to hear more. What're these teachings called again?"

"Nondualism, is what a lot of Westerners call it. Or Advaita Vedanta. Yeah, call me any time. Blessings . . . for you and Elizabeth. Give her my love."

34.

To Elizabeth, Big Cove seemed a magical place
—so different from the asphalt and traffic of Asheville.

For some reason he couldn't explain, Nate looked forward to hearing more of Mac's talk about the spiritual awakening work he'd been doing. They'd been friends for a while, of course—so he also just liked talking with him, especially now. Their relationship was almost like brothers, but on some level he thought of Mac more as a confidante and guide. In his first couple of years in recovery, Nate had used Mac as his "sponsor" in AA—which may have been essential to his maintaining sobriety. And so, a week after their last long conversation on the phone, Nate called him again. This phone call reinforced the thought that he needed to talk to Mac in person—and sooner rather than later.

Elizabeth's health steadily declined, and near the end of September she wasn't leaving the house anymore. Nate now spent almost as much time at home with her as he did at work, leaving Steve to keep the business going much of the time. In the past week Elizabeth had trouble with fluid building up around one lobe of her lungs, and a shunt was put in to drain it. She had some degree of pain almost continuously now, so the doctors stepped up the frequency of her pain-killing meds. A Hospice care nurse was scheduled to visit twice a week through the Gila Valley Medical Center.

It was a period of angst and suffering that Elizabeth was merely enduring—with Nate enduring it vicariously. For him, the spiritual talks he had with Mac were one of the few bright spots in this otherwise dark period.

~ ~ ~ ~ ~

Half-asleep, Elizabeth opened her eyes for a moment and saw that the strong autumn sun was blazing into the bedroom, warming the bed and blankets but not uncomfortably so. The oxycodone that she took as a painkiller now oftentimes made her groggy and tired. She'd been having the chills, lately—especially in the evenings—but the sun-warmed bed felt just right. And as soon as her eyelids grew heavy she fell asleep again.

The humidity in the warm air clung to Elizabeth like honey, as Grandma Weaver led them up onto the hogback ridge rising above the Big Cove area. Elizabeth was eleven, her younger sister Jean was nine— and they were staying with their grandmother for a whole week, now that school had let out for the summer. Grandma Weaver had moved back onto the Cherokee reservation southwest of Asheville, North Carolina, after Grandpa died. The main reason being her desire to live close to her two remaining sisters. Her sisters both lived—with extended families nearby—in the Big Cove community, along the cold mountain stream known as Raven Fork.

As Grandma led them up a faint trail that branched off of the hot, red-clay road and into the lush, shadowy forests of the Great Smoky Mountains, she spoke to them in colorful stories about the land of her ancestors. Grandma wasn't full-blooded Cherokee, but nearly so. As she wove her tale, Elizabeth looked at her eyes, sparkling against medium-dark skin. Her hair still black but streaked with gray.

Grandma talked to them about how her people had lived in these mountains for thousands of years. And how, in the 1830s—when the white man's government forced the Cherokees to relocate west, to Oklahoma—some of them escaped into the mountain wilderness nearby. They called the forced relocation of her people the "Trail of Tears" because so many died on the trek. After living secretly in these mountains for years, this Eastern Band of the Cherokee was later given a small reservation in the Great Smokies. And the U.S. government, about fifty years later, created the Great Smoky Mountains National Park right next to the reservation.

Elizabeth loved hearing her grandmother talk. Grandma Weaver was a wealth of knowledge about nature and wildcrafting in these mountains—showing Elizabeth and her sister how to recognize the witch hazel trees, and how to pick the leaves and twigs to make medicine.

She taught them about ginseng, and the way it mostly grew on the cooler, north-facing hillsides. After finding one particularly nice ginseng plant, she thanked it for giving its medicine to the people and then dug it up to show them the root. A few of the old-timers in Big Cove wildcrafted witch hazel and ginseng to make money. And some of the best ginseng, she said, was over the boundary in the national park—where you weren't supposed to dig it, of course. But some of them did anyway. She cut up part of the ginseng root, and handed pieces of it to the girls to chew on, telling them it was good medicine for the heart and kept one strong. It tasted bitter and hot, but Elizabeth kept it in her mouth while her sister spat hers out as soon as Grandma wasn't looking. Grandma told them all about the woods, with its many medicines that came from the plants. And that Creator put them here to help the people—and put animals on the earth to keep the people from getting lonely.

In the late afternoon they walked back to her little house near the river, and she showed them how to steep the witch hazel in spring water. Later, she would simmer it down into a tincture. After dinner, Grandma took the girls into town to get an ice-cream cone. On the drive back home the air felt too chilly to leave the car windows down, so they rolled them up most of the way even though it was June. A large black bear crossed the road, in the car's headlights—and Grandma stopped the car to listen, as the bruin snapped branches while galloping into the woods. To Elizabeth, Big Cove seemed a magical place—so different from the asphalt and traffic of Asheville—as the early summer crickets filled the night with their song. After she took a bath, Grandma sat her down and combed her hair. Although her grandmother was a bit unusual—and surely wouldn't have been much at home in the streets of a big city like Asheville—Elizabeth knew without a doubt that her dad's mother loved her as one of her own. Unconditionally. Later, sharing a bed upstairs with her sister, she fell asleep to a duet of hoot owls in the misty nighttime air behind the house.

When she awoke the sun was already up quite high. Elizabeth squinted her eyes against the glare, reflecting off the white comforter . . . *Looks like afternoon sun. Where am I? Oh, I was dreaming* . . . She felt wrapped in a deeply caring love, fostered by her memory of Grandma Weaver. It reminded her of a similar feeling of unconditional love she'd experienced, sometime recently . . . *Something about the bright sunshine. Oh . . . The Casa . . . Brazil* . . . She closed her eyes with a quiet smile, and when she fully opened her eyes again, blinking a bit, she recognized Nate sitting next to her on the bed.

He was perched on the edge of the bed, maybe to avoid awakening her. He smiled. "Hey there, Sweetie. I was just checkin' on you . . . to see if you needed anything." Elizabeth's hair was a bit disheveled, no longer having the same luster it once did. A slightly dry, wiry look to it. She hadn't been eating well lately, maybe wasn't even getting adequate nutrition. Foods that for years had been her favorites were becoming hard to stomach now, and she had little appetite.

Nate rubbed her arm softly. "I made you a chicken salad sandwich. Will you try and eat some? I made it your favorite way . . . in a 'pita pocket.' I even put some greens in it—I think you'll like it. Good vitamins and stuff."

"Okay. I'll try. Funny . . . I was just dreaming about Grandma . . . and the Great Smokies. And something made me think about the Casa de Dom Francisco."

"Oh?"

"It really *was* a pretty special place, wasn't it?"

"Well, yeah. I always thought so. I liked it there."

A half-smile came to her face. "I'm sorry we didn't go back there, Hon'."

"Oh . . . water over the dam. We can go back there sometime, if you want to."

Elizabeth was quiet for a moment and fixed her gaze calmly on Nate. "I think I want my ashes to be spread in the Smoky Mountains . . . in the woods near Big Cove, where my grandma used to live."

Nate looked at her silently, thinking her gray eyes absolutely beautiful, though tired.

"It always felt so peaceful and *ancient*, there," she continued, ". . . in those green, green mountains. I guess I've always loved the mountains. Just like you do. I could never live in the flat lands, really. Maybe it's the part of me that's Cherokee."

When Nate got up to go to the kitchen, she noticed him squinting, his eyes looking a little bleary. "I didn't mean to make you sad, Honey. I don't like talking about that stuff when I'm feeling crummy . . . but I feel pretty good right now. I had a good nap."

"Excellent," Nate said, sitting down on the bed again, taking his boots off. He climbed over her, on the bed, and lifted up the covers to get in beside her, not caring that he had his clothes on. In a cracked voice, he said, "I love you so much, Liz." He snuggled up close to her, and Elizabeth turned to face him.

Nate pulled her close. "I hate that I'm goin' away for a couple of days. Beverly's gonna be here tomorrow, you know. You sure things'll be okay?"

"Oh yeah . . . they will be. I almost forgot that she's coming tomorrow. It'll be good to see 'er."

"Are you still okay with my going up to visit Mac? I'm only going if you're *sure* things'll be okay, while Bev is here."

"Oh, yeah," she said, "you *go,* now. Didn't you say you guys are gonna go backpacking?"

"Yeah. That's the plan. Maybe the Pecos Wilderness . . . you know, around Truchas Peak. Where you and I went up there once, remember?"

"I remember. It's beautiful there. And it'll be nice, this time of year . . . with the aspens turning. Or already turned. Far out. You go, now. *Seriously.* Bev'll probably be waiting on me hand and foot."

Nate raised himself slightly to kiss her forehead, and then kissed her mouth. His tongue exploring a little. He let his lips leave hers. They lay face-to-face, noses touching, as they gazed into each other's eyes. He kissed her more insistently, and pressed his body against her. He didn't want to hurt her in any way, in her weakened condition. But also wanted to make love to her. Elizabeth reached down to his belt and noticed he was aroused. She began to undo his belt buckle. "Oh . . . let's get your jeans off. What the heck."

Wriggling out of his jeans, Nate pulled her close. "The kids won't be back for a while."

"They're at Jean's?"

"Yes. And y*es* . . . I want to make love to you. I want to make love to you always."

35.

"You already possess infinite wisdom and knowledge.
We all simply forget this, amid the confusion
and trance of this world."

It was a crisp fall evening, in the high-desert air of Santa Fe, when Nate parked his truck in front of Mac's house. The first stars beginning to shine like jewels in the depths of a cobalt blue sky. He knocked on the door and opened it, poking his head in. "Hey, buddy! Guess who?"

Mac came into the living room and with a smile welcomed him in. "Come on in, brother, it's gettin' chilly out." He hugged Nate and closed the door.

Nate had stopped and called from the road, saying he wanted to pick up some take-out Chinese food if Mac was game. From a good Chinese restaurant that he remembered—and was still in business where it had always been on Cerrillos Road. "Hey, man . . . I hope this stuff is still *warm.*" He scooped up a bulky oil-stained paper bag from where he'd set it near the door. "Smells good, anyway."

Sitting down on the threadbare couch, which had a Mexican Indian blanket draped over the back of it, Nate opened the bag, producing four white cardboard cartons with red Chinese-style designs on them. Mac went to the kitchen to fix some tea to go along with it, brought out a couple of plates, and they settled down to eat.

Mac had asked Nate to get him some kind of spicy tofu dish, and he stirred a sticky pile of rice into the sauce on his plate. He glanced at Nate. "So the drive was okay?"

"Yeah," Nate said. "Fine. No *problemo.*" Mac was being less talkative than usual, he noticed. And there was something a little different about the man's eyes. "Yeah, uh . . . when did you start eating *tofu,* anyway? I thought you were always a meat-eater."

"Oh, I just got used to having vegetarian food while I was in India . . . and thought I'd continue with it for a while."

"Gotcha." Nate talked for a while about the latest, regarding Elizabeth's condition. Beverly had arrived in the early afternoon, and he knew Elizabeth was in good hands for the moment. Luke and Joey seemed to be dealing with her illness, but that part was very troubling to Nate. "I don't know how they're gonna take it—," he said, tearing up, and in a cracked voice he continued, "when she passes."

"Yep," Mac said. "This is very tough stuff."

Changing the topic, Nate spoke for a while about the earthship, how it was working for them, and about some of the other sustainable-type houses that had been built in their community. As they finished their meal, Nate took a long gulp of his tea, now just tepid. "I'd like to hear some more about the teachings, Mac—the teachings you were exposed to in India. The stuff just sounds intriguing to me."

"Yeah. Sure thing. If you're drawn to it, we'll talk. I'm just gonna clean up a few things in the kitchen—so I won't have to deal with it in the morning—and we'll talk for a bit, out here. You're on."

A half hour later, or so, they sat down again—Nate taking his place on the couch as before. Mac suggested they first spend some time in silence, in meditation, saying that it was usually helpful to quiet the mind before this kind of dialogue. "Just sit back, and get comfortable. Close your eyes, if you want—or leave them half-open but without really focusing on anything. You know how . . . you've practiced meditation before."

"Yep. Sounds good." For a while, with his eyes softly closed, Nate couldn't stop the racing thoughts in his mind. As if he was still coursing down the highway, like he had been an hour earlier . . . *The traffic . . . Elizabeth! . . . Beverly . . . Cancer . . . Brazil . . . Ben . . . Religion . . .* Finally, in the silence of the room with only the infrequent soft whoosh of a car on the street outside, his mind quieted and came to a halt . . . *Silence, now . . . at least for the moment . . .* He slowly opened his eyes and raised his gaze to where his friend sat. Mac was looking at him, a half-smile crossing his face for an instant.

Mac cleared his throat. "Some of us are drawn to *Advaita satsang,* in this lifetime. But, really, there's only a small number of people—all around the world—who are ready for it and pulled toward it. Those of us drawn to satsang are the lucky ones. The journey's almost over."

"Journey?" Nate asked. But he felt peaceful and didn't feel

emotionally or intellectually invested in the question. As if everything was okay no matter what Mac's answer was.

"The soul's journey. Maybe you're an 'old soul'—have been here many times before—and have reached the point where you're done with samsara and its suffering. Only you can know that . . . or have some inkling of that. That's a good place to be. The soul—over its numerous lifetimes—finishes its work here and merges into a state of permanent union with Consciousness. That's the permanent awakening. . . . Where the game of *Leela*—playing hide-and-seek with God—is finished. And the individual's soul isn't born into the suffering of this world anymore."

Nate gazed quietly at a mug sitting on the coffee table . . . *Done with suffering. Finished with suffering. I've heard of this, somewhere. Maybe this is the real alternative—the other way, of being in this world—that I've been aware of in the back of my head for so many years* . . . He exhaled loudly. "Kind of like the end-game, huh?"

"You *could* say. Or just the beginning—of the end of suffering. I've had periods of awakening to my true nature—Consciousness—with Papaji. But I guess I'd have to say that I'm not sure I'm permanently fixed in that state. Papaji *does* seem to be permanently in that state . . . he's like, permanently resting in stillness. And blissful at the same time. He giggles and laughs almost constantly—the happiest person I've ever known. I want that, too. Sometimes—in satsang with him—everyone in the room breaks out into laughter. Over some silly business when we all realize how insane it is, the way the human mind works."

"No kidding."

"Yep. This teacher says that laughter is a state of 'no-mind.' A state where the mind cannot function in its 'normal' way. We get relief from our thoughts—in laughter—even if it's just for a few moments."

"Huh. . . . Makes sense. I guess that's why we pay comedians to make us laugh."

There was a silence, for a minute, maybe more, neither of the men needing to break it or fill it. Nate felt an unusual quietness within him, pondering what Mac had said.

Mac spoke again, "You know, if you're drawn to the Advaita teachings, then you're actually drawing it to *you*. The teacher appears when the soul is ready for the teaching. When the soul is ready, the guru manifests. But eventually . . . you learn that the guru is really your own true Self. No difference. No separation. You already possess infinite wisdom and knowledge. We all simply forget this, amid the confusion and trance of this world. You see, the true guru—or *satguru*—doesn't actually give you *anything* you don't already possess. He or she only points out to you, indelibly, where it's located—and how to awaken to it

and realize it, in your life. They point out to us what we already know . . .
but forgot, in the chaos of this world."

An expression akin to surprise came over Nate's face, his eyebrows
raised. "Whew. This stuff sounds heavy. But simple, at the same time . . .
the simplicity of it sounds to be true. I've always thought that religious or
spiritual truth *has* to be simple. I 'spect it's the human mind that
complicates these things—like the mind does, in forming organized
religion. And the mind complicates most everything else that we create,
actually."

"Yes. The human mind is the trickster. And not really trustworthy.
It's been necessary, of course, in the evolution of our species—and in
ensuring our survival. But it's not really trustworthy."

"Not sure what I think about having a guru, though."

"Well, I'm just playing my part in this, Nate. I'm not saying that I
could or should be your teacher or guru. If you weren't ready for these
teachings . . . well, our conversation here wouldn't even be happening. It
wouldn't make any sense to you . . . and we wouldn't be talking about
it."

"You're right. We wouldn't. . . . So you, and some other folks are,
like . . . spreading Papaji's teachings, here in the States, now?"

"They're not *his* teachings," Mac said. "He's just one of the more
recent awakened masters—in this sort of lineage of spiritual concepts.
He's been able to reach a whole lot of people—just by word of mouth,
and from folks being drawn to him. Many have had permanent
awakening in his presence . . . through his grace. Or I should say,
through *Grace*. . . . Papaji had his final awakening through *his* satguru,
Ramana Maharshi. But enlightenment always *comes* from Grace—
though it's often *through* the satguru. I think there's little doubt, though,
that all spiritual paths and religions have had awakened masters
throughout history. Spiritual awakening or enlightenment—and the
desire to share that experience—unfortunately just gets bogged down by
the people who decide that there needs to be a religion built up around it.
And pretty soon, that vital knowledge about enlightenment just gets
buried under religious dogma and ritual. And gets lost to the world.
Again."

"Totally. That's kind of what I've suspected about organized religion
all my life."

"My teacher believes that there will be more and more people born in
the West—people who are 'old souls'—and ready for enlightenment.
And so, yeah . . . there *are* more and more teachers beginning to bring
Advaita—nondualism—teachings to the West. The Americas. Europe. . .
. Very possibly it's in the highly developed and technologically-minded

societies where these teachings are needed the most. This human race probably won't survive another World War."

"Huh. No," was all Nate said. . . . *Yeah, we're in real trouble, in this world. I've been wondering if we're gonna make it, here, or self-destruct . . . been wondering this, for a long time* . . . "Yeah, the Americas, and Europe, are pretty much the most powerful countries in the world. And the wealthiest. And the most materialistic."

"Yes. Materialism has run its course, here. There are no more answers here in the West—in scientific knowledge, technology, materialism. It sounds simplistic or even obvious, but the human mind can *never* really solve the complications and problems caused by the human mind. But nevertheless *that* carrot will always be dangling in front of us, here. . . . For example, the hope that better technology—or more 'stuff'—will *fix* things. But it never does. That carrot, that hope, is all part of the suffering game . . . the suffering game of this phenomenal world."

"Huh. And, funny, how it's the Americas and Europe where Christianity and Judaism have been running the show, for millennia."

"Yes."

"Well, maybe," Nate said, "we *do* need some new blood, here. Some new ideas."

"I'd say so. The 'Abrahamic' religions—Judaism, Christianity, and Islam—are *very* dualistic. With the exception of their mystical branches. . . . In fact, I'd say that most *all* of the world's organized religions seem to foster dualistic concepts like 'the Chosen' people . . . and the *others*. Us . . . and *them*. God . . . and *Satan*. And the concept of God, as being a separate, frightening, judgmental entity. These dualistic ideas and beliefs cause tremendous suffering in the world. And the more crowded our world gets—the more population pressure we have—the more suffering they cause."

"Yeah. Really. But you know, man . . . I got a pretty good feel for Hinduism years ago, when I lived at Morningstar. The commune. It was pretty much a Hindu-based commune . . . and isn't the Hindu religion pretty freaking dogmatic, too? Full of ritual?"

"Oh, you bet," Mac said. "And I'm not peddling Hinduism at all. Orthodox Hinduism has been the cause of the same types of craziness other religions are subject to. Segregation. Classism. Racism and genocide. These Advaita or nondualism teachings aren't specifically Hindu. Or Indian, either. They're universal. No, from what I've seen, *all* organized religions eventually run amok. Even with the best of intentions, things go astray. It's just in our human nature, I guess . . . possibly a function of our lower consciousness. Our tribal instincts helped us survive during our evolution in a harsh environment—and in that environment, the concept of *us and them* was actually helpful. But it isn't, any longer. The Truth can be found in all religions, but it has to be teased out. Separated from the chaff."

"You know," Nate said. "I've been talking with Liz about these things you and I've been rapping about—and she's really curious about it. But like I told you, she's accepted Jesus into her life. And been pretty busy, for really the past year and a half, doing the Christian religion thing. Praying at all hours. Reading scripture in the Bible. Going to church regularly. I've been taking her to the church in Deming, the past couple of weeks. Sometimes Ben comes down from the city, and he takes her there. She finds peace in it, I think. But she also likes hearing about your experiences there, in India. Would you want to come back down, to visit? And talk to her about this? It might help her."

"Well, I *could*, Nate. I'd certainly love to see Elizabeth. And I *will* come down to your place—maybe next weekend. But it's really *you* I'm conveying this to. *You're* the one who's feeling drawn to these teachings. And I'm not sure anything I say will be helpful to Liz."

"How do you *know* I'm drawn to these teachings? And she's *not?* . . . I mean, I *am*, but—"

"I know you pretty damn well, Nate. You'd have cut me off in the first two minutes if you weren't curious about it. You're not *that* polite." Mac chuckled.

"Huh! Yeah, you're right."

"Actually, that's one of the things I appreciate about you—you're pretty straight up, about what you are and aren't interested in. You don't mince words. And you don't waste time with stuff you have no use for." He chuckled again and raised his eyebrows. "You'd have told me where to *shove* it—that first time we talked, after I'd gotten back from India. Seems to me that you've always been somewhat of a seeker, from what I've heard and seen. Living at that spiritual commune, a while back. Getting into a meditation practice, getting involved with sweat-lodge. Most of us alcoholics actually *are* looking for spiritual answers—answers to this messy thing called life. Just looking in the wrong places. . . . No, you're drawn to these teachings—I can feel it. Otherwise we wouldn't be having this conversation."

36.

"... at times, when I was in India—where it can feel
so incredibly crowded and hot—I thought of this place.
And how good it would feel to get back up
into the mountains here."

Mac's pickup truck had high ground-clearance, so the two loaded their gear into it since the forest roads where they were going might be washed out from summer thunderstorms. And they managed to pack up and leave at an early hour of the morning. At an outdoor sporting goods store in the city, they picked up some lightweight freeze-dried food, and Mac picked up a new set of aluminum tent stakes—saying he couldn't find them in the garage, the night before.

Leaving Santa Fe, they veered off the interstate at Española and took the old "high road to Taos." It was still quiet in the tiny Hispanic mountain town of Truchas when they drove through it, mid-morning. On the east side of the town, Mac downshifted and steered the truck onto a rutted dirt road, one of the network of unpaved logging roads in the national forest, roads that led up to the Pecos Wilderness boundary.

It was just as well they had brought Mac's truck, because the steeper sections of forest road were badly washed out, with spider webs of eroded trenches running downhill. The roads probably hadn't been graded in a couple of years. Mac's pickup chugged up a short but steep hill to a two- or three-car parking area at the trailhead. The Pecos Wilderness boundary. He squeezed his truck alongside a red pickup. A rusty gate blocked off the road here, which continued on for a mile or so as a Jeep-trail leading eastward up a small river cañon into the wilderness area—a road probably intended for access in the event of a forest fire. The fall air was crisp and cool as the men stepped out of the truck, though the morning sun was quickly warming things. Nate noticed a damp odor of watery vegetation and wet rock, hanging in the air around the chuckling streambed. The North Fork of the Rio Quemado drained off the high alpine country of the Truchas Peaks area—and even after the winter snows had long since melted, this rugged valley stayed moist all summer.

Pulling his backpack out of the truck, Mac set it down and looked around at the surrounding hillsides and trees. He inhaled deeply with a faint smile. "Ahh. *Won*derful! I tell ya . . . at times, when I was in India—where it can feel so incredibly crowded and hot—I thought of this place. And how good it would feel to get back up into the mountains here."

"No doubt," Nate said. "I haven't been here in *years* . . . not since Liz and I did an overnight up here, the summer that we moved to Silver City. It's an amazing place."

Without much discussion, they divvied-up the supplies and gear. Mac's tent was large enough for both of them, and he strapped that to his pack frame. Nate organized most of the food and cookware into his own pack. It was late morning when they finally set out on the trail. The Jeep-trail crossed the rushing stream several times in the first half-mile of gradual ascent, but they were able to cross using the river rocks without getting their boots wet. Nate's backpack felt heavy, massive . . . *Huh. Seems it's always like this, when I'm first starting a hike. Ridiculously hard . . .* At less than a mile into the high country they stopped for a break.

The men gulped water out of their water bottles, though Nate thought the water in the stream looked tempting . . . *And probably clean enough. But it'll be cleaner, farther up . . .* He found a tree branch on the ground, roughly the right size for a walking stick, and whittled a smooth handle on it while they rested. The scent of evergreens, in this heavily wooded lower part of the valley, helped Nate to shed his worries and dark thoughts.

As they picked up their packs and started again, Nate looked up at the beefy tree branches above them—strong, large-girth trees, here, not logged in many decades. Ponderosa pines, though as they gained elevation these were giving way to larger numbers of Engelmann spruce and firs. By mid-afternoon, if they kept up their pace, they would be getting up into the alpine country . . . *Osha! Maybe we'll find some Osha plants growing up there . . . Nothing like fresh Osha root. It'd be really good for Liz's chest congestion . . .* Nate sighed—his thoughts heavy again . . . *Shit. Osha root sure couldn't hurt, though . . . and just might help . . .*

In the early afternoon, after a lunch break they were back on the trail again—and at this point it had gotten much steeper and rockier. The altitude was becoming more apparent to Nate, his breath more strained and raspy . . . *Must be around ninety-five hundred or ten thousand feet, here. And this pack feels even heavier . . .* His dark thoughts about Elizabeth's condition returned, as if to join in with the punishment his body was taking. There wasn't enough extra energy in him, though, to let him talk out loud about it with Mac.

At their next stopping point he vented, a bit, though. As they sat down next to the stream, he gulped from his water bottle, halfway choking on it as he tried to get some words out. "I don't know what I'm supposed to do," he gasped. "I can't raise the kids *without* her. We've always been a team. There's no one else I want, in my life . . . she's *it.* I know that now. Damn it."

Nate spilled his guts while Mac listened quietly, glancing at his friend's reddened face and then back to gazing at the stream near their feet. Nate's face registered, by turns, rage and sadness, as he stabbed at the dark earth near his feet with his walking stick. "What the *hell!* And the damnedest part of it is . . . well, I can't swear to it, but I'm almost certain Liz would've recovered completely—if we'd just gone back to Brazil, and Joseph of God. She was damned near *cured,* by the time we left the Casa! But she just wouldn't do it. Too many years of southern Baptist upbringing, I guess. And I think she knows it, now."

"Maybe . . . " Mac said, "it's just not her karma. This time."

"Her *what? Huh? Karma?* What d'ya mean?"

". . . Let's see if I can put this into words. Maybe she just wasn't *ready . . .* for some kind of radical, spiritual healing. Probably most folks wouldn't be ready for that."

"Maybe so." Nate squinted, as if to see some picture more clearly. "Maybe so . . ."

Mac stood up rather slowly, and moved his backpack into the "ready" position—for hoisting it up and slinging it around onto his shoulders. He looked at Nate before he made the effort. "If it makes things any easier, I can tell you that I'm quite sure, now, that birth and death are only concepts. And I know it may not make sense to you—but these events are only a *relative* reality."

With a frustrated expression, Nate watched as Mac hoisted his backpack, wrestling it onto his shoulders and adjusting the shoulder straps. "What are you saying? More of this 'Elizabeth isn't her body' stuff?"

Mac glanced at Nate, with a concerned expression. "I only meant what I said—and I don't mean to sound callous. Birth and death are only a relative reality, as I understand it. They're manifested by our karma . . . by our attachments and unfulfilled desires from a previous life. I think I talked to you once before, about *samsara*. Samsara—referring to this manifest world and the cycle of birth and death—in its simplest terms means 'repetition of desires.' By that, I mean the desires of the soul."

Nate wore a frown, his mouth slightly agape. "I don't get you."

"We'll talk more about it later, if you want." Mac waited for Nate to shoulder his pack, and they began again the slow trudge up the trail.

The sun was strong at this elevation, though the sweat had dried on the two within minutes of stopping for a break. And it was cool whenever they passed into the shade. Nate watched his friend, ahead of him, hiking with his formidable backpack in a detached, businesslike manner. Mac had tied a rolled-up red bandana around his forehead. Nate glanced at his back from time to time, the man's medium-length unkempt brown hair restrained by the bandana. They'd been friends since shortly after the time Nate moved to Santa Fe . . . *Almost fifteen years ago. I've known him longer than I've known Liz . . . Not sure I really know him anymore, though. He's changed. But change is good. Usually . . .* He thought again about Elizabeth's deteriorating condition . . . *Well, I guess change is just change. Inevitable. As much as we might, or might not like it—inevitable. That, I can wrap my mind around . . .*

But Mac couldn't possibly know what Elizabeth, and he, had been going through. It was irritating, his blithe comments about life and death . . . *The enlightened Mac McGuinn—master of space and time—Hah! And making these sweeping, omniscient remarks about the nature of life. What arrogance! . . .*

Around a bend in the trail, they reached the lower end of a large aspen grove, stretching up the valley, many of the trees still clinging to fluorescent yellow leaves. Their pace—since the last rest stop they made—was slower, neither of the men feeling the need to break any land speed records at this altitude.

At this current stride, Nate felt a second wind—and had the spare energy and a niggling urge to argue with Mac. Something the guy said about karma didn't make any sense, and Nate was aware of a scowl on his face as he thought about it. Making his words loud enough so Mac could hear him without turning around, he said, "What did you mean, Mac . . . about it maybe not being Liz's karma to get well?"

Mac turned around, halfway, as he slowed his pace for a moment. He looked at Nate, but with no hint of defensiveness in his expression. He turned back to trudging the incline in front of them.

Nate continued, "And what do you mean about death being just a concept? I don't really *get* that."

Mac spoke, over his shoulder, taking his time between breaths, "I didn't mean to upset you in any way, brother . . . or to minimize what you all are going through. I'm sorry if what I said was out of place. I just speak what feels to be truth, to me."

"Well, you act like you know all *about* death. . . . And that what you say is the bottom line about birth and death and everything."

Mac turned halfway round, again, looking at Nate with an untroubled expression, though his eyebrows were raised. He stopped on the trail, allowing Nate to step up the few yards to where he stood. Waiting a good half-minute or so to catch his breath, Mac said, "I *have* looked into my own heart—about these things. And I've experienced the death of someone close to me. You and I probably never talked about it . . . but my older brother died when he was eighteen. Just a couple years older than me. Hugh was killed in a car accident—a drunk driving accident. He was decapitated. I've had questions about life and death ever since."

"Oh . . . I'm sorry, man. No, I didn't know that."

"Through Papaji's teachings—the Advaita teachings—I've come to some peace around it. And I'm no longer afraid of death. At least . . . when I'm resting in Consciousness, I'm not afraid of it. Not concerned about it. But I guess I'd have to say that I'm *not* there all the time. And sometimes I just plain miss him . . . Hugh, I mean."

"Sorry. I didn't mean to sound like I—"

"Not to worry, my friend. I'm sorry if I offended. . . . Do you want to take the lead for a while? It's probably just another mile or mile and a half up to that alpine meadow below the peaks."

"Sure," Nate said. "I'll take the lead for a bit. And I'll try to keep up the pace. We're makin' pretty good time. We should be up there near timberline, by . . . what d'ya think? Around four? We could even set up camp quickly, and hike up to the peaks before sunset. If we wanted to. That might be cool."

"Yeah. Sounds good. If we've still got the juice for it. And, what do you think? . . . maybe we could try this . . . Let's just stay quiet, for the rest of the hike. Okay if we try that?"

Nate smirked . . . *Sounds like he's tired of hearing my voice. Huh! 'Course, he's about talked my ear off about this Advaita stuff, the past few weeks . . .*

Mac continued, "We could just stay in, sort of, what the Buddhist's call 'noble silence' . . . for a while. And try to be absolutely in the present—without any thoughts about the past or future."

"Yeah, I'm game." Nate sighed. "My thoughts are *killing* me, anyhow. I'd love to at least try and catch a break from 'em."

"Right. Our thoughts *do* have the power to kill us. Literally. . . . Okay, let's do this. Let's just be silent and in the present moment. Don't engage the mind—or make any effort of the mind—which is a kind of movement. And just see what happens."

"Okay. I can dig it."

"The mind is *always* of the past . . . and the past is always *of* the mind. How could it be otherwise? . . . Since the past doesn't really exist except in our memory?"

"Huh. . . . Yeah, I get that."

Mac turned partway uphill and waited for Nate to pass him, taking the lead. As if talking to himself, Mac ruminated, "Ramana, also . . . I mean, Ramana Maharshi—Papaji's teacher. He used to say, over and over to people, *'Summa Iru.'* Keep quiet. . . . Keep quiet."

Nate nodded, grunting agreement. He continued up the rocky trail, noticing that he was leaning on his walking stick much more at this elevation than he had lower down. It was also much more of an effort to put one foot in front of the other—his muscles crying *rest*. And he was taking much smaller strides. His bit of arguing with Mac seemed to have used up his energy reserves, but he tried to keep up with as fast a pace as he could manage. Nate's t-shirt, beneath his unbuttoned flannel shirt, was soaking wet where it pressed against his back . . . *Man, this pack is really heavy again . . .* Each time the trail turned smooth—where he didn't have to watch his footing—he turned his gaze toward the stream on their left. Where it was once a rushing stream, down below, it was now just a rivulet. Sometimes it was right alongside the trail—sometimes down in a ravine, ten yards away or so, with small cascades . . . *Beautiful . . .* The rocky slope beyond it, on their left, stretched up to become a high hogback ridge, well above timberline.

When he focused on his increasingly mechanical footsteps, Nate noticed his mind slipping back into the broken-record groove of sad rumination over Elizabeth and the family. But at those other times when he fixed his attention on the rushing stream—or on the ridge beyond it—he found his mind got quiet . . . *Yeah, buddy. I've been needing this, for a while, now. Nature's always a good thing to clear the mind. Glad that Mac was able to come and hike with me . . .* He halfway turned around to look at Mac, but the man was gazing at the stream with an undecipherable expression. Nate felt a momentary urge to say something but didn't.

As his attention returned to his depleted stride, he became aware of how his eyes automatically focused on the location where his next footstep would land—making sure, picking a safe and level spot. And then his focus would instantly shift to the next spot where his other foot would land, assessing each location with a split-second thought. Left foot—good location? Right foot—good location? Left foot—good location? Right foot . . . *How is Luke gonna do his homework for school without Liz? Shut up!* . . . He focused on the gurgling sound of the stream, and the noisome thought disappeared. Came and went . . . back to wherever it was that it had originated . . . *Yeah, Mac's right. My thoughts are like my worst enemy, sometimes. Probably most of the time. Come to think of it, my thoughts are never very friendly to me* . . .

While they trudged up the trail, the aspen grove petered out as it gave way to spruce-fir forest again. Nate noticed that the trees weren't as tall as they were in the forests down below—the largest being no more than twenty or thirty feet high . . . *No doubt there's some hellacious winds up here. Frigid winds, in the wintertime* . . . Occasional clearings in the woods allowed for views of the rocky slopes and cliffs on both sides of the valley, now—and a view of a green alpine meadow some distance ahead. The hogback ridge on the left marched upward to join the ridge on the right side of the valley. And where the ridges met, they thrust up into a rocky alpine 'cirque'—encircling the top of the river valley which the trail had been ascending. Close by but invisible from here, the several promontories of the Truchas Peaks presided.

A couple—backpacking also—passed them, heading down the valley. A man and a woman, smiling and chattering about some bighorn sheep they'd seen higher up. They said "hi" as they passed. Nate hesitated, wanting to talk with them, but then just nodded with a "hi." They reminded him of himself and Elizabeth, a few years ago . . . *She'll never hike up here again* . . . Another wave of sadness swept over him. He consciously surveyed the gray rock cliff towering above them on the right, and the gloomy thought disappeared. The muffled sound of the hiker-couple's talk—behind them now, on the trail—vanished into the silence. Just as his dark thought did.

37.

"But, you know, the craziness is all around us—and mostly is within us. Even here. This place—peaceful and beautiful as it seems—is not immune."

A few minutes passed, and they reached the lower end of the long, green alpine meadow—which stretched up eastward into the cirque of rugged cliffs and rocky peaks enclosing the valley. Small groups of stunted trees scattered the meadow, the last stragglers of the forest, scarcely surviving up in this rarefied alpine country. Clusters of dwarf aspen trees, their leaves mostly gone. Colorado blue spruce, here and there, and Rocky Mountain Douglas firs. It must have been a mild fall up here, Nate thought, as he noticed scatterings of wildflowers still in bloom. Orange splashes of some Western yellow paintbrush. Yarrow, and blue patches of mountain harebells. The grass, which had looked like a smooth green carpet from a distance, was actually over a foot tall, and reached up into the boulder fields and scree slopes at the base of the cliffs. A slow-moving ripple of the stream's headwaters—the sign of a showery summer in the high country—suggested it wouldn't take any effort to get water for their camp.

The men dropped their packs and sat down on a hummock of grass near the edge of the stream, actually more like a seeping spring here near its origin. After a couple of minutes of rest and drinking the last gulps of water from his water bottle, Nate stood up, consciously—feeling like an aging athlete—and tested his muscles and joints. He heaved a long sigh and staggered over to the stream's edge. "Whew! I'm tired, for *sure.* Just about played-out. But maybe, after a break, we could set up camp and head for the top. If you want to. . . . Probably only an hour's hard hike up to one of the peaks, right? And we won't have our packs on." Nate bent down and splashed his face with the spring's icy water. He walked back and slumped down onto the grass again, and after a moment turned to Mac. The man still seemed to be observing silence—and smiled at Nate, nothing more . . . *Man, this guy's really into it. He wasn't kidding around . . .*

For quite some length of time, the men took a conscious and deliberate rest in the grass—during which Nate said nothing more but simply appreciated the sun, welcome at this time of the afternoon and at this time of year. They both finally stood up and broke the silence, talking for a few minutes about a good location for the campsite and tent. Nate suggested they pitch the tent on the south side of the meadow, closer to the south ridge. If a storm came up, though unlikely, it would most likely blow up from the south—and the mountain would be close to them on that side, shielding them from the wind. Mac agreed.

Finding a level spot near an old fire pit, they began setting up the tent. But, being Mac's tent, he was more familiar with it—and Nate left him to finish setting it up himself, while he scrounged around for some firewood. Wandering a good distance off, over to a stand of fir trees, he yanked some dead branches down and gathered a few up off of the ground. He glanced back at the campsite, amazed at how quickly the tent was up—a hurried but sound home away from home . . . *The last time I was up here, Liz and I set up the tent . . .* She had wanted to dig a little trench around the tent, to divert rainwater if it showered . . . *But I thought that was overkill . . . And I told her so. Shit . . . I wonder if I'll ever have a woman in my life again, if she passes. God help me, shut up!* . . . He took a deep breath, taking in the scenery of the valley around them, and dragged the firewood over to the campsite, wondering if he'd thought to bring his camping saw.

The two men—without much talk about it—decided to hike up to the peaks in the remaining afternoon sunlight. In a few minutes' time, they got the camp somewhat organized. Nate put most of their food into a bag, and with a rope suspended it up in a solitary tree—to keep it away from bears. Mac removed a section of his backpack, which apparently could be used as a small knapsack, and stuffed a couple of emergency items, a few snacks, and a water bottle into it. He slung it onto his back. Nate filled his water bottle at the stream and tied a hooded sweatshirt round his waist. They tossed their regular backpacks into the tent and were ready to go.

Nate took one last look at the campsite, and they made their way through the grass to the bottom of the rocky slope banking up to the towering rock wall at the head of the valley. There was no discernable footpath leading up this bastion of rock—most of the access to the Truchas Peaks being trails from the other side of the mountains, through the Pecos Valley. Mac said he'd only been in this valley once, at a time even further in the past than Nate had. And wasn't at all sure how to approach this climb.

From what seemed like ages past, Nate remembered how he and Elizabeth had found an unmarked trail up the slope, on the right side of this rocky cirque. He pointed out what looked to be a navigable way over and around boulders, to the right—up close to the massive cliff on the south side of the valley. The cliff already brooded in deep shadow. "Yeah, I'm sure that's the way we went up . . . it puts you up on top of the cirque, not far from the peaks. But Liz and I, when we hiked up here, came down near sunset. And you have to be careful, there—" He gestured with his head toward the sheer cliff on the right. The cliff towered over their campsite and, further west became the ridge which towered alongside the river valley they'd just ascended. "Because, coming back down, it's easy to go too far west along that ridge. . . . And then you wind up at the top of those cliffs. There's no good way down *there*, unless you're a monkey, or have technical rock-climbing skills." . . . *Yeah, that's the quick way back down to the campsite, for sure . . . quick, but fatal . . .*

Mac grinned. "Yep—I don't think we have either of those qualities. Let's not make that mistake. We'll just keep that in mind, on the way back down."

Over a slope of slippery scree that shifted underfoot—gravelly brownish-gray rocks—they found a faint trail up the cirque. Where Nate said it would be. The two rested for a water break, at a place where the scree gave way to a more solid boulder field and the ground was stable. After their break, they made an exhausting nonstop slog to the top of the cirque, the air becoming more rarefied with each step. At the top of the cirque was a knife-edge ridge, which divided the valley they'd been climbing up all day from the basins and valleys to the east.

They clambered along the ridge southward, to where it eventually became a series of rock promontories and the Truchas Peaks. At one point, the ridge was so narrow that a stumble could mean death. A couple of alpine lakes were visible on the east side, a half mile away and at a lower elevation. While Nate surveyed these lands to the east, a dark brown bird with an enormous wingspan sailed over their heads, gliding along the ridgeline northward. Nate checked his footing and then gazed up at it, gliding only thirty feet or so above them. It passed over in silence, and on along the ridge behind them . . . *My God, what a bird.*

Looks to be a golden eagle . . . and it hasn't migrated yet . . . One stroke of its wings lifted it fifty feet or so, and it glided over to the rocky heights on the north side of their valley. Perhaps hunting for marmots or carrion. Mac also followed the bird with his eyes.

"Yeah, man," Nate said, almost whispering. "Wouldn't it be great to fly like *that?*"

After the men topped a jagged promontory, finally the peaks were visible: North Truchas, Middle Truchas—and further south, the highest point of Truchas Peak. All three of these high spots over thirteen thousand feet high. Close enough that you could touch them, it seemed. But the sun was getting low in the sky, and it was already after six when they made their way toward the peaks. The days were shorter now, it being the beginning of October, and the valley where they'd camped was already mottled with deep shadow. It might stay light on the peaks for a good while, yet—and they both had headlamps with them—but Nate suspected it might be dangerous hiking down, if they didn't descend off the top of the cirque before nightfall . . . *That knife-edge ridge, after dark? I don't think so . . .* "You know, Mac—why don't we head straight for the big one? Truchas Peak? We're not gonna have a whole lot of time up here before it's dark. And that ridge that we have to negotiate down to our valley is a little *spooky.*"

"It is. Sure, let's do that. Actually . . . even if we *did* get stuck up here after dark, you know . . . it's almost full moon. In fact, it'll be comin' up soon. It ought to be spectacular up here."

"No doubt, it would be. Spectacular. But I don't want to find out. 'Cause, even if the moon is blindingly bright, it ain't gonna help us much, going down the west side of that ridge. We'd be in shadow there."

"Yep," Mac said, "you're right."

"And it could get cold as hell up here on these big boys if the wind starts up."

Once they'd set their course, it was just a matter of clambering over boulders and quick walks over soft grassy tundra—about twenty minutes—to reach the highest point of Truchas Peak. A chilly draft blew from the south, and the men sat down beside a Volkswagen-sized rock that blocked the wind. The air smelled clean, of sun-baked grass and rock. Nate twisted round and gazed over at the eastern sky. Hazy with distance, fushia and light purple darkened by degrees into cobalt and navy blue at the horizon's edge. A lighter spot on the horizon suggested where the moon might be preparing to rise. Mac stood up, surveying the lands to the west, glowing in dusky amber and gold. He made a long, sighing whistle. *"Beautiful.* We made it."

Nate squinted at Mac's silhouette, against the intense late-afternoon sun. "Yeah. We did. . . . I needed this, man. Thanks for takin' the time and hiking with me." Mac turned partway round and grinned.

Nate looked over the lands to the west and sighed. A long, tired sigh. "The world, and all of its suffering and craziness, seems a long way from here. . . . Elizabeth's illness. The war in Yugoslavia. Genocide in Africa . . . *God!*" He gazed west across a large valley, to a distant mountain range where the lights of a city perched on its slopes were already lit, lighting up the mountains' shadow. "You know? . . . And right over there—across this valley, at Los Alamos—they're probably at this moment working on some new kind of nuclear weapons. . . . Insanity. But it feels far away from here."

"Yeah," Mac said. "Nature can be very healing." He looked at Nate and sat down opposite him, a few feet away. "But, you know, the craziness is all around us—and mostly is within us. Even here. This place—peaceful and beautiful as it seems—is not immune."

"Yeah? What d'ya mean?"

"What I'm saying is . . . if we bring our desires, or attachment to things, here. Then peace won't be found here. . . . Or if we bring fear. . . . Fear of death. Fear of anything. That's another kind of *attachment*. . . . Then no peace, but only suffering, will be here, too."

"I guess . . . I guess that's true."

"You see . . . at this moment, you feel calm. And like everything is right with the world, at this moment. Am I right?"

"Yep. I feel like things are really *okay*. But maybe that's because I'm too tired to think of anything."

Mac took a deep, slow breath. "Well, man . . . being physically tired is only a small part of it. You see, you feel calm now because at this moment you're feeling the *absence* of desire. . . . Like, a temporary state of desirelessness."

"*Desirelessness?* Huh? What do you mean, desirelessness?"

Mac looked at him, raising his eyebrows, though Nate couldn't see his face clearly with the evening sun's glare silhouetting the man. Mac continued, "Well . . . for the past few hours—or maybe *all day*—you've wanted to reach the top of this mountain. Right?"

"Yep. True."

"And now you've reached the top of this mountain. . . . So *that* desire is gone. That's where your peace and calm is coming from. Not because you've 'bagged a peak'—or because now you've got some kind of bragging rights, from climbing one of the highest peaks in New Mexico. And it's not because you're tired. . . . No. The peace you're feeling is because the *desire* is gone. And it hasn't been replaced yet, with another desire. See what I'm saying?"

"Yeah . . . I do." Nate was silent for several long moments. "Huh. I wouldn't have thought of it that way. But it sounds about right. . . . More Papaji teachings, I guess?"

"Truth," Mac said. "As far as I can tell. Whether it comes from Papaji, the Buddha, Mohammed, or Christ. Or even from little old *me.* Truth always comes from Grace. . . .

"And the only way I know this to be true, is from observing it in myself. I watch the way my desires, and the thoughts and angst they produce, rise and fall. They rise—are either fulfilled or frustrated—and then they fall back into the emptiness where they came from. They are nothing . . . and don't in fact exist outside of our minds. And yet our desires and attachments *rule* us, in our lives as tenants of this world."

"Huh. . . . I guess I'm not aware of myself the way you seem to be. Self-aware. . . . I wish I was. Seems to me you have a real peace, about you, that I don't remember you having before. . . . Like you've found some answers."

"It all comes from Grace," Mac repeated. ". . . It's something I already *had,* but just wasn't conscious of. And, as it turns out, I didn't have to go to any effort to achieve it—" Mac chuckled softly. "because it's already *here.* Papaji merely pointed it out to me . . . helped me to realize it. And helped me make it a more permanent part of me. I *became* it. It's in you, also—no difference. It's in all of us. Our true nature . . . the Self. Consciousness. You could call it our God-nature. Or Grace."

Confusion welled up in Nate. An annoying butterfly feeling in his chest—fluttering with anger, sadness, joy, frustration . . . *What's this weird feeling I'm having, now? Where's it coming from?* . . . "Mac, why don't I feel it? Peace, I mean? The peace that you seem to have. Or contentment? Why do I feel it only once in a damned *blue moon?*"

"You do feel it . . . at least at times, you do. We all have a core of peace and contentment that we're only aware of when our thoughts and desires—our distractions—are silent. You've just said to me that you feel peace now. And once in a while, in the past. . . . When's the last time that you felt *silence,* in your mind? And felt the peace that comes from that?"

Nate scanned his memory for a moment . . . *That sunset I saw, just last week. Back at the house. So beautiful . . . that everything just stopped, in my head. That was wonderful* . . . A feeling of wonder and peace came over him again, at the memory of that moment. "It seems like I only feel silence—and peace—when I experience something beautiful in nature. Like an incredible sunset, or something. It somehow stops my mind. It makes me realize there's something bigger, running the show and taking care of things. . . . Like we're not all alone here."

"Yes. So you, at least sometimes, have *satsang* or communion with

Nature. Nature is great for that . . . for helping us renew our connection to Grace. Without the distractions—and the trance—of the world that's created by the mind. Even if that connection is just temporary. The point is: we can stay here, all the time. Stay here in peace. In contentment. With Consciousness. With Grace. With The Beloved."

"The *Beloved?*"

"Yeah." Mac chuckled. "That's what we like to call it. 'The Beloved.' Consciousness. The Self—with a capital 'S'. It's what we're *all* secretly looking for—we just look for it in all the wrong ways. Money, sex, drugs, alcohol . . . material things. Or we even look for it with spiritual methods—meditation, mantras, austerities, prayer. Going to church. . . . Fact is, there's no *method* for finding it. There's no method *needed,* for finding it! That's the absurd part. No method. No teacher.

"Papaji always tells us that he's not really a teacher at all. Some of us call him our guide. Teachers and preachers can only lead you to something from the past. Or they try to give you something they *think* you need. But that's all *of* the mind—and the mind is *always* from the past. The truth is . . . we don't need *anything.* It's all here, right *now.* Anything that can be given to us—or can be gained, in the material world—can also be lost. And ultimately, *will* be lost. My teacher, or guide, Papaji, is always very clear—that he doesn't *give* us anything. As an awakened master, he's just very adept, and able, to point us in the right direction. Pointing out to us, clearly, *what is already here.* Within us. But is overlooked, in the trance state we're in. This is what the true guru does . . . points out to us our own inner guru—the final, true satguru. Our own true nature. Consciousness. The Self. God.

Mac chuckled again. "There's this Westerner—an American guy named Adyashanti, who's another guide in this vein of the Advaita teachings, and he says it pretty well. He says, 'all of us are walking around—*in God's hand*—searching for God.' You see, God, Grace, Consciousness . . . is all *around* us, all the time. And within us. . . . We just have blinders on. "

A crooked smile came to Nate's face, replacing the puzzled frown. "And it's *here? Now?*"

"*Yes.* Where else would it be? No need for heavenly gates, here, my friend."

Nate felt the confused butterfly in his chest again, and chuckled for a second . . . *But why is it I can't seem to get what he's saying? And yet . . . everything he's saying (and what we've talked about, recently) sounds familiar. Like I've heard it somewhere before . . . Or I have some knowing, about this. Like part of me knows this already . . .*

Mac's face was hard to focus on, with the sunset glare behind him.

But he was smiling. "Yes, part of you *does* know this, already. And you *have* heard it somewhere, before. That's the only reason we're having this conversation. Maybe you learned some of this in a previous life, I don't know. Time doesn't really exist. In fact, time only exists in a relative way—in this manifest world of samsara. From what I understand, all of our lives—this present life, and all of our previous lives and incarnations—are actually going on simultaneously, in God's time. In the *big* picture. . . . It's all part of Leela—God's play, or God's game. God playing hide-and-seek with Itself. Through all of this manifest life, here on this planet. And on all other inhabited worlds that can or will exist. The individual soul—the *jiva*—eventually, inevitably, finds its way back to Consciousness. Back to God. And, in this realization, is reabsorbed back into That. Your soul . . . your consciousness . . . like all other souls, is on this journey. Through millions of years in human time. But in truth this journey doesn't happen in *time*."

Even with the large rock next to them as a windbreak, a cool breeze wafted over the two. Nate had put on his hoodie as soon as they'd reached the peaks, but hadn't noticed till now that the air was chilly in the waning sun. Still wearing a confused half-smile, he looked down at his hands and his legs stretched out in front of him. His faded blue jeans were dry now, after getting damp from the sweat of the climb. What Mac had been saying seemed important, somehow. Profound, maybe even crucial. In the back of his mind, Nate felt a readiness for these concepts, and he yearned for more. But his thoughts were confused, and they drifted again . . . *Man, a fire will feel good, down at the campsite . . .* He looked down at a patch on the knee of his jeans. Elizabeth had sewn it on, over a month ago, with some spare fabric of a green plaid design . . . *Wonder how she's doing . . . with Beverly there, and the kids . . .* A wave of sadness and loneliness swept over him again, and his eyes felt hot with tears for a moment . . . *I'm not really getting this . . . this stuff Mac is saying. Am I just wasting time, talking with him about this? . . . But it all sounds so familiar . . .*

Mac looked into Nate's eyes. "Your thoughts making you feel a little sad?"

"Yep." . . . *Seems like Mac can read my mind, now. That's weird . . .* A premonition of Elizabeth's death crossed his mind, and Nate felt nauseous for an instant, reaching his hand up to smear away some tears.

"Why don't you look into yourself, in this moment . . . without the thoughts of Liz, or of anything else, and find out how you *really* are, *right now*. In this moment. This *instant*. Just let go of the mind—don't follow it. Don't follow it, for even a fraction of a second . . ."

Nate blinked his eyes and gazed, without any thoughts, at the sunset valleys and mountains behind Mac. His eyes took in the scenery without any story involved. And saw beauty. Instantly. And felt, without a doubt, a benevolent animating force behind it all. A genuine grin came to his face.

"Well?" Mac asked.

"I feel okay. Everything's *fine.*" He paused, and then heard himself say, "Maybe even *perfect.*"

"*Excellent.* Now stay here. Don't *move.* Don't even *start* a thought . . . because thought is movement. Allow your mind to simply *not* start a thought. *Don't **move.** "*

Nate slowly closed his eyes. These last words—though coming from his friend sitting in front of him—oddly enough, also came from within himself. He heard the words *"Don't move"* pronounced in his own voice—as he himself would have said it. Or as if a voice within him echoed the words . . . *There's some part of me that's the same as Mac . . . one and the same . . . or is it just his voice sounding like mine? A coincidence . . .* But this feeling didn't puzzle him enough to encourage any further thought or a question. And silence followed—without thought—for several minutes.

Nate looked in Mac's direction but with a soft gaze that refused to focus on anything. So he closed his eyes again . . . *There's something huge here. Right on the edge of my perception . . .* He was aware of an immense silence beneath the sensation caused by the words "Don't move" . . . *Emptiness? Or a sense of oneness? Oneness, that I'm aware of? Oneness with Mac, oneness with Everything . . .* The feeling of oneness and mystery ripened into awe. And awe remained. Not as a thought, but as a feeling, a state. A truth. It didn't feel frightening—in fact it felt comfortable. As if something huge, unfathomable, and awe-inspiring—but benevolent—was welcoming him home after a *long* trip afield. All fear and suffering—as well as joy and desire and pleasure— were absorbed into this vast silence and emptiness. And were seen, in their true perspective, as being transitory and not real. It didn't feel to be a lonely or terrifying emptiness at all . . . *It's not the way I've felt about emptiness before—like the primal horror of outer space. A profoundly horrible vacuum. No, not at all . . .* It was an emptiness that contained everything. With an aspect of vast benevolence, or love, to it . . . *My God, it's true . . . Everything is right here . . . right now . . .*

The butterfly sensation in his chest no longer felt confusing—but began to feel funny, ticklish. And he felt an ecstatic, ticklish feeling also on the crown of his head. With his eyes still closed, Nate began to giggle. And then laughed out loud for a couple of minutes—his body and features pulsing with laughter. Mac laughed along with him. Emotions didn't seem to function here, and tears blurred Nate's eyes as he laughed and cried at the same time. A thought arose, again—starting like an infinitely small bubble . . . *Pointless* . . . But it raised a question nonetheless . . . *But how?*. . . It became a coherent thought . . . *How did Mac do this? How does he know what I'm*— . . . Nate opened his eyes. But because of the tears—or the glaring of the sun, close to the horizon—he again couldn't seem to focus on anything.

A voice spoke. "I'm not the one *doing* this. . . . If a thought arises— don't *follow* it. But look for its source. Look for its source. And there you'll finally *know* who the Seer is."

A minute or two followed, with silence reasserting itself. Nate giggled and then laughed again—a profound, quaking belly laugh.

"This is *Grace,* your own Grace. Grace itself, calling you home."

Feeling contented, even ecstatic on some level, but with emotions that didn't work, Nate laughed again with tears in his eyes. His story: the story of Nate—that he'd been told and had told himself for decades— was reabsorbed, dissolved back into the immense emptiness from where it came. And *That* was simultaneously filled with Everything.

Suggested Further Reading

Alcoholics Anonymous World Services, Inc. ; *Alcoholics Anonymous*, Fourth Edition, 2001

Casey, Susan ; *"Leap of Faith : Meet John of God"* ; O, The Oprah Magazine, Dec. 2010

Cumming, Heather, and Karen Leffler ; *John of God : The Brazilian Healer Who's Touched the Lives of Millions* ; Atria Books / Beyond Words, 2007

Godman, David ; *Papaji : Interviews* ; Avadhuta Foundation, 1993

Godman, David ; *The Fire of Freedom ; Satsang with Papaji, Volume 1* ; Avadhuta Foundation, 2006

Hammond, Frank, and Ida Mae Hammond ; *Pigs in the Parlor : A Practical Guide to Deliverance* ; Impact Christian Books, Inc., 1973

Kay, William K. ; *Pentacostalism ; A Very Short Introduction* ; Oxford University Press, 2011

Lemkin, Jim, and David Godman ; *"Call Off The Search ; Freedom Here and Now with H.W.L. Poonja"* (video format) ; Avadhuta Foundation, 1993

Nave, Orville J. ; *Nave's Topical Bible* ; Hendrickson Publishers, 1907, 2002

Pearlman, Myer ; *Knowing the Doctrines of the Bible* ; Gospel Publishing House, 1937, 1981

RavenWing, Josie ; *The Book of Miracles ; The Healing Work of Joao de Deus* ; 1st Books Library, 2002

Reynolds, Michael ; *Earthship ; Volume 1* ; Solar Survival Architecture, 1990